The Lighted Rooms

The
Lighted Rooms

RICHARD MASON

Weidenfeld & Nicolson
LONDON

First published in Great Britain in 2008
by Weidenfeld & Nicolson

1 3 5 7 9 10 8 6 4 2

Extract from 'The Old Fools' from *Collected Poems* by
Philip Larkin reproduced courtesy of Faber and Faber.

Extract from *The Ageing Brain* by Dr Lawrence Whalley
reproduced courtesy of Weidenfeld & Nicolson,
an imprint of the Orion Publishing Group.

A CIP catalogue record for this book
is available from the British Library

ISBN 978 0 297 85319 0 (hardback)
ISBN 978 0 297 85320 6 (trade paperback)

Typeset by Input Data Services Ltd, Frome

Printed in Great Britain by Clays Ltd, St Ives plc

The Orion Publishing Group's policy is to use papers that
are natural, renewable and recyclable products and made
from wood grown in sustainable forests. The logging and
manufacturing processes are expected to conform to the
environmental regulations of the country of origin.

Weidenfeld & Nicolson

An imprint of the Orion Publishing Group
Orion House, 5 Upper St Martin's Lane,
London WC2H 9EA

www.orionbooks.co.uk

Perhaps being old is having lighted rooms
Inside your head, and people in them, acting.

– Philip Larkin

Chapter 1

Number 17 Kingsley Gardens presided over a leafy street on the south side of the river, protected from the traffic of Wandsworth Bridge Road by its own substantial grounds and a low-rise 1950s development of flats and shops. A flight of stairs led to an imposing front door, beside which a brass plaque engraved *The Albany* was discreetly obscured by a well-pruned yew tree in a terracotta pot. Only a wheelchair ramp spoiled the illusion of an exclusive gentleman's club, though its expansive width and polished gold rails implied a superior sort of disabled access.

Eloise helped her mother from the taxi and put her arm around her shoulders. 'Here we are!' she said.

'Yes,' said Joan. 'Here we are indeed.'

They stood together on the pavement, admiring the building's exuberant exterior. As The Albany's full-colour brochure informed potential residents on its opening page, the home occupied a 'Grade II listed Victorian mansion, sympathetically restored to the highest standards and retaining many of its original period features'. Above them, the architectural fashions of a thousand years competed for prominence on a densely crowded façade across which turrets, cupolas and bay windows had been liberally scattered by an effusive architect of the late nineteenth century. Medieval arrow slits sliced through Jacobean gables; slate roofs rose steeply, dotted with *oeil-de-boeuf* windows. Gothic arches, Norman columns and Corinthian pilasters jostled for attention across a frontage of white stucco stamped, above the door, with ornately intertwined Gs and Cs.

'Goodness me,' said Joan.

'This looks like the best one so far.' Eloise spoke with the slightly hysterical optimism of one who has spent too many successive Saturdays examining residential-care facilities for the elderly.

'It's certainly better than that place in Enfield.'

'I'd never have let you live there.'

Joan squeezed her daughter's hand affectionately. She did not remotely condemn Eloise for putting her into a home. She had not brought her into the world, given her life and loved her, raised her and cared for her as best she could, in expectation of return. She reminded herself of this and gripped her hand more tightly. Aloud she said, 'No, of course not, darling.'

They rang the bell and were met in the pillared entrance hall by a smartly turned out nurse in a uniform of grey and white, whose nametag read *Sister Karen*. 'And you must be Mrs McAllister, or may I call you Joan?' She enunciated each word with sprightly professionalism. 'I am the Nursing Manager here. Welcome to The Albany!'

There was something representative, Joan thought, in the tone of Sister Karen's voice. It carried in it the well-scrubbed tiles of The Albany's entrance hall floor and suggested scrupulously tidy, air-freshened public rooms. She was amply built and moved with careful purposefulness. 'If you'd just follow me,' she said.

Joan glanced behind her to make sure that the pair of burnished brass piano pedals that had materialised in the taxi were with her now. They were. She was glad of that, for this was their first visit in a week and she was eager for their company. They had not made a single appearance at the nursing home in Enfield, a fact that had heightened the impact of its dank passageways and concrete-paved 'garden'. Buoyed by their lively presence, she followed Eloise and Sister Karen to the reception desk and waited behind them while Eloise wrote 'JOAN MCALLISTER, ELOISE MCALLISTER, 10.53 a.m.' in a Visitors' Register and the Nursing Manager asked them if they would like a hot drink.

Eloise worked long hours, Joan knew, and she was anxious that this visit should not consume more of her daughter's precious free time than was necessary. She was also eager to enjoy the pedals' unexpected reappearance in private, as one never knew how long they would remain for once they had come, or where one might find oneself without their kindly guidance. So she said, 'I'm quite all right, thank you. Perhaps we could begin the tour?' and turned expectantly towards a majestic staircase, the banisters of which appeared to end in a pair of winged mahogany angels.

Joan was quite accustomed to seeing extraordinary things in matter-of-fact places, and the sight of these heavenly figures did not unduly astonish her. The first visit of the piano pedals had been shocking, to be sure; a little disturbing, even. They had materialised over her bed in the early hours of a dark morning three years before: an alarming spectacle at first, though once she had put away her fears and learned to befriend them, they had taken her on many adventures. She was now seldom, if ever, surprised by the curious things she sometimes saw.

'Not even a slice of cake?' Sister Karen was herself a little peckish. It was her custom to entertain potential clients to refreshments in her office, while she explained to them the advantages of the world-class geriatric care provided by the *TranquilAge*™ chain of nursing homes.

'Go on, Mum. You always have a snack around this time.'

'Do you, now?' Sister Karen smiled approvingly. 'One of the advantages of our staff-to-patient ratio', she went on to Eloise, lowering her voice, 'is that we can continue any little routines the old dears are used to. We have the personnel to treat each client as the unique individual they are.'

Joan, whose hearing and eyesight were rather more functional than her joints, pretended not to have overheard this aside. Instead she said, 'Well I do like my elevenses.'

'That's settled then. Why don't you follow me?'

The Nursing Manager led them down a corridor tiled in stylised cornflowers, its arched ceiling reminiscent of a cathedral's nave. 'We acquired this property nine years ago,' she said, beginning her routine, 'with the aim of making it TranquilAge's European flagship. Can you believe it was once a family home? Though, of course, we still think of it as such because' – here she put her arm around Joan's shoulders, and squeezed – 'each and every resident becomes a member of the TranquilAge family.' She opened a solid-looking door and ushered her guests into a large, pleasantly furnished room, lavishly adorned with silk flowers. 'Let's get some tea on the way, then. Would you prefer carrot cake, or coffee-and-walnut?'

Sister Karen's Pre-Registration Talk took around twenty minutes, sometimes more, sometimes less, depending on the self-confidence of her audience. Some prospective clients found her air of clinical omniscience so intimidating that they asked no questions at all, and very few who heard her friendly and sincere exhortation of the

'*TranquilAge*™ Experience' did not sign on the dotted line a short while later. Those who held out tended to be daunted by the exorbitant costs involved, which was why, on the whole, Sister Karen preferred having the dear old people present while she got down to basics with their younger relatives. In her experience, middle-aged professionals were reluctant to appear stingy in front of their elderly aunts, uncles and parents, and she was expert at inferring tactfully that they were welcome to look at cheaper alternatives – provided they remembered that you got what you paid for in life.

She was quite taken aback when Eloise did not once mention the expense of a private room at The Albany, and further surprised to encounter a series of detailed, technical questions that suggested an unusual familiarity with the workings of geriatric institutions. She went through, at some length, the qualifications of The Albany's staff; the extensive background checks undertaken before any offer of employment was made; the arrangements in place to deal with a wide variety of medical mishaps. As she did so, she wondered whether Eloise had, perhaps, some personal knowledge of geriatric medicine. She hoped not, because relatives with experience in the field were prone to interfere – and this, though understandable, was an aggravation and a distraction. Was she, perhaps, a medical professional? Sister Karen glanced at the file on her lap. In the *Occupation* box Eloise had written 'Fund Manager' – which was a relief. 'I do like a client who has done their research and thought about the issues,' she said, leaning forward and smiling.

Joan listened vaguely to her daughter's interrogation of the Nursing Manager, content in the knowledge that Eloise was sure to get to the bottom of things. Had she known the cost of care at The Albany, she would have intervened and chosen a different establishment; even, if necessary, that hideous place with the concrete garden in Enfield. But she knew nothing of The Albany's rates – Eloise, in any case, handled all her money now – and in blissful ignorance she composed her face into an expression of placid concentration and looked about her for the piano pedals. These materialised, moments later, on top of Sister Karen's filing cabinet.

Quite unbeknownst to Eloise, Joan inhabited a rich inner world which she disguised from her daughter, and from everyone else, with a feeling that had begun as embarrassment but was now rather closer to the delight with which certain children hoard a secret. The piano pedals were a portal to adventure – but she should not, she knew, begin her games now; she was sure to be disturbed in the middle, which was tedious. So she drank her tea and ate a slice of over-sweet carrot cake, thinking that there was more than a little of Astrid in the Nursing Manager: they had the same, slightly damp air of unquestioned authority.

For a moment her mother-in-law came vividly to her, but a glance at the pedals banished her; and betraying no sign of this small victory she waited patiently for the conversation between Eloise and the nurse to subside. Once it had, she answered the few questions put to her as best she could and said that she would, indeed, very much, enjoy a guided tour. Then she followed both younger women out into the cathedral-like corridor and back to the entrance hall, where the winged angels remained where she had left them. Were they real? Perhaps.

'These are original,' said Sister Karen, confirming their tangibility by patting an intricately rendered wing feather. 'As is the picture window. We did our best to preserve period features, where consistent with our Health and Safety policies.'

Above the staircase, three portraits of a woman in radiantly stained glass gleamed down and made the shadows gaudy. In the first, her hands were raised in welcome above a Latin greeting, *Salve*. In the second, her arms were thrown open beneath a banner proclaiming *Hospitalitas*, and she stood before a sumptuous feast. She was sorrowful in the third, waving goodbye above the legend *Vale*. The effect of the whole was somewhat spoiled by burglar bars which interrupted the vivid shadows and suggested the sinister possibility of forced confinement, but Joan turned her back emphatically on this thought.

'Do you use a Zimmer frame?' asked Sister Karen, kindly.

'No, dear.'

'Aren't we independent! Good for you.' The Nursing Manager pointed to her right. 'The Dining Room is down there. To the left over here is the Smokers' Recreation Lounge. Are you a smoker?'

Joan shook her head.

'Well we'll just look in quickly then.'

She took them to a large door, recessed within a neoclassical pediment on which was mounted a red electric sign that read SMOKERS ONLY. 'This is one of our two Recreation Lounges,' she said grandly, leading the way into a substantial room in the centre of which a group of people on pine armchairs were clustered, as if for warmth, around

5

a television set. The walls, doors and ceiling were painted magnolia and the air was thick with cigarette smoke. 'Yoohoo!' she cried. 'We have visitors!' But this news attracted the attention of only one resident, an elderly man in a wheelchair who turned wide, startled eyes to Joan and Eloise and raised a hand in an enigmatic gesture that fell somewhere between a welcome and a warning. The others remained intent on the television set, which showed a haggard-faced woman screaming at a man in a pub. Sister Karen approached the elderly man and patted his shoulder. 'Hello, Lionel! And how are we today?'

Lionel nodded but said nothing. Sister Karen shook her head and took Eloise's hand, drawing her away. 'We care for people across the ability spectrum,' she said in an undertone. 'Medical science can only do so much. Often it's a case of providing emotional support and the right kind of comforting routine.' She pursed her lips in a smile of appropriately concerned resignation. To Joan she said, more loudly, 'What luck you're so sprightly! Your daughter tells me you're a pianist. Is that so?'

Joan nodded.

'Well I've got a treat in store for you, just you see if I don't.'

She led her visitors back to the staircase, which boasted an electric chair on a reinforced steel rail. 'You'll find that we combine the latest in modern functionality with respect for our heritage,' she said, helping Joan onto the grey leather seat and sending her up the stairs at a sedate pace that somewhat belied her enthusiastic talk of a 'home fairground ride!'

Noting with approval Sister Karen's deft manipulation of the equipment's safety harness, Eloise followed her mother up the steps. They were shallow and wide, carpeted in a pattern of green and puce, their banisters gleaming with polish. It would not be so bad, she thought, to live for a few years in a place like this. There was no trace of urine beneath the smell of disinfectant, a fact which distinguished The Albany from a number of its competitors, and the rooms were decently sized. The staff were excellent and there were more than enough of them. She thought of the activities schedule that Sister Karen had just shown her and tried to imagine her mother passing a happy afternoon with the Trivial Pursuit Club. She would surely settle down and make friends. She spent too much time in her flat, sitting alone all day.

Reaching the first floor, Sister Karen helped Joan down and led them both to an imposing door, identical to the one on the ground floor except for the fact that it was painted mushroom and sported a red electric sign that said THANK YOU FOR NOT SMOKING. 'We're very proud of this room. I'm sure you'll remember it from the brochure.' The Nursing Manager stood back, ushering them inside.

The Recreation Lounge (Non-Smokers) had once been the principal reception room of 17 Kingsley Gardens, in the days when the property had been a private house. It ran the length of the building and its seven windows looked out over the 1950s development and onto the busy lanes of Wandsworth Bridge Road. At one end stood an ornate mahogany fireplace, garlanded in flowers and supported by two figures of mythic proportion; at the other, a series of classical bookcases, in the style of Robert Adam, displayed a large selection of romantic novels and ageing magazines.

'Wow, Mum!'

Eloise could not, Joan thought, be exclaiming over the grey non-slip tiles on the floor. She looked at Sister Karen, who pointed upwards. 'Have you ever seen anything like that? It's all original – we found it when we checked for asbestos.'

The ceiling above them was painted in pale blues, greens and pinks, in a floral pattern arranged around four gilded roundels. At the centre of each was a portrait of a woman – perhaps, thought Joan, the woman in the window downstairs? She looked about her for the piano pedals. She had known them to elucidate such mysteries, but they did not seem to have followed her from Sister Karen's study. She arched her neck. The lady looked contemplative, a little sad.

'Now what do you think these images represent?' asked Sister Karen.

Joan examined the panels above her. In one, the mournful figure wore a dark cloak and leaned low over a fire of burning twigs; in another, she was draped in russet against a background of falling leaves. She wore a pretty blue dress and held a posy of spring flowers in the third, and carried a sheaf of wheat in the fourth. 'The Four Seasons?' she ventured.

Sister Karen looked disappointed. 'Very good. You're the first person I've known to get that right first time.' She patted Joan's arm, encouragingly. 'Now what do you think of that?' She was pointing at a rickety upright piano that, along with another set of pine armchairs and a widescreen television set, completed the room's furniture. Joan did not know what she was meant to think of it. 'You'll be giving us concerts before you know it! You see if you don't!'

An hour later, Joan made her way down The Albany's front steps on Eloise's arm. It did not seem to her that it would be worthwhile to spend many more Saturdays looking at old people's homes.

'What did you think?' asked Eloise.

'I liked it very much, darling. It seems extremely well run.'

Joan was seldom critical of the institutions Eloise showed her, and this forbearance had heightened her daughter's sensitivity to the subtlest nuances of tone. 'It's meant to be the best, you know,' she said.

'I can quite see why.'

'They have an excellent staff-to-patient ratio and the building, I think, is well done.'

'Oh, very.'

Eloise helped her mother into the minicab and they sat beside each other in silence as the car moved off.

'I really don't think,' said Joan, after a moment, 'that we should carry on wasting your time like this, looking at places.'

'We'll look as long as we need to look, Mum. What matters is that you're happy. We've got to find somewhere you feel at home.'

It would be unkind, thought Joan, to remind Eloise that she already had a home and did not need another. For a moment, she could remember none of her daughter's excellent reasons for deciding – or *suggesting*; to be fair to her, she had only suggested – that a live-in carer would not be practical. She looked out of the window, concentrated for an instant and remembered: there was no space at Wilsmore Street and the lease was almost up in any case; she would have to get a bigger flat to accommodate a full-time nurse, and if she was going to all that trouble she might as well move to an environment dedicated to geriatric well-being. It was Eloise's phrase, 'geriatric well-being', and Joan did not altogether like it. 'Well I—' she began, but a violent electronic rendition of Bach's *Air on a G String* interrupted her.

Eloise chased her phone determinedly through her cluttered handbag, aware that the coming conversation with her mother might be decisive and eager for any postponement. She hesitated when she saw Claude's number, but only momentarily. Joan would be cheered by news of Claude. 'Now this is a surprise,' she said warmly, into the receiver. 'What are you doing up?'

'What is life without surprises?' Claude sounded tired. 'Anyway, I am not in Boston. I am visiting my parents in Paris, so I am in your time zone for a change.'

'I thought they hated Paris.'

'They do. But I can only be here for two days, and the journey to Toulouse is too long. One of their friends has lent us his apartment on the rue Louis David. Isn't that where you lived when you worked for those people with the awful children?'

Almost thirty years before, Eloise had indeed spent six fraught weeks living on the rue Louis David. 'Such recall,' she said.

'I thought of you when I saw the address. Is this a busy time?'

'I'm just with Mum, as it happens.'

'Oh! How is Joan?'

Eloise looked at her mother, now staring anxiously out of the window for the pedals she had last seen on top of Sister Karen's filing cabinet. 'Doing very well,' she said.

'Will you tell her I send my love?'

'Claude sends his love, Mum.'

'Are you speaking to Claude?' The thought at once soothed Joan's anxiety. The pedals sometimes disappeared for days at a time, but they always came back in the end. 'Could I say hello?'

It was an open, though unacknowledged, fact that Joan desperately wished that Eloise had married Claude. In Eloise's opinion, this had more to do with Claude's eminent suitability as a son-in-law to Joan than with any merits he may or may not have possessed as a husband for her. From the beginning, Joan and Claude had got on famously, sharing recipes like a pair of old ladies and drinking themselves dizzy while cooking fabulous dinners, exclaiming delightedly over *Aile de Raie aux Câpres*, or *Rognons de Veau flambés au Madère* as they tossed back the Sancerre.

'Claude! Dearest boy. How *are* you?'

Eloise listened to them, vaguely irritated by their enduring intimacy. At least, she thought, Joan would be in good spirits when she told her what was, after all, only the truth: that The Albany seemed to deserve its reputation, and that if she were ever to secure a place she should put her name on the waiting list now.

'How is your work on osmium going?' asked Joan into the mobile phone, gripping the slender receiver with unnecessary force as though it might slip from her hand at any moment. 'Really? But that's *marvellous*! You know I've always had the greatest faith in you. You must let me know. Yes, of course. Well' – regretfully – 'I had better pass you back to Eloise. I'm sure this call must be very expensive.'

'I do adore your mother,' said Claude, when he was once again speaking to Eloise.

'I know. It's mutual. How have you been?'

'Oh, you know.'

But Eloise did not know and was not sure she wanted to. 'What was that you were telling Mum about osmium?' she asked, instead. 'Don't tell me you've completed your life's work?'

There was a pause.

'Well, have you?'

Claude hesitated, then said – evenly; in the tone of voice he had used, long ago, when she had wrung secrets from him – 'We're in the home straight. It's a matter of months now.'

'That's fantastic.'

'Thank you.'

There was another pause, more awkward than the first, which Eloise ended by saying, decisively, 'Give my love to Ingrid and the kids. You should bring them to England, some time. We'll celebrate your triumph.'

'Yes, I will. Good idea.'

'Great.'

'Well— Goodbye, then.'

'Thanks for calling.'

And with a beep, he was gone. Eloise put the phone back in her bag, gathering her courage; and then, hoping to divert Joan's inevitable recollections of Claude's culinary talents, she turned to her and decided that the moment had come. 'It's up to you, of course,' she began, 'but it seems to me – I mean, I think – that The Albany's really one of the best, in fact *the best*, of all the homes we've looked at. By a long way, wouldn't you say?'

'It seems excellent, darling.'

'Well I think it is, Mum. It's not easy to get into, either. There are only private rooms, no wards. It could take a very long time to get a place.'

This last detail was of interest to Joan, who intended to spend as long as she possibly could in her cosy little flat before bowing to the inevitable. 'Really, darling?'

Why was it, wondered Eloise, that she who had such a reputation for straight talking should be so tongue-tied now? Forcing herself to make eye contact, she straightened her shoulders. 'Don't you think you should put your name down on the waiting list?' she asked, gently. 'To keep the space open, if nothing else.' She paused, and when Joan did not break the silence she went on more gruffly than she had intended: 'I would, if I were you.'

For an instant, the suggestion hung in the air, almost visible between them.

Then Joan spoke, choosing her words carefully. 'If you would, darling, then I would.'

And in this way the thing was settled.

Chapter 2

Eloise woke a second or two before the hateful beeping of her alarm clock. She had slept on her side and cut off the blood supply to her right arm – which made it harder, when heavy with sleep, to locate and activate the Snooze function. A frustrated stab in the dark connected only with a glass of water, which broke as it fell from the table and forced her to begin the day on her knees, frenziedly mopping the blurring columns of a ruined spreadsheet. It was an April morning about six months since she and Joan had first visited The Albany, and although the days were lengthening it was not yet light.

She got up slowly and pressed a dimmer switch on the wall, which bathed the room in a soft, 'mood-enhancing' glow. Standing in front of the full-length mirror she had acquired as an incentive to dedicated exercise, she fought briefly against the idea of crawling back into bed: an idea she fought against every morning, in what was by far the most challenging conflict of her day. She was wearing a silk slip she had bought for herself the previous Christmas; it was a pale aquamarine and caught the colour of her eyes, which were large and deceptively gentle. She was a tall woman, almost five foot eleven, and big-boned. She examined herself critically – for she had intensified her training regime around the time of her first nursing home visit with Joan, and she monitored her progress daily.

Nature had not intended Eloise for a life of deftly tailored executive suits and the struggle to fit into them was a long and wearying one. She regretted last night's impulsive portion of egg fried rice.

As she rolled out a yoga mat, her day's To Do list flooded her head. She considered it as she lay on her back, breathing in through her mouth and out through her nostrils. She tried not to think of her yoga instructor's sultry injunction to 'breathe in acceptance of yourself, breathe out acceptance of others', but she found the memory hard to silence – and the irritation it prompted powered her through her first set of twenty stomach crunches. When she had finished, she stood up and examined herself once more in the mirror, encouraged by the fact that hints of her abdominals were visible if lit from the right angle. She returned to the yoga mat and repeated the process. As she neared the top of the final crunch, breathing out to intensify the contraction, she felt her grip on consciousness strengthen. She was never at her best in the very early morning and found it difficult to abandon the dreamless refuge of sleep: the sheer volume of each day's activity was too daunting. Once awake, however, things seemed more manageable; and by the time she was at the office, sixteen hours would pass reliably in an eye's blink.

She reached under her bed for a thin, grey disc and placed it over her breasts as she began a third set of crunches. The weight made the final contractions – seventeen, eighteen, nineteen ... twenty! – exquisitely painful. She lay on the floor as the lactic acid subsided, inventing reasons for postponing her morning jog. The relentless monotony of running and the absurd half-greetings it obliged her to exchange with other joggers irritated and bored Eloise. She had tried swimming as an aerobic alternative, but seemed to have forgotten the lessons of her childhood and was ashamed to repeat them decades later. She looked at her watch. It was 4.25 a.m. She had, she reminded herself, jogged twice this week already. She stood up and consulted the mirror once more, deciding that its verdict would be final: she was slightly underweight and acceptably well defined; her thick blonde hair, just the right side of lustrous, and her calves – though they would never again be thin – did not embarrass her. She went to the window and drew back the curtain. It was dark as night outside and the empty street was distinctly uninviting.

She decided against the run and went to shower instead.

By 6 a.m. Eloise had washed her hair, dried it, dressed, eaten a bowl of muesli, resisted the temptation to sugar it, had three cups of strong coffee, answered thirty-eight emails, listened to a voicemail message left at 2.26 a.m. by Claude (unlike him to call so late; he had sounded tense), stopped herself from phoning her mother to make sure she was ready for the movers, checked the temperature in Bloemfontein, South Africa, and packed a suitcase of clothes for the Trip of a Lifetime.

Standing in the hall with her case, she surveyed the chaos that stretched from living room to bedroom. There was only so much disciplined effort one person was capable of, and domestic maintenance was not one of Eloise's priorities. The crusted remains of three oat-based breakfasts stood dejectedly beside a cluster of cartons that contained the remnants of the previous evening's Chinese takeaway. Several shirts, selected then rejected for travel, lay in tragic attitudes where she had dropped them. She went to the desk in the living room and righted a small framed sketch of a roast chicken, in rusty brown, that had fallen over. It stood beside a photograph of her grandmother, and she blew the dust from both frames and returned to the door, patting her coat pockets for her keys.

Claude had never been able to abide her messiness. A coffee cup left unwashed for more than a few hours had, towards the end, been enough to inspire rage in him – a fact that had left her quite incapable of washing anything up for years. Now that an ocean separated them, and the only physical trace of him was a lump of blue-white metal in a sealed perspex cube, she could admit that she had (secretly) quite enjoyed provoking him. It had amused her to see his usually serene face contorted in fury, for there was a time when Eloise had been mischievous. She smiled at the recollection and decided to call Claude later, when it was breakfast time in Boston.

She double-locked her apartment and took the lift to ground level, feeling alert and purposeful. As she opened the mansion block's front door and stepped into a street now pleasantly full of crisp spring light, it occurred to her – as it often did, even now – that she far preferred sharing her life with a well-paid, part-time Kosovan housekeeper than with an unpaid, full-time French lover.

Eloise lived on Stratton Street, six blocks and a zebra crossing from her office on St James's. The traffic on Piccadilly was stationary and fuming, an endless line of five-seater cars bearing solitary commuters, and she hurried past them holding her breath, pulling her suitcase behind her. On entering the building in which most of her waking hours were spent, she nodded to the security guard and took the lift to the fifth floor – from which Green Park was just visible, its grass twinkling in the morning dew.

It was odd, all things considered (and she sometimes did consider such things), that Eloise's professional life should have taken her so close to Claude's own discipline, though in truth she had little grasp of metallurgy or any interest in acquiring one. Making money in niche commodities did not require hands-on experience of the goods traded, and over the years she had bought vast quantities of exotic ores that she had never seen, and sold them again without seeing them, and in the process – because she had an instinctive understanding of mass hysteria and the tendency of individuals to think as those around them do – she had grasped the essentially arbitrary nature of Value. She had not, it was true, read a novel in over a year, or had more than four consecutive days' holiday since 1998; and she had lost touch with every one of the friends who had once clustered so eagerly around Claude's dinner table, swearing lifelong intimacy with her.

Still, she thought, pushing open the office's swing doors, she would much rather have her life than Carol's.

Derby Capital occupied half a floor of a 1930s office block with a prestigious address. The fund's letter-headed paper was discreetly expensive, the business cards of its employees stiff and lavishly engraved. None of these details betrayed what was in fact the case: that besides Eloise McAllister, Patrick Derby and Carol Wheeler, only two other people worked there.

Patrick Derby ('Packet' to his friends) was already at his desk. He was a short, sweaty, ferociously bright man on the far side of fifty who had poached Eloise six years before from Kleinberger Dresden, in whose equities division they had once worked together. Behind him, five televisions conveyed the international news.

'Another fucking disaster in Iraq.' Patrick nodded at a screen which showed a smiling, fresh-faced American girl of extraordinary prettiness pointing a gun at the exposed genitals of a hooded prisoner. 'You're not flying British Airways, are you?'

'No.'

'I don't want you travelling on any British or American airliner until this crazy war is over – if it ever ends. Which reminds me.' He picked up a phone and barked at it, as though the object itself had caused him some kind of acute offence. 'Chloe? I need to go to New York. Four days, leaving next Thursday. Get me a corner room at the Four Seasons, nothing higher than the fifth floor, and a seat on Air France.' He pushed a button to cancel the call. Patrick never said please or thank you or goodbye on the telephone. Looking at Eloise for the first time that morning, he smiled briefly. He cultivated an air of formidable misanthropy that caused administrative assistants to avoid him in corridors but which had never terrified Eloise. This was partly why he had asked her to leave the bank and join his venture: she had an ability to withstand his rages and to stick to her guns. Patrick admired that quality in a person.

He leaned back in his chair and took a new plastic biro from a box of them on his desk, held it wistfully for a moment between index and middle finger, like a cigarette, and then bit through its lid with savage decision. Chewing plastic biros absorbed some of Patrick's excess nervous energy. 'How's osmium doing as it prepares for the big time?'

Eloise sat down and consulted her Bloomberg monitor. 'Rising steadily. Looks like the markets know something's up.'

'You sure this source of yours isn't sharing his secrets more widely?'

'I couldn't say.' She bit her lip. 'It's possible our own buying is driving the price up by itself.'

'What's our position?'

'When we put our first $25 million in, about six months ago, it was at $100 an ounce.'

'And the rest?'

'We've been building steadily since then, averaging about $10 million a month – a bit more in December, a bit less in March. We've got about $65 million in play now.'

'And what's osmium worth this morning?'

'A little over $200.'

'Sure we shouldn't just clean up while we can?'

She turned to face him, thinking of Claude's airy laboratory with its glass walls and ranks of white-suited technicians: a far cry from the dingy quarters he had occupied as a graduate student. 'There aren't many people I'd trust to deliver, but Pasquier's good,' she said. 'Besides which, the numbers tell a persuasive story. If you look at the cost of industrial diamonds—'

'You going first class?' Patrick had a habit of changing the subject abruptly.

'She wouldn't let me. Said it was obscene to spend that much money.'

'Cheapskate.'

'You try dealing with her.'

Patrick clamped another biro between his molars, which were small and square and capable of withstanding significant pressure – rather like the man in whose gums they grew. 'No thanks. As you know, mothers aren't my favoured leisure activity. No disrespect to yours, of course. Anyone lucky enough to spend several years fondling your bottom gets my vote, but from a distance.'

Patrick's mother was currently installed at his expense in a private nursing home recommended personally by one of Derby Capital's most valued clients, an African dictator whose mother-in-law had proved impossible to tolerate at the Presidential Palace. Patrick visited her once a month and complained about doing so for at least three days before and after each encounter. The idea of spending an entire fortnight in the company of a geriatric with whom he had nothing in common but a few temperamental genes was unthinkable. He had made this point more than once to Eloise.

'Thanks for the pep talk. I'm looking forward to it, actually.'

'No need to get all defensive.'

Eloise was making a point of ignoring this jibe when the lift doors at the end of the corridor opened and Carol Wheeler walked through them. She was shorter than Eloise and could have been older or younger, though from this distance she looked as she might have done a decade or so before: slim; studious; with a strong nose and long, curled, dark hair. Carol was wearing her habitual navy-blue business suit, its skirt cut well below the knee, and wedge heels which drew attention to the fact that she was not as tall as she would have liked. As she came closer, her exhaustion showed itself more plainly and inspired in Eloise a sympathetic distaste which she disguised beneath a warm gesture of greeting.

Eloise McAllister and Carol Wheeler disliked each other intensely, but politely. Patrick knew this, and exploited the dynamic's competitive potential. In fact, he had hired Carol mainly because he approved of the way she would inevitably clash with Eloise. Experience had taught him the value of a brilliant risk-taker, but he knew also that Eloise's heady intuition required the ballast of a sober rationalist. This Carol undoubtedly was. She was also kinder than Eloise suspected, or was able to glimpse – though Carol felt for her colleague an envy so vicious it woke her, sometimes, in the night.

'Are we expecting good things from Anglo-Titanium?' asked Eloise, when Carol had closed the door.

'Hard to tell.' Carol took off her jacket, hung it on a hook and went to her desk. 'Apparently almost seventy per cent of the workforce is now HIV positive, and they've been forced to provide free anti-retrovirals after dragging their feet for ten years.'

'Corporate cunts.'

'Quite, Patrick.' Carol knelt down. Her one eccentricity was to work at a kneeler rather than a chair, in order to mitigate debilitating back pain. This meant that she not only faced Eloise but knelt towards her: an irking necessity that she obviated, where possible, by addressing her colleagues from a standing position. Now she seemed to decide against the kneeler in the act of slipping onto it, and she rose unexpectedly and shuffled some papers. Then she said, 'I think we're over-exposing ourselves on osmium.'

The timing of this announcement illustrated one of the many things that Eloise disliked in Carol: a timid Machiavellianism that combined deviousness with a complete absence of the necessary style. She could, of course, have raised her objections to the fund's steady build-up of osmium reserves at any point in the last six months, but had chosen to do so a few hours before Eloise left the country on a ten-day trip. The manoeuvre's lack of finesse was astonishing.

'Go on,' said Patrick.

Carol cleared her throat and began. 'We've bought up $65 million of osmium so far. That's thirteen per cent of the entire fund in a commodity that hasn't shown any significant upward movement in the last decade.'

'When MaxiTech's research is published, there'll be movement,' remarked Eloise, pleasantly.

'Maybe. But I'm anxious about relying on the word of a single scientist. I know Pasquier's given us good leads in the past, but I've read his CV and research history and—'

'Yes?'

'And the fact is he's too emotionally involved. He's been working on osmium for too long and can't see the situation clearly.' She glanced at a list of Claude's publications on her desk. 'Interestingly, he's written nothing on the subject since 2001 – which suggests to me that he has run out of ideas. That certainly seems to be the opinion of the scientific community at large: that the osmium project is simply not going to work. I wonder if you've seen—'

'Yes,' said Eloise. 'I've seen the work of the Lawrence Livermore National Laboratory. I believe it was published ten years ago?'

'That's the last time anyone, apart from Pasquier, published any-thing on osmium.'

'You've certainly done some timely research, Carol.' Eloise smiled dangerously. 'Why don't we all sit down and talk it through?'

There was a moment's awkwardness, a silent duel of made-up eyes, that resulted in a first-round victory for Eloise, whose smile grew warmer as her colleague sank to her knees.

'I can understand your caution. Really I can,' she said graciously, once Carol's eye level was appropriately lower than her own. 'And I think it's healthy for there to be a cautious voice in any discussion. You know I do.' She stopped smiling. 'But you've misread the situation and the research. What the scientists at the LLNL proved – or think they've proved – is that osmium is not, in fact, harder than diamond, as Pasquier originally proposed. They didn't suggest for a moment it was anything other than a super-hard substance, and the fact that it is the least compressible of all metals is undisputed.'

Carol opened her mouth.

'As you so rightly note,' Eloise went on, 'osmium has been con-sistently undervalued for decades. To date, no one but Pasquier has really looked into its possible industrial applications. You might find some in the tip of an expensive fountain pen, but you won't come across any in a factory.' She leaned forward, aware of Patrick's eyes on her. 'Traditional thinking goes that diamond is the material best suited to industry's cutting requirements. But it's also an imperfect solution to a lot of major problems. Diamond can't, for instance, slice through hot steel. Why not? Because the iron in the steel absorbs the carbon atoms in the diamond. Importantly also, diamond's brittleness means that when it fails it does so catastrophically.'

It was astonishing, she thought, how those early conversations with Claude had burned themselves into her impressionable brain. She remembered him leaning forward in bed, shoulders hunched, in the grip of a quasi-mystical desire to bear witness to an element's extraordinary powers. 'For years', she went on, 'people have been looking to diamond to point the way to the durable, super-hard compounds that industry in the twenty-first century needs. The problem is, no one has found a workable solution.'

'But—'

'Granted, there's a theoretical possibility that a diamond compound called beta-carbon nitride could – and that's *could* – be harder than diamond, but so far no one's been able to make a piece big enough to test. And all attempts to insert *non*-carbon elements into diamond-like tetrahedral structures have so far come to nothing.'

As she spoke, the part of Eloise's brain that was watching her performance found time to recognise that she had no idea what 'diamond-like tetrahedral structures' might be, though she had heard Claude declaim against them on many occasions. 'The reason Maxi-Tech has given Pasquier almost unlimited resources,' she continued, 'is that he has vision.'

'I just don't think—'

'Imagine what will happen to the price of osmium when its durability and strength are harnessed effectively to the needs of industry. World reserves are tiny, and what mines there are have limited capacity. Sinking new ones will take serious investment and a lot of time. If we buy now, we could dry up the market's liquidity, which will send the price through the roof when everyone starts buying.

Feeling that the situation was veering dangerously out of control, Carol stood up from her kneeler. Having done so, however, she was seized by one of the paralysing spells of inarticulacy that occasionally came over her in the presence of Eloise. 'That's *if* osmium's durability and strength are harnessed effectively,' was all she managed to say.

'I said "when" for a reason. Let's weigh some probabilities here.' Eloise noted, with satisfaction, that Patrick had begun chewing his biro again. 'Claude Pasquier went to the Sorbonne at seventeen and graduated top of his class. He had a doctorate by the time he was twenty-seven and a full professorship by the age of twenty-nine. At thirty-five he was Head of Materials Science at the School of Earth and Planetary Sciences at Berkeley, and by the time he was forty he was running the place – which he did for almost a decade. For the last seven years he's been Head of Research and Development at one of the world's most aggressively pioneering companies. If anyone can do it, he can.'

Since liquidating her mother's share portfolio in the harrowing aftermath of the dot-com implosion, and sacking the hapless financial adviser who had decimated Joan's savings, Eloise had scrupulously kept from her the precariousness of her situation and covered her monthly outgoings from her own salary, knowing that it was useless to trouble her brother George for funds. She was, however, sufficiently alive to the vagaries of professional fortune to know that this could not go on indefinitely. What Joan needed was an independent income. She might, after all, live another twenty years, and the costs of doing so at The Albany were staggering. Only a major lump sum, invested in safely dependable bonds and ring-fenced from Eloise's other earnings, could provide Joan with long-term security; and such an investment, in the context of a life as expensive as Eloise's, demanded a bonus of significant proportions. She was not about to let Carol interfere with the most likely opportunity that had presented itself in years. 'We know Pasquier's the man for the job,' was all she said, turning to her computer as though the discussion was concluded.

'But that's exactly the problem.' Carol raised her voice now. 'Pasquier's been working on osmium for years, with world-class research facilities behind him. He hasn't come up with anything.'

'Yes he has. He told me so.'

'But he wasn't specific.'

'He said—' Eloise tried to remember, precisely, what Claude had said in that taxi with Joan six months before, but the only phrase that came to her was her mother's enigmatic 'If you would, darling, then I would.' Banishing this recollection, she summarised for him: 'He's on the verge of a breakthrough. It's months, not years.'

'We can't wait around indefinitely in the hopes that a miracle will happen.' There was something taut in Carol's voice now. 'Even if you do have *a personal relationship with him.*'

Eloise had not shared her and Claude's romantic history with Patrick and Carol, presenting Dr Pasquier instead as a useful contact – whose tips, over the years, had been lucrative. She ignored this bait now and said, 'If I thought we'd have to wait indefinitely, I wouldn't have suggested it. But you'll remember I visited his lab last year, when I was in Boston for the World Metals Fair. He's got some of the best minds in metallurgy working under him. So when he tells me he's almost there' – she looked straight into Patrick's eyes – 'I believe him.'

It was at moments like these that Eloise most enjoyed being herself. She had a gift for grasping the essentials of an argument, for absorbing them and making them her own. This allowed her access to a livelier, more intuitive truth than that available to unimaginative rationalists like Carol; and though she could have told her colleagues nothing about beta-carbon nitride, if pressed, or distinguished a diamond-like tetrahedral structure from a tetrahedral structure that was not diamond-like (if, indeed, such a thing existed), the concepts had ceased to be hazy ideas to her. Osmium and diamond were now protagonists in an eternal drama, a battle between opposing forces of titanic strength, and in some mysterious way they had become subject to the indisputable laws of narrative. It would be osmium, the poor relation – ignored, neglected, dismissed – that triumphed over its glittering rival in the end, and secured an old lady's future.

The effect of this romantic vision, coupled with the temptation to put Carol firmly in her place, was irresistible. Argument always had this capacity to crystallise the uncertain for Eloise, to lend opinion the quality of truth, and when she spoke next it was with a victor's calm authority. 'I think we should double up,' she said, quietly. 'If we put twenty-five per cent in osmium and the price rises, say, five hundred per cent – which is conservative – we'll double the fund. Last year was pretty lacklustre. We need to raise our risk profile to stay with the pack, and if we really want to take this business places we shouldn't be thinking of off-loading the position. We should be putting another $65 million into play.'

Patrick's molars stopped grinding.

'That's – No!' Carol's interjection came as an indignant squeak, which she instantly regretted. 'That's more than a quarter of the fund. We can't . . .' But she did not finish her sentence.

There was silence, broken only by the droning of the fluorescent lights above them.

'Let's do it,' said Patrick.

Chapter 3

A little later that morning, Joan stood in the remains of what had been her sitting room, watching two New Zealanders wrap her beloved upright piano in blankets and begin to hoist it onto a wheeled trolley. In a corner, propped against a wall, its five ornamental griffins patiently bearing the indignity of suffocation in bubble wrap, was the chandelier her mother had given her and Frank on their honeymoon visit to Cape Town sixty years before, and on whose behalf she had fought so fruitlessly against Astrid.

She went to the reproduction Queen Anne bureau by the door and put the note she had written her daughter into an envelope. The shaky letters seemed inadequate to the message they conveyed, but the voice in her head as she read them was unmistakably her own: *You are my firstborn*, she had written, *and I have loved you deeply and tenderly, and watched with pride as you have lived your life, since the moment I first held you all those years ago. Being your mother has been one of the greatest privileges I have known.* She would present her gift in person once they were back from their trip, but she wished to have everything well prepared in advance. There was something forbidding about Eloise that Joan feared might inhibit her at the crucial moment; and there were certain things, too rarely expressed, that she did not wish to leave unsaid.

'You want this at the nursing home with you?' asked an unwashed young man.

'Yes, please,' said Joan. 'I'm going to be giving it to my daughter.'

'No worries.'

'Thank you, dear.'

She watched as he lifted the light fitting gently into the box she had wrapped for it the night before, burying each of its tissue-swathed shades among the cushioning wedges of styrofoam. When he had finished, she taped the package closed and tied a ribbon around it, thinking how pretty it looked. Then she slipped her card beneath the bow, satisfied with a job well done, and examined the room hopefully – but the pedals had not come.

It was clear that she would have to face this moment of parting alone.

Joan had lived at Flat 3, 16 Wilsmore Street, South Kensington, for a little over twenty years. With the exception of nine delirious months in Soho in 1947, the interval between her arrival in London and her marriage, she had never lived alone except behind its comforting stucco façade; and as she watched the morning sun creep across her sitting room floor for the last time, she felt the sense of bereavement she might have done at the bedside of a departing loved one. Though Eloise had insisted, absolutely *insisted*, that she should store whatever she could not bring to The Albany, it was clear to Joan that she would not see again whatever she allowed these young people with their big hands and unfamiliar vowels to take away with them this morning.

Unable to bear the presence of strangers any longer, she left the sitting room and shuffled down the corridor to her bedroom. On the bed, awaiting attention, were neatly tied stacks of cardboard folders: eight decades of letters and photographs, en route to oblivion. She had intended, at some point in a future that had too quickly become the present, to go through them all and live her life again, in old age; but now that the moment had come she found that she had no stomach for it.

On the bedside table was the single box of personal possessions permitted by the management of The Albany. Peering into it, she saw that she had saved a certificate congratulating Eloise on five consecutive wins of the Princess Louise Merit Cup; Frank's Croix de Guerre, Silver Star; some family photographs and trinkets; a picture of her bedroom at Nooitgedacht, the paper peeling from the walls where the rain had leaked through the roof; a few books. It was a haphazard collection, but how could it be otherwise? To choose between objects one loved was no choice at all.

She thought of the ferociously lush grounds of her childhood home, of the tangled confusion of pampas grass that had once rioted behind its disused slave quarters. The smell of the marguerite bushes came to her, and the dankness of the space beneath the floorboards as she crawled through it, with Rupert in close pursuit. As an adult, on her honeymoon visit to introduce Frank to her mother, she had tried to share with her

24

new husband the happy mysteries of this early world, but her nanny's stories of the *tokolosh*, and Rupert's of the white witch who lived in the cypress tree on the lawn, had left him unmoved.

She shook her head firmly, as if to shake out the heavy realisations of that time. Over the years at Wilsmore Street, her recollections of her marriage had resolved themselves into two or three comforting scenes, which were all she cared to dwell on: the way Frank had seized her hand in a darkened cinema, shortly before his stammered proposal; his spontaneous sobs on the morning of Eloise's birth, so out of character in an otherwise tight-lipped man. She had forgotten the evenings of suffocating monosyllables; the dinners cooked with passion and eaten in silence; and of Astrid she had thought as little as possible for twenty years.

She sat down on the bed. The sheets had been stripped and were waiting to be given away, and the mattress beneath her bore a large brown stain – but that hardly mattered, because the bed was going too. What else should she save? She lifted a cardboard folder at random and put it into the box. The act was tiring and left her dejected, for the little space that remained was so unequal to the task of containing a lifetime. She resolved to choose just one more keepsake and to leave its selection to chance; so she closed her eyes and extended her arm, running her fingers along the smooth board of the folders, and pulled something out.

It was a photograph of a large, substantially bosomed woman, sitting stoutly on a straight-backed chair under a pergola of roses. She wore a long dark skirt and bodice, both heavily fringed with beads, and her head was bare, her hair scraped severely back. She was about forty and her eyes stared narrowly at the camera, mistrustful of this strange new device which so impudently did the work of a human artist with such accuracy and speed.

She looked like a woman who was mistrustful of speed.

The veranda she sat on belonged to a long, single-storey thatched dwelling, made solidly and without ostentation of roughly hewn stone. Four shallow steps led from the lawn to the front door, which was open and offered a glimpse into the room beyond. A girl of sixteen or seventeen stood in the doorway, tall and strongly built, wearing a starched white pinafore with a white band across her forehead that restrained a tumble of thick dark hair. Large, long-lashed eyes looked straight into the camera with a saucy bravado that reminded Joan of Eloise, when she was that age.

In the hall, the telephone rang. Joan put the picture down and attempted to stand up. She had left her stick in the sitting room and had sat down without thinking of it. How vexing! The phone continued to ring. It seemed unlikely that the removals men would answer it. Really she must get up. She was sure it was Eloise.

She edged down the bed until she was within grasping distance of the dressing table. Leaning forward, she put her hands on it and tried to pull herself up. But the angle was all wrong. The phone stopped ringing. This removed the sense of urgency and left her calmer. She sat upright again and rested for a moment before bending over once more with renewed vigour and launching herself forward. Achieving lift-off, she clung to the dressing table and used her arms to pull herself further from the bed, at which point the door opened and one of the hulking Antipodeans entered the room to find her in what was (she could not help thinking, with irritation) an embarrassing position.

'Your daughter's on the phone,' he said, coming towards her and lifting her effortlessly to her feet before handing her the cordless handset.

Joan took a deep breath. 'Thank you.'

'No problem.'

She put the speaker to her ear.

'Mum? Are you all right?'

'Hello, darling.' Joan did her best to sound alert and cheerful, as she always did when she spoke to Eloise. 'I was just in the bedroom.'

'Is everything okay with the packers?'

'Absolutely. They're doing a very thorough job.'

'Well that's good.'

'Yes.'

'Very good.'

'Yes.'

'Are you all packed and ready?'

'Absolutely.'

'Well that's good, too.'

'Yes.' Joan's conversations with Eloise often tended towards these monosyllabic exchanges, which was partly why she had written a letter to accompany her gift of the griffin chandelier. 'And how's your day going?'

'Mine? So busy you can't imagine. I'll tell you all about it on the plane.'

'Right.'

'I *am* looking forward to our holiday.' Joan spoke with sudden enthusiasm.

'So am I.'

There was a moment's pause, which a flash of inspiration allowed Joan to fill. 'You'll never guess what I found this morning, darling, while I was sorting through the last of my papers.'

'What?'

'A photograph of your great-grandmother with Hannie.'

'The one who played the organ when the—'

'Yes, exactly. She looks a little like you, I think.'

'Make sure you bring it.'

'I will.'

'And I'll see you at seven o'clock.'

'You don't think that's cutting things a bit fine?'

Eloise and Joan had had this conversation before.

'No, Mum, I promise you. If we leave any earlier we'll just get stuck in the rush hour. Our flight only takes off at half past nine and it doesn't take any more than half an hour to get from your house to the airport when there's no traffic. We'll be there with two hours to spare, at least.'

'Well if you're sure.'

'I'm sure.'

'I suppose you do do a lot of travelling.'

'Yes I do.'

'So you would know.'

'Yes I would.'

'All right then.'

'Goodbye, Mum.'

'Goodbye, darling.'

And so their conversation ended.

'What is it with mothers and airports?' asked Patrick at Eloise's end of the line. 'Even before she lost her mind, mine would want to arrive six months before check-in opened.'

Eloise shrugged her shoulders and picked up the telephone again. 'Emily?' Beyond a glass partition at the far end of the room, her assistant picked up her telephone. 'You've arranged a car?'

'Yes, Eloise.'

'Good. Get the driver to pick me up here at six-thirty, please. We'll stop by my mother's at Wilsmore Street and then go on to Heathrow.'

'All taken care of.'

'And you're sure the plane will be an Airbus 340-500?'

'Yes. South African Airways has just introduced them on the Johannesburg route. Fully flat beds in business class. And I've ordered a gluten-free meal for you.'

'Excellent.'

'Anything else I can do?'

'Schedule a call with the chairman of Anglo-Titanium for three-thirty. It'll need to be a conference with Patrick.'

Patrick was looking at his Bloomberg monitor when she put down the phone. 'Osmium's just passed $203.'

'That'll be small change by the time we're done. You'll have to sell your body to cover my bonus.'

'You wouldn't accept payment in kind?'

'So tempting, but no.'

Patrick bit through the end of the pen in his mouth and removed the thin cartridge cylinder. Inserting the dry end into his ear, he rotated it, emitting a low whistle of pleasure. 'No better itch to scratch than an ear itch.'

'I'll bear that in mind.'

For several minutes they worked together in companionable silence. Then Eloise said: 'You made the right decision this morning, you know.'

'I know.'

'I think Pasquier's going to come through for us.'

'I believe you.'

'I'll have Emily make up a dossier of the relevant research for you this afternoon. You can study it over the weekend.'

'No need.'

'No need?'

Patrick picked up a fresh biro and took a meditative puff on it. 'I made my bet when I hired you, McAllister,' he said. 'If you believe in something this strongly, so do I.' He leaned back in his chair. 'Of course, if it turns out you're wrong, or Pasquier's some dodgy Frog scientist you slept with once' – he smiled broadly, displaying defiantly uncared-for gums – 'I'll simply have you hunted down, tortured appropriately, and left to roast in your own burning house.'

'How gallant.'

Patrick put the pen in his mouth and chomped it in two, emphatically. 'If it's any consolation,' he said, 'I'll do the same to him.'

Chapter 4

Eloise had arrived at the idea of taking her mother on the Trip of a Lifetime by a circuitous, occasionally fraught mental process fired chiefly by guilt. She had spent enough money on therapy to know that this was at best an unreliable motivation, but there was nothing she could do about that. Life was a series of decisions and consequences. It was clear – and had been becoming clearer for some time – that Joan could no longer live alone on the third floor of a building with no one but a shift-working porter to deal with any emergencies that might arise. Some sort of consequence-laden step had to be taken.

Eloise's younger brother George, who at forty-six might reasonably have been expected to share the responsibility for their mother's well-being, had absconded deftly to Sydney five years before. He lived there with his second wife, an artificially pneumatic Australian who had been his PA, in a glass-walled apartment on the North Shore with panoramic views of the harbour and the Opera House, paid for by the advertising agency whose Youth Media department he ran.

Both siblings had known, in the weeks before his departure, that George was leaving Joan's welfare in Eloise's hands, but neither had spoken of it. Now that ten time zones and a nineteen-hour flight separated him from his only surviving parent, he safely discharged his filial duty by issuing an annual invitation for Christmas, secure in the knowledge that it would be regretfully declined. On his occasional visits to England he made a point of having dinner with his mother every night for a week. Otherwise he left the management of her declining health and prospects to his sister.

'Put her in a fucking home.' That had been Patrick's advice.

'I couldn't do that,' Eloise had said, but she had known even as she spoke that she could. Over time, that knowledge had transformed itself into an understanding that she would. And now the moment had come: on their return from South Africa, Joan would be moving in to The Albany with a new set of fire-retardant sheets.

Eloise felt terrible about this, but she knew that the alternative was more terrible.

Eight years before, when a lavish bonus from Patrick had permitted a decisive ascent to the upper reaches of the property ladder, she had instinctively avoided any advertisements that boasted detached outhouses. Joan, who had insisted on accompanying her on her many outings with over-tanned estate agents, clucking all the while about the expense of property nowadays, had fastened on a beautiful Edwardian villa in Richmond, with a coach house at the end of the garden that might have been refurbished as eminently suitable semi-independent accommodation. 'How useful it would be, for guests,' she had said, significantly.

Though neither of them had mentioned its implications, Eloise's choice of a Mayfair maisonette – with a second bedroom she had converted emphatically into a home office with impressively durable built-in bookcases – had decided Joan's future. From that moment, her removal to a home had ceased to be a matter of 'if' and become a question of 'when'.

The answer to that question was now available to them both.

As Eloise entered the lift that evening, after a shortened working day of just twelve hours, she felt a momentary and uncharacteristic desire to burst into tears. A long, hard cry would have provided relief, but there was no time for it in an elevator with only five floors to travel between. Outside, a suited driver loitered against a black Mercedes, waiting for her. He was stocky and fresh-faced, vaguely insolent, and made confident eye contact as he asked her where she wanted to go. It was a strange thing, being older, she thought. You never knew when a look was a *look*. She smiled and gave him her mother's address, and his white teeth, bared in return, lifted her mood.

She got into the car and leaned back into the soft leather seat. Though she could not live with her mother, she could – and was about to – provide her with an experience she would never forget; a swansong to vitality that would ease the coming transition for them both. Reaching into her bag, she took out her Blackberry and switched it off with a gesture of devil-may-care finality, remembering just as she had done so that she had not returned Claude's message.

She hesitated, about to switch it on again. Then she put it back into her bag. She had to be in a certain mood to get through conversations with Claude, and the lateness of his call suggested drama – of which she'd had quite enough already today. No, she thought: too late. She would tell him about the morning's events when she got back from her trip, and until then her only focus would be her mother.

As her daughter's car edged through the traffic, Joan stood in her now empty sitting room and wished earnestly for the pedals. She had known, ever since Eloise bought that ugly 'luxury apartment' in a post-war block on a noisy street in Mayfair, that she would one day leave Wilsmore Street for an institution of some sort. She had accepted this fact as she had accepted other inevitabilities in her life: with as much cheerfulness as possible. Her contented routine and the gentle pleasure she took from it had a permanence that made its future destruction unreal, somehow, and strangely unlikely. Now that crushed sections of carpet were all that remained of the furniture that had once made the space so cosy, the bare walls with their pretty blue-grey paint seemed to mock her, and for a moment the space threatened to become the overheated, brightly furnished housekeeper's room, on the top floor of a London boys' school, in which Frank had taken her to meet his mother.

She held her nerve against this possibility, though without the pedals she was rarely able to influence the itineraries of her internal excursions. The sound of Astrid singing Ivor Novello seeped, unbidden, from a deep crevice of memory, and brought with it a trace of the numberless hours she had spent at the piano accompanying her mother-in-law's penetrating renditions of the hits of her youth. 'No!' she said, aloud, for there was no one to hear her; and as she spoke the pedals materialised on the window sill and she stepped forward and grasped them, with a sharp inhalation of gratitude.

The room at once assumed its former identity, undoing all traces of the morning's lumbering men and the destruction they had wrought. Her piano reappeared on the far wall, beneath the watercolour of Nooitgedacht that Rupert had painted three weeks before his death, and with it came two small sofas, whose embroidered antimacassars she had stitched herself. Her mother's favourite rug stretched at her feet, evocative of the many dogs that had slept on it in the years before its arrival in England, and books crowded into bookcases once more, in amicable disarray. Above her the griffin chandelier shone with familiar benignity, its etched shades casting intricate shadows on the ceiling.

The only false note in this delightful illusion was the presence on a side table of the small porcelain box, painted with peonies, in which she had hoarded the little orange pills Astrid had started giving her in the months after Eloise's birth, as her lengthy stay extended into full-time residence in the McAllister household. Joan had broken this box, emphatically, and refused all further medicaments on the morning of George's sixth birthday party. It could not possibly be there. And yet it was. She closed her eyes to banish it, but when she opened them again the entire room had vanished, as if offended by her quibbling. She was standing once more on a piece of crushed carpet, and the emptiness around her spoke eloquently of finality. As the street lights buzzed to life beyond the curtainless window, she struggled for control, and then abandoned the effort and began to cry.

Joan had not cried for many years – not since George had left for Australia and taken with him the possibility of an old age enjoyed in the raucous company of tousled grandchildren. Her frame, no longer as sturdy as it had been, shuddered at the force of the sobs that welled from some long-closed place within her; and for a moment she was twelve years old again, called by Beauty to the breakfast room at Nooitgedacht to hear that Rupert had died in the night.

For ten minutes she wept. Then she stopped. Eloise would be arriving soon and could not possibly see her in such a state. She went into the bathroom and splashed her eyes with icy water. Reaching for a hand towel, she remembered that there wasn't one. All that was left of the collected treasures of a lifetime was half a roll of toilet paper, with which she dried her face. Peering into the mirror, still screwed into the tiled wall, she saw that she looked haggard and drawn and experienced a moment's unusual vanity. She had been a good-looking woman in her day. This was no way to face old age, dejected and defeated. She went back into the hall and opened one of her suitcase's brass locks with difficulty, retrieving her vanity case from an inner compartment. Most mornings she applied nothing more than some powder and a dab of rouge. Now she put on lipstick and eye shadow too, bringing her features vividly to life.

By the time the doorbell rang she felt better.

*

32

A thickset, good-looking young man opened the door of a sleek black car for her and Joan's spirits rose. She was not entirely unsusceptible to the glamour of her daughter's success, though she pretended to be.

'You look wonderful,' said Eloise, gripping her hand.

'Nonsense.' But the compliment pleased her. As the car accelerated on the motorway she looked at her daughter's striking profile, at the high cheekbones and glowing skin that turned so many heads, and was sorry that Eloise should feel guilty about putting her into The Albany. That she did was clear to Joan, who had too much experience of her confident façade to be deceived by it. The very lavishness of this holiday spoke volumes, and she wished she could tell her that she harboured no resentment. Why should a child devote the best years of her life to taking care of an ageing parent? She had given her love freely, without reciprocal obligation; and though she wished, perhaps, that things had turned out differently, that was not the same thing as resenting the way things *had* turned out.

'Did you bring the photograph of Hannie?' asked Eloise.

Joan thought for a moment. She had certainly intended to bring it. She tried to think where she had put it, but could only remember leaving it on the bed when the telephone rang. She must have left it on the mattress, which meant that it was now in a van heading to a storage facility, that it was evermore lost to her.

'Do you know, I think I've forgotten it.' She heard the irritation in her voice and worried that Eloise would feel responsible for it. 'It's my fault,' she added hastily. 'There was just so much on today. You'll find it in my papers when I'm gone.'

She wished, as the words were spoken, that she had chosen others. Eloise's shoulders tensed and Joan saw that her remark was open to misinterpretation. It sounded bitter and was not meant to. 'Or perhaps we can both go down to the storage place when we get back, and find it,' she said quickly. 'Once you've seen where your family came from, you'll want to see what they looked like.'

'That's what we'll do.'

'Yes.'

'As soon as we get back.'

'Yes.'

'Which terminal are you flying from?' asked their dashing driver.

Chapter 5

At the door to the business-class lounge, a middle-aged stewardess in a viscose uniform handed Joan a newspaper whose front page was devoted to a photograph of a blonde, white-toothed young woman helpless with mirth, pointing delightedly at a naked figure with terrified eyes who appeared to be dripping wet and suspended from an overhead bar by wires attached to his wrists. A picture editor of delicate sensibilities had blurred the hanging man's groin area, as though the sight of a flaccid penis was in some way more shocking than this image of squalid brutality.

The lounge was full of smartly dressed men and women eating stale canapés and watching the television sets that were mounted in each of its four corners. Two were displaying different games of football while the third was tuned to a long procession of bony women wearing outlandish make-up and very little else, who appeared to be striding purposefully but going nowhere. On the fourth, a kindly-looking man was reassuring the world that 'the images we see today from Abu Ghraib prison are the work of the few, not the many. The behaviour of these individuals does not in any way reflect the actions of our fine soldiers in Iraq. We will not rest—'

No one seemed to be paying the least bit of attention to him.

As Eloise led her to a right-angled grouping of expansive armchairs, Joan felt ashamed of the self-indulgence of her earlier tears. What was the loss of an upright piano, or an antique light fitting, by comparison with the sufferings of this poor unnamed man? There was something shocking about the way the prisoner's blurred genitals were reproduced, with so little apparent impact, in the carelessly discarded newspapers scattered over low veneer tables.

'We are in Iraq to help the Iraqi people,' said the friendly man on the screen.

'Would you like a glass of champagne?' asked Eloise.

'No, thank you.'

The knowledge that her daughter, too, saw nothing worthy of comment in the newspaper headlines depressed Joan immeasurably. Perhaps she had not seen them. She put the newspaper carefully face up on the table between them, as Eloise summoned a pale young server.

'Anything for you, madam?' he asked Joan.

'Come on, Mum. Have something. You're on holiday.'

Joan looked at her daughter's smiling face. 'How could I—?' But she faltered. Drawing attention to her own outrage seemed suddenly ostentatious. They *were* on holiday, after all. Perhaps Eloise was being cheerful for her sake.

'We are serving an excellent Veuve Clicquot tonight,' said the waiter, handing them a plate of tiny smoked-salmon sandwiches on a tin tray.

'Go on.' Eloise almost added, 'It's free.' Her mother's resistance to the spending of money had always irritated her and she asked for two glasses. 'I'll drink yours if you don't want it,' she said teasingly, reminding herself that she was here to make the experience fun for Joan.

'All right then, darling.' Joan shifted in her seat so that Eloise's head blocked the callous eyes of the kindly-looking man on the television screen behind her. Steeling herself, she took a sandwich from the tray. It was cut into a tiny, painstakingly equilateral triangle. 'How delicious!' she said. 'I'm being spoiled rotten.'

'Of course you are. We're here to enjoy ourselves.'

'Of course we are.'

They smiled at each other in silence for a moment, but Joan had prepared for this. 'You said your day was busy?'

Eloise leaned back in her chair in a gesture of exhaustion. 'I can't tell you how glad I am to get out of the office.'

'Why?'

'Oh, no particular reason. I'm just exhausted.'

'You don't get enough sleep.'

This was another conversation that Eloise and Joan had had before. Seeking to divert its course, Eloise embarked on a simplified anecdote about Derby Capital's buying-up of osmium reserves; but though she had tried diligently for years, Joan had never been able to grasp the finer details of futures trading and arbitrage around which her daughter's professional life revolved. Now, as the kindly man disappeared from the television screen to be replaced by a blow-dried reporter silhouetted against a burning building, she found it even harder to follow the thread of the narrative. Eloise, reading her abstraction for boredom, hurried through her day and put things in the simplest possible terms, explaining what was in fact all that mattered: that she had just bet a sizeable sum on Claude being right about osmium.

A further relevant question suggested itself to Joan. 'What do you mean by a "sizeable sum", darling?'

'About a hundred and thirty million dollars.'

To Joan, who had never spent more than £48,000 – the price of a twenty-two-year lease on Flat 3, 16 Wilsmore Street, South Kensington – on a single transaction in her life, the figure was unimaginable. 'Goodness me,' she said. 'But what happens if Claude's wrong?'

'He won't be.'

'But what would happen if he was?'

'The price would fall.'

'By how much?'

'Difficult to say. By a lot, probably.'

'And could you lose all the money you've put into it so far?'

'Not all of it. A lot of it, perhaps.'

The possibility, however slight, of losing any part of a hundred and thirty million dollars was so alarming to Joan that she took a sip of champagne to steady herself, and then another. This emboldened her unexpectedly. 'So you've been speaking to Claude?'

'He called last night.'

'How is he?'

'I don't know. He left a message and I forgot to call him back.' Eloise sensed that she and her mother were drifting dangerously close to another conversation they had had before.

'Claude was the cleverest of all the men you've ever gone out with,' said Joan, confirming her daughter's fears. 'You need a clever man, someone you can't run circles around. And he was so good-looking.'

'If the emaciated academic look works for you.'

'So good-looking,' repeated Joan, wistfully. 'How kind of him to let you know in advance about his research. Although' – a thought occurred to her – 'isn't that illegal?'

'There's no such thing as insider dealing in the commodities markets, Mum,' said Eloise, patiently reiterating a point she had explained many times before. 'It's not like equities. There are no rules against exchanging information like this.'

'So you can't get into trouble?'

'No.'

'Well that's good, darling.'

'Yes.'

Joan paused. 'Imagine if you *do* make' – she steeled herself, as though taking a physical leap – 'all your money back.'

'We'll make more than our money back, hopefully. If Claude's right we could double the value of the fund.'

'You'll owe it all to Claude.'

'I'll send him flowers.'

'You should do more than that, darling. A visit of some description, at least. A holiday. Something he would really enjoy.'

'Perhaps,' said Eloise with emphasis, 'I should give Claude *and his wife* a weekend break at a romantic hotel.'

But Joan was lost to sarcasm now. 'Do you remember that wonderful dinner he cooked for your birthday? When was it? You were living in Paris, in the eighteeth – with that beautiful view of Sacré Coeur. It must have been your twenty-fifth or -sixth. Do you remember?'

The fact that six railway lines terminating in the Gare du Nord had formed the foreground of the beautiful view in question was one of the many irritating little details that time had smoothed from Joan's memory.

She's going to start talking about the duck, thought Eloise.

'I don't think I've ever eaten such exquisite duck,' said Joan.

By the time their flight was called, Eloise had consumed four glasses of champagne in an effort to maintain the cheery intimacy with her mother that the situation demanded. Joan, whose reminiscences of Claude's cooking had taken her on a delightful journey through some of her happiest memories, was feeling better than she had all day. Even the wheelchair which a smiling attendant helped her into did not dampen her spirits. Where was the advantage, after all, in trudging the long miles to the gate on foot, as the more able-bodied were compelled to do?

'Good evening, Mrs McAllister. Good evening, Ms McAllister. Welcome aboard,' said a statuesque black steward at the aeroplane door.

'But how wonderful of him to know our names!' whispered Joan to Eloise as they took their seats.

Eloise resisted the temptation to explain to her mother that the steward had read their names on their boarding cards. She was more preoccupied with something she had understood as soon as she entered the cabin – that this was not, as Emily had assured her it would be, an Airbus 340-500. That meant, unless she was much mistaken, that she would not find a fully flat bed; and a cursory examination of the control panel by her side as she sat down confirmed her suspicion.

Joan was right. Eloise did not get enough sleep. The adrenalin of her work days kept her mind spiralling long after her return from the office. 'Take a fucking pill,' Patrick advised her regularly, proffering a blistered sheet of Xanax. But Eloise was resistant to the idea: the independence of spirit that made it impossible for her to live with a lover or a parent made her equally unwilling to form a partnership with a tranquilliser. As a child, she had been what Joan called 'a fussy sleeper'. She had refused the comforting glow of a night lamp, requiring total darkness from a very young age, and her sensitivity to noise had made George's sleep mutterings unbearable – so much so that, at the age of nine, she had demanded to be moved to the guest bedroom on the floor above.

Eloise was unable to sleep at all unless stretched out, at full length, on her back. This made her an awkward romantic bed partner, as the tangle of heavy limbs that other lovers understood as intimacy was a torture for her. It also made aeroplane journeys difficult; and as the years had passed and her disposable income risen, she had bidden what she felt was a well-earned farewell to sleeplessness on international flights. Now she was faced with the prospect of twelve hours of dry-mouthed restlessness with no privacy from her happily snoring fellow travellers. The thought depressed her. So too did the fact that there was nothing she could do about it: Joan had so stridently resisted the idea of first class that any attempt to alter – or even complain about – the situation was impossible. She switched on her Blackberry to change her answer machine message, but felt a pressure on her arm.

'I have a serious favour to ask, Eloise.' Joan spoke gravely. Punishments had been Frank's domain, and she was uncertain how to be strict with her children. Nevertheless, she had given considerable thought to the request she was about to make and intended to get her own way.

'Anything, Mum.'

'I want you to switch that wretched thing off, and keep it off the whole time we're away. You have an assistant to take your messages. You'll never be able to relax with it pinging all the time, and neither will I, and we both deserve a holiday.'

The speech was so earnestly delivered that Eloise began to laugh, and a flood of old affection for her mother entirely changed her attitude to the missing flat-bed seat. 'I'll do one better,' she said conspiratorially, holding her hand up to silence Joan as she pressed the button for the office.

Emily answered.

'It's Eloise,' said Eloise. 'I'm calling from the plane. I left my bloody phone at home, so I'm going to be completely out of contact for the next ten days.'

'Should I divert calls to your hotel?'

'No point. Nothing's going to happen that Patrick can't deal with.' She hesitated, aware of her boss's need for a sparring partner, and the fact that Carol could only be a punchbag. 'If he gets pissy and threatens you for my number, tell him you have no idea where I am, and that I booked the hotel myself.'

'I'll drink to that,' said Joan, as the plane began to taxi.

Chapter 6

Joan was as good as her word, and under Eloise's influence she consumed a glass of dry white wine during dinner, which made her daughter's subsequent tutorial on the operation of her seat and its in-flight movie selection a little hard to follow. It seemed impossible to Joan that so many films could be stored in the armrest of a chair. 'If I need anything I can always ask the steward,' she said, giving up the attempt to comprehend such marvels. 'You should get some sleep.' And Eloise, anxious to end their first evening on a high note, accepted this suggestion and kissed her warmly as she drew a grey silk mask over her eyes.

Able to act unobserved, Joan congratulated herself on settling the issue of the intrusive telephone and turned to look at her daughter. Eloise had her van Vuuren grandmother's bone structure, and a powerful frame that bore further witness to Boer heritage. There was so little of Frank in her face or body, and yet she alone of them all had been able to withstand him; to *understand* him, she thought, for Eloise had always had a bewildering and instinctive sympathy for her father. She remembered the lunch, months before, when with something of the commanding enthusiasm she brought to the boardroom Eloise had outlined three visions for the trip: 'Holland', 'South Africa 1' and 'South Africa 2'.

Joan had decided against 'Holland', a visit to the Amsterdam house in which her father, Peter van Hartesveldt, had been born; and she did not think she could bear to see 'South Africa 1', her own birthplace of Nooitgedacht, as the block of luxury flats it had apparently become. Eloise had suggested hiring one of the holiday bungalows in its grounds: a horrific idea, which Joan had refused as gently as possible. She wondered if the cypress tree still stood on the oval lawn at the centre of the drive, and for a moment the cabin filled with the scent of its leaves burning in Rupert's dugout behind the abandoned piggery. No, she thought; she had acted wisely to leave that place a memory.

Under her eye mask, Eloise was thinking about Samantha Parry, who had begun the chain of events that was about to result in a seven-figure bonus for her former victim. She wondered if she remembered her, if she ever thought of her as she did part-time secretarial work for a legal firm and looked after three children and an accountant husband in the five-bedroom house about which she had boasted so smugly on FriendsReunited.com. They had been best friends from eleven to fourteen, Eloise McAllister and Samantha Parry, the intense competition of their relationship held at bay by the ritual sharing of break-time hot chocolate; and it was only Samantha's betrayal in the matter of the Princess Louise Merit Cup that had severed their intimacy beyond repair.

She had made the fateful remark carelessly, elegantly, at the end of the Christmas term at St Monica's – a skilful piece of one-upmanship about her progress through that year's French textbook, *Tricolore Trois*. Although the course was designed to take a year to complete, both Samantha and Eloise had finished *Tricolore Un* and *Tricolore Deux* a full month before the end of the previous two academic years and won glowing praise from Monsieur Pellier, their glamorous French master, as a result. Now, with the rest of the class barely a third of the way through – and with the Princess Louise cup too close to call – Samantha calmly announced that she had finished it. 'I'm going to make my fair copies over the holidays and give it to Monsieur Pellier at the beginning of next term,' she told Eloise sweetly. 'I expect I'll have to go on to *Tricolore Quatre* while I'm waiting for the rest of you to catch up.'

'What's wrong?' Frank had asked his daughter as he kissed her goodnight ten hours later.

'Nothing, Daddy.'

'Are you sure?'

'Yes.'

But in the dark, once her father had turned out the light, Eloise lay in bed and applied her full attention to the situation. She had won the Merit Cup twice in a row and did not intend to relinquish her chance of a hat-trick to her best friend; but although she was at least two months ahead of the rest of the class, she was nowhere near the end of the book. This led to urgent calculations: the Christmas break was seventeen days long and four of them would be wasted by the family's annual visit to her aunt and cousins in Bracknell. That left thirteen days to complete seventy-two pages of exercises and vocabulary lists: a daunting challenge to lesser fourteen-year-olds, but Eloise was not faint-hearted. She dreamed restlessly of carousing verbs and impregnable prose translations and woke the next morning resolved to live to a strict routine.

For the next two weeks she rose at 5 a.m. and completed two of the day's six target pages of *Tricolore Trois* before breakfast. After three games of draughts with George, whom nothing less would silence, she usually managed another page before lunch – unless her mother's obsessive practice of a piece of nervy Liszt, at unpredictably varying tempi, made concentration impossible. She slept briefly for twenty minutes each afternoon before completing a further two pages of exercises, leaving the final page for the quiet of the night.

She shared her endeavours with no one but her grandmother, whose belief in her abilities was total and sustaining; and at breakfast each morning she greeted Astrid's questioning glance with a discreetly satisfied nod. In this way, she reached the end of *Tricolore Trois* with two days to spare and arrived at school exultant. Four periods passed with frustrating slowness before Monsieur Pellier appeared, and his charmingly crooked smile widened thrillingly as she said, 'Please, sir, I'm ready for *Tricolore Quatre*.'

It was the glee on her rival's face that betrayed what the rest of the sniggering class already knew: that Samantha Parry had lied on purpose to win a bet with Laura Parker, and that none of the girls were any further than they had been at the end of the previous term. 'Swot! Swot!' yelled the class in unison as the colour rose in Eloise's cheeks and the glory of the Princess Louise Merit Cup faded, never to return.

As a move designed to cement her transition from the Swots to the Cool Group, Samantha Parry's stratagem was devastatingly successful. She was no longer excluded from Rattna Jandoo's sleepovers (at which supplies of Kentucky Fried Chicken were limitless) as Eloise was, and the denizens of the school bus's back row now welcomed her as enthusiastically as they cried 'Swot!' on the rare occasions that the weather prevented Eloise from walking home alone, as she usually did to avoid such torment.

Frank and Joan wondered why their eldest child absolutely forbade them to display the Princess Louise Merit Cup as they had done the year before, but they accepted her decision unquestioningly. Though tight-lipped on the subject with her parents, in the privacy of her grandmother's bedroom Eloise confided her grief tearfully, and Astrid – whose allegiance to family was total – threatened such violence on Samantha that her granddaughter, smiling through her tears, was comforted.

What the teenage Eloise did not understand is that even the social credibility of a back-row bus seat must fade. As it did and the girls of St Monica's moved through senior school and on to university, so the truly enduring consequence of Samantha's mean trick revealed itself: the grammatical foundations laid by Eloise's intense absorption of the rules and vocabulary of *Tricolore Trois* developed over time into a natural facility for the French language, a facility which led not only to an excellent degree but also, indirectly, to the first stratospheric orgasm of her life.

Eloise met Claude Pasquier during her third year of a Modern Languages degree at University College London. She was spending three semesters, as required, in Paris, and it had become clear to her soon after arrival that the *placement* arranged by the university would not suit. Though she had ticked the *Professionnelle* box on the application form, the mysterious workings of the university's bureaucracy had produced a position as an au pair in the household of two successful attorneys – a job she had foolishly accepted in an uncharacteristic collapse of will.

Trapped in the Récamiers' apartment in the sixteenth *arrondissement* with two pampered and impossible twelve-year-old twins, she lived for the three hours of daily freedom permitted by the arrival of the assorted extra-curricular tutors retained by their absent and guilt-ridden parents. From two to five every afternoon, while Thomasz and Hubert studied a bewildering array of subjects – bridge, Czech, perspective drawing – she took the Metro to St-Germain-des-Prés and strolled the boulevard, imagining herself in love.

She was beginning her second month in the city, and reaching the conclusion that her current situation could not continue much longer, when she saw Claude for the first time. It was raining and she had hurried into a café. Standing by the door, scanning the room, unwilling either to approach the forbidding *maître d'hôtel* or to retreat into the drizzle, she saw to her relief an empty seat at a table occupied by someone close enough to her own age to be approachable.

'*Permettez-moi?*'

He hardly looked up. The Formica before him was strewn with notebooks, some of them open and dense with neatly swirling numbers. Taking a burning Gauloise from between two seductively full lips, he placed it in an ashtray and cleared a space. '*Avec plaisir.*'

She sat down, pleased with her own *savoir-faire*, and took out the diary she kept to record just such thrilling moments: sitting in a Parisian café, in the rain, while a handsome man with green eyes and olive skin smoked cigarettes at her side.

In the days before her income stretched to an expert colourist, Eloise's hair was its natural dark chestnut. Her face was rounder, too, than it later became, her body more carelessly voluptuous. She had a perennial anxiety about the size of her bum that made her much prefer the seated to the standing position, and she was glad that the dashing stranger had paid her no attention while she hesitated at the café's door. As he continued to work with enticing concentration, she had an opportunity to study his face. Though she would later deny this to Joan, Claude was in fact extremely good-looking, if a little on the thin side. Discreetly taking in the length of his legs under the table, she calculated that he was at least six foot three, and noted his dark, tousled hair and elegantly masculine hands with approval. His tongue protruded with unconscious sex appeal from stubbled lips and drew her attention downwards, to the rows of neat calculations that so absorbed him.

For forty-five minutes he worked without hesitation or interruption. His progression through a ritual so alien to her was fascinating to Eloise, who watched as he completed his work with a neat *QED* and leaned back, stretching and for the first time meeting her eyes.

He smiled.

The combination of the city, the rain and the eye contact was heady, and inspired courage in her. '*Un verre pour célébrer votre aboutissement?*' she asked.

'*Tu es Canadienne?*'

He slipped deftly, immediately, into the informal *tu* form. The suggestion that she might be Canadian, and so a first-language French speaker, was subtly flattering. When Eloise explained, in carefully exquisite French, that she was, in fact, an English student studying *la langue des anges*, he said that in that case it was he who would buy her a drink. Three *Kir royales* later, Claude knew all about Thomasz and Hubert and the daily indignities of an au pair's life. She knew that he was a research fellow at the Sorbonne, a physicist, that he was twenty-six years old and had lived in Paris for eight years. The difference in their ages made her feel delightfully grown-up, as did the seriousness with which Claude listened to her hastily constructed views on the sculptures she had seen at the Musée Rodin the week before.

'I find them very erotic,' he said, significantly, holding her gaze a fraction longer than was necessary.

She had never seen such long lashes on a man.

When she realised, after her fourth *Kir*, that it was almost six-thirty and that she was over an hour and a half late for Thomasz and Hubert, Claude offered to give her a lift on his *vélomoteur*. There was a decisiveness about the way he called for and paid the bill that silenced all memory of the health-and-safety lectures given termly at St Monica's. As Eloise got onto the back of a stranger's motorbike, the fact that he had consumed four cocktails and that he neither wore nor offered a helmet seemed only to heighten the glamour of the moment, as did the reckless path he cut through wet, traffic-filled streets. As her hair flew behind them in the wind, her hands linked above his waist could not help but press against the solid ridges of a set of abdominals noticeably tauter than those of the pasty English youths who had been her previous sexual partners.

As they sped along the Quai Voltaire, with the floodlit Palais du Louvre facing them across the river, Eloise felt deliriously alive. Alighting in the rue Louis David, outside the apartment where Thomasz and Hubert, unsupervised, were in the throes of ransacking each other's bedroom, she lingered in the street as she said goodbye, desperate for Claude to kiss her. He did not, but he did ask her to dinner the following day, giving precise instructions for a restaurant called Le Petit Trésor.

'I will see you there?'

'*Peut-être.*' She smiled, to show that she was joking.

'*À demain, ma belle Anglaise.*'

And with that he was gone, leaving her to tackle the twins, and the mess they had made, with less than her usual dedication.

*

The next twenty-four hours were among the most agonising of Eloise's life thus far. Time had not passed so slowly since the Christmas Eves of her childhood, and taking advantage of the twins' absence at school and the well-stocked vanity unit in Madame Récamier's bathroom, she shaved and plucked and moisturised the next morning with frenzied attention to detail. Having exhausted all possibilities for personal grooming by 11 a.m., she locked herself in her bedroom and masturbated, though this offered only temporary release. While the twins' Spanish instructor guided them through their irregular verbs that afternoon, she attempted to calm herself by playing the piano – but this had never worked for her.

The time that might have been enjoyably spent deciding what to wear was severely curtailed by the fact that she had only one vaguely acceptable dress, and no money to buy another. Her only option was an electric-blue creation in satinised polyester, scooped low between the shoulders. In London, in the ladies' department at Selfridges where Joan had bought it for her, it had looked elegant, the height of Parisian chic. In Paris, it looked cheap and *faux*. Standing in front of the mirror, blow-drying her hair, she was seized with doubt: perhaps a dress was too much, after all. Claude was only a student, and so was she.

As she took it off, she was brought face to face with another, even more serious problem: her Marks & Spencer knickers, in white, no-nonsense cotton – a far from ideal accessory for Gallic love-making. Looking at her watch, she saw that her employers would shortly be returning from the office. The occasion demanded a snap decision, which she took without hesitation. Hastily putting on her jeans and a sweater, she left her bedroom and stood in the hall, listening for the reassuring monotony of the twins' verb declamations. Then she opened the door to the Récamiers' bedroom and crossed to the armoire under the window, the drawers of which proved to contain an astonishing array of designer lingerie. She selected a peach silk set from Maison Femme and retreated to her room.

Ten minutes later, her trophies in place, she felt more confident. Madame Récamier was smaller than she was and the bra bit into her back, but its very inadequacy to the task of supporting her breasts drew attention to their luscious fullness. The pants were tight too, and also painful to wear, but they firmed her bum. Thus lavishly accoutred, she decided that her exterior should be casual, almost careless. Slipping a tape of Olivia Newton-John singing 'Me and Bobby McGee' into the portable cassette player Frank had given her for her birthday, she lip-synched ecstatically in front of the mirror as she finished dressing. Consigning the satinised polyester to the closet, she selected instead a stretch bandeau top of geometric pattern and a sexy black miniskirt, which she wore above cream tights and a pair of navy clogs. Blue eyeshadow completed the effect, though she did not add this until the twins had had their supper and their parents were back from work, in even filthier tempers than usual.

Eloise took a taxi to the Place de la Chapelle, through a floodlit city seemingly illuminated just for her, and asked the driver to stop a few streets short of the square in case her mode of transport should seem ostentatious to a graduate student. She was precisely fifteen minutes late, and walked past the Metro station with a soaring heart.

It was the absence of interior lighting that first alarmed her. As she drew closer, she saw that Le Petit Trésor was closed; that it had, in fact, been closed for weeks if not months. Brightly coloured circulars littered its dusty floor and the menu that still hung outside its door was drizzle-stained and illegible. The shock of the anticlimax was almost overwhelming. She leaned against a lamp post to steady herself. Though not a smoker she yearned suddenly for a cigarette, some suitable prop to do justice to the tragedy of her shattered plans.

'*Merde!* But you are very late. I had begun to think you would not come.'

Claude touched her shoulder, emerging from the crowded square with quick, graceful strides. It was all she could do to control her voice and answer light-heartedly. '*Quel choix charmant*,' she said, attempting a sexily sceptical smile.

'Now be serious, *ma belle Anglaise*. Do you mean to say that the thought of eating off sawdust does not appeal?' He slipped an arm round her shoulder and kissed her on both cheeks. He had shaved and smelt faintly of citrus. 'I realised my mistake as soon as I had given you the address – it closed two months ago and I have been too busy since then to think of dining out. I decided, instead, to take you somewhere slightly more *particulier*.'

'Where?'

'Over there.' He pointed across the street to an iron grille, behind which a toothless concierge sat smiling at them. With one large hand in the small of her back, he guided her across the road.

'*Bonsoir, Monsieur Pasquier.*' Twinkling eyes in a fat face ran Eloise up and down. '*Bonsoir, mademoiselle.*'

'*Bonsoir, Madame Vaudrillon.*'

'Where is this, Claude?' asked Eloise as he led her across a courtyard and into a rickety lift.

'This', he said, 'is *chez moi*. Welcome to my home.'

The apartment was tiny and candlelit – just two rooms and an open kitchen in the eaves under the roofs. Narrow windows looked towards a ribbon of railway lines, beyond which Sacré Coeur rose serenely white against the night sky. The few pieces of furniture were strictly functional: a low sofa and a desk in the living area, a bed and a small chair just visible through the open door to the bedroom.

What struck Eloise first was how clean it was, how sparsely neat. Besides those of a small pot of well-watered purple heather on the desk, she could see no other curves; she was surrounded by right angles aligned with other right angles. Standing awkwardly by a bookcase while Claude opened a bottle of champagne in the kitchen, she scanned the brightly spined volumes and saw that they were arranged alphabetically by author and epoch. The shelf in front of her, labelled *18ème Siècle*, held books by Balzac, Doudet, Hugo, Labiche, Mérimé, Montesquieu, Musset, Taine, Voltaire and Zola – in that order. The tape cassettes stacked in two aluminium towers beside a sophisticated hi-fi system were also arranged alphabetically by artist. On the desk, a jar of perfectly sharpened pencils stood eagerly to attention.

She moved towards the windows and looked out, thinking to arrange herself appealingly against the romantic backdrop of the view. She had imagined a dirtier, more bohemian apartment; a place strewn with velvet cushions and Indian throws, with perhaps a half-smoked joint in an ashtray perched on a tottering pile of books. The way Claude rode a motorbike had suggested it.

'*Voilà!*' He appeared from the kitchen and placed a chilled champagne glass in her hand. 'Welcome, *ma belle Anglaise.*'

They ate *coquilles St Jacques*, bought in their shells that morning from the Marché de la Chapelle two streets away. Eloise stood in the kitchen with her drink – it took two quick glasses of champagne to still her racing heart – and watched Claude as he cooked. He moved decisively, efficiently, his attention stretching easily across several simultaneous tasks as he talked. 'When they're fresh,' he told her, holding up a *coquille* and grinning, 'they're very … feisty.' He slipped a long sharp knife into the shell's crack. 'As you open them they try to close – almost to bite you. Isn't that how you English respond to intimacy?'

Her astonishment at the question caused him to throw his head back and roar with laughter. Until he did so, it had never occurred to Eloise that an Adam's apple could be sexy.

'The trick', said Claude, standing close to her, 'is to get inside it. Then the whole thing will open up.' He made his point deftly, flicking the shell open and scooping the creature from its last refuge.

He served the *coquilles* pan-fried, with a pea-and-mint purée and a crisp Pouilly Fumée. They ate them side by side on his sofa, as the city's lights threw baroque shadows from the building's trellis work across the crazily angled walls. They sat so close that Eloise caught traces of Claude's scent as he moved his head in talk – a vigorous, well-scrubbed smell suggestive of long, strong limbs and taut skin.

They discussed the Récamiers and the chaos to which Eloise had returned the previous evening. She told him about Astrid and Frank and Joan and George, for Claude was an avid researcher of context, and asked him about his work and the streams of figures that had so absorbed him in the café. She discovered that he was researching an element called osmium, that he was about to show, conclusively, that it was harder than diamond.

'But do not think I was so distracted by my rare metal that I did not notice a beautiful woman sit down at my table,' he said playfully, putting his empty plate on the coffee table and stretching back.

The knowledge that they would soon be naked together settled deliciously over them both.

Chapter 7

Eloise, lost in lascivious recollection, not even thinking of sleep, fell asleep with the sudden unconsciousness of the truly exhausted and woke only as the orange juice was being handed round the next morning. Beside her, Joan was filling in landing cards and hesitating over the selection of brioches proffered by the strong-jawed steward who had welcomed them on board at the other end of the world the night before. 'I'm so glad you're awake,' she said, gripping her daughter's arm. 'I'm always a bit nervous about landing.'

Johannesburg International Airport was markedly more like an international airport than it had been during Joan's last passage through it, when with the six-year-old Eloise and four-year-old George she had come to South Africa to organise the sale of Nooitgedacht in the weeks after her mother's death. A gleaming marble concourse now surged before them as they emerged from customs, and although they had a tight connection she attempted gamely to make the journey to Domestic Departures on foot. Leaning on Eloise's arm, conscious of the vast expanse of polished stone and plastic store fronts that lay between her and the gate, shuffling slightly because her left hip was playing up, she thought how much of her life she had spent hurrying and wondered whether she would ever hurry again.

'Are you sure you wouldn't like a wheelchair?' asked Eloise.

'Perhaps that would be best, after all,' said Joan.

The flight to Bloemfontein, the capital of the old Boer Republic of the Orange Free State, took just over an hour. Joan had not been to the city since, as twenty-two-year-old Miss van Hartesveldt on her way to music college in England, she had come with her father to tend Rupert's grave and bid farewell to her ageing van Vuuren grandmother.

Peter van Hartesveldt had decreed that his son and heir be buried at Nooitgedacht, in a grandiose mausoleum of his own design, but by the time of Rupert's death the balance of power between him and his wife had shifted drastically and he was no longer able to legislate in this way. Joan's mother Cecilia, with her genius for 'making do', had quietly arranged for Rupert's body to be transported to her family's Free State farm and placed in the earth among the still-blackened ruins of Die Ou Plek. Joan had never seen this building, burned long before her birth, but she had often visited Die Nuwe Plek, or 'New Place', that replaced it: a house set at the furthest extent of the farm, as though in flight from the steadily encroaching suburbs. Her father had stopped for a night on his way to Johannesburg and left her with his mother-in-law, in whose company he was prone to fidget.

When Joan last saw her grandmother, Gertruida van Vuuren was ninety years old, with a back as straight as a coffin lid. Since the recent Allied victory she had lost her appetite, sickened by the injustice of Britain's escape from pillage and defeat; and after a plump middle age she gave the unsettling impression of being too small for her collapsing body. She relied for all her wants on 'Elsie', her maid: a Zulu woman named Nqobani who had worked for the van Vuurens since the age of ten.

Now sixty herself, with a back half-broken by the birthing of six children, it was a struggle for Nqobani to run the house on her own; but she had promised Miss Cecilia that she would look after the Madam as she would her own mother – and because of this Cecilia had accepted Mr van Hartesveldt's proposal of marriage, having rejected so many during her teens and twenties. It was Nqobani who tended the roses on Rupert's grave, for he had come into the world through her agency also; and the fact that Cecilia had been spared a daughter as gifted and healthy as Joan made her tearful sometimes as she refilled the flowers in her room. She had no intention of letting this miraculous prodigy cook, and banned her from the kitchen and all domestic tasks.

Used to a more demanding regime, Joan found the uselessly passing hours effortful. She went to Rupert's grave in the early morning and at sunset, and watered the rose bushes that grew over him in an enclave of three charred stone walls; but the grey granite cross that marked the place so inadequately evoked him that the observance became mechanical. The monotonous creaking of her grandmother's chair was irksome to her; and on the third afternoon, thinking to distract herself and her demented relative, she took the van Vuuren *Psalms en Gesange* from its shelf in the *voorkamer* and began to play from it on the family's portable organ.

She was beginning the twenty-third psalm when a rasping voice interrupted her.

'Hannie? *My eie dollie?*'

Gertruida, who had not risen unaided for almost a decade, was standing in the doorway, shaking violently. Joan did not know what to do.

'Hannie?'

Her grandmother was shouting now. The urgency of her voice, its sheer *hopefulness*, rendered Joan mute, unable to deny or confirm. She gave silent thanks when Nqobani appeared, and watched as the maid took her employer's hands with such gentleness that she allowed herself to be led back to her rocking chair without complaint.

'You mustn't play that organ, Miss Joan,' said Nqobani quietly, once Gertruida was resettled. 'We can't be giving an old lady frights.'

'But why should it frighten her, Elsie?'

Nqobani's round, jovial face grew wistful. 'Hours and hours Miss Hannie would play and sing. When we were all children together – at the Old Place, the one that burned.' She rested heavily, with creaking joints, on the arm of a brown velvet armchair with tasselled antimacassars. 'Oooh, but she was very good. You can't imagine how quickly a person's fingers can move. We used to stand watching her, your mother and me and – the others. So many things Miss Hannie used to play. You just had to begin singing a hymn and she could do it, even without the music. The gentlemen would come from as far as Kroonstad to hear her.'

She reached beyond Joan to the organ and closed its lid.

'She was playing hymns when the English came,' she went on softly, almost with reverence. 'They had to carry her out onto the grass on the stool because she would not leave it. That whole afternoon she sat just where they put her and played and sang. Oooh, they were mad, those English. But what could they do? They told her they would burn it but she said then they must burn her, too.' She touched the ornate scrolling with tenderness. 'One little girl, shaming all those men. When the English left, my uncle Nongamso wrapped it in blankets and put it in the barn, so it was waiting for the Baas and the Madam at the end of the war. But Miss Hannie never played it again.' She looked gravely at Joan, and stood up. 'And neither should anyone else, now.'

Joan's first language was English, and she had a little Xhosa for the servants. In the opinion of her mother's surviving brother and his family of deep-voiced, barrel-chested farmers, her spoken Afrikaans left much to be desired. She did not know many of the family's stories of the Anglo-Boer War, or *Boere Oorlog* as her cousins called it; and those she did know were at second hand, for her mother never spoke of the deaths of her siblings.

The discovery of Hannie's instrument rooted an established legend in vivid reality, and when Nqobani brought the tea Joan slipped inside and retrieved the family psalter – for she had more than one means of hearing its music. As her grandmother rocked back and forth she listened to the psalms in absolute silence, assigning them to four richly voiced singers and a small chamber orchestra. The settings were old-fashioned, their harmonies simple but proud, and she offered the music heavenwards as a tribute to the aunts and uncles she would never know, who had been Rupert's aunts and uncles, too. She listened until sleep overcame her, and at intervals all the next day, and finished only as long shadows were spilling onto the lawn and the crickets were tuning for their evening's courting. Turning the last psalm over, she was surprised to see that the end pages of the hymnal were covered in dense, handwritten script.

Carefully, like a child just learning to read, Joan made out the sounds: *O God, hou U nie stil nie, swyg nie en rus nie, O God!* It was not until her grandmother's voice joined hers – softly, as though coming from far away – that she realised that she had vocalised her efforts.

With the profound calm of a woman in a trance, old Mrs van Vuuren began to sing. She required no prompting from Joan as she finished one verse to begin another; and from some long submerged place deep within her, beyond the obscuring mists of old age and disease, whole hymns of trial and consolation welled upwards. As the shadows lengthened and the sun dipped behind the orange clay of the four surrounding hills, grandmother and granddaughter sat together, singing.

They sang late into the night. Nqobani brought lanterns out into the warm darkness and stood silently by, watching them. *God staan in die vergadering van die gode; Hy hou gerig te midde van die gode,* they sang. After some time, Gertruida's fingers, wrapped in a tissue paper of wrinkled, transparent skin, moved towards Joan's. She took

53

her granddaughter's hand in her own and held it tenderly, stroking the knuckles, and when they finally went to bed the old lady drew Joan towards her and kissed her, straining her bowed shoulders upwards to meet the young girl's lips.

The city through which Eloise and her mother were driven almost sixty years later bore only the faintest resemblance to the town of Joan's memories. The handsome buildings of Voortrekkerstraat were now impudently diminished by cheaply built towers of concrete and glass, and only the weather was precisely as she remembered it from countless childhood visits. Even in April, as autumn approached, the midday sun radiated an intense heat that gave the dust-filled air a viscose quality, like hot orange syrup dripped down the lungs. 'Goodness me,' she said. 'I do hope our hotel has air conditioning.'

The Volksraad Hotel, Bloemfontein, did have air conditioning, because it was the best hotel in the city, but it did not have many of the other conveniences Eloise expected from the establishments in which she stayed. Its decoration, she thought, checking in beneath a vast arrangement of plastic proteas, gathering dust, was a fine example of the Apartheid period at its most monstrous: oddly angled, concrete wall features; acres and acres of orange and beige.

Eloise always had a massage after a flight. This was not available. She asked instead where the pool was. It was closed, 'for upgrading'. She followed her mother to their rooms, along a corridor carpeted in rococo swirls of orange, brown and lime green, and reminded herself that she was in Bloemfontein, not New York. 'It's wonderful to be here, with you,' she said decisively as a middle-aged black bellhop whose nametag read 'Big Boy' put her mother's case at the foot of her bed and opened the interconnecting door between their rooms.

'Marvellous,' Joan agreed.

Standing in her shower a few minutes later, Eloise noted with relief that the water pressure was adequate. She stepped out of the avocado plastic cubicle, tied her hair in a brown towel and walked naked into the bedroom to stand by the air-conditioning vent. There was something almost sinister, she thought, about the indifference of menopausal hot flushes to air conditioning. As she waited for her body temperature to normalise, the reflection of her stomach in the blank television screen reminded her that she had not done her crunches this morning – but it was too hot to think of exercise.

Day one was almost over. Only nine more to go.

The room's clock was not working. She switched her Blackberry on to check the time and her heart sank as it shuddered painfully through a series of alerts. She pressed the speed dial for the office, but as she did so her mother's instruction came to her, and her promised obedience, and with emphasis she switched it off and returned it to her suitcase – just as Joan, knocking once, entered the room through their interconnecting door.

'Gracious. Sorry, darling. I didn't know you weren't decent. Don't stand by the window like that.'

'Sorry, Mum.'

'I rather thought we might begin our tour. Unless you're tired and would like to sleep?'

'I'm raring to go.'

'Then I'll meet you downstairs when you're dressed.'

Chapter 8

The driver provided for them by the hotel was a fresh-faced young man in his early twenties called Simbongile, who drove a second-hand Toyota Corolla that smelled strongly of disinfectant. He had a shaved head and full, sensual lips. 'They say at reception you are VIP visitors from UK,' he said. 'It is a cold place, so I've heard.'

'Just at the moment,' said Joan, 'it's not too bad. But last winter was awful.'

'I would like to go to UK,' said Simbongile, thoughtfully. 'But that is a long way off. Where are you liking to go to now?'

'Well . . .' Joan leaned forward from the back seat, confidentially. 'I last came to Bloemfontein when I was a young woman. My grandmother had a farm. It was called Van Vuuren's Drift. You wouldn't happen to know it, would you?'

Simbongile looked at her doubtfully.

'It was a little way out of town. A stream ran across it that fed into the Modder. There were some low hills, too.' Joan looked helplessly at the concrete cubes that now dominated the city's wide streets and rose-planted traffic islands. 'Have you ever heard of it?'

'Not in these days, ma'am.' Simbongile spoke regretfully. He had a granny about Joan's age. She had brought him up, while his own mother did domestic work to support a family of five children. He had an instinctive respect and affection for elderly women.

'Oh well,' said Eloise brightly. 'I suppose it was always a long shot. Why don't we go and look at the concentration camp?'

'There may be', said Simbongile, stretching his arms wide, 'a way to find your granny's place. My uncle Harold is very old man now. He is driving a taxi for a long time. Perhaps he knows.'

'Is there a way of reaching him to ask?'

Simbongile considered. 'He lives in the location,' he said hesitantly, as though that might be the end of the matter.

'Could you take us to him?'

'I don't think we should be going anywhere dangerous, Mum,' said Eloise in an undertone.

Joan feigned deafness. 'What is the location like nowadays?' she asked their driver. 'Is it safe?'

'Oh, ma'am. It is much better than it was. There is not so much violence now that we have voting in this country.'

'Splendid. Would you take us there?'

'*Mum.*'

Simbongile turned round in his seat and flashed both of them a smile of dazzling whiteness. 'When people hear you are visiting from UK, they will welcome you,' he said.

And so it proved.

Joan was amused to observe her daughter's rising anxiety as the Toyota Corolla left the thronged streets and garish signs of the town centre and took them through a series of dusty fields planted with dejected *mielies*. She was used to Eloise being decisive and assured; there was something endearing about her uncertainty now.

Their journey took almost forty minutes and ended in Mangaung, a bustling metropolis of brightly painted tin shacks built on fine orange clay. Everywhere one looked were signs of economic activity: ingeniously devised advertisements for corner hair salons; markets full of strange fruits and plastic baubles; teenagers slaughtering sheep and roasting their heads on open fires, to sell later as 'smilies'. On a hot day like this one, the scene looked cheerful from a distance – until one noticed the flies. Joan did not like to imagine what it would be like to live here through a cold, wet winter.

The presence of two well-dressed white ladies in the back of his cab spoke to the showman in Simbongile, who slowed the car as though transporting exotic beasts. Eloise, reading violent robbery in every glance, surreptitiously removed her watch and bracelets, while Joan, wondering what had become of Elsie's descendants, thought happily that South Africa was on her way to peace at last. A similar journey to a black township would have been unthinkable in 1962. Now she had the status of a social curiosity, and did her best to smile back at the stares that followed the car's majestic progress along crowded dirt roads.

'We have electricity, in these days,' said Simbongile. 'Maybe next year, a latrine in every house. Perhaps the Football World Cup will one day come here.'

As he spoke, he pulled up outside a shack with a greater air of permanence than most. Its walls were brick and painted a radiant blue, with a roof of corrugated-iron sheets waterproofed with black plastic bags. A series of sturdy upturned rubbish bins did duty as chimneys. He hooted twice and leapt out, leaving the women alone in the car.

'I hope you know what you're doing,' said Eloise, as a group of children surrounded them, smiling shyly.

Simbongile emerged from the shack and opened the Toyota's door with a flourish. 'This is the house of my family,' he said. 'And it is always open to our visitors from UK.'

Simbongile's uncle Harold, who seemed to Joan and Eloise far too old to be his real uncle (and whose proper name, in any case, was Sifiso), was sitting in a chair in the kitchen of the shack. He seemed oblivious to the tiny cockroaches whose purposeful movements made the walls and surfaces shimmer with life. His hair was a wiry grey, and springy whiskers leapt from his cheeks and provided resting places for the flies that buzzed continually about his head.

From nowhere, a piece of childhood etiquette recurred to Joan. '*Sabona, baba,*' she said.

The old man turned keen eyes on her. '*Sabona, mama.*'

'These are visitors from UK,' said Simbongile, by way of introduction. 'This lady is looking for her granny's place.'

'It was a farm,' said Joan, 'called Van Vuuren's Drift. It used to be a little way from town, beside a group of low hills.' She felt, as she spoke, the inadequacy of these few distinguishing details.

'Do you recognise it, *baba*?' asked Simbongile, placing a hand on his relative's shoulders.

Harold thought for a moment. Eloise's spirits rose as he began to shake his head; she was not at ease in a context so far removed from her own and longed to escape. Thinking guiltily of the crisp roll of banknotes in her handbag, she wondered how she might give one of them to this family without revealing how many she had on her.

'How many hills?' asked Harold.

Joan sat down at the rickety kitchen table and tried to think. How useful the pedals would be now! But without their gift of perfect recall she could see nothing but the long shadows cast over the lawn before the *stoep*. She counted these carefully. 'I think there were four.'

'In which direction they face?'

She thought of where the sun had set. 'To the west.'

A rapid exchange took place in Zulu between the young man and his uncle.

'He says he knows the hills!' cried Simbongile. 'But he has not visited them for many years.'

'Could you take us there?'

The young man nodded. Uncle Harold resumed his attitude of placid contemplation.

'Let us go,' said Simbongile, waving away the note that Eloise had just succeeded, with some difficulty, in extracting unobserved from her handbag. 'Your granny is watching and waiting.'

Their journey led them back into town and across the busy thorough-fares of Presidentslaan and St George's Straat. In the presence of Simbongile, Eloise did not wish to discuss what she had just seen. She did not yet have the words to describe the unexpected combination of squalor and optimism that they had witnessed, but Joan chattered on excitedly. She asked Simbongile questions and learned about his granny, who lived in Lesotho, and about his mother, who still worked for a family in town. She heard how his father had left his mother when he was three weeks old and discovered that he could still be seen around the location, buying expensive trinkets for new lady friends. 'You know,' said Simbongile, 'but my mother is a hard-working woman. One day, when I have paid off this car, I will earn the money to buy her a house.'

They were on the motorway, heading for the suburbs. To their right, a line of four small hills was visible. Joan took Eloise's hand, her heart rate rising. 'I think those are them! Can we get any closer?'

Simbongile left the highway at the next exit and they found them-selves in an area of square plots and rusting fences. 'This is where the poor whites live,' explained their guide. 'And they are even poorer now they cannot all work for the railways.'

The houses were large, but ramshackle. Dogs barked invisibly in hidden yards and the lawns were coarse, yielding regularly to the fine orange clay that also covered the windscreens and bumpers of the beaten up Passats and Nissans that filled the driveways. The street had been planted with jacarandas once, but they looked as though they had last flowered long ago.

'Maybe they will help us at the Mall,' said Simbongile, turning right onto a wider street that ended in the parking lot of a shopping centre, extravagantly adorned with false cupolas.

'Stop the car!' cried Joan.

'What, Mum?'

'Can we go back to that last street sign, please?'

'No problem!'

To Eloise's horror, Simbongile looked once over his shoulder and threw the car into reverse, sending them backwards at terrific speed towards the oncoming traffic. With a screech of hot rubber on tarmac, he rounded the corner out of harm's way just as the first car swept past them, hooting.

He smiled.

They were on a smaller street of cracked pavements, dominated by an ancient fig tree with a gnarled trunk of splendid proportions. 'That tree,' said Joan. 'There is something familiar about it.'

It was all that Eloise could do to silence the observation that a visit to a fig tree, however familiar, was hardly worth braving death for. She saw to her alarm that her mother was winding down her window and doing her best to look out. 'I don't have the right glasses with me,' said Joan, exasperatedly. 'Can you see the name of the street from where you are, darling?'

'Katrienstraat, Mum.'

'Could we carry on driving to the Mall, please, Simbongile?' asked Joan quietly. 'And do drive slowly, won't you, dear? I want to check the street names. Could you read them out for me, Eloise?'

The Toyota swung into the traffic once more and Eloise read the signs at each passing intersection. 'Katrienstraat ... Johanstraat ... Naomistraat ... Ceciliastraat ... Jacobusstraat ...' They reached the parking lot of the Mall and Simbongile drew to a stop in a bay by the main entrance.

'What're you doing, Mum?'

Joan had opened the door and was attempting, unsuccessfully, to leave the car unaided. Simbongile, springing from his seat and to her side, lifted her gently out and deposited her on the pavement. Joan looked behind her, towards the hills. The sun was still high in the sky. She leaned on Simbongile's arm and closed her eyes.

'Are you all right, Mum? What are you doing?'

'I am saying a prayer, darling.'

To Eloise, who had grown up in a family where her mother's regular church attendance was never discussed, the admission was striking.

Indicating a road that exited the parking lot at right angles from where they stood, Joan turned to Simbongile. 'What does that sign say, *buthi*?'

He squinted in the bright light. 'Hann – Hanniestraat,' he said eventually.

'Then this is the place.'

'How do you know?'

Joan looked at her daughter, as though the question were somehow impertinent. 'Each of the streets we have just passed is named after one of your great-aunts or uncles,' she said at last, 'in ascending order of age. Wherever the house was, we must at least be standing on a part of the farm now. How else could you explain the coincidence?'

'So we've found it?'

'Yes.'

Eloise looked around her, hoping for something she could remember with pride. She had not imagined tracing her roots to the parking lot of a downmarket shopping centre.

'Do you want I make photo of you?' Simbongile, raised in a culture of ancestral respect, was visibly moved. His obvious emotion made Eloise feel ashamed.

'Please,' she said, handing him a wafer-thin digital camera and putting her arm around her mother. 'With the hills in the background.'

'I will count from one to three,' said Simbongile. 'When I reach three, you must smile!'

Chapter 9

On the recommendation of the manager of the Volksraad Hotel, they had dinner at the Waterfront, a complex of restaurants and shops built on an artificial lake filled with orange pedaloes. The surreality of eating to the sound of gently lapping waves, at such a considerable distance from the sea, produced for Joan a pair of gulls like the ones that had nested in the water tower at Nooitgedacht. 'I do hope we can get Simbongile to drive for us tomorrow,' she said.

They ate thick steaks of exceptional tenderness and drank a voluptuously full-bodied local Shiraz. The friendliness of the black servers astonished Eloise, who could not understand why the luxury they serviced did not provoke a murderous bloodlust in them. To wake in a tin shack and return to it at night, after fifteen hours spent frothing cappuccinos and polishing crystal glasses, must be – but she could not find the word and realised with a twinge of discomfort that she had never imagined the struggles of such a life. As soon as she got her osmium bonus, she decided, she would write a sizeable cheque to one of those organisations that paid for black-and-white images of starving African children to be printed on the front pages of national newspapers.

This resolution soothed her.

'What's the plan for tomorrow?' she asked Joan, vivaciously. 'We have tickets to a lecture at the War Museum in the afternoon, but our morning's free.'

'I want you to sleep late, darling.'

'I never sleep late. Six-thirty is a lie-in for me.'

'Even on holiday?'

'*Especially* on holiday.'

'In that case, if you're sure.' Joan took her hand. 'I thought we might go to the concentration camp. I asked that nice man at the hotel about it. He says it's not open to the public, but he can get us the keys through a friend of his at the Bible Centre. Apparently the army uses it now. For rifle practice, I'm told.'

Eloise focused intently on her mother as a crème brûlée was served to a diner at an adjacent table. 'Great idea,' she said.

'That's settled then. Now what about a pudding?'

'Peppermint tea will do me.'

'Come on, Eloise, choose something. I'm going to have the mango sorbet.'

'Honestly, I'm stuffed. That steak.'

'What about the crème brûlée that lady's having? It looks delicious.'

'Really, I'm fine.'

'Go on.'

'I'm *fine*, thank you.'

But her mother's prolonged temptation depleted Eloise's reserves of self-control, and on their return from dinner she kissed Joan goodnight and locked the interconnecting door between their rooms. She had left the air conditioning on high and it was freezing. Shivering, partly from the cold, partly from the thrill of impending transgression, she took from the minibar six miniature bottles of Scotch and four bars of Swiss chocolate and consumed them purposefully. Then she sprawled across the bedspread, her make-up smudging the pillows, and fell into a grateful oblivion.

Joan woke early the next morning, disturbed by her daughter's steady progress through three hundred stomach crunches on the other side of the connecting door. She had slept well, despite the nylon sheets which caught her toenails and reminded her unpleasantly of Astrid.

Forty-six years before, while Joan was in hospital giving birth to George, Astrid had donated the soft, worn Nooitgedacht linen Cecilia had left her to the Salvation Army, and replaced it with nylon sheets and comforters in a variety of fashionable hues. Joan looked warily about her. Though her mother-in-law would have commended the colour scheme, there seemed to be nothing more of her in this ample, sunny room. She got out of bed, her toes forging channels through the olive-green shag pile as she shuffled to the window. Observing the jostling billboards below, she thought how unlikely – and yet how inevitable – it was that the once fragrant gardens in which her mother had played as a child should now be a desolate car park.

Joan had a horror of the encroaching city. She disliked the defiant absence of nostalgia that went with 'progress', the complete finality with which a car park and a shopping centre could obliterate the evidence of a century or more of passionately lived family life. The original homestead of Van Vuuren's Drift, like the house that so dejectedly replaced it, had been built room by room, its stone hauled from the quarry at Boomspruit twelve miles distant. What other treasures lay buried beneath the dreary little office buildings all around her?

She thought of Frank, so bent on destroying the past. In her opinion, everything had started moving too quickly after the last war; too little had been done to counter the standardising forces of mass production and economies of scale. She thought of all the cinemas and shops and airports she had known, each one more like another with every passing year; and the fact that those who were now young would never know that things could be different – that they *had* been different, not so long ago – troubled her. She thought of her grandmother's farm, of the cacophonic beauty of its fields as night fell: lost forever. How fortunate that Nooitgedacht remained recognisable as itself, that people still lived there. She considered her father's vainglorious attempts to rescue it, and remembered that his study in the tower was now the sitting room of a maisonette flat. A strange, clogged sorrow crept up her chest and made her wheeze; and in it was the fact that she would never play Schubert to him again, or sit on the window ledge with her legs dangling over his chair.

She closed her eyes and said a prayer for each of her parents, which she concluded with an acknowledgement that was only fair: that it was not Peter, but Cecilia, who had saved her first home from extinction.

Peter van Hartesveldt was accustomed to cutting a dash in the Cape Town of the 1920s, and when he bought the tangled wildlands of Nooitgedacht for his bride Cecilia, *née* van Vuuren, he still retained the conviction of his own future glory which events were sadly to extinguish in him. The place had been so elegant once, yet was now so devilishly cheap; it presented an admirable solution to his problem of how to live on a generous scale, as a handsome man with a handsome wife, on an income that would have kept lesser men in check and could only, he was certain, increase.

Faced with a choice between re-slating the roof and re-papering the principal rooms, Peter silenced his new wife's objections and insisted on making the house 'habitable' for her, which required the daily attendance of the city's finest furniture dealers and the retention of eight indoor servants to replace and periodically reposition the buckets that caught the rain. The land had been carved from the side of the windswept mountain in 1708, an irregular pentagon bound by three vigorous streams which only an intricate drainage system, long since beyond repair, had prevented from swamping the house during the wet season. For a century a humble wooden dwelling had stood there, demolished and replaced by an extensive neoclassical mansion in 1812. This house had once possessed its own ballroom, which was in truth the property's chief attraction for Mr van Hartesveldt; and though its parquet floors now peeled and vines crept through the windows, it was rapturously romantic in the moonlight.

Peter invited his friends and backers to meet Cecilia at a reception for *La Belle au Bois Dormant* and doused them in cocktails dispensed by footmen in the silver livery of an enchanted castle. The entertainment established the new Mrs van Hartesveldt as one of the first hostesses of the city, despite her rather guttural English; and the way she looked in photographs subtly contributed to the impression her husband gave of being a man with Capital and Prospects.

Joan was five and Rupert seven when the Great Crash of 1929 brought an abrupt end to their father's pretence of means, and the true resource of the family emerged in the person of Cecilia, then forty-five years old and desperate to be free of the self-satisfaction and constricting shoes of her neighbours. In the weeks after Peter's ruin, she sold her fine clothes with a haste that suggested relief and kept her hair long in defiance of the fashion, confronting the future with an implacable defiance to which, in the months that followed, she sacrificed all the showy trifles her husband had bought her.

The van Hartesveldt sale at the auction rooms of Messrs Hoare and Driskell, of number 21 Long Street, so sharply censured Peter that he remained subdued for the rest of his life. Cecilia retreated behind an impression of quiet dignity and watched with disdain as her friends bought for three shillings objects they knew to be worth five pounds. She arranged for new employment for each of the servants and kept only Elsie's child Beauty, who had come with her from Bloemfontein at her marriage. She did not despair, for she had witnessed far graver human savagery, but she did withhold two treasures from the public scavenging: her sister Hannie's organ, which she sent back to Van Vuuren's Drift to preserve it from the Nooitgedacht damp; and the griffin chandelier that her mother had given her as a wedding present. This continued to hang in the drawing room as everything else of any value was taken away: the heavy furniture, the gilded mirrors and ruined, rain-sodden hangings, bought so recently at such great cost. It remained there until the afternoon, long after Peter's death, when Cecilia presented it to Joan and Frank, with the assurance that it would watch over their future happiness.

How lovely it was, thought Joan as she brushed her teeth, that Eloise would own it now.

Chapter 10

'Where to today?' asked Simbongile, holding open the door of the Toyota Corolla for Joan, whose left knee had started playing up at breakfast. 'Will we still be searching for your granny's places?'

He was wearing a loud checked shirt, a size too small for him, and a pair of chinos several sizes too large. A tan leather belt kept them firmly in place, but the resulting, inelegantly bunched waistline distressed Joan. Simbongile was such a charming young man, such a good-looking and helpful young man – she wished she could buy him something that fitted properly.

'I think we'd like to look at the concentration camp this morning, dear. Do you know where it is?'

Simbongile nodded, closing the door after her and taking his place at the steering wheel. In the seat behind him, Eloise was focusing on the back of his headrest. She had long ago conquered the motion sickness of her childhood but her grumbling stomach was in no mood to be provoked; and as they drove through the hotel gates she realised that she had not brought any painkillers with her. 'Thank you for being so helpful yesterday,' she said, by way of distraction, to Simbongile.

'Anything for VIP visitors from UK!'

The last wisps of the morning smog had lifted and the temperature was beginning its inexorable rise. As they left the town centre and took a long, straight road out of the city, Eloise realised that she had chosen the wrong clothes and regretted her defiant disregard for the causal link between alcohol consumption and hot flushes. Her skin began to prickle unpleasantly and her temples to throb.

On either side, a sprawl of industrial warehouses crowded to the highway's edge. It was not impossible, thought Joan, that she had ridden out over this land as a young girl, that the plot now occupied

67

by an abandoned distillery was the site of one of the Sunday-school picnics of her youth.

'Can I ask', said Simbongile, 'if your granny was in the camp?'

'She was.'

'My great-granny was in a camp, too. But not the same camp as your granny.'

'There was a separate camp, I understand, for' – Joan hesitated – 'Africans.'

Simbongile nodded.

'I would very much like to see the site of the Africans' camp, if you think that would be possible.'

'Oh no!' A hollow chuckle emanated from the front seat. 'They did not make preservations for them. There is nothing left of my great-granny's camp now.' Simbongile slowed the car and turned right into a paved driveway. 'And I'm sorry about it,' he said, turning round in his seat as the car came to a standstill, 'but there's not much left of your granny's camp either.'

They were in another parking lot. A large sign of freshly painted red letters reserved it solely for the Bloemfontein Bible Centre and its visitors. This organisation was housed in the only nearby building, an apartheid fantasy of mauve and grey with a jaunty, plastic-coated rhomboid pediment above its glass doors.

'I'll wait for you in the car,' said Simbongile.

'Don't worry, Mum. I'll go.' Eloise left the Toyota and strode purposefully towards the Bible Centre, hoping to snatch a few solitary moments on a clean toilet.

'Ask for Mrs du Toit,' called Joan, winding down the window.

Eloise did so, at a large reception desk of mock, mauve-tinted granite. The receptionist, a young Zulu woman with complex braids and a look of fathomless boredom on her wide, pretty face, led her across an atrium lined with Bibles and evangelical pamphlets in a variety of pastel shades. Asking Eloise to wait, she disappeared for a moment and returned trailing Mrs du Toit, a friendly woman of indeterminate age whose golden fringe glinted in the fluorescent light. She wore a great deal of carefully applied make-up and had perfect nails of a length Eloise had last attempted at the age of seventeen.

'Be sure you lock up properly,' she said kindly, holding out a purple plastic key chain. 'I've checked with the army and there isn't any rifle practice today. But there's a pony in there and we don't want him out on the highway, do we?'

'No, of course. Thank you so much.'

Alone in a blissfully air-conditioned bathroom a few forced pleasantries later, Eloise leaned her cheek against a cool mauve tile and closed her eyes. She counted very slowly to ten, then to fifteen. Forcing her eyes open again, she took a long drink from one of the taps and examined herself in the mirror. It was difficult, when confronted with such unanswerable evidence, to ignore the fact that she too would one day be old. Already, her eyes looked more like her mother's than her own.

She thought treacherously of feigning sickness and spending the rest of the morning in bed; but she knew, too, that this was impossible, and with a smile of determined brightness she steeled herself against the day to come.

'Were there any problems?' asked Joan when she returned to the car. 'I was beginning to worry.'

'Oh no, Mum. Everything's fine. Apparently the army has no plans to use the site today. But there is a pony we should watch out for.'

'Goodness me.'

'Yes.'

Simbongile was helping Joan out of her seat. 'It is best to leave the car here,' he said. 'Follow me.'

He led the two women across the car park to a short ornamental path that twisted under some jacarandas to the back of the Bible Centre and ended in a high wire gate with a padlock of comical proportions. Taking the keys from Eloise, he unlocked it with a solemn flourish. 'Your granny is watching us again,' he said gravely to Joan.

The plot of land before them was square and flat and fenced in with wire, a lifeless stretch of orange clay punctuated haphazardly by clumps of hardy grass. It struck Joan how odd it was that she had never been here, even on one of her childhood visits to her grandmother. She had imagined the camp, of course, but imagination had over-furnished the scene. She had expected something more than the dusty nothingness that stretched before her in all directions.

All she knew was what the guidebooks told her: that the camp had been established in December 1900, intended originally to house the refugee families of surrendered Boer commandos; that it had soon become a prison for the loved ones of those who fought on. She thought of Gertruida van Vuuren, of her scorn for those *hensoppers* or *rooipootjies* who had abandoned the fight before the bitter end, and of the thousands who had refused to give in even after their homes and farms had been burned by the British. The sheer number of prisoners, recorded on a brass plaque nailed to a cemented pile of orange rocks, seemed unreal to her: 1,200 by the end of 1900; 3,700 just four months later; 6,586 by the August of 1901. She knew that the inmates had lived in neat rows of bell tents – she had seen the photographs – but she could not imagine how six and a half thousand people could have coexisted in such a confined area. Where had they done their washing?

As if reading her thoughts, Simbongile indicated a narrow man-made incline at some distance from them. 'They call that the Dam of Tears,' he told her. 'It is where your granny washed her clothes.'

'But where did the water come from?'

'That I am not knowing.'

'Are you all right, Mum?'

'Quite all right, darling, thank you.' Joan felt an overwhelming desire to sit down. There was not a bench in sight, nor even a tree under which to shelter from the sun. She became conscious of the heat, rising steadily from the baked ground; of the cracks in the dried soil. She took a few steps forward and swayed slightly.

'Mum, are you all right? Should we go back to the car?'

Joan shook her head. She wished – though she only half-acknowledged it, even to herself – that her daughter was not with her. Like Frank, Eloise had no tolerance for contemplation or stillness. 'I'm quite all right,' she said, and walked purposefully away from the others, wondering where the van Vuurens' tent had been, where the hospital had stood in which Hannie had died. For the first time in decades she thought of her parting from her grandmother fifty-eight years before, of the rush of lucidity that had accompanied the old lady's final words to her.

As a taxi waited in the drive with Joan's bags in its boot, Gertruida had brushed aside Nqobani's ministrations and risen unaided for the second time in a week. The effect was alarming: a last manifestation of life and purpose, as though the old woman's youthful self were struggling to clamber out of the collapsed mineshaft of her body. Once on her feet, she had taken the *Psalms en Gesange* from the table and set it resolutely before her granddaughter. 'This is for you, *my kleintjie*,' she said urgently in Afrikaans, panting from exertion and taking the young woman's hands in her own. 'And in return you must make me a promise, *my liewe* Joan.'

It was the first time for many years that the old lady had used Joan's name.

'Anything, *Ouma*.'

Gertruida fastened a pair of small, dark eyes on her and drew breath. 'If you must go to England,' she said hoarsely, tightening her grip on her granddaughter's hands, 'then promise me, whatever you do, that you will never marry an Englishman.'

Joan had made the promise lightly, as a mark of respect to an eccentric relative. She had not even thought of it when Frank proposed, or when she accepted him, or on the showery April day on which, in a new dress made possible by Astrid's hoarded coupons, she had married him. How different her life would have been if she had kept her word!

She walked slowly towards the Dam of Tears, now half-full and stagnant. The water had a vile, viscose quality to it, suggestive of the water-borne diseases that had once flourished in its murky depths. She wished to offer prayers for the eternal rest of those who had died in this terrible place, but she did not care to be observed. She had a horror of false piety and was unable, more than twenty years after his death, to shake the embarrassment that Frank had always made her feel at any suggestion of the numinous. He had not liked her to pray and had forbidden her to compel the children's attendance at church or Sunday school.

She glanced at Eloise, standing some way off, and thought how worldly she looked, how greatly she might have profited from regular spiritual instruction in her youth. She was wearing a crisp black linen trouser suit that would be ruined by the dust and a pair of expensively inscrutable sunglasses. The sight of her, possibly bored and certainly restless in such a hallowed place, prompted a flash of uncharacteristic anger in Joan. She should, she knew, have stood up to Frank more. Perhaps their children would have grown up kinder, less selfish, more inclined to devote their lives to worthwhile causes had she felt freer to discuss the great imponderables of life with them. In this shameful place, so eloquent of the sufferings of her forebears, she felt that she had not done enough to help Eloise and George develop into decent human beings. Such gifts they had, so uselessly squandered!

She turned from her daughter and faced the water. However fancy the terminology, the simple truth was that Eloise used her energy, her quickness and flair, to make rich people richer. And George – well. All that childish affection he had once shown her, all that warmth and generosity of spirit. Where had it gone? As an adult he had proved himself capable of abandoning his wife and his mother, of devoting his considerable talents to the incitement of greed.

She sat stiffly on the dam's bank and felt something sharp beneath her. Rising painfully, she found a shard of thick brown pottery and picked it up. How could anyone leave litter in such a sacred place? She turned towards the others and caught something white on the ground; an unplaceable shape. She blinked, for such things often disappeared when so prompted, but when it did not she leaned down very slowly and retrieved it. It was a piece of china, about an inch long, coated in fine orange clay but of visibly better quality than the other fragment. Turning it over, she saw that its reverse was decorated with a still visible pattern of red leaves, pricked out in tiny dots.

For an instant, it seemed that a multitude was moving restlessly along the waterline. She heard a cry and the splash of bathing bodies; then all was silent once more. 'Goodness me,' she said, straightening up. She began to walk, her eyes on the ground, and by the time she reached Eloise and Simbongile she had found three further fragments, all of differing patterns, and one piece of viciously barbed wire. Under the influence of these relics the field lost its barren emptiness; shadows swarmed about them, women and ragged children, old men on their deathbeds, raging against their confinement.

'Ah yes,' said Simbongile, examining her outstretched hand know-ledgeably. 'These are Victorian sponge ware.'

'Victorian what?' asked Eloise.

'Victorian sponge ware.'

Had Simbongile been white, or as educated as she was, Eloise would have asked him how on earth he could be so sure. As it was she held her tongue, but he seemed to sense her scepticism.

'My cousin is a professor,' he said. 'He has found many things in this place.'

'But how did it get here?'

'The prisoners brought it with them. And this wire was used to keep them in.'

'So it's a hundred years old?'

The young man nodded. 'See there,' he said, pointing to the piece of glazed clay that had been Joan's first discovery. 'If I am not mistaken, that was being part of the British Tommy's rum-ration jar. The ladies were often using the soldiers' ration jars to carry water. They were not having so many buckets.'

'Maybe,' said Eloise. 'But there's no way of knowing for certain what this fragment is.'

'Wherever you look here,' Simbongile went on, ignoring her, 'you will find things. Come with me.' He led them over the parched earth, pointing out coins and the fragments of dinner services, retrieving from a ditch a sawn-off can of Lyle's Golden Syrup.

Eloise endured it as long as she could, and then said, 'I think we should go back to the car. We'll all fry in this sun.'

'Not me,' said Simbongile quietly. 'But maybe lunch would be welcome.'

Chapter 11

They ate again at the Waterfront and Joan insisted that Simbongile join them, rather than wait in the Toyota with a sandwich. She was moved, but also excited, by the discoveries of the morning. 'I am ashamed to admit how little I know about the war,' she said as they sat down.

'Well you don't have long to wait now.' Eloise took a photocopied itinerary from her handbag and consulted it. 'Our lecture begins in an hour and a half, at the War Museum.'

'Who is giving it?'

'I can't read the name. Dr – Somebody.' She passed the sheet to Simbongile for clarification.

'Dr Xolile Kakaza. He is my cousin, the grandson of my uncle Harold.'

Though neither woman would have admitted it, both were surprised to learn that a taxi driver who lived in a tin shack could be related so closely to someone who gave lectures at museums.

'It is the New South Africa,' said Simbongile cheerfully, acknowledging their unasked question.

'But—' Joan hesitated.

'But it hasn't been new for that long,' said Eloise, completing her mother's sentence. 'Weren't students of colour only permitted to attend white schools in 1990? I thought that very few of them – I mean, of you – made it to university.'

'That is right,' said Simbongile. 'Even today it is not easy for everyone to get the good education. But Xolile was lucky. He was having lessons since a long time from the priest who employed his mother.' He smiled. 'Oooh, but he was a very good man, Mr Reverend Booysen. Even though he was also an Afrikaner. Never mind the police were trying to arrest him, he carried on teaching – many children, not

74

just my cousin. When Xolile was thirteen, he found people to help him. UK people. They give him money for a scholarship, so he was going to a white school.' He looked at Eloise. 'Us blacks could go to private schools in those days. The problem was, we never had money for the fees. Xolile is the only person so far in my family to go to university. He is going to Cape Town first. Then he is getting a scholarship to America.' Simbongile said this with reverence, as though 'America' were a talisman, a place to which a single visit, like the touch of a charmed object, could guarantee lifelong good fortune.

'And would you like to go there one day?' asked Joan.

Their driver leaned forward with the air of one about to impart an important confidence. 'My plan', he said, 'is this.' He stretched his delicately made hands before them on the starched tablecloth. 'I will work hard. One day I will pay off my car. Then I will work hard to afford money for a minibus. That is the way to make progress as a taxi driver. You must have a minibus.' He paused and breathed deeply, emphasising the solemnity of this fact. 'When I have a minibus, I will work hard to get my mother a house because she cannot be working much longer and a shack is too cold in winter for an old lady. Then I will employ my cousin Thabo to drive my Toyota while I drive the minibus. When the minibus is paid off, I will work hard to earn money for my own house. And then—' he leaned back in his chair, as though the vision of this glittering future were almost too much to contemplate – 'I will earn money to visit UK and America.'

Eloise had long ago made her accommodation with material success, and for the first time her insistence on first-class air travel embarrassed her. 'What hours do you work?' she asked.

'I am getting up at four o'clock a.m.,' said Simbongile. 'I drive four times from the location to the city, taking people to work.' He shook his head. 'That is why it is better to have a minibus. With one journey you can take eighteen, maybe twenty people. At the moment, I can take seven only.'

'Seven? In your Toyota?'

'Oh yes. Two on the front seat and five in the back. At nine o'clock I am going to the hotel. Sometimes there are guests who need me for the whole day. Guests like my VIP visitors from UK!' He grinned at them. 'These are the best days. Other days, I must drive around and look for passengers. Then at six o'clock I am taking people from work to the location. I am eating at eight o'clock, then resting until midnight when I am coming here to collect the restaurant workers.'

'But how much sleep do you get?' asked Joan.

'From ten o'clock until midnight every day,' said Simbongile, brightly. 'Then from one o'clock until four o'clock.'

'But that's just five hours.'

'It is okay for me because I sleep all day on Sunday.' He smiled reassuringly at the two women. 'I am lucky. At my place we have electricity and a latrine. Except when it rains, everything is very okay.'

'And how were you able to buy your car?'

'Xolile get a job in a university and give me the money for the down payment.' He wiped his mouth with a napkin. 'I am glad you will meet Xolile. He is a good cousin to me.'

The museum to which Simbongile took them after lunch was set in a large park of dry grass which also contained the *Vrouwemonument*, a memorial to the tens of thousands of women who died in the concentration camps and to Emily Hobhouse, the English lady who drew the world's attention to the sufferings of the 'refugees' detained at Her Majesty's pleasure.

Eloise, whose hangover had been painfully exacerbated by a morning spent in the scorching sun, was relieved to find herself in a dark, air-conditioned lecture theatre. She knew, from her mother's slight prickliness as she helped her into her seat, that she had not acquitted herself well at the concentration camp: Joan had expected more piety than she had been able to produce, and Eloise longed to tell her that it was precisely this expectation that had inhibited her expression of profound feeling. Though she did not admit this to herself, she was irritated by Simbongile's cheery equanimity and its implicit criticism of her own stress levels; and she diverted this energy into a sharp burst of applause, which galvanised the slack hand-clapping of the other audience members as Dr Xolile Kakaza entered the room and took his place behind a steel lectern.

He was tall and sinewy, quite unlike his sturdy cousin, and he spoke English with studious precision and American vowels, his accent disorientingly close to Claude's.

'Ladies and gentlemen,' he began. 'I am going to tell you a sordid story of greed and pride and an attempt by a great nation to seize control of another's natural resources in the name of Democracy. I am going to tell you about a conflict that was avoidable, opposed by many before it started, pursued with ever greater ferocity while it lasted. My story concerns the Anglo-Boer War of 1899–1902.'

He paused and cleared his throat.

'Let us begin in the years 1834–40. In that period fifteen thousand people trekked away from British dominion in the Cape Colony and struck out for what they thought was virgin territory in the heart of the country. They were Boers, descendants of the first Dutch people who came to this continent, and they engaged in bloody skirmishes along the way with the established inhabitants of their newfound lands.'

Eloise listened vaguely as Dr Kakaza described the foundation of the Boer Republics of the Transvaal and the Orange Free State in the 1850s; the discovery of diamonds at the confluence of the Orange and Vaal rivers in 1867; Britain's subsequent annexation of the Transvaal; the successful Boer uprisings against British rule in 1880 and 1881; and the eventual restoration of self-government. Although her job required her to read seven daily newspapers and four weekly news magazines, Eloise followed politics with the kind of resigned cynicism available to those whose lives are not profoundly effected by external events. She listened as Dr Kakaza compared the economic importance of gold in the nineteenth century to that of oil in the twenty-first, and heard without surprise that the discovery of vast deposits outside Johannesburg in 1886 had tempted the world's major superpower once again.

'The British invaded the Boer Republics ostensibly to uphold democracy,' Dr Kakaza told them. 'Popular feeling at home was stoked with tales of Boer savagery and the threat it posed to civilisation itself. The British believed their vast military superiority would ensure a quick and painless victory, and lead to long-term control of the world's largest goldfields.' He cleared his throat. 'But the British were wrong. The war became the most expensive conflict in the history of the world, and set a new threshold of civilian suffering.'

The unfolding of this tragedy had a heavily sedative effect on Eloise, and the fact that succumbing to sleep would cause unforgivable offence to her mother made the lure of it doubly resistible. Drowsiness, she thought, as Dr Kakaza's well-modulated tones filled the room, regular and resonant, was like laughter: the more intensely one resisted, the more impossible resistance became.

She tried shifting in her seat, digging her nails into the flesh of her palms, but saw that this gave the appearance of restlessness – which was almost as unforgivable as unconsciousness. She knew that her body language must betray no sign of internal struggle and fixed her eyes on the lecturer's charismatic face, adopting a pose of rapt attention which threatened to unleash a flood of fatigue, the accumulated exhaustion of many months. In the darkened room, the seductive illusions of a dream state fused subtly with the reality of the present as Xolile's voice, so reminiscent of Claude's, cocooned her in mellifluous sound.

Claude had made love as he did everything except argue: precisely, painstakingly, his eye trained calmly on his goal. That first night, as the trains shuddered beneath his window and the traffic threw writhing shadows across the bare walls, he had laid her on his bed and rested gently on top of her, allowing her to feel his weight while supporting himself on his arms. She had never touched the hard ridge of a man's triceps before; nor, she thought with a thrill as he kissed her, holding his body a fraction of an inch above hers, entirely controlled, had she ever seen a man with such an athletic body naked.

It was Claude's deftness, his unhurried control, that allowed Eloise to enjoy herself from the very beginning. Her previous sexual encounters, with English boys in their late teens and early twenties, had been fraught affairs, a physical cacophony of inserted digits, pinched nipples and – on one or two memorably unpleasant occasions – bad breath. Claude's breath was sweet, like wind passing through a vineyard. She could taste the *coquilles St-Jacques* they had shared on his tongue, a subtle flavour that mingled with the lean saltiness of his skin. He undressed her expertly, his fingers finding the clasps of Madame Récamier's bra with a practised ease that was indescribably sexy in its knowingness.

Claude kept his clothes on at first, in a manner both restrained and respectful. The apartment, suffused with the heat and aromas of good cooking, was the perfect temperature for love-making. His tongue on her ear lobes, a little scratchy, like a cat's, so different from the saliva-drenched slobbering of previous partners, alerted Eloise's entire body to the possibilities of unhurried sensuality. She was soon twisting beneath him, running her hands under his shirt, along the rippling expanse of his back. Thrusting upwards against him, she felt the rigid compliment of his erection barely constrained by his trousers – but he pulled away, teasing her, finally slipping his T-shirt over his head, exposing a tapered torso lightly dusted with hair, the indentations of his ribcage and the clean lines of his abdominals lit from behind by the city's radiant skyline.

When he touched her, the calluses at the base of his fingers sent ricocheting tingles across her skin. As his tongue danced downwards – from her ears to her neck, in deft pirouettes around her nipples, down and down towards the tight lace of Madame Récamier's panties – she felt herself, as she had never felt before, completely present in the moment. Eloise's internal commentator, the critical voice that planned and schemed, analysed, exhorted and threatened, the constant companion that only sleep could quiet, was not so much silenced as obliterated. She tried to fumble with Claude's belt but he gently pinned her arms behind her head, his lashes kissing her cheeks. The anxieties that sex had induced before – was her bum too big? what, precisely, should she do with this strange piece of hard, warm, male flesh in her hand? – dissolved in the solvent of Claude's sensitive expertise. It became clear that he expected nothing in return, that he gave pleasure for its own sake; and this knowledge allowed Eloise to relinquish her insecurities, to relax into herself and to savour the liberation of erotic release.

When Claude's tongue reached its object, she cried out so loudly she disturbed the neighbours, a middle-aged couple who recognised the significance of what they heard with an admixture of nostalgia and bitterness. Expecting him to enter her, she was first surprised, then maddened, then ecstatic when he did not. She had never understood the rush to penetration, had often found – though she felt ashamed to admit it, a failure in some way – that it hurt. What committee of adolescent boys had decided that no woman could climax without it? On whose authority?

Sliding further down the bed, away from her, Claude focused his attention on the smooth expanse of her recently waxed inner thigh. For a long time – how long? – he made feints at her clitoris, sensing instinctively when she drew close to orgasm and displaying the utmost patience as he allowed the pleasure to subside, only to be rekindled. She was conscious, at one point, of the floodlights of Sacré Coeur being extinguished, but otherwise no marker gave form to the passing hours save the gradual silencing of traffic as the city slept. The scent of her own arousal filled the room, mingling with his smell, drenching his sheets, and when he lifted himself over her again, returning to the position in which he had begun, and kissed her, she could taste herself in his mouth and on his lips.

'Isn't it *fascinating*?' whispered Joan, seizing her hand and causing Eloise to leap as though she had been scalded. 'Would you take some notes for me?' She proffered a pen. 'He's going too fast for my fingers.'

For a moment, the thick felt tip in her mother's hand seemed vaguely obscene. 'Of course,' said Eloise, weakly.

'The British didn't have much difficulty in "winning the war",' Dr Kakaza was saying, 'and by September 1900 both Boer Republics had forcibly been made colonies of the Crown. But even though the number of Empire troops eventually exceeded the entire civilian population of the Transvaal, the British still could not conclude the war. Why not? Because they were fighting a people for whom freedom from foreign interference meant everything. Facing insuperable odds, the Boers began the first guerrilla war of the twentieth century, using their mobility and knowledge of the country to prolong the struggle long after their main towns had fallen.'

'Military might not necessarily effective against passionate, inventive resistance,' wrote Eloise.

'By August 1900,' Dr Kakaza went on, 'with the war still not concluded, the British Commander, Lord Roberts, turned up the heat – quite literally. A policy of farm burning was instituted, designed to clear the country of hostile Boers, though a pretence of fair play was initially maintained. "No farm is to be burnt", ordered Roberts, "except for acts of treachery." He ignored the fact that one man's treachery is another's patriotism, and that Boer farms were so large that the women and children left on them by their husbands and fathers had no control over the presence of commando forces on their land. This did not prevent their houses from being burned and their livestock slaughtered in what became known as the "Scorched Earth" policy. Neither did it prevent their own forced removal to what were first called "refugee" and later "concentration" camps.

'In the country as a whole, more than thirty thousand homesteads were burned to the ground. Around Bloemfontein alone, dozens of farms were destroyed, among them one described by an English journalist, writing for the *Manchester Guardian*, as "the very example of a modern working farm" – an estate called Van Vuuren's Drift which used to lie just a few kilometres to the east of where we are sitting today.'

Joan gave a sharp cry and reached for Eloise's hand.

'It required the "total war" attitude of Roberts's replacement, Lord Kitchener, to combat the Boer tactics successfully. In March 1901 he began to build what one might describe as a gigantic cage, a grid of 8,000 blockhouses connected by 3,700 miles of wire fencing and guarded by 50,000 soldiers, to hem in the Boers and reduce their freedom of movement. As he did this, the inadequacy of planning and supplies for the concentration camps led to the death of more than twenty-eight thousand adults and children in them.

'It took a brave Englishwoman, Miss Emily Hobhouse, who visited the camps and was outraged by their state, to alert the world to the suffering behind the British government's fine talk of "humanitarian aid" – but her reward was to be refused permission to disembark on her next voyage to South Africa. And though the world was shocked by what it learnt, conditions did not begin to improve for several months, blocked by official denial and delay.

'By the time the Boers finally capitulated, more than ten per cent of their population had perished. Faced with the prospect of a never-ending war, the British abandoned their original aim of total victory. They agreed to give the Boers eventual self-government and made good on that promise five years later. They also agreed to leave the management of "native affairs" in Boer hands, dashing African hopes of an extension of the liberal franchise of the Cape Colony. The consequences of that decision, and the psychological legacy of the concentration camps, coloured the history of South Africa throughout the twentieth century.'

He paused theatrically, then flashed a brilliant smile.

'For those interested in pursuing this subject further, I take the immodest step of recommending my latest book, *An Ominous Peace*. It is available from the museum gift shop.'

Chapter 12

'What a shame', said Joan, 'that your cousin couldn't stay longer. There is so much I would like to have asked him.'

It was, Simbongile agreed, deeply regrettable. He had been looking forward to showing Xolile off to his new English friends, and the fact that he had had a plane to catch annoyed him. Xolile was always catching planes. 'Next time you are visiting,' he assured Joan, 'he will be here.'

Having reached an age at which repeat visits could no longer be guaranteed, Joan smiled affectionately at the young man. At least, she reflected, Dr Kakaza had found time to say hello, to express astonishment and delight that she had known Van Vuuren's Drift as a girl. With the air of one conducting a polite retreat, he had introduced his cousin's friends to the museum's assistant curator and disappeared.

This official was a flushed Afrikaans woman in khaki trousers and a leopard-print blouse named Sarie Reitz. As Joan moved stiffly towards the main exhibition hall on Simbongile's arm, Eloise lingered behind with her and began a conversation about the museum's history. She had intended, in the first flush of her enthusiasm for this root-tracing trip with Joan, to organise a personal tour of the private collections for her mother; and though she had not done so, she was confident that this outcome could still be achieved. It would be a charming, tranquil end to the day, and engender just the right mood in which a suggestion of separate room-service dinners in bed might be made without offence.

Ten years before, Eloise had obtained the early declassification of her father's War Record and SOE Personnel file, the contents of which she had kept resolutely from Joan. Sarie Reitz could not possibly be more difficult to manage than the egotistical bureaucrats at the Ministry of Defence; and the plastic photo frame that dangled from her key ring suggested the appropriate opening. 'What *stunning* children,' she said.

'Ach man, shame. Do you think so?' Sarie removed the chain from her belt and held it to the light, the better for Eloise to see. 'That's Johan, and that's Koos. But they're a lot older now. Almost seventeen. Twins.'

'You must be enormously proud of them.'

This succinct articulation of Sarie's most profound feelings touched her, and made her a little less afraid of the commanding woman in her expensive clothes who was being so nice to her. 'Ach man,' she said, 'not really. But they're good boys.'

The conversation moved quickly through Johan and Koos's childhood illnesses and hopes for the future, before Eloise elegantly returned them to the question of the museum and its archives. 'What a huge responsibility they must be for you,' she said, sympathetically.

It transpired that Sarie Reitz's job would have been entirely manageable had she not also had to perform the archivist's duties for her; and judicious concern from Eloise prompted various revelations of her colleague's haplessness. 'We have hundreds and thousands of letters and journals, various accounts of the period. They need to be properly indexed,' Sarie told her. 'And then there's all the stuff in the basements. A lot of it hasn't even been catalogued.'

'Could we see it?'

But Eloise had asked too soon. 'Applications must be made six weeks in advance, in writing to the Museum Director,' said Sarie automatically. 'Members of the public are entitled to see all documents, on payment of a fee and provided that due notice is given in the proper manner. The artefact collections are open only to academics with full accreditation.'

'I see. And for the descendants of camp victims?'

'They have to give three weeks' notice.'

'Of course.' Eloise retreated temporarily and allowed the conversation to return to families and children. As Joan and Simbongile walked ahead, examining cases filled with mannequins bending over plastic campfires, she mentioned casually that she and her mother were probably on the last holiday they would ever take together.

'Ach no,' said Sarie. 'Shame.' And then, after a pause: 'Do you have children?'

'Unfortunately not.' Eloise understood now what was required and heard herself admit – quite untruthfully – that she had always wanted kids, that it was a tragedy she was too old to have them now. 'I just don't know how I could ever live up to the bond I have with my mother,' she said.

'Oh but you *will*.' Sarie gripped her arm, then remembered herself and let it go. 'Of course you will bond with your own children. And there's always IVF.' To the assistant curator's untutored gaze, Eloise did not seem much beyond her mid-thirties. 'It's not too late until you think it is.'

By the time they reached the display case devoted to objects made by Boer prisoners of war on St Helena, the deal was done. 'We're closing for the day now,' Sarie told Joan and Eloise, confidentially, 'and tomorrow's Sunday. But give me your details and let me see what I can do.'

That night, Eloise got more than eight hours' sleep, a feat she had not managed in over a decade. She woke at 8 a.m. and lay in bed, relishing the bustle of the city outside and the fact that she did not have to join it for at least an hour yet. Joan had said she should get some rest – well, she was getting some. She got out of bed and stretched languidly, then made herself a cup of instant coffee. It tasted like walnuts, but the caffeine brought its customary sparkle and a long, cool bath improved her mood still further. Emerging from it, her eye caught the bright-blue cylinder of her electric toothbrush on a shelf by the avocado basin; and twisting her hair into a beige towel, she returned to the bedroom and got back into bed with it.

Two nights of use had softened the sheets. Closing her eyes, Eloise summoned her favourite erotic companion. He had Claude's smile but was hairier and more sturdily built, with thighs that resembled those of the captain of the French rugby team whom she had met the year before at a corporate-hospitality event hosted by Kleinberger Dresden. Today he was blond, like the driver who had brought her and Joan to the airport, and more commanding than usual. She was cresting the wave of a deliciously unfolding climax when there was a knock on the door.

'Darling? Are you decent?'

'I'm just – brushing my teeth.'

'Do you want me to order some breakfast for you?'

84

'Yes, please!' Eloise was very close now. She redoubled her concentration.

'Would you like the Continental breakfast or the Full English? The Continental comes with a basket of pastries and a complimentary orange juice. The Full English has a choice of eggs, boiled, scrambled or fried, and—'

'Continental's fine.'

'And would you prefer tea, coffee or hot chocolate?'

Almost there.

'Tea, coffee or hot chocolate, darling? I've got them on the line.'

'Coffee!'

'What's that? Oh yes, I'll tell her. They say they're out of croissants. Would you mind a *pain aux raisins* instead?'

It was no use. Eloise switched off the toothbrush.

'A *pain aux raisins* would be fine,' she shouted, trying to keep the tension from her voice. 'I'm just going to take a shower. See you soon.'

Ten minutes later, as she dried her hair for the second time that morning, she retrieved her Blackberry crossly from the suitcase and put it into the pocket of her shorts. There was only so much she would give up for Joan, and she had never gone for more than three days without checking her messages.

'Morning, darling,' said her mother as she unlocked and opened the connecting door. 'I didn't like to wake you until I heard you up and about.'

'Morning, Mum. How did you sleep?'

'Like a log. And you?'

'Very well.'

'I'm so glad. Can I pour you a cup of coffee?'

As Eloise sat down on the edge of Joan's bed, eyeing the basket of icing-drenched pastries on the tray with suspicion, the telephone rang. It was Sarie Reitz.

'And how are you this morning?' she asked chirpily.

'Very well, thank you. How are Johann and Koos? Did their rugby match go well?'

'Ach shame, man! You remembered. Yes, they're at swimming practice now. They're triathletes too, both of them. But Koos always breaks the records. He—'

But Eloise had had enough of Johann and Koos. 'I'm just having breakfast with my mother,' she said sweetly. 'Could I call you back?'

'No need. I just phoned to tell you I've got together a few things I think Mrs McAllister might be interested in. Should I lay them aside for you?'

'That would be so kind.'

'Just ask for me when you come to the museum. The archivist doesn't work weekends, but I'm here.'

They were at the museum within the hour, the pastry selection of the Volksraad Hotel having failed to tempt either of them. Well slept and dressed for the heat, Eloise's optimism returned, while Joan thought that maybe she had judged her a little harshly the day before. As Sarie Reitz ushered them into her cluttered office, she felt a surge of gratitude for all the care her daughter had shown her. 'What an angel you are to me,' she said as she sat down.

'Now,' began Sarie, 'I have a surprise for you.'

She reached into her desk drawer and withdrew a green cardboard folder, bound with orange ribbon. 'This came into the museum's possession when the state archives were re-evaluated at the beginning of 2001. It took a while to find it, as our archivist is somewhat behind schedule and hasn't got as far as V yet.' She waved away Joan's thanks. 'No, no. Please. I'm always happy to help' – she nodded, significantly – 'a *relative*. Yes, yes.' She chuckled at her audience's astonishment. 'It seems that we are distant cousins. An Ellie Reitz married an Elijah van Vuuren around the time of the Great Trek – I found it in a reference book last night; I have terrible trouble sleeping – but the really exciting thing is what I have here.' She undid the folder's neat bow to reveal a decaying calfskin notebook. 'Would you like to know who wrote this?' She lifted its stitchless frontispiece reverently to reveal a page covered in narrow lines of tiny copperplate. 'Well?' She leaned back, a look of delighted satisfaction on her carefully made-up face.

Eloise, who had been expecting some title deeds, at most a birth certificate, was now excited herself.

'Your very own grandmother!' cried Sarie. 'Gertruida van Vuuren.'

'Goodness me,' said Joan.

'And because you are a survivor's descendant, and in the city for a short time only, the Director will grant you full access to the artefact collections. Those', she added, lest her visitors underestimate the importance of this privilege, 'are not usually open to the public. Even professors from overseas have to apply six weeks in advance.' She rose and picked up a large bunch of keys. 'After you!' She waved Joan in the direction of the corridor; and as Eloise stood up to follow her mother, she lowered her voice and stood on tiptoes to reach her ear. 'I went on the internet for you last night,' she said warmly, putting an arm around her shoulders. 'In Great Britain, you can get IVF treatment *for free*!'

The museum's storerooms were in the basement, protected by a succession of iron grilles. 'Yissis, man,' said Sarie, 'I keep telling them to get an alarm. These keys are so heavy and each one looks the same. I don't know what we'd do if there was a fire.'

Standing in the dark behind her, Joan felt the same giddy excitement she had experienced as a child in the anticipation of unknown wonders. 'Bless you for going to all this trouble,' she said.

'Yes, well. I don't usually, it's true. But since it was such a special case. I just wish there was more light down here.'

As if in answer to this request, the door at the top of the basement steps opened and revealed a figure it took Joan a moment to recognise: Mr Engelbrecht, the manager of the Volksraad Hotel.

'Miss McAllister? Is that you?'

'Keep that door open!' called Sarie. 'And don't block the light!'

Mr Engelbrecht hesitated, unsure how to accede to both requests at once. 'Miss McAllister?' he called again.

'Yes?'

'I have an urgent message for you.'

'For me?'

'Yes. From England. From a Mr Derby. He said you were to call him at once.'

'At once?'

'Yes.'

Eloise knew that Emily would have revealed her location in only the most extraordinary circumstances. She reached for the handrail, to steady herself. 'Did he sound excited?'

'Most certainly.'

'Are you all right, darling?' asked Joan.

Be calm, Eloise. 'Fine, Mum, fine.' She did her best to sound unconcerned. Had Claude called, too? Was it good news?

'He said would you please be so kind as to phone him back

immediately?' Mr Engelbrecht delicately paraphrased Patrick's rather more emphatic message.

'He sent you out here to find me?'

'Yes, ma'am. I called Simbongile and he told me he'd driven you to the museum. I came straight away.'

Eloise closed her eyes. 'Thank you,' she said.

'Is it urgent, dear?' Joan kept all disappointment firmly from her tone. 'Do you need to make a call?'

Eloise considered the situation. She knew in her bones that Patrick was calling about osmium, which could only mean one thing: the long-awaited announcement from MaxiTech. Equally, she was about to participate in a unique moment of root-tracing with her mother: the very purpose of the whole trip. She hesitated, and only understood many years later that this was no neutral action – because it encouraged Joan to say, as she had known that she would: 'If he's sent Mr Engelbrecht all the way from the hotel, it must be urgent. You'd better telephone him at once.'

'Perhaps you're right.' Eloise attempted unsuccessfully to infuse a note of regret into her tone; and then, as if to verify the falsehood that it was her mother's wish she was obeying, rather than her own: 'If you really think I should.'

Joan said nothing as her daughter bounded away up the stairs, but Sarie Reitz understood what had happened and took the old lady's hand in hers.

'We'll wait for her,' she murmured, consolingly.

Chapter 13

Eloise emerged from the sombre gloom of the museum's galleries into bright sunshine and felt that even the weather was applauding her. How delicious this triumph was, how sweet! She thought joyfully of the grudging admission Carol would be forced to make, of the infuriating graciousness with which she would receive it. It was so like Patrick to send the manager of her hotel across town to get her; she sensed in this theatrical gesture the contagious euphoria that came over him when he backed a winner. And she *was* a winner.

She thought with sudden affection of Claude. It was thanks to him that they had salvaged a friendship of sorts, sporadic though it was, from the embers of their wrecked domestic experiment. She laughed girlishly, throwing her head back at the memory of their fights – for they had fought as passionately as they had made up. What a pity he had turned out so impossible to live with.

Eloise had left the Récamier apartment ten days after her first night with him, never to return, and in their early years together they had lived mostly on the proceeds of his various graduate scholarships, supplemented by the translation work Eloise did for a travel magazine. Money was yet to assume its importance for either of them, and they found an answering morality and taste in each other that led to a life of riotous contentment. Claude took care of the household chores and cooked astoundingly. He woke his *belle Anglaise* in the mornings with freshly ground espresso and home-made pastries, laced with gooey strips of dark chocolate. Together they gave inventive dinners for his friends, predominantly chain-smoking graduate students with romantically stained teeth, who in time became their friends, and conformed precisely to Eloise's idea of the bohemian intelligentsia.

Over langoustines grilled lightly in Pernod-infused butter, or smoked wood pigeon with a beetroot and Merlot *jus*, Eloise learned the deft art of French social discourse: how to draw blood without bruising and to parry the return blow with nonchalant unconcern. Welcomed into this new world, she began to taste the suasive power she would later wield, and with elegant efficiency she transferred to the Sorbonne and entered the second year of a degree in *la littérature française* – though much of her real learning took place on Claude's sofa, with his favourite books.

Claude did not believe in debating trivial subjects, and chose to bear his frustrations with Eloise's shoddy domestic habits as quietly as he could for as long as he could. Perhaps he should have told her sooner what pain her carelessness caused him, for she was not callous or incapable of change – only young and glad to be out of her parents' house. But Claude did not. And a week before their second anniversary, returning from a conference to find three spore-filled mugs under a pile of Eloise's knickers on his side of the bed, he lost control.

The drama of the ensuing scene, so entirely without precedent, unsettled Eloise profoundly. It revealed a temper in Claude that she had not imagined and which she could not forget, for she had already lived under the roof of one violent man. Her lover's control of his environment, at first merely eccentric, began to seem sinister and to resemble her father's. The apartment's straight lines and clean sheets became oppressive to her, and Claude's insistence on them was intolerable. In a reference to the Ovidian myth of the man who begs Aphrodite to breathe life into a statue, having found no living woman worthy of his love, she began calling Claude Pygmalion; and over time this sly joke became something else: a linguistic marker of the limits of his authority.

Such unavowed tension led to more frequent eruptions. Humour became Eloise's shield against Claude's articulate fury, and she learned from several heated skirmishes that the impeccable Dr Pasquier had his weaknesses too, that mockery could undo him.

The apparent perfection of their situation only inhibited the acknowledgement of their difficulties. Too proud to negotiate, too young to see what would happen if they did not, they resisted – each for their own reasons – the frank discussion of difference that might have saved the situation, and were drawn as a consequence, by tiny degrees, into a cycle of explosive conflict and sexual reconciliation.

It took Eloise several years to realise, as she did at first with surprise, that Claude could be jealous. It had not occurred to her, in the dazzling months after their first meeting, that someone with so few apparent inadequacies could be moved to agonising self-doubt by the simple act of her having coffee alone with a male friend. When it became clear that he could, she had coffee alone with male friends as a matter of principle. This led to further rows, their causes often deceptively trivial. It was after one of these, as they lay in bed in the flushed aftermath of a passionate ceasefire, that Claude gave her the only gift she had taken with her when she left him: a small perspex cube, in which a nugget of osmium gleamed darkly.

'I give this to you because it is a part of myself,' he had said. 'And because in some ways the loves of my life are the same. Like you, this is rare. Like you, it shines somehow from within. It seems malleable, but really it can resist enormous pressure.' He leaned forward and kissed her penitently. 'It is an element with hidden properties.'

Sitting on a bench in the park of the War Museum in Bloemfontein, more than twenty years later, Eloise smiled at the recollection and switched on her phone to call Patrick.

'Eloise? Have you forgotten how to use an answer service? Where the fuck have you been?'

'Great to hear your voice, too, Patrick.'

'That retarded secretary of yours pretended she had no idea where you were staying. I've had to call every hotel in Bloemfonfuckingtein to find you.' She heard the unmistakable crack of a splitting biro. 'You heard from that French boyfriend of yours?'

'No, and he's not my boyfriend.'

'Well you need to fucking get hold of him. Because I've got some good news—'

'Yes?'

'And' – he spat something from his mouth – 'some bad news. Which do you want first?'

'Good news, please.'

There was silence. Eloise's heart rate rose. She was reminded of Speech Day at St Monica's and the tension before the awarding of the Princess Louise Merit Cup. 'Come on, Patrick.'

'The good news is that osmium tetroxide—'

'Yes?'

'Is a super-hard substance. Tougher than a witch's tit.'

Just as it had at long-past prize-givings, exhilaration washed over her. *Thank you, God. Thank you, Claude.* 'That's a beautiful image,' she said, trying to keep her voice level as she did the sums in her head. With \$130 million in play, even a small—

'But the bad news, honey pie, is that it's about as toxic as a witch's tit, too. A few sniffs and you're irreversibly blind, a couple more and your lungs fill with fluid. They call it "dry drowning" – nasty way to die. I'm considering sending some to your mate Pasquier, after I've dealt with you.'

'Who told you that? Carol?'

'No, sweetheart. Pasquier's old buddies at the Lawrence Livermore National Laboratory published their research in *Science* the day after you left. Crappy timing, I know. It's why I've been calling you every fifteen fucking minutes. They're "confident" they've "exhausted all the options".'

'But how can they be?'

'Don't ask me. They're the world-renowned scientists. I'm prepared to take their word for it.'

'So—'

'You want some more bad news?'

She stood up. She needed to move, to think clearly. 'Go on.'

'The price has *tanked*. Fell twenty per cent on Friday afternoon – thank God the market's closed for the weekend. We're offloading it as fast as humanly, but \$130 million worth of osmium isn't something you can shift overnight.'

'Listen, I'm—'

'Hang on.'

A tinny rendition of *Für Elise* informed Eloise that she had been put on hold.

She sat on the bench, listening to mutilated Beethoven. She had played the piece as a child, at one of the St Monica's Christmas concerts, and her fingers twitched in memory of many hours of supervised practice with Joan. *Of all the times for a fucking crisis*, she thought – what a godsend for Carol. She breathed deeply, to steady herself, and the details of the scene around her assumed a heightened vividness. She was conscious of a squirrel cavorting through the leaves above her head, of the precisely right-angled corners of a swastika that someone had drawn onto the white seat of the bench. The obscenity of such a symbol, within sight of a monument dedicated to concentration-camp victims, caught her attention and distracted her momentarily.

The paint was peeling off the warped planks and she lifted a section free and pulled it away.

Eloise knew Patrick in this mood. When very large sums of money were at stake he was apt to lose some of the strident self-belief that was, at other times, so unshakeable in him. How like an overgrown, foul-mouthed baby he was – prone to tantrums but ultimately dependent on the reassuring presence of a strong woman.

Reassurance was not, Eloise knew, what Carol would provide. Had she known of the LLNL research and kept it from them? She weighed the possibility. Surely not. Carol was scheming and duplicitous, certainly, but she didn't have the nerve to lay a trap of this magnitude or to risk the fund's future in a bid to oust her rival.

'Eloise?' The muzak came to an abrupt halt. 'Eloise?'

'Yes, Patrick?'

'That was Carol. I sent her home to shower – she was here all night but she's coming in now.'

'On a Sunday?'

'Yes, on a fucking Sunday. There's a lot to sort out before the markets open tomorrow.'

'You need to calm down.'

'Don't you fucking tell me to calm down. Save your charms for the people who really matter and get your arse to the airport. You're on the early-evening charter flight tonight, from Johannesburg. You land at 4 a.m. and we'll need to meet at 6 a.m. to plan what the fuck we're going to do. The connection from Bloemfontein leaves in an hour and a half.'

'But, Patrick—'

'What?'

'I'm with my mother.'

There was silence on the other end of the line, and when Patrick spoke again there was no trace of pugnacious bravado in his tone. 'Listen to me very carefully,' he said softly, enunciating each syllable with chilling precision. 'I. Don't. Give. A. Fuck. About. Your. Mother.'

Chapter 14

Joan was in Sarie Reitz's office, admiring the photographs of two blonde children, when Eloise knocked on the door. She saw immediately that her daughter had something to say and tried to stand, only to be reminded of the futility of the effort by a crippling pain in her left knee. The resentment that Eloise's abrupt departure had inspired, and the cold rage to which it had condensed during the thirty-five minutes of her absence, disappeared at once – for Joan had not lost the maternal habit of prioritising her children's dramas over her own.

'So, are we ready for our tour?' asked Sarie, brightly.

'Do you know, dear' – Joan glanced at Eloise – 'my leg is troubling me so much I don't think I could make it down all those stairs again. Would you mind very much if we put off our visit to tomorrow? I would so like to be fresh for it.'

'Ach shame, man.' The assistant curator was disappointed, but she sympathised with old ladies at the mercy of uncooperative limbs. 'Of course not.'

'Are you sure? That would be so kind.'

'Not a problem. Just make sure you come before eleven o'clock in the morning. I'm going on a training course and you don't want the archivist showing you around, believe me!'

'I can't tell you how grateful I am for all your efforts,' murmured Eloise, helping her mother from her seat.

'No problem at all. I'll see you both tomorrow morning.'

'We'll be bright and early.' Joan made this promise cheerily, though she knew in her heart that she would be visiting the museum alone. She took her daughter's arm and leaned heavily on it while Eloise guided her from Sarie's office, through the building's dark foyer and onto the steps outside. Then, adopting her most tender tone of voice, she said, 'What is it, darling? Is there a problem with Claude's osmium deal, the one you told me about on the plane?'

How like her mother, thought Eloise, to understand at once what had happened. 'No, it's nothing to do with Claude,' she said. 'There's been a crisis in the copper market and – God, I can't believe this – Patrick says I have to come home. He's scheduled a meeting with some big private investors. I told him I couldn't go, that I was absolutely committed to—'

'But of course you must.' Joan led her over to the car. 'We can always take another trip. I won't have you risking your career just to keep me company for a week.' They reached the Toyota and Simbongile held the back door open for them. 'We need to go to the hotel as quickly as possible, please,' Joan told him, briskly. Turning to Eloise, she put an arm around her shoulders and squeezed. 'Just get your passport and change into something warmer. I'll pack for you and bring your things home with me when I come.'

'I told Patrick I couldn't leave you here, and I'm not—'

'Nonsense, darling. I'm quite all right with Simbongile and the nice people at the hotel to look after me.'

There was something unflattering, thought Eloise, about the equanimity with which her mother bore the news of her departure. Standing outside the door of Sarie Reitz's office, she had prepared a moving account of her refusal to return to England, of Patrick's ultimatum and her eventual bowing to the inevitable. None of this seemed necessary as Joan sat in an armchair in her room at the Volksraad, watching her pack a small shoulder bag. 'Use this to pay the bill and buy anything you need,' she said when she had finished, kissing her mother on the forehead and pressing a piece of black plastic into her hand. 'I've written the PIN number on a piece of paper for you. It's 0912, my birthday.'

'Well I could hardly forget that, darling.'

'Good. And don't be afraid to treat yourself.'

'I won't.'

'Well …'

'Well …' Joan smiled at her daughter. 'I'll come down with you in the lift.'

They parted unostentatiously, and when she had waved Eloise off in Simbongile's car the drama of Mr Engelbrecht's concern – had there been a family emergency? Was everything quite all right? – seemed quite overblown to Joan. As she stood in the lobby, reassuring him that all was well, she noticed a shady veranda at the back of the hotel that she had not seen before; and with the help of the attentive manager, whose courtesy did much to excuse his over-reliance on aftershave, she succeeded in reaching it and sat under its striped awnings for an hour or more, nursing a cup of steadily cooling Earl Grey.

Should she have returned to London with Eloise? Perhaps. But then again, what could she possibly have done, she who knew nothing at all about the copper market? Besides which, Wilsmore Street was empty. There was no room for her at Eloise's, nor had there ever been. Unable to offer practical assistance, she closed her eyes and said a prayer for her daughter – not for a speedy resolution to her difficulties, for Joan's God did not participate in the financial markets any more than He made parking spaces available for harried Christian mothers, but for her to find the strength to tackle the situation with dignity and calm.

Mr Engelbrecht, watching his elderly guest through the glass doors to the terrace, thought fondly of his own grandmother's habit of falling asleep over a cup of afternoon tea. Seeing a waiter emerge from the lobby to clear the table, he waved him away and put his fingers to his lips.

By the time that Joan, prompted by the lengthening shadows, had left the hotel terrace and repaired to her room for a hot shower – it was one of the curses of old age that she could no longer enjoy baths, unaided – Eloise was landing in Johannesburg. She hurried from Domestic Arrivals to International Departures, ransacking her bag for her Blackberry and ignoring the bombardment of helpful offers from resolutely cheery taxi drivers and porters. Standing in line to check in for the London flight, she listened to her messages.

The first was from Emily. 'Hi, Eloise. Patrick keeps asking for the number of your hotel. I've told him I don't know it, but I'm not sure he believes me. Could you give him a ring? I'll hold out until I hear from you.'

The following eighteen were from Patrick, who seemed to have had her on redial for the better part of two days and whose language set a new standard of telephonic indecency. The twentieth was from Emily, an hysterical plea for her to call Patrick; the twenty-first was from a

96

company offering her a plasma television screen if she spent more than £15,000 on a new kitchen; and the last three were from Irina, her Kosovan housekeeper, telling her that the washing machine had broken down and flooded the kitchen.

Claude had not rung, and her attempts to reach him at home or at the office resulted only in voicemail assurances that he would call her back as soon as possible. Eloise did not leave detailed messages, for experience had taught her to establish the facts before committing herself – and she had no way of knowing, yet, how serious the situation really was. Commodities routinely ducked and dived and the market had been skittish lately. Patrick's panic probably owed as much to the unchallenged doom-mongering of Carol as it did to the bleak forecasts of the LLNL scientists – and she spent the journey pleasantly planning the boardroom vengeance she would wreak, for her mother's sake as much as her own, on the woman who had spoiled their once-in-a-lifetime trip.

Chapter 15

Joan was delighted to find, as she tucked into a deliciously creamy serving of scrambled eggs the next morning, that they did them very well at the Volksraad Hotel. Though her appetite was no longer what it had been, she ate them all and managed half a rasher of bacon; and it was only when she had reached the editorial section of the morning's newspapers, from which pictures of terrified Iraqis had miraculously disappeared, that she realised that she had not thought of Eloise. She thought of her at once, sending dutiful prayers heavenward on her behalf and ignoring – or doing her best to ignore – the possibility that she was, perhaps, just a little, if truth be told, glad to be on her own.

'*Sabona, mama,*' said Simbongile a short while later, holding the door of the Toyota Corolla open for her.

'*Sabona, buthi.*' Joan noticed that Simbongile now guided her to the front, though she and Eloise had shared the back seat together. She took this as a compliment.

'Where to, today?'

'The War Museum, please,' she said, cheerfully.

'Ach man, shame! And how are you feeling this morning?' were the words with which Sarie Reitz greeted her half an hour later. 'Ready for all those stairs? I'll help you.'

They made a rapid descent to the basement, Joan clinging to the assistant curator's shoulders as she was lifted down the steps.

'My mother lives with us, at home,' explained Sarie. 'I'm used to helping old ladies around! Where's your daughter?'

Joan gave an even vaguer account of the reasons for Eloise's abrupt departure than the one she had herself received.

'Ach shame, man! Modern business is so demanding.'

They exchanged a smile of tacit understanding.

It took some time for Sarie to locate the proper keys to the store-room's outer security door, and more for her to navigate two further metal grilles. When she had done so – and made several parenthetical allusions to the uselessness of the archivist, to whom responsibility for colour-coding the keys should have fallen – she stood by the final door and gripped its handle with a flourish. 'Welcome to the special collections!'

The room beyond was dark. Sarie groped gingerly into its depths and found a light switch. A strip of fluorescent tubing buzzed sullenly to life and illuminated a shelf on which several white cotton gloves had been left. Feeling rather proud of her professionalism, Joan reached for a pair and put them on.

'Oh, you can if you like!' Her guide marched on. 'I don't usually bother – my hands are always clean.'

It was not her place, thought Joan, to mention that the gloves were not designed to protect the artefacts from dirt, but from the oil on human skin. She was, in any case, too distracted by the room in which she found herself: long and narrow, its lengths lined with yellow-wood drawers.

'Make yourself at home,' Sarie told her, conspiratorially. 'I must just go upstairs and prepare for my workshop. I'll order you some tea.'

Joan closed the door and stood for a moment, listening to Sarie's retreating steps and the steady hum of the lights that eventually drowned them. She sniffed. The room had the ticklish, faintly spicy aroma of old manuscripts, though none were immediately visible. She took a few steps forward and consulted the handwritten label on the first drawer, *0001: Pipes*. The sweet smell of pipe tobacco, tissue-wrapped in dust, rose to greet her as she opened it. Inside, as the label had promised, were pipes – of ivory, wood and bone. Some were elegantly simple, others carved with delicate bas-reliefs of hunting scenes and ox wagons, and their smell took her at once to her father's study with its smoke-infused velvet curtains.

The pipe in her hand was labelled *A. B. de Waal, 1900*. It seemed improbable, almost magical, that something this old should retain its smell so powerfully. She tried another drawer, which contained a box of Viennese fruit-shaped soaps, elegantly wrapped and labelled *Toomfontein Farm, 1899*. She lifted its lid and found the contents untouched, the pineapple and pear in pieces but the others recognisable as the handsome, unused gift they had once been. A less appealing stub of something that bore a suspicious resemblance to candle wax was labelled *Bethulie Camp, 1901.*

Above the drawers, on one side of the room, were cupboards with sliding wooden doors. The first of these bore the legend *0049: Undergarments* and contained a bewildering array of slips, drawers, corsets and handkerchiefs. The drawer beneath it, *0104: Children's Clothes*, held an exquisite collection of miniature bonnets and Sunday dresses, taken from the nursery of a farm called Ooktevreden. Joan was astounded at the quality of the workmanship. The children's underwear, in particular, was a marvel: petticoats of fine muslin edged with lace, intricately embroidered; tiny corselets of whalebone and linen. She opened the next drawer and discovered a regal collection of dolls' clothes: an evening dress of black satin with a sliding fan of pink feathers, barely two inches high. She was leaning down, attempting to remove a large black box from a low cupboard, when Sarie returned with a tray of tea and biscuits.

'Let me help you there!' The assistant curator reached down and lifted it heavily onto the table. 'This used to play the most wonderful tunes – we used to listen to it all the time.' She sighed, for she was sentimental about such things. '*Ja-nee.* It hasn't worked for over ten years now.'

The box was handsomely inlaid with ivory and tortoiseshell. Inside its lid, fourteen song titles were listed in painstaking copperplate. 'Our ancestors loved their music boxes,' said Sarie. 'They loved them so much they even took them out onto the veld with them, when they were on commando duty. See here' – she reached down and picked up a heavy portrait of Paul Kruger – 'I think this one works better.'

The portrait was, in fact, a music box. Sarie removed a key that had been Sellotaped to its back and wound it decisively, in the manner of one who shows an inanimate object who is boss.

A whirring filled the room, bringing with it, as though from far away, the silvery tricklings of a tune. It was not the melody that the device had originally played: though she could not see the mechanism, Joan could hear that it had wound down; it seemed that some of the tines on the sound comb had rusted away, too. What she heard was an echo of the tune that this strange portrait had first sung, a spirit air that strayed between keys with a whimsical carelessness – as though relieved to have outlived the pressures of public performance.

'Where did these things come from?' she asked.

'Here there and *everywhere*,' cried Sarie, throwing up her hands. 'All this stuff is pre-war. Some of it was found in deserted houses that nobody ever went back to. Some of it was hidden away in barns and only discovered decades later. A couple of items were given by the owners' immediate descendants.' She stopped and looked thoughtfully at the floor. 'Now where is that old dress?'

It took a few minutes' rummaging for Sarie to find what she was looking for: a black skirt with a matching corset and bonnet. They looked exactly like the clothes Gertruida van Vuuren had worn for the photograph of her and Hannie on the *stoep* at Van Vuuren's Drift. 'Now there', she murmured, holding them up, 'you've got something. A complete set, as worn at the concentration camp in Bloemfontein. Can you imagine how hot you'd get in all that on a summer's day in the Orange Free State?' She smiled at Joan's evident emotion. 'I'm so sorry now, but I really must go. Feel free to stay here as long as you like. Is there anything else I can do for you?'

'I wonder,' asked Joan, 'if you would mind calling my driver?'

'Ooooh,' cooed Simbongile, his face a pattern of awe, when Joan opened the first drawer for him. He was looking at a pair of black lace gloves and a matching collar of lace and jet. 'I am not knowing anything about this place, myself.'

'Could you help me, do you think? There are some things I'm afraid I can't reach.'

'No problem.'

'And do put on a pair of these gloves, won't you?'

The young man put on a pair, a little too tight for his large hands. 'Where you want me to get things for you, Miss Joan?'

She directed him to a tall closet on one wall, whose handle was too high for her to reach with ease.

'Just long drawers,' reported Simbongile, craning his head.

'And in the drawers?'

He pulled one out and peeped over the top. 'There are some bright things in here,' he said. 'Shall I take them out for you?'

Joan hesitated. She was too instinctive a rule-keeper to feel easy about the unsupervised exploration of a museum's private collection. On the other hand, Sarie herself had bustled about as though in the comfort of her own attic – and Simbongile, at least, was wearing gloves.

'If you could, dear.'

He fetched a chair and stood on it. 'Yissis,' was all he said. And then: 'You look at this, Miss Joan.'

Joan gasped as a cascade of protective tissue paper fell to the ground.

'It seems very pretty to me,' offered the young man.

It was. The dress Simbongile held up for Joan to see was of silver satin, edged in lace. It seemed made for a woman of mythic proportions, almost six foot tall with an eighteen inch waist, and its long train fell in delicate folds to the floor. The label informed them that it was a wedding dress, bought for £100 just before the outbreak of the war. Laying it carefully over a plastic chair, Simbongile stood on his own and reached to a further, more distant drawer. This yielded a tea gown of pale apricot silk, trimmed in vermilion. Another, closer to the floor, held a stunning confection of aquamarine and green, and a pink silk jacket trimmed with fur.

'They seem to have been dressing better than us,' said Simbongile, articulating both their thoughts.

To Joan, whose memories of her grandmother were tinged with the dowdy regret of that lady's middle and declining years, the discovery of these bold and beautiful clothes was a revelation. They reproached and overturned her unconscious notion of the past as a place where people knew their destinies and, knowing them, despaired. They were confident, these dresses, designed to be worn confidently by vigorous young women in whom the ruddy health of an open-air farm life was refined and enhanced by the decorous addition of drawing-room manners.

'You sit in that chair,' suggested Simbongile. 'I will read the labels out to you. When you are wanting a drawer opened, just let me know.'

In this way they spent the afternoon, the young man daring further and further into the reaches of the basement, returning with ever more glorious discoveries: dinner services, in patterns that matched the shards Joan had found at the site of the concentration camp; shoes; European hunting rifles; bound volumes of sheet music. One far-off drawer yielded a collection of ornaments made by the male Boer prisoners in the comparative comfort of St Helena, who had sent them to their starving wives in the concentration camps. They were made of whatever was to hand, these love troths: bits of tin, pigeon feathers, the melted gold of a concealed cigarette case. Many of them bore the name of their recipient, the swirling letters of 'Elria', 'Naomi', or 'Johanna' carved delicately into wafer-thin slices of bone.

It was clear that much of what they found had not been looked at in years; had, quite possibly, not been touched since it was first put into the yellow-wood drawers. The more distant compartments and their contents were unlabelled, and here Simbongile found pens and embroidered curtain swags; christening robes of hand-stitched muslin; sturdy copper cooking pots. He returned from one expedition, moist-eyed, with a bouquet of flowers in his hand – not dried, but made of icing, preserved as a keepsake from a wedding cake eaten more than a century before.

The objects in the room, relics of a world so painstakingly built and so brutally destroyed, began to rejuvenate under the reverential attention of Joan and Simbongile. There was no need for the piano pedals, Joan saw – for Simbongile, wiping the dust from intricate surfaces with a gloved hand, required no magical assistance to make the muted colours glow again. He held up dress after dress, demonstrating the stylishness of each for the first time in too many long years, and from a collection of scent vials he chose one and held it open for her. Sniffing gently, teasing out the fragrance from the shadows of the past, she caught the scent of violets and her nanny Beauty flickered across her consciousness. 'I do wish that music box still played,' she sighed.

The young man opened it. The humility of this movement touched Joan and silenced her reservations about untrained enthusiasts tampering with historic antiques. Simbongile bent over the machine with the happy attention of one with a lifelong love of mechanical workings. He retrieved its key from where it had fallen in the cupboard and began to wind it. 'Oooh,' he said, stopping at once, 'someone has been winding this too much. That is not the problem.' He brought the box closer to Joan, so that she might look at it too. On an inlaid platform, a silver cylinder lay ready to turn and disturb the complete set of tines, releasing the music held captive for a decade. There seemed to be no obvious damage, but though the butterfly spring began to whir it failed to inspire the cylinder to motion.

'Oh well,' said Joan. 'Never mind.'

But Simbongile was lost in thought, his lips tracing a soundless conversation with himself. He examined the outside of the box and shook his head; then the inside, and shook his head again. He ran a finger delicately along the comb and a cluster of notes tinkled, like the release of doves from a magician's top hat. He frowned and peered closely at the spring.

Joan's heart was leaping; she had not wished so fervently for something for more than thirty years.

'*Yebo, mama*,' said Simbongile, at last. 'I think I have found the problem.' He leaned over the box and put the tip of his baby finger between the soundboard and the butterfly spring, which spun to life. This time, it brought the cylinder with it and a waltz began to play, the sound quality eerily rich and true. 'There was a clasp here,' said Simbongile, 'which is being broken. So long as you hold your finger over this pin, everything is very okay.'

Chapter 16

In London, Eloise stepped onto the soft cream carpet of her entrance hall and felt her foot sink, as though through a marsh. Braving the stench, she walked through to the kitchen where she found Irina's note, a confused jumble of English nouns that included the words 'wall', 'water', 'plumber' and 'no show'. The severity of the smell – it's lung-draining awfulness – served, if anything, to intensify her mood, which was distinctly combative.

She showered and dressed and left the building once more, pausing on Piccadilly to purchase two *pains au chocolat* and a double espresso from a chain café in which a pimpled *barista* with a northern accent attempted, unsuccessfully, to say 'hello', 'please', 'thank you' and 'goodbye' in Italian, in accordance with the company's branding initiative.

'No I don't have a loyalty card,' she said, more aggressively than she intended.

'Well *grat-zee* anyway and *arriva-der-chi* to you.'

She ate the pastries as she walked to her office, thinking with regret how repetition had dulled her appreciation of Claude's home-made efforts. Taking the lift to the fifth floor, she paused outside the swing doors of Derby Capital and drew herself together, visualising her colleague's smug little face and drawing energy from it.

It was inevitable, perhaps, that Carol Wheeler should dislike Eloise McAllister, and understandable that this feeling should be sincerely returned; and though neither woman admitted this, their mutual antipathy was grounded in something more profound than a simple clash of temperaments. Even Patrick, who spent eighty hours a week with them both, had little notion of the undercurrents of feeling that ran between them – though a woman in his position might have guessed them.

To her mother's secret horror, Eloise had decisively rejected the possibilities of childbirth and motherhood when she left Claude. She had done so freely, after a lengthy interrogation of the notion that female fulfilment required the bringing forth of new life. Deciding that it did not, she had spent twenty-one years creating for herself the kind of existence that seemed, to harried parents like Carol, enviably free of responsibility; and now that there was no going back, she did not often revisit the choices she had made.

Eloise liked living alone. Eight years with Claude had taught her more than she cared to remember of the sacrifices required of romantic life partners, and no one she had met since him had inspired her to make them again. She was not a person given to might-have-beens; and when she did consider them it was not the sight of bawling babies in pushchairs that prompted her to do so, but the occasional, flickering fear that once her mother died there would be no one left who really cared about her.

This dark thought did not come to her often and was not, of course, strictly true – as she reminded herself on the rare evenings that the solitude of her empty flat became heavy to bear. Besides, the idea of creating a consciousness merely to ward off loneliness was ridiculous, and ethically distasteful. Eloise had friends, certainly, and was god-mother to a number of their children, though her job somehow complicated the maintenance of social intimacy. By and large, she did not mind this; and when she thought of them at all, she looked back on the frenzied confidences of her twenties with something like wonder.

To Carol, Eloise's life choices acted as a constant provocation; and there were moments – usually in the dead of night, when her husband's snoring woke her – when her failure to choose similarly appeared the gravest mistake of her life. She admitted this to no one and kept the thought guiltily within her, afraid that her family might read it in her eyes. She would not, for anything on earth, give up her children: she repeated this regularly to herself, but she found it easiest to believe when they were asleep, their heads tousled and angelic on the pillow.

Carol's children were not often angelic, and their father did not seem inclined to aid her efforts to make them so. She had a fifteen-year-old daughter and two ten-year-old twin boys and none of them seemed to get on with each other, which meant that she returned from the office each day to a household riven with tension and noise. The idea of solitary evenings, with no one to answer to but herself, was so painfully tempting that the thought could bring tears to her eyes; and Carol despised Eloise for inspiring this treacherous envy in her. It made her yearn, with an intensity she found shocking, to inflict pain on her adversary: a desire that was clear to Eloise, who responded in kind.

'Morning, Patrick. Morning, Carol.' Eloise entered the boardroom, took off her coat and sat down, smiling ruthlessly.

'Have a look at these.' Patrick pushed a pile of photocopies in her direction, without greeting her. 'This was published on Friday, in *Science*. As I said on the phone, osmium's dead in the water. Selling started before the close of play for the weekend and the stock has dipped twenty per cent from its high. Thanks to Carol's quick work we've found buyers for about $10 million worth without too much trouble. But the shit is going to hit the fan when London opens in two hours, and we need to have a coherent strategy in place by then.'

Eloise turned to her boss, her posture indicative of polite attention. 'I think you're confusing blind panic with coherent strategy, but let's hear what Carol's got to say.'

In her rare moments of leisure, Carol was a devoted consumer of self-help manuals with titles like *Potent Persuasion* and *A Billionaire's Guide to Body Language*. These unanimously stressed the importance of holding the floor at critical junctures, and she was determined to act on their wisdom now. 'It's not so much the original stake in osmium that's the problem,' she began, speaking quickly and activating a Powerpoint display. 'You'll remember we invested $65 million during the period that it doubled in value, from $100 to roughly $200 an ounce.' She indicated a red dot on the low end of a steep curve marked 'Entry Point' and met Eloise's laconic gaze defiantly. 'Because the commodity has traditionally traded so stably, prices shouldn't fall much further than the level we began buying at. The real problem is the $65 million you invested in osmium last Thursday, when it was priced at $200.'

Eloise noted the accusation in the pronoun and smiled.

'As you'll recall,' continued Carol, her voice rising a semitone, 'I felt that risking a quarter of the fund on an uncorroborated boast from a scientist who hasn't published anything on the subject in three years was an unjustifiable risk.' She had written this sentence out longhand the evening before, and memorised it. 'Had we dumped our reserves before you left, we would have realised a profit of about $48.5 million – a figure that will, in any case, be significant, because it forms the benchmark for our fee. We obviously won't be able to charge clients anything until we're beyond that point again.'

'I knew that, as it happens,' remarked Eloise.

'Well, yes.' Carol took a sip of water. 'Of course. Anyway, that's one of the worries, but not the biggest. As of the end of trading on Friday, we were down twenty per cent. A crisis, but not one we can't survive. It's when the price continues to fall, as it almost certainly will, that we start entering, um, *difficult territory*. And the further down it goes, the further we are from the average price we bought at, and the more money we lose.'

'Talk Eloise through the figures, if you would,' growled Patrick.

'Okay.' Carol took a deep breath and told herself that she was doing quite well. 'We began our buying at $100 an ounce and kept at it while the price rose to $200. Then we put another $65 million in, which forced our average purchase price up to about $155 – which is fifty-five per cent higher than osmium's historic market value. There's no easy way out of this situation and we're going to take a hit whatever we do. But if we don't dump our reserves as soon as possible, and at least before the price has bottomed out, then – well. Our losses will exceed $80 million, by a conservative estimate. Clients will start withdrawing funds, forcing us to liquidate other, potentially viable stocks, which will only increase our position in osmium. As more clients haemorrhage, as they almost certainly will – well, you know what that means.'

There was silence. Eloise favoured her with an encouraging nod.

'We're looking at potential losses of more than $100 million,' said Carol, pressing grimly on. 'And the timing's unfortunate, too. A number of two- and three-year lock-in clauses expire in December, and then those investors will also be free to withdraw their money. Between them they represent, let me see' – she made a show of consulting a spreadsheet on the desk, though she knew the figure by heart – 'almost forty-two per cent of the entire fund. That's $210 million. If they're not happy with our performance this year and take their money out, it's Game Over for us all.'

Looking at Patrick, Eloise was momentarily distracted by a bead of sweat that was trickling down his forehead to his nose. She watched it gather into a drop and fall as she selected her tone, understanding that Carol had too successfully destabilised him for straightforward aggression to work now. She picked up a pen and began a visibly large doodle on the pad in front of her, deciding on a patronising reasonableness; and very slowly, as though quite unaware that Carol had finished speaking, she drew a large dog. Then, with deliberate gentleness, she smiled indulgently. 'Excellent presentation,' she said. 'And let me begin by saying that I agree with every point you've made. Or, rather, that I can see how the premise you started from led you to make them.'

'Right. Well, the other—'

But Eloise raised her hand. 'The only problem with your analysis, Carol – I mean, apart from its essentially simplistic view of a complex set of factors – is that it entirely fails to utilise our secret weapon.'

'Which is?'

'Which is that *we* know something the market does not.'

'You mean Pasquier?'

'That's right.' Eloise took a biro from a pot on the desk and handed it to Patrick, on whom she now focused entirely. 'There's not a lot of liquidity in the osmium market. Investors are going to be watching closely this morning, and if we kick off the week by trying to offload more than \$100 million, we can kiss this fund goodbye.' She sat up straight. 'There's no particular reason osmium should stabilise at the level it began at. The panic we induce could drive it down much, *much* further, and in the end you won't be able to pay people to take it off our hands. That's when we're properly fucked. And Carol's strategy' – she glanced regretfully at her colleague, as though it pained her to say this – 'is the surest way to disaster.'

Patrick took the lid off the biro and scratched his inner ear with it.

'Let's look at some less drastic alternatives for a moment. We have until the end of the year before we have to worry about performance bonuses, and seven months until the really significant lock-in clauses expire. The only thing that's changed since' – she looked at Patrick, reminding him of their shared responsibility – '*we* agreed to put twenty-four per cent of our capital into osmium, is that a group of disgruntled scientists has shown that one of its alloys is highly toxic. It's a pity they didn't publish their research last week, or we could have got the stuff on the cheap. Of course they *say* they've exhausted the possibilities of the subject – but that's exactly what the "experts" of the ancient world said when they decided the earth was flat.'

'What you should remember—'

'If we believed in Pasquier last week, we should believe in him this week. Let's ride out the price fluctuations and hang on to our reserves. That way, when the research comes through we'll be there to clean up.' Eloise leaned forward and glanced pointedly at Carol. 'You've got to have balls to run a hedge fund. If Pasquier doesn't deliver in the next seven months, we've got a major crisis on our hands – but why anticipate disaster? The only way we're going to keep our clients believing in us is by believing in us ourselves. Which is why these apocalyptic narratives are, ultimately, so fucking unhelpful.'

There was silence again, though this time it was a different silence than the one that had greeted Eloise's entrance to the room. It hadn't occurred to Carol that her rival would suggest riding out the storm. 'That's *a hundred million dollars* we could lose,' she repeated, with emphasis. 'Or more. There's no coming back from a loss like that.'

Eloise rose from her chair, sensing correctly that Patrick's mood was shifting. 'For God's sake, grow a backbone,' she said. 'You're playing with the big boys now.'

Chapter 17

J oan woke early the next morning, with the painful certainty that it was going to be a bad-knee day. Crossing to the dressing table of her bedroom, she switched on the complimentary kettle and opened the curtains. She should not, she knew, have removed the green folder in which her grandmother's decaying journal was preserved from the institution entrusted with its care. In fact, she was a little shocked at her own daring, and inclined to blame it on the headiness of her unsupervised adventure through the museum's vaults the previous afternoon.

I am a thief, she thought, not without a certain agreeable tingle.

Outside, lengthening shadows whispered of approaching day. Joan looked at the object on the desk before her. She had taken it impulsively, unable to contemplate the thought of reading it in the company of strangers. 'Thief' was a strong word, she decided as the kettle hissed to life. Surely it did not apply to those who intended to put back what they had merely borrowed without permission?

She drank her tea meditatively, standing by the dressing table. When she had finished, she took a pair of purloined white gloves from her handbag and put them on. She picked up the green folder in both hands and lifted it to her face, savouring its complex smell of dust and age. Standing straight and tall, she closed her eyes and prayed silently, holding her grandmother's journal with reverence. She prayed for Eloise, far away; for the women who had worn the dresses that Simbongile had so carefully rewrapped in tissue paper the day before; for the men who had made the trinkets and smoked the pipes that now lay forgotten in the museum's yellow-wood drawers. Then she sat down at the desk and opened her spectacle case. Her eyes had served her better than her joints; that, at least, was a blessing. She put on her glasses and untied the binder's ribbon. Before her was a small notebook, bound in calfskin. She turned the first page with a gloved finger and began to read.

TO WHOM IT MAY CONCERN:

I, Gertruida Naomi Van Vuuren, née Maritz, of the farm Van Vuuren's Drift in the region of Bloemfontein, Orange River Colony, do give under oath this day, the third day of October, nineteen hundred and three, a full and accurate testimonial of my experiences during the recent War of Independence. I make my deposition in English, not out of any love for this language but because, as God is our witness, the Dutch already know quite well what terrible sufferings they have endured.

I was 43 years old and in the twentieth year of my marriage to Martinus van Vuuren, Burgher, when war came. We were living on my husband's farm of Van Vuuren's Drift. At the time of the Declaration of War we had six children: Hannie, seventeen years; Jacobus, sixteen; Cecilia, fifteen; Naomi, eleven; Johan, five; and Katrien, three years. In addition, we had a little Kaffir girl named Elsie, thirteen years old, whose parents were no longer living and whom we loved as our own.

My husband was the fourth generation of his family to work Van Vuuren's Drift. At the time of the outbreak of hostilities, we had a flock of some 2,000 sheep, not to mention a stable of eight fine horses. The house itself was airy and well appointed, containing drawing room, dining room, eight bedrooms, kitchen, and pantries.

When the call to arms came, my dear husband called us together and addressed us thus, as General Smuts had addressed his own wife a few weeks before: 'The moment is come at which we must choose between surrender and war to the utmost, war without end,' he said. 'I have duties to you, wife, and to our children. But you, I, and our children, we have also duties toward the country. And if we are true to these duties, then we must sacrifice ourselves.'

Never before have I felt such pride. 'Go, dear Martinus. Farewell and God speed,' I said. And that night, with his saddles and bridles and biltong sufficient for ten days, he departed. It was 24th October 1899.

For some months, nothing occurred to trouble us, but in the second week of March, 1900, the English came. At first we saw only a small group, led by Lieutenant Macklethwaite. He was a good man and assured us that we should be left in peace and not harmed. But this promise was no protection against the next party of soldiers. These, led by Captain Bryars, took possession of every vehicle in the wagon-house, leaving us no means of getting about, and helped themselves liberally to our food stores.

Throughout the winter, the visiting soldiers grew bolder. Then, on 16th September 1900, a group of imperial yeomen came to the farm and arrested Jacobus, saying that he was of fighting age and must be resting from his commando duties.

In vain I pleaded with them not to take my son. Then, when I saw that it was inevitable, I refused to beg any more. I was not permitted to say goodbye or to pack any possessions that might have been a comfort to him, and the next day we received a message from the British Commandant at Paardekop, addressed to my husband. This told us that if we did not surrender our farm it would be burnt, and the cattle taken within a fortnight. How glad I was not to know the whereabouts of my dear husband! For nothing in the world would have persuaded me to pass on such a low threat.

In the event, the English did not wait even the full fortnight they had promised. Five days after sending their notice, a squadron of troops under Captain Bryars arrived.

There were ten or fifteen English soldiers and they went through the pretence of searching the homestead for Boers and weapons. By the time they had finished I could not believe my eyes. No book remained on its shelf. The china cupboard was torn from the wall and thrown forwards, so that much inside was broken. Eiderdowns were ripped open and their feathers displaced. Despite the heat, it seemed as though a snowstorm had taken place. I was in such a distracted state that I could do almost nothing but save the barest necessities from the carnage. I was calling for Cecilia and Elsie, telling them to find blankets and warm things for the night, when one of the soldiers struck up *Home Sweet Home* on the organ. He played it so sadly that I found myself imagining what he must be feeling, so far from his own home. Then I thought, But what about *my* home?

Before the first verse was finished, there was a cry. I hurried downstairs. Hannie was asking the soldier who he thought he was, to make so free with another person's instrument? He replied that she had better things to do, just now, than worry about him playing a little music to entertain his friends. At which, she threw him bodily off the stool and sat down to play herself.

The young soldier, becoming enraged, got some of his friends together. They lifted the organ to carry it outside, but as soon as it was in the yard Hannie sat down at it immediately again.

I was too preoccupied by the sight of all this, and by the pride that a mother must feel for her daughter's courage, to notice the kerosene until I saw one of the soldiers pouring it across the floor. That was the first time that I fully understood what would happen, though I was not the first of those I knew to suffer such treatment. I called to Elsie to make sure Katrien and Naomi were safe and anxiously counted my children in the yard. Seeing that the inevitable must shortly take place, I ran into the dining room and took the family Psalter from the cabinet there. We had already taken the precaution of burying our Bible, with my jewellery and other valuables, in a chest behind the stables. Among these was a handsome chandelier of gilded griffins sent to me from Amsterdam by my aunt, Mrs Naomi de Leeouw, on the occasion of my marriage. These few things, alone of all my family's possessions, remained to us after the war.

We sang Psalm 83 while the house burned. When the flames reached Naomi's bedroom, a shelf collapsed and threw one of her dolls against the window pane. She did not see, the poor child, but it was as if the little doll had been consigned to hellfire.

Though I could not say why, this sight upset me more than all the others. Not wishing to give way to undignified grief, I walked some way off. The soldiers were running amok in the farmyard. They had devised a game of trampling on the chickens' heads, and there was a great deal of commotion. I went into the threshing barn. I did not wish to cry, but I wished to rest my face. It can be hard to betray no emotion when your life is being destroyed before your own eyes.

On entering the barn, I heard a sound that astonished me. Someone was sobbing. Thinking that it must be one of the farm labourers, I went into the machine room. Imagine my surprise to find the very same English soldier who had played *Home Sweet Home* on Hannie's organ. He was standing against the thresher and there was blood at his feet.

'Are you injured?' I asked.

'No,' he said, stiffly. 'I have killed your dog, on the orders of Captain Bryars. He said we were to leave nothing living here.'

By his side, in the shadow of the thresher, was the body of our sheepdog, Piet. He had been shot through the head. 'I am sorry,' said the soldier. 'I would have kept him for myself if I could, but the regulations do not permit pets.'

I could see that he was ashamed to be surprised by me in his grief.

On leaving the barn, I encountered once again Captain Bryars. 'And what are we to do now?' I asked him. 'You have stolen our goods and destroyed our home. My support, and that of my family, must now fall to the British authorities.'

'You Boers are used to living rough,' said he. 'You will have to spend the night in the Kaffir kraal. Tomorrow, you shall be taken to a place of safety.'

Then he and his men remounted their horses and herded the sheep, cows and the remaining oxen away. They also took our horses with them. 'You have President Kruger to thank for this,' cried Captain Bryars. 'Why do you Boers not come and give in, why do you go about the countryside like robbers?'

'We will never give in,' I replied, 'because we are fighting for our country.'

Joan placed the volume of her grandmother's reminiscences carefully on the desk. In earlier days, she had developed the habit of pacing about when troubled by whatever she was thinking or reading. As she pulled herself upwards now, using the bureau's sturdy legs for support, she cursed her body's failing agility.

It took some time to stand, and when she had done so she knew that the pain in her left knee was too acute for prolonged movement. Accepting this, she compromised by taking Gertruida's journal over to the window and opening it once more on the sill. She stood still, remembering her brother's games on the farm that was now a parking lot, and continued to read:

The English left us alone for three days. Then Captain Bryars returned. We were put onto one of our own wagons and taken to the Concentration Camp. At our arrival, the guard at the gate saw Elsie. 'What is she doing here?' he asked. 'She is with us,' I said. 'She is as a daughter to me.' 'This is a camp for Europeans, not Kaffirs,' says he. 'She cannot stay here. She must go to the Native Camp.' It was not in his power to make me let go of my little Elsie's hand. I threw myself on my knees and implored him not to take her away.

It was all to no avail. Two more soldiers were summoned to prise Elsie from us. 'Have you no sympathy for a little girl of only thirteen years?' I asked them. 'There are regulations,' says he, sternly. 'I must do my duty.'

So Elsie was taken away, and I truly believed that she was lost to us.

Then everything we had brought, all our foodstuffs, candles, matches, pen, ink, hammer, pillows, etc., was taken from us. We were permitted only to keep one blanket each.

We were all placed together in a single bell tent, with no groundsheet and so many holes that scant refuge was offered from the elements. When it rained we often found ourselves ankle-deep in mud. On many a night, Hannie and I had to stand and hold the babies on our hips, lest they drown in the mud beneath us. Truly, it was God Himself who gave such mighty strength to two poor women.

On hot days, it became impossible to breathe in the tents. The slightest breeze was sufficient to cover everything we owned, as well as the bodies we lived in, in dust. In addition, the situation of the camp on open, flat ground exposed us terribly to the wind.

Keeping our standards in these conditions was difficult, but we swept the tent every morning and aired what linen we had. Our neighbours did so also, and we always had a cheery greeting for one another. Some, in an effort to make themselves feel more settled, even named their tents. When our neighbour Mrs Herbst called hers Bellevue Tent, Cecilia promptly christened ours Bell-Tent View.

For people used to good, wholesome food, the rations were hard to bear. Those who had not willingly brought themselves to the camp were given almost nothing to live on. Each week, I received: $\frac{1}{2}$ lb fresh or tinned meat; $\frac{3}{4}$ lb either meal or rice; 1 oz coffee; 1 oz milk; 2 oz sugar, $\frac{1}{12}$ of a can of condensed milk. Often the weight of the food relied more on the quantity of creatures that lived in it than on its nutritious value. The smell of the camp was terrible and no amount of exposure made it more bearable. It was impossible to be within fifty yards of the latrines without covering one's nose and mouth. The slop buckets were never removed before eleven o'clock in the morning, and often stood later in the heat of the sun.

Little Cecilia queued from morning until late afternoon for our water. On frequent occasions, we were forced to draw our water from the dam, in which many people bathed daily. The water was a dirty yellow colour, with a surface of greenish foam. Several newborn native babies were found dead in it, and the smallest sip was sufficient to cause vomiting and diarrhoea. One night, soon after our arrival, Mrs Booysen and her two daughters took ill. Their only receptacle for night soil was a Golden Syrup tin. When it was full to overflowing, they suffered agonies to preserve their decency.

We continued to exist in this way throughout the summer of 1900 and into the winter of the following year, which was the bitterest I have ever experienced. After two months, I learned that Jacobus had been sent to Ceylon as a prisoner. I prayed each night for his well-being and for that of my dear husband, of whom I had heard nothing for almost two years. The most earnest requests yielded no information concerning Elsie, and in the dark of the night I could not rid my mind of the thought of her, alone and defenceless.

Life in the camp was very hard for my children, used as they were to living in a clean, airy house, with good food and exercise in abundance. Without candles or medicines, it was very difficult to nurse them when they fell ill. In May 1901, little Johan began to cough. He refused to eat and grew dangerously thin. Hannie and I went without condensed milk so that Johan might have enough, but he could only manage a few sips at a time. In his fevers, his little body would tremble as I held him against my heart, praying to the Lord to hear my prayers for his recovery.

I applied to the camp doctor but was told I must wait three days before I might see him. When at last my turn came, I was told simply to go away, for 'Did I not know all children under the age of five must die?' The word he used to me was 'frek', which in Afrikaans refers to the death of animals, not of human beings.

Understanding that there was to be no help from this quarter, I continued to nurse Johan myself and to treat the red spots that covered his body as best I could, though I had no medicines. He was received into God's merciful care on 29th June, 1901.

Johan was not the only person to die during that terrible winter. Wherever one went throughout the camp, one heard rasping coughs and groans. I will never rid my memory of those sounds. The air was so full of infection it was a wonder that anyone was spared. Cecilia, Naomi and Katrien became ill also. My only consolation was the strength and continuing health of my dearest Hannie, who nursed her brothers and sisters with tireless devotion.

I cannot write more of that time or of the harshness with which the doctors treated my dear little ones. Truly, acts worthy to shame the sternest advocate of war were perpetrated in that camp hospital, itself as filthy a collection of tents and huts as one could find. From those few who lived to return, we heard terrible things. Children being tied by their hands and feet to the posts of their bed, obliged to lie in that stretched out position for hours at a time, blankets used for several sick, without any effort at disinfection. We heard reports of the gravest cruelty and ill-treatment, among them doings too terrible to mention. When Naomi became ill, the medical inspectors removed her to the hospital, against all my entreaties. They refused to let me accompany her or to visit her. A week later, they told me that she had died of measles. She left this world on 16th July, 1901.

I became frantic with anxiety that the English doctors would remove Katrien to the hospital. I saw that I had abandoned a true mother's sacred duty, to nurse her children herself, and I repented bitterly that I had not done more to keep Naomi under my own care. We resorted to every possible means to keep Katrien and Cecilia with us. During one medical inspection, we even hid the little one in an anthill we had hollowed out for a bread oven.

So we spared Katrien the attentions of the English, and in this way she survived longer than her brother and sister. But I was powerless, without medicines or clean linen, without so much as a candle to light the tent at night, to help her as she needed. She was taken from us on 28th July, 1901.

I began to fear that all my children would be taken from me. In truth, I could not begrudge them the joy of heaven. God, I knew, had offered them refuge from the sorrows of this world. This did not make the want of them, or the memory of them in happier days, any less bitter. I began to lose all hope.

The crisis point of Cecilia's illness came on 15th August, 1901. For three days and two nights, Hannie and I sat with her. With nothing to give her but rancid coffee and condensed milk, I sat by her side and held her hand while the fever wracked her. For two days she was not lucid. I felt her drifting from me.

On the morning of the third day, at about three o'clock, while Hannie was sleeping in her chair, Cecilia opened her eyes. Her fingers moved. 'I am at peace, my dear mother,' she said to me. 'I am ready to go to my heavenly Father.'

Never, I think, has a mother prayed so earnestly as I did then! For a time I was lifted out of the camp, away from the cries and the fever. I knew that if I slept, that if I took my eyes from her blessed face for a moment, she would be lost to me forever. I beseeched God to spare her.

There is no force on earth so powerful as a mother's love. Throughout that long night, not once did I move, nor take notice of anything but my dearest child. When she awoke the next morning, the fever had lifted. She was able to take a little bread. I knew that God had answered my earnest wish and I sang for joy.

Truly, even the water in the dam was beautiful to me that day.

In this way, we reached the end of the terrible winter of 1901. I will not describe how it felt to sleep on the bare ground, in an unlined tent, during the terrible snows of that year, and I could not rest easily about Cecilia, who grew fearfully thin after her sickness had passed. She had never been as sturdy as Hannie, and now not only her ribs, but the bones of her knees, were visible through her skin. Hannie insisted that she take a portion of her own rations, but even this did nothing to help her gain weight.

Spring came. It was a blessed relief after the hardships of the winter months. Then – oh bitterness! – Hannie began to cough. At first she insisted that she was well, but I knew the sound of that awful throat rattle too well. So, too, did the English medical inspectors, who removed her at once to the camp hospital. In vain did I protest. 'You dirty Boer,' they said to me. 'You know nothing about hygiene!'

On 19th September, 1901, Hannie was taken from our tent, leaving Cecilia and myself alone, and very wretched. I went every day to the hospital but was not allowed in to see my daughter. On the fourth day, I called out to her from beyond the tin walls. 'Hannie! My dearest daughter, my beloved child! I love you and pray for you.' There was no reply, and the English guards forced me back, but I took some small comfort later from the knowledge that she had heard me.

Mrs Taljaart, who had once been a neighbour of ours on her farm, Waterval, was one of the few to leave the English hospital tent alive. The day after she left the hospital, she came to see me at my tent. She wished to tell me that Hannie still lived, and that she cried earnestly for me but was refused by the English nurses.

This news reminded me that, though I had been treated as such, I was not an animal but a lady. I marched to the hospital at once and demanded to see my daughter. Again I was refused. This time I would not budge, but insisted on a mother's right to see her children. For two hours, in the heat of the sun, I refused to move. The nurses were vicious to me, calling me all sorts of names. I would not be cowed. 'You harpies!' I cried. 'Have you not children of your own? Do you understand nothing of the bond that binds a mother to her child?'

'You will only bring infection, you dirty Boer,' they said. 'Look at you.'

'If I am not as clean as I would like,' I replied, 'that is to your account, for there is almost no soap in this camp and I must shift as best as I am able.'

The encounter grew heated. A soldier was called. By chance, he was the officer who had played *Home Sweet Home* on our organ on the day our troubles began. He recognised me, I saw, but gave no sign. 'Please, sir,' I begged him. 'My daughter lies in that tent. I must be allowed to go to her.'

At first he refused. He had not the power, he said, to bend the regulations. But there was something tender-hearted about this Englishman. He was moved by my entreaties, for I abandoned all dignity and let him see my distress. 'Very well,' he said. 'Let me see what I may do.'

He disappeared and entered the hospital. I waited outside, giving thanks to God for his simple human kindness. For almost half an hour I waited. Then the Englishman returned. Without a word, he beckoned me towards him and into the hospital tent.

It was a small, close structure, crowded with beds. I saw Hannie at once, at the end of the row, and went to her. Her eyes were closed and her wrists were bruised, as though she had been bound. I took her hand in mine and stroked her fingers. They were soft and cold. As I touched them I knew that I was too late. The English soldier came up and stood behind me, putting his hand on my shoulder.

'I am sorry, madam,' he said. 'Truly, I am very sorry.'

It was 26th September, 1901.

Chapter 18

The violent ringing of the telephone brought Joan, with disorienting suddenness, back into her brown-and-green bedroom at the Volksraad Hotel. How long had she been there? She reached for the handset but thought better of it. What if the caller were Eloise? It would never do for her to discover her mother in tears, half a world away. Looking up, she caught sight of her reflection in the mirror over the desk and was alarmed by the streaming eyes that met hers. No, she must recover before speaking to her daughter.

She waited for the telephone to stop ringing.

When it had done so, she closed Gertruida van Vuuren's notebook and returned it to its folder, carefully retying the green ribbons and placing it in a desk drawer. Her eyes, no longer used to such uninterrupted concentration, were aching; her left knee, forgotten in the absorption of the last few hours, was reasserting its claim to her attention with painful stridency. She would finish her reading later. As she closed the drawer she thought of her mother, broomstick-thin to the end, and of all that they had never discussed. She found herself wishing with childish urgency that she were still alive.

The telephone rang again. Joan took three deep breaths and answered it, as cheerily as possible.

'Miss Joan?' It was Simbongile. 'I am waiting for you downstairs for half an hour now. Are you not wanting me today?'

'No, no, dear. I'm sorry. I was – distracted. Could you give me a few more minutes?'

'Is everything okay with you?'

'Yes, of course.'

'If you are needing to rest, I can come back for you this afternoon. Or even tomorrow.'

Joan hesitated. 'No thank you,' she said at last. 'Perhaps some sunshine would do me good. I'll be down shortly.'

'I think', said Simbongile gravely, as he helped her into the passenger seat of the Toyota a few minutes later, 'we should not be going to the museum today.'

'Would you prefer to go somewhere else, dear?'

'It is not for me, Miss Joan. I am happy to take you wherever you are wanting. I am just thinking that the museum makes you sad.' He looked at her, sympathetically. 'Your granny won't mind if you have one day off.'

There was such sincere concern in his eyes that Joan's denial died on her lips. It occurred to her that Eloise's abrupt departure had removed her obligation to enjoy herself at all times. 'I do feel rather sad,' she confided. 'I am learning a great many things I never knew, and all the people I might talk to about them are dead.'

They drove in silence through the gates of the Volksraad and past a string of car dealerships.

'I know a place', said Simbongile, 'that is good for sadness.'

'Really?'

'It is some way away from here.'

'How long?'

'About two hours' drive. Perhaps more.'

The thought of open countryside, after the confines of this dusty city, was deeply appealing. 'Do you think we could go there today?' asked Joan. 'Is there time?'

'That depends on how happy you are with fast driving.' Simbongile smiled widely and tapped the accelerator, causing the Toyota to surge forward. He said the words 'fast driving' as though they were a single verb, with a meaning entirely distinct from what one usually did in a car.

Joan put her hand on the dashboard to steady herself. She was not, as a rule, at all comfortable with speed. And yet – If one couldn't take risks at her time of life, with nothing to look forward to but years of gradual decline in a nursing home, then when could one take them? 'I don't mind a little – vigour,' she said.

Simbongile gave a grunt, suggestive of quiet satisfaction, and the force of the subsequent acceleration pressed Joan back into her seat. It was rather thrilling to be going this fast. She glanced at her driver, whose posture was reassuringly indicative of concentration, and as they slid onto the motorway Joan felt a surge of affection for the young man. Really, he was a wonderful tonic. She was glad to be with someone who understood silence, glad also to be facing the prospect of a swift journey through unfamiliar country. She felt unequal to the challenge of her grandmother's memoirs, and thought with relief that at least she did not have to summarise her responses for Eloise.

It was at times like these that Joan most missed the piano. She did not belong to a generation that set much store by the articulation of private sorrow – and there were no words, in any case, for the shifting complexities of what she now felt. She folded her hands in her lap and examined them surreptitiously. The gnarled joints of her thumbs were incomprehensible; it was impossible that these aching, liver-spotted digits could belong to her. She flattened her palms and stretched her fingers as far as she could: they would barely span a sixth now, let alone the easy tenth for which Eiko Miyanishi had once so envied her. She thought of her friend, so delicately made that she had cracked a wrist during a second-year master class on Prokofiev. The fact that she would be old now, if she was alive at all, was astonishing.

An image of the muscles in Eiko's shoulders leaping above her quick thin fingers came to Joan, and brought with it the last time they had seen each other, at the Wigmore Hall in the summer of 1964. Astrid had arranged the outing as a treat for her daughter-in-law's fortieth birthday and spent the two hours of the concert unwrapping and sharing a succession of chocolates with Eloise and George, while Frank slept. There was nothing novel in such distractions, and they had not interrupted Joan's wonder at the athletic invincibility of Eiko's performance – little Eiko, who had once been unable to make an accurate four-octave leap in public.

As a student at the Royal College of Music, Joan had dearly loved her clumsy, diminutive friend; but the contrast in their situations on this evening inspired an uncharacteristic meanness of spirit. She watched sceptically as Eiko composed herself for the Hammerklavier Sonata. Surely she wouldn't risk making the opening jump with just the left hand? But she did, and with such nonchalance that Joan's skin prickled. The Ravel of the second half was easier to bear, for Eiko's pedestrian ear was unequal to the haunting sadness of the second movement of the Piano Concerto in G Major – a fact that allowed Joan to admit that she had been better than Eiko once, that she would surpass her again if only she had a decent piano and more than forty minutes a day to spend with it. By the end of the concert she had recovered sufficiently to plan a nicely turned speech of congratulation, which she would have delivered with aplomb had the audience not thunderously demanded an encore. Even Frank woke up.

Dear Lord, no, she thought, as five people in the third row stood up; then two in the sixth; then the entire first row, after which an ovation became inevitable. *They must be friends of hers,* she decided, resolutely still herself; but when even Astrid rose heavily to her feet it occurred to Joan that Eiko would soon appear, and perhaps see her thus ungraciously sedentary. She leapt up and began to clap, and on the third collision of her hands the friend of her youth emerged from the wings.

Eiko Miyanishi was a little over five foot in height, with short black hair and deep-set eyes that had worn a hunted look in her student days. There was no trace of apprehension in them now. She looked fierce, almost hate-filled as she marched to the piano and sat down at it, pausing sternly before throwing herself into the opening *acciaccaturas* of Liszt's first Mephisto Waltz.

By the time of the C sharp minor *marcatissimo* Joan was feeling nauseous, and Eiko executed the repeated *fortissimo* chords with such precisely honed violence that George covered his eyes with his hands. Joan comforted herself with the certainty that Eiko could never play *espressivo amoroso*; but when the moment came she rose to it so lushly, with such compassionate comprehension, that Joan realised with a start that Eiko – who had once lived for her work alone, and shunned all men – had experienced romantic sexual love at some point since she had last seen her. As the piece ended, she glanced at Frank, whose pale hairless body sensitised her nails unendurably. Perhaps she would never know what Eiko now felt. George's hand found hers and held it tightly, for he read the dismay in his mother's face; and to cover it Joan let him climb onto his seat, and jump up and down on it, causing Astrid to intervene with a sniffed suggestion that they leave.

Such a dishonourable memory had no place on this sacred day, and Joan pushed it from her decisively. She would not torment herself with the recollection of her famous friends. She looked again at her fingers, wondering when a sequence of chord clusters, in rapid semiquavers, had last come easily to her? She could not remember. The arthritis had gained ground gradually and her retreat before it had been almost imperceptible. What would she not give to play freely again!

She looked about her for the pedals. Had she not befriended them, resolved not to fear them? Had she once betrayed their existence to any of the Harley Street clinicians whom Eloise had insisted she see? *I was true to you*, she said to them. *Be true to me.* And as she spoke, with the benign alacrity of a well-invoked marvel, they appeared above the dashboard.

'Are you okay, Miss Joan?' Simbongile took his eyes for an instant from the road. 'Am I going too fast?'

'No dear, I'm quite all right. Thank you.' She looked out of the window, feigning unconcern, her mind racing with the possibilities now before her. But the release she sought could only be achieved through self-denial, and she resolved to limit herself to the work of one composer. Who should it be?

Though Joan had played this game many times before, she liked to take her time arriving at her decision. She ran through the great composers of the last four hundred years, dismissing one after another – Handel, Rameau, Haydn, Beethoven, both Scarlattis – with bittersweet regret. At one time, when she was very young, she had adored Mozart, but she had ceased to care for his piano music after Eloise's birth and the bed-bound months that followed it. She lingered over Schubert and Brahms, like a prince in a ballet choosing his bride, before sending them both sorrowfully away. She rejected Schumann and Schubert and Debussy, too, and sent the atonal Schoenberg about his business, putting Rachmaninov and Rimsky-Korsakov aside also. Sighing gently, she reached the inescapable conclusion that she would play Chopin.

Observing her discreetly, Simbongile saw with satisfaction that his elderly passenger seemed calmer. As the buildings thinned and the ground began to rise, contentment settled over Joan's features, for she had reached her favourite part of all: the selection of a programme. 'I might just have a little nap, dear,' she said, shutting her eyes and tapping her feet in a wordless indication that she was ready to begin.

When Simbongile stopped the car some time later, Joan did not open her eyes. She was playing the Second Étude from the second Book of Études, Op. 25, and the delicate balance of semiquaver triplets in her left hand against demisemiquaver triplets in her right required total concentration. The skill was not so very different from the child's trick of patting your head while stroking your stomach, but in the context of this performance it demanded a great deal more energy. She took care to play it lightly, effortlessly, and when it had died away on one lingering, repeated note, she opened her eyes and saw Simbongile sitting on a rock, some distance away, with his back to her. The landscape was lunar. In the drowsy half-consciousness of her return to reality it seemed that they were floating on a tranquil ocean of stone.

She opened the door.

'I too get sleepy in the car,' observed the young man, coming at once to help her. 'But never when I am driving – don't worry!'

He lifted her from her seat and deposited her gently on the gravel. Below them the ground fell away in a steep valley. Around and above, like statues of forgotten gods, the Maluti mountains stood tall and proud against the sky.

'Goodness me,' said Joan. There was something awe-inspiring in the vastness of the layered rocks. Pale stone rose into promontories of red, capped in the ochre of ancient sand dunes through which fingers of black basalt dripped devilishly. A perfect circle had been blown through a peak on the opposite side of the valley, as if by a giant's breath: the joint work of time and wind.

'I am feeling small when I come here,' murmured Simbongile. 'And that is making me feel better, too.'

They sat together on a patch of hardy grass as the light turned crimson, its rays polishing the pedals in rose-tinted gold leaf. Neither of them spoke, but for Joan the landscape was alive with the notes of the Thirteenth Nocturne in C Minor. The valley beneath them filled with the stately sadness of its opening chords; the crashing octaves of the second section bounded from the rocks; and in the end the mountains themselves acknowledged the truth of the tune's return, with its promise of meaning in a harsh and brutal world. She sat beside Simbongile, her fingers twitching in silent tribute to their former agility; and though no one knew this but her, it was the performance of her life that she gave.

She dedicated it to her great-aunt Hannie.

Chapter 19

Carol's mother, who had lived under her fair share of dark clouds – among them the early death of her husband and the arrest of a teenage son for small-time drug-pushing – had often stressed the importance of looking for silver linings. It was a lesson her daughter drew on in the aftermath of her meeting with Patrick and Eloise, and which seemed to be confirmed by the behaviour of the markets. Though Carol would not have used this phrase herself, the shit did, indeed, hit the fan as soon as London opened; and as she watched the numbers spin on her Bloomberg monitor it occurred to her that, though Eloise had won an early battle, the war was just beginning.

In the week following Eloise's return to London, osmium dropped a further eight per cent in value, leaving Derby Capital more than $46 million down on its previous high and ensuring a steady accumulation of gnawed biros in Patrick's overfilled bin. Surely, thought Carol, someone – a major investor, Birgir Lindqvist or Clive Stamp; one of the bigger funds – would notice and get cold feet? That was the kind of thing that would knock some sense into Patrick; shake him free of Eloise's bewitching self-confidence. She watched her rival closely, impressed despite herself by her infuriating calm, and asked her as often as she dared what Pasquier had to say about his colleagues' disparaging research.

Eloise pretended not to hear Carol's questions, unless Patrick was in the room – in which case she repeated the lie she had first told: that the MaxiTech board were out of reach on a corporate retreat in Aspen. In fact, Claude had not returned any of the three calls she had made to him, and this was not a piece of information she thought it advisable to share. Carol and Patrick would read more into Claude's silence than was necessary, for they had no experience of his intellectual frenzies or the isolation he required when lost in them. In Paris, she had known him go for days barely speaking, and her intimate acquaintance with his moods was not something she could share with her colleagues. So she did what she was known for doing well: she held her nerve. She did not bombard Claude with messages and at the office she focused her attention on titanium, interspersing her professional phone calls with a stream of emails to The Albany to finalise Joan's reception there.

The previous January, when the hefty deposit paid by Eloise had propelled Joan to the top of The Albany's waiting list, two rooms had unexpectedly become available at once. One was on the second floor: a 'standard single' with a view of ugly shops; the other was on the first floor and cost three times as much. 'It's the second-largest subdivision in the mansion's former Music Room and has its own en suite,' said Sister Karen, who believed in the subtle sell. 'You said your mother was musical?'

Eloise knew that Joan valued beauty, and had looked with approval at the stucco cherubs that joyfully shared the burden of a harp in the lintel frieze above the pillared entrance. 'Where does the second door lead?' she asked.

'That's blocked up. We keep it for ornamental purposes.'

It was indeed, thought Eloise, exceedingly ornamental. So were the eight Corinthian pillars, their bases carved in complex bas-reliefs. In Paris, in the icy winter of 1979, she had done a hundred extra hours of translation work so that she and Claude could spend their fourth anniversary in a suite at the Ritz. A similarly generous possibility came to her now and she made rough calculations. She had budgeted on a 'Classic Deluxe' room for Joan, which was in the respectable centre of The Albany's price range. The weekly rate of a 'Prestige Apartment' was much more than even she could consider with equanimity, but—

'We're having it entirely repainted,' volunteered Sister Karen.

Eloise hesitated, imagining her mother spending her last days in such a majestic space. How well deserved its elegance would be, and how appreciated. If she tightened her belt for a few months she could probably bear the cost until Claude announced his findings – at which point she would set aside her bonus to pay for this luxury in perpetuity. She considered negotiating, for she rarely paid the advertised rate for anything; but it struck her that this was not a decision to haggle over. 'I'll take it,' she had said abstractedly, as if the price was the least of her considerations. 'I mean, my mother will.'

As Eloise emailed Sister Karen for the fourteenth time in forty-eight hours, her mother sat on her bed at the Volksraad, cautiously prodding her left knee. She had never known agony like that which had woken her the night before and left her wakeful during the long, dark hours before daybreak. The ageing aspirins she had brought with her from London hadn't helped a bit.

She attempted cautiously to rise, and found that she could do so quite well. It was as though she had imagined the pain, but she knew that this could not be. What she needed was some fresh air, perhaps a little light exercise to get the blood moving again. Yes: a gentle walk to the pharmacy for something stronger than aspirin, followed by an afternoon in bed. She would give Simbongile the day off and ask him to come for her again tomorrow.

She went to the dressing table and touched the green folder containing Gertruida van Vuuren's journal. She had decided to steal it. She could not, she knew, read it once and be parted from it; she could not bear that. Neither would she accept a photocopied substitute, her great-grandmother's handwriting reproduced on shiny modern paper that held within it no trace of the past. So she took it to her suitcase and wrapped it gently in a towel, before zipping it safely into an inner compartment. Its contents needed time; she would finish it when she got home and could be alone with it at her leisure. It would be a talisman, of sorts: a companion in that dreadful, well-scrubbed nursing home.

This was Joan's first theft. Shortly after completing it, she went downstairs, wrote a note for Simbongile and left the hotel armed with a set of directions from the obliging Mr Engelbrecht. He had offered to drive her up the road – there was a pharmacy on the second street on the right, just past the car dealership – but she had declined: the helplessness of the previous night had left her anxious to reassert her physical independence.

It was a bore how long everything took when one was old. She admitted this as she tottered down the Volksraad's drive, past the well-tended rose bushes at its gate. And yet— Perhaps one saw things more clearly with more time to observe them. She thought of all the rushing she had done in her life. What had it really accomplished?

As she emerged onto the main road, the speed of the traffic astonished her. What on earth could explain such urgency on a weekday afternoon in Bloemfontein? The drivers who screeched past her were going at seventy or eighty miles an hour, at the very least. There was something comical about the tension on their faces, and the purposefulness with which they overtook one another. The fumes were choking. She thought of the poor roses, condemned to absorb them all day. She did not keep up with Science and its varied mysteries, but she knew what the Greenhouse Effect was and how it was exacerbated by the burning of fossil fuels. It was outrageous that, knowing this, people refused to share their cars or to take more public transport: she could not see a single vehicle that carried more than one person.

By the time she had reached the end of the first block, Joan had counted seventeen cars containing solo drivers and was feeling mildly indignant. The appearance of a minibus taxi, bursting at the seams, was briefly cheering – until it veered abruptly towards her, seemingly intent on running her down. She made a futile attempt to get out of its way, which was greeted with raucous laughter by the vehicle's occupants as it skidded to the other side of the road, honking loudly. Watching it disappear in a cloud of black soot, she felt a little foolish and in need of a place to sit down. The distance to the next block was far greater than Mr Engelbrecht's sketched map had led her to believe. She looked about her, hoping for a café of some description, but this was clearly not the right part of town for such conveniences. All around her were cars: rushing down the road; standing, mutely pristine, on the showroom floors of the dealerships which lined the street. She was deciding that she had better press on when she caught sight of – could it be? Yes it was – a sofa, nestled among the gleaming models arranged beyond the glass wall behind her. Further investigation revealed a water cooler beside the sofa and a young man, presumably a sales assistant, who caught her eye as she looked through the window and beckoned her inside.

'How can I help you this morning, *mevrou*?' he asked, holding the door open. He smelt freshly laundered and inviting after the pollution of the street.

'A glass of water would do very well, please, to begin with,' said Joan.

André du Plessis, whose name was advertised in loud orange letters on his lapel badge, led her politely to the sofa and filled a plastic cup from the burbling cooler. He was tall and thin, with a large pimple on his neck and a sizeable loan to repay from his university days. 'What kind of vehicle are you looking for this morning?' he asked, enunciating the words with exaggerated precision in case the old lady was as deaf as she looked.

The question embarrassed Joan; it made her feel as though she were obtaining refreshment under false pretences. She cast her eye about the showroom. On one side were some flashy sports cars, intended for men who cheated on their wives. Further off were family saloons in a range of metallic shades. She thought that this was probably not the moment to mention that she had never held a driver's licence.

'I've got a nice little Toyota,' offered André brightly, 'which would do very well for you. Is it yourself you're looking for?'

Joan nodded absently. She did not like to lie, but felt that she had gone too far not to. She allowed the young man to help her from her seat and take her to a distant corner of the room.

A familiar shape loomed ahead of them.

'Oh, but a friend of mine has this car!' she exclaimed. 'Or one very like it, at least.'

'The Toyota Corolla is very popular just now. Would you be interested in the 1.3 litre model or the 1.4? There's also a new 2 litre diesel. Very economical.'

Joan attempted to look as though she had understood the question and was considering it. She felt suddenly tired again. 'Would you mind if I sat down for a moment and thought it over?'

'Not a problem, ma'am. In fact, if you'll give me a sec . . .'

André disappeared briefly and returned with a grey plastic chair which he positioned in front of the Toyota, for it was as well to keep the client's mind focused.

'Thank you,' said Joan, rummaging in her handbag to avoid his hopeful gaze.

'You just let me know when you're ready, ma'am.'

'I'll do that.'

'It will be my pleasure to assist you.'

'Thank you.' She removed her diary from her bag, as if intent on making notes; note-taking, she felt, was a suitably serious occupation for a person about to make an important purchase. As she did so, a piece of discreet black plastic caught her eye and revealed itself, upon further investigation, to be the credit card Eloise had left before returning to London. A thought occurred to her. She banished it immediately, but it returned almost at once with a host of pleasurable associations.

She silenced it again – no, no, really, it would never do.

Watching her from the far end of the showroom, André du Plessis's heart sank: the old lady was talking to herself now and rocking gently to and fro. Clearly a basket case. He imagined what his boss would say, returning from his tea break to discover that he had installed a senile geriatric in the middle of the showroom, blocking the view of the BMW Z3. The thought was distressing. It inspired him to return, with almost undignified haste, to the vicinity of Joan's plastic chair and to ask her, with challenging gruffness, if there was anything further he could do for her.

This sudden interruption caused Joan to abandon the struggle with her own better judgement. 'Do you have any minibuses?'

The shock on the salesman's face was most amusing. It cheered his client up, and emboldened her to say, 'I'm looking for the very best one you have. Something with – as many cylinders as possible and' – she thought of the belching taxi in the street – 'some sort of emissions control.'

'I'm sorry, ma'am?'

'A minibus is what I'm after,' she repeated, more authoritatively. 'I would like to see the best model you have available.'

'This would be for yourself?'

'Does it matter?'

The tone in which Joan said this reminded André of the fact that the customer – particularly if a well-dressed customer, with an English accent and hard currency to spend – is never wrong.

'Of course not,' he said, meekly. 'Follow me.'

Chapter 20

The delivery of a sleek silver minibus to Mrs Joan McAllister of Room 302, the Volksraad Hotel, Bloemfontein, caused no little consternation among the staff of that establishment. Mr Engelbrecht, receiving the keys from the spotty young man who delivered it, cast an expert eye over its interior and noted with approval the pre-installed six-change CD player and fawn leather seats. The Head Porter, summoned to adjudicate a dispute between the Doorman and the Junior Porter, found for the former and confirmed that electronic parking sensors did not come as standard – not even on such luxury vehicles.

'What can an old lady want with such a thing?' asked the ageing bellhop, whose name tag read Big Boy.

'Ach man,' sighed the receptionist, an Afrikaans woman of advancing years with startlingly red hair, 'I expect she is planning a road trip and will sell it when she gets to the other end.'

Had Joan known of the commotion inspired by her purchase, she would perhaps have felt the tremor of guilt which was, she knew, the very least she owed Eloise under the circumstances. In fact, she did not feel remotely guilty – just as she felt no guilt about the theft of her grandmother's diary that morning. She had been anxious, perhaps, when tapping in her daughter's PIN number on the keypad of the showroom's billing machine: the number of zeros flashing on the screen had alarmed her. Raised in a generation for whom the extension or acceptance of credit was no small matter, Joan had worried that perhaps the transaction would be refused.

When it was accepted with a squeak of electronic delight, she had been gripped by a wild excitement quite unbecoming to a woman of her age. She had allowed André du Plessis to drive her first to the pharmacy, the initial object of her morning's journey, and then back to the hotel. She had impressed upon him the necessity of a swift delivery and been assured that she would receive her purchase before sunset. Alone in her room after these excitements, she was quite unable to compose herself for the afternoon nap she had planned and felt entirely – almost alarmingly – tranquil about the spending of large amounts of someone else's money. She thought of the tireless care she had bestowed on Eloise over the course of forty-eight years, of the graceful quiescence with which she had accepted her daughter's decision to put her into a home.

She had never asked for a thing in return, until now. What would the sacrifice mean to her? A few first-class aeroplane journeys and a couple of pairs of those ludicrous shoes of which she had too many in the first place. *I jolly well can spend this money*, Joan had thought earlier in the day, deliberating over the optional addition of an electric sunroof – and she jolly well had. Now she felt almost dizzy with anticipation and looked forward to the next morning with the breathlessness of a schoolgirl.

'With pleasure,' said Mr Engelbrecht, delighted to be given the chance of driving the vehicle that had spent the previous night raising the tone of the entire forecourt. 'I can move it round the back for you, no problem.'

'And string,' said Joan. 'I'm going to need an awful lot of string.'

'Also not a problem.'

It was six o'clock in the morning and Joan was awake and dressed, supervising the arrangements over which she had spent a fitful night deliberating. 'How much ribbon do you have?' she asked, anxiously.

'Well, there you've got me.' Mr Engelbrecht scratched his stubbled chin. 'I'm not sure we have any, to tell you the truth. How much were you after?'

'About fifteen metres, ideally.'

'Yes, well, no. We wouldn't have that much on the premises.'

Joan, who had imagined a gigantic bow stretching right round the minibus, looked crestfallen. The string she had asked for had another purpose entirely, and would not do for wrapping a gift of this magnitude. She looked around the lobby, suddenly disconsolate. Then her eyes fastened on the display of plastic proteas that was its chief adornment, and she smiled: rosettes of blue and orange ribbon were placed artfully within the arrangement, intended to suggest its recent delivery by a florist. 'Could I possibly—' she asked, finishing the sentence with her eyes.

'Just give me a moment to fetch the ladder,' said Mr Engelbrecht.

The rosettes were dusty and had to be wiped clean before they were at all serviceable. They were not, of course, what she had intended, but they were better than nothing. She attached the largest and best-preserved to the steering wheel once Mr Engelbrecht had parked the minibus in the service yard. It looked jaunty, she thought, and the blue sat well against the black of the dashboard.

She was in the breakfast room, as arranged, when Simbongile arrived for her. From its wide windows, she saw the Toyota Corolla draw up in the parking lot and watched with affection the con-centration on the young man's face as he reversed it into a tight bay. This task accomplished, she settled herself expectantly into her chair to wait for him; but Simbongile did not immediately leave his car. Thinking himself unobserved, he unclasped his safety belt and slumped motionless over the steering wheel. Joan watched in alarm, wondering at what point she should alert Mr Engelbrecht to this developing medical crisis. She was about to do so when Simbongile, having remained in this unorthodox position for several minutes, raised his head once more and opened his mouth in an extended yawn.

The poor boy was exhausted, she thought, and yet he never betrayed a hint of such exhaustion to her. She waited impatiently as he got out of the car, stretched, shook his head violently from side to side, and made his way up the steps and into the lobby.

'Won't you have some breakfast with me, dear?' she asked, as he was shown into the dining room.

'Surely, Miss Joan. I was not getting a chance to eat before leaving my house.' He sat down at her table and waved his hand in greeting to the two waiters on duty, who were regular passengers. 'How are you on this fine morning?'

'*Extremely* well,' she said.

'You look excited about something. Are you looking forward to going home?'

Joan considered this question. She was not, in fact, going home; she had no home to go to any longer – a sad fact that had no place on such a happy morning. 'Could we have some pastries, please?' she called to Mr Engelbrecht, with a significant nod of the head.

'I am preferring bacon and eggs, if possible,' said Simbongile.

'Of course, dear. We'll just have something sweet to get ourselves warmed up.'

She could barely contain herself as Mr Engelbrecht brought a plate of pastries to the table and set it before the young man. 'What can I get for you to drink?'

Simbongile was considering the rival merits of coffee and orange juice, and deciding that he could not ask for both, when his deliberations were disrupted by a shrill squeal from his hostess.

'Whatever is that?' cried Joan, pointing to a string emerging from the coagulated icing that so injudiciously decorated a *pain aux raisins*. 'We should investigate, don't you think?'

The pastry chef at the Volksraad Hotel was a friend of Simbongile's, who had no wish to get him into trouble for this strange oversight. 'No, no,' he said. 'It's quite all right. Nothing to investigate.'

'But there's a *string* in your pastry, dear. And, look, it stretches right to the door.'

Simbongile took a decisive bite and surreptitiously slipped the offending object from his plate to the floor. 'Where would you like to go today?'

But Joan was not to be deterred. 'We must find out where that string comes from. And if you won't then I will.' She made an effort to stand up, which forced Simbongile to his feet.

'Really,' he said, a note of desperation intruding into his voice, 'everything is absolutely okay.'

His friend the pastry chef, observing this loyal interaction, felt ashamed of the envy with which he had greeted the news of Simbongile's extraordinary good fortune as it spread through the hotel's kitchen that morning.

'Come on!' cried Joan. 'I can't follow it all by myself.'

With great unwillingness, the driver leaned down and picked up the string, guiding the old lady on his arm as they followed its trail. It led to the dining-room door, down the steps onto the terrace, around a clump of rose bushes, under a small door in the wall which, to Simbongile's astonishment, was unlocked at that hour, and into the service yard of the hotel.

'It is attached to that minibus,' said Simbongile.

'And what is the registration of the vehicle, dear? I don't have my glasses with me.'

'It is S-I-M-1, Miss Joan,' he said, peering at it intently.

'Isn't it strange,' murmured Joan, 'that a string from your breakfast pastry should lead to a minibus with the number plate SIM 1? It might almost stand for Simbongile.'

There was silence.

Simbongile did not move or speak. Neither did the Head Porter, the Junior Porter, the Manager, the Receptionist or the Bell Hop, all watching the scene from an unoccupied bedroom on the first floor. In the end it was Simbongile's friend the pastry chef, observing the proceedings from the hotel terrace, who broke the tension. 'Come on, man!' he shouted. 'Let's see you drive it!'

Simbongile looked at Joan; then at the minibus; then at Joan again. He opened his mouth and closed it. He took three steps in the direction of the vehicle and stopped.

'Come *on*, man!' called the pastry chef. 'If you can't drive it, she must give it to someone who can!'

Still Simbongile seemed incapable of movement. Finally, with what appeared to be a great effort of will, he crossed the remainder of the service yard and opened the door of the minibus. The onlookers, moved by the drama of the scene and led by the moist-eyed Mr Engelbrecht, burst into spontaneous applause as he did so. Oblivious to them, Simbongile slid into the driver's seat and put his hands on the steering wheel. He sat there for some time in silence. Then, finding the key in the ignition, he turned it with a delicacy approaching reverence and the vehicle sprang to life.

'Do you like it, dear?' asked Joan, stepping painfully towards the passenger window.

But there was no reply from the minivan's new owner – for Simbongile, his body hunched forward over the walnut-finish dashboard, was unable to speak.

He was sobbing.

Chapter 21

Eloise looked at her mother, squeezed her hand and smiled reassuringly. 'Everything's *fine*,' she said. 'The market's very frisky these days. It's the war. There's absolutely nothing to worry about.'

They were in the back of a taxi, leaving Heathrow Airport and joining the lines of stationary vehicles queuing for the dubious privilege of entering central London in the rush hour.

'So copper's all right again?' repeated Joan, in the tone of voice one might use to enquire after a younger relative, always in and out of trouble.

'Yes, Mum.'

'You're sure, darling?'

'I'm sure.'

'Well that's very good.'

'Yes.'

'A relief.'

'Absolutely.'

Joan detected a certain tension behind Eloise's glossy optimism. Misreading it as guilt, she gripped her hand tightly – for she could not bear her daughter to reproach herself for abandoning her. To change the mood decisively, she made the confession she had been planning on the plane. 'I have done something impetuous,' she said. 'I have bought Simbongile a minibus.'

'You bought him – *what*?'

'A minibus.'

Joan's posture as she said this – hunched forward in her seat like a penitent schoolgirl, a trace of defiance in her eye – was unintentionally comical. Eloise began to laugh. 'How much did it cost?'

Joan leaned towards her and whispered the sum into her ear.

'Where did you get so much money?'

'I put it on your credit card, darling. The little black one you gave me for expenses. I'm afraid it was a bit dear, but the young man at the showroom assured me I was getting a very good deal.'

'I'm sure he did.' Eloise leaned back in her seat. The thought of her mother in a Bloemfontein car dealership, purchasing a minibus, was deliciously absurd and distracted her from the tension that had been building all morning. She had woken resolved – as if her certainty could influence the outcome – that Claude would call today, and her nervous anticipation now vented itself in laughter. She laughed and laughed, and laughed still more to see how taken aback her mother was by this response.

'It's an awful lot of money, I'm afraid,' ventured Joan.

It was, but the financial implications of the purchase seemed insignificant in the context of Derby Capital's recent losses. Besides which, Eloise was not an ungenerous person. She would not, herself, have given a minibus to someone she had only known a week, but she liked Simbongile and she loved the warmth that had inspired Joan to help him. It was not something Frank would have done. 'For a person who can't decide between a starter and a main course in a restaurant,' she said affectionately, wiping her eyes, 'how did you ever settle on the colour?'

It took them an hour to reach Wandsworth, and as the taxi turned into Kingsley Gardens Eloise put her arm around Joan. Her mother's shoulders surprised her whenever she touched them; it seemed wrong, somehow, that they should be so frail and bony. 'How are you feeling?' she asked.

'Oh, very well, darling.' Joan patted Eloise's leg. 'Quite excited, in fact.'

'It's certainly a beautiful building.'

'Yes.' Joan looked up at the cluttered façade of The Albany, wondering whether *beautiful* was the word she would have chosen. It was more becoming, certainly, than any of the other geriatric institutions they had visited, but there was something monstrous about it, too, something defiantly imposing that was, perhaps, a little self-conscious for her tastes. 'Well, here we are,' she said.

They were met in the hall by the Nursing Manager, attended by a young Asian man in a smart suit and plastic-soled shoes that squeaked as he moved. 'Welcome, Joan!' Sister Karen took Joan's hands and squeezed them in hers, a greeting somewhat spoiled by the dampness of her palms. 'I understand you've just been on a Rather Exciting Trip!'

'Yes, indeed,' said Joan. From the corner of her eye she caught a flash of something bright. The pedals, perhaps? She looked for them among the stylised cornflowers on the tiles at her feet, but they did not appear.

'You must tell me what fun you had, but first things first.' Sister Karen nodded at the young man. 'This is Sunil. He will bring your bags in from the taxi. Everything else is waiting for you in your room.' She smiled widely, as though encouraging a child to face her fear of the dark. 'Let's get you settled in, shall we?'

Together, they crossed the hall – the winged angels were still there, supporting the banisters of the staircase – and entered a lift on the far side. Joan was glad, all things considered, to be spared the indignity of the electric chair lift. Emerging on the first floor, Sister Karen led them down a wide corridor carpeted in a repeating pattern of green flecks that reminded Joan of the Arrivals Hall at Heathrow. They passed a row of doors, on which the names of the rooms' occupants were displayed on small cards, and stopped outside the last one on the right. 'We've had it especially repainted for you.' The Nursing Manager ushered them inside. 'Welcome to your new home!'

The shock of the colour threatened to send Joan hurtling into the summer of 1962 – for it was the precise shade Frank had chosen to paint over the exquisite design of twisting vines and birds that had once decorated the ebony aesthetic-movement sideboard in the dining room. He had called such destruction 'updating'.

'I always think yellow's so cheerful,' said Sister Karen, echoing Astrid's view with uncanny precision.

'Don't you, Mum?' asked Eloise.

It required an effort of concentration for Joan to remain firmly in the present and adopt an expression of appropriate pleasure. 'Absolutely,' she said. But the yellow was *not* cheerful; it was a sour, acidic yellow, with a trace of green in it.

'This used to be part of the Music Room,' her daughter went on, indicating a pair of yellow cherubs strumming a yellow harp above the doorway. Further children in a state of acute jaundice danced wantonly in the bas-relief at the base of a nearby pillar, waving at the window that looked onto The Albany's well-tended garden and mews. A cherry tree, its blossoms littering the lawn, gave Eloise something further to exclaim over while Joan recovered herself and examined with melancholy interest the space she would occupy until she died. She wondered whose death had freed it up for her.

'I'll leave you to get settled in and spend some time together,' said Sister Karen, brightly. 'Sunil will be along with your bags shortly.'

Beyond the pillars was a single bed on a substantial metal frame, with a control pad like the ones Joan had seen on the aeroplane to South Africa. Beneath the window was a simple, modern desk in the glossy pine of which the room's other furniture – an armchair, a small bookcase, a built-in cupboard – was also constructed. The bed was made up with a duvet in a stiffly crinkled cover of purple and maroon which matched the curtains and the seat of the chair, and combined with the shade of the walls to suggest another of Astrid's favourite colour schemes. She supposed sheets and blankets were a bother for the staff.

'What a marvellous bathroom!' cried Eloise, opening a door on the opposite side of the room.

'It does look very convenient,' agreed Joan, crossing to her and peering in.

The bathroom was tiled in white, with a non-slip floor of dove grey. There was no bath, she noticed, but then she could no longer take baths unaided – and the idea of being helped to wash by the efficient Sister Karen was vaguely alarming. The shower, in any case, was as 'spacious' as the brochure had promised, with a grey plastic seat and as many handrails as a person could reasonably require. She felt a sudden and intense urge to be alone.

There was a knock at the door. Eloise opened it and admitted Sunil, who put Joan's suitcase down at the foot of her bed and smiled shyly at them. 'If you need to be taken anywhere, or to have anything collected for you, just sign in at the reception desk and reserve a time slot,' he informed them. 'I will be happy to assist you in any matter.'

'That's very kind of you, dear,' murmured Joan. 'I'm quite all right for the moment.'

'Well, let me know if anything comes up. You will find a box of your personal possessions on a shelf in the closet.'

When he had closed the door, Eloise said, 'He seems very nice.'

'Yes he does, darling. Very nice indeed.'

There was a pause.

'Shall I unpack for you?'

'Goodness no. I can do that by myself quite well. Shouldn't you be getting back to the office?'

'I can be here as long as you need me.'

'I think I'll be all right on my own now. You've been marvellous to ferry me about like this.'

'Are you sure?'

'Quite sure, darling.'

'There's going to be a Residents' Induction course later. Would you like me to stay for that with you?'

'Why ever would I? I'm sure Sister Karen will explain everything perfectly.'

'You're right.'

'Yes, darling.'

'You will call me if you need anything at all?'

'Of course I will.'

'Good.'

'Yes.'

'Well, goodbye then.' Eloise leaned down and hugged her mother.

'Goodbye, darling.'

Eloise turned and went to the door, pausing as she reached it to look back and wave. Joan was standing by the desk, very small under the high ceiling. 'I love you, Mum,' she said.

'I know you do, Eloise. I love you too.'

Chapter 22

Joan waited until she was quite sure that her daughter had left the building. She counted the minutes slowly in her head, allowing ample time for Eloise to have a conversation with Sister Karen and to call a taxi. Then, having attempted and failed to lock the door, for there were no interior locks at The Albany, she sat down in the pine armchair, rested her head in her hands, and began to cry.

She cried quietly for fifteen minutes, almost furtively – as she had cried in the weeks following Eloise's birth when Astrid's domestic intentions, and the uselessness of resistance to them, had become plain. Then she stopped and went into the bathroom, where she rinsed her eyes and dried her face on a scratchy maroon towel. The day had turned cold outside and the thin spring light emphasised the bareness of the room. Taking a deep breath, she opened the door of the built-in cupboard to find, among her own clothes, already hung up and neatly pressed, the black dress that her grandmother had worn on the *stoep* of Van Vuuren's Drift.

The sight of it, on a grey plastic coat hanger stamped in gold with the word *TranquilAge™*, prompted penitence. There were, after all, many whose troubles far exceeded her own. She resolved to be more cheerful and reached into the closet. Where was the griffin chandelier? In the shock of her sudden return to the early 1960s, she had forgotten to effect its touching presentation to Eloise.

But an examination of the cupboard's depths revealed no tenderly wrapped gift. She began to hunt for it, without result; and when she had looked in every conceivable place – even in the desk's drawers, which could not possibly accommodate it – she accepted defeat and told herself that the movers must have made a mistake. Eloise had a knack for dealing with service professionals who made mistakes, and Joan did not doubt that she would succeed in retrieving it.

Reminding herself of the need for calm, she lifted her cardboard box of personal possessions and opened it on the bed. The photographs were in their familiar frames: a black-and-white shot of Frank in uniform; a colour snap of Eloise and George as young children; Eloise, aged sixteen, in the finals of a Shakespeare declamation competition; George, tanned and shirtless, grinning cheekily on a beach. And finally (she felt a tremor of guilt as she removed it) a photograph of herself with Claude, in the kitchen of that adorable apartment he had had, overlooking Sacré Coeur.

How different things would have been if Eloise had married Claude! Joan returned the photograph to the box, but she could not silence the cruelly tempting possibilities it had summoned. Claude and Eloise would have had children, she felt sure. She could have lived, if not with them, at least near them; near enough to bake cakes for her grandchildren and swap recipes with her son-in-law. She saw herself in the carriage house of that lovely villa she had so hoped Eloise would buy: surrounded by her own things; the cosy confidante of a loving family.

With some difficulty, she lifted the cardboard folder she had chosen at random from the many so painstakingly preserved, and set it on her lap. It was full of birthday and Christmas cards, made by her children with such enthusiastic innocence that she could not bear to look at them. She put them hastily away, and as she did so a picture of her mother-in-law fell out of a mottled envelope. She was wedged into a narrow armchair, which she filled to overflowing, and Eloise was leaning over her, laughing. The easy affection on her daughter's face reminded Joan of a time when Eloise had been gentler than she was now, and prompted a flicker of irritation at the disloyalty of her fondness for her grandmother. She put this emotion aside – for she had, of course, encouraged good relations between her children and their sole surviving grandparent – but Astrid continued to stare up at her from the maroon duvet cover: an impudent reassertion of the past.

Although they had met in her sitting room on the top floor of a private London boys' school, Astrid had never once mentioned to Joan her years in domestic service there, or the fact of her seduction, at seventeen, by the Scottish-born French master – who had done the decent thing and married her, and then gone and died when Frank was eleven. Only a careful adding-up of dates and age differences had revealed this chronology; and in the beginning it had explained something of Astrid's fanatical devotion to her son, and so excused it. Now, the sight of her threatened to summon the sound of her singing, and as a pre-emptive measure Joan returned the photograph to the folder and began to put the other volumes of sheet music she had brought with her in the bookshelf. She was extracting from her suitcase the green cardboard folder that contained Gertruida van Vuuren's journal when a sharp knock at the door made her jump painfully.

'Well aren't we making ourselves snug!' Sister Karen stood in the doorway, smiling broadly. 'No time for reading now, Joan. We're going to plan some wonderful activities for you, and introduce you to your new friends!'

It occurred to Joan, as Sister Karen led her up and down The Albany's long corridors, babbling brightly about the home's mentorship system, that she had not, for many years, met someone who inspired in her a keener dislike than this patronising official. There was something despair-inducing about the Nursing Manager's relentless breeziness. She thought of the numberless quiet, solitary evenings she had spent – oh, how contentedly! – at Wilsmore Street, and wondered at which point she could politely escape the attentions of the nurse.

'Do you know,' she began hopefully, 'I'm feeling a little tired. I wonder if I could possibly have dinner in my room and meet my mentor tomorrow?'

'Goodness gracious! No need for nerves!' Sister Karen put a fleshy arm around Joan's shoulders. 'It's the same for *everyone* on their first night – but you'll soon feel a part of the family. Trust me.'

They had stopped outside a door which bore a card that read *Sylvia Fraser – Chairwoman, Entertainment Committee*.

Joan's heart sank.

'Sylvia! A new arrival for you!' Sister Karen rapped smartly on the door and entered the room, just as she had Joan's, without waiting for a reply. 'Sylvia Fraser, Joan McAllister. Joan McAllister, Sylvia Fraser.'

A short, plump woman with a square jaw and crooked teeth was sitting on the bed, in a room noticeably fuller and more individual than Joan's was. On the wall behind her was a large noticeboard, covered in leaflets. In fact, wherever one looked there was paper – piled on the desk, stashed between books on the pine shelves, scattered over the duvet cover, which looked much softer than Joan's and was an appealingly cheerful print of roses and ribbons. On either side of the bed were two brightly polished marble pillars that reached to the ceiling, on which were stuck various To Do lists.

'Well, my,' she said, 'a fellow artist at last.'

As Joan shook Sylvia's hand and said how glad she was to meet her, accepting Sylvia's assurance that this sentiment was as mutual as could be, she was unnerved by the thought that they had met before.

'No, no, believe me, we haven't. I never forget a face.'

'Sylvia's here to guide you through your first few days,' explained Sister Karen. 'Sometimes you'll want a friend closer to your own age, not a spring chicken like me, to confide in. Sylvia knows *everyone*. She's the Chairwoman of the Entertainment Committee.'

'I'm from Charleston, South Carolina, but I married a Brit,' remarked Sylvia, at something of a tangent. 'I don't play an instrument, but I'm a very keen appreciator of music. It just thrills me to have a pianist with us.' She smiled widely at Joan, who succeeded abruptly in placing her: she looked just as she had always imagined the Red Queen, bearing down on Alice in *Through the Looking-Glass*.

'The good news', Sylvia went on, apparently following her own train of thought, 'is that we're a man short for the Trivial Pursuit league. Dear old Charles McFadden – gosh, he was a darling, now wasn't he, Sister? – died last week, so you've come at just the right moment to take his place.' She took Joan's hand. 'Now I'm going to take you right down to the dining room and introduce you all round. Then you'll have to come back up here with your coffee and tell me everything. Husband, kids, loves, losses, *everything*. I just know we're going to be great friends.'

Chapter 23

Joan woke early the next morning. The room was far too hot. Unused to the height of her new bed, which seemed an unnecessary distance from the floor, she got up gingerly, taking care not to hurt herself. The process took some minutes and left her panting. Only when she was in her dressing gown, and had opened the window, did she remember the control panel that might have lowered the mattress to a more convenient height. Perhaps there was a temperature setting on it? She went back to the bed and examined it carefully, but the rows of buttons and flashing lights were indecipherable. Giving up the attempt, she thought how wasteful it was to have the radiators on this late in the year; in her own home, she had stopped them promptly on the first day of March, whatever the weather.

There was a knock on the door.

'Morning, Joan! Morning, morning.' Sister Karen opened the door and bustled in. 'Oh, you've got yourself up, I see. Well done! Would you like some help with washing? I can send one of the nurses up to take care of you.'

It was the first time in her life that Joan had been congratulated on getting out of bed, unaided. 'No, thank you,' she said. 'I am quite used to showering by myself.'

'Well you'd better get a move on! You've only got an hour before the aerobics class!'

'I don't think,' said Joan, firmly, 'that I will be participating in the aerobics class.'

'Nonsense. The only way to stay youthful is to keep active. You don't want to be stuck in a wheelchair like some of the poor dears you met last night, do you?'

'I really don't think—'

But Sister Karen had already left. 'I'll send someone up in forty-five minutes to escort you to the Recreation Lounge,' she called from the corridor.

Joan, who was not a confrontational person (she often marvelled, in fact, at Eloise's capacity to command a situation), stood in the centre of her room, fighting the dawning realisation that she was helpless to resist the cheerful instructions of Sister Karen. The notion that a person half her age could take charge of her, in such a breezily peremptory fashion, was infuriating; and yet there was, apparently, nothing to be done about it. On her desk, untouched since the night before, was her grandmother's journal. How she longed for some peace and quiet to finish it! Sensing, however, that she would get neither this morning, she put it in a pine drawer and made her way to the bathroom.

She was just finishing dressing when there was another knock: a meeker tap, this time, than the rat-tat-tat that indicated the Nursing Manager's imminent intrusion. Joan waited for the door to open, and when it did not she felt absurdly grateful for this courtesy. 'Come in,' she called.

A young nurse entered the room, carrying a plastic tray on which a grapefruit had been sliced in half and divided into segments. She was delicately boned, with pale golden hair that fell in wisps from the ponytail in which it was tied. 'Good morning,' she said. 'My name is Nurse Fleur. I'm going to take you along to the aerobics class shortly.' She handed Joan the sliced grapefruit. 'Just a little something to get your blood-sugar levels up. You'll work up an appetite for breakfast while you do your exercises, and they're very good for your mobility.' She smiled at Joan, who still looked doubtful. 'I'll be back for you in ten minutes.'

The aerobics class took place in the Recreation Lounge (Non-Smokers). It consisted of a group of residents, many of them in wheelchairs, sitting in a circle while a young woman with an exposed midriff and tauntingly toned abdominals exhorted them to movement.

The widescreen television was on and another group (enviably exempted from the aerobics session) was facing it, its members apparently untroubled by their more energetic peers. On the screen two rather plain, thirty-something women were savagely humiliating a plump, attractive lady whose friends – to whom Joan doubted she would ever speak again – had entered her for a televised makeover. No one seemed to be watching. In one corner an old woman with the face of an impish young girl sat under a duvet on a makeshift bed composed of two armchairs pushed together. Her eyes were closed, her skin like wax; she did not talk or move, though she occasionally half-opened her lids. She did so now, and took Joan in. 'You're not Nora,' she said, testily.

Joan was wondering how best to respond to this perfectly truthful statement when Sylvia entered the room. 'Morning, Nurse Fleur! Morning, Joan! How are you today? I was so disappointed you didn't come up yesterday for a chat.' She hurried towards the exercise group, miraculously mobile in this aged company. 'Do you recognise everyone from last night?'

Joan had met some of the participants of the exercise class at dinner the previous evening. Sister Karen had made her stand in the middle of the dining room, like an animal at auction, and had called out people's names so quickly that she had no recollection of them now. She nodded at those whose faces seemed familiar and received nods in return.

'This is Sabrina,' said Nurse Fleur, guiding her further into the group and introducing the physiotherapist. 'Don't bother about Mrs Hawkridge.' She nodded at the impish old lady in the makeshift bed. 'She's a little confused. Her sister Nora has been dead for seven years. Why don't you take a seat here?' She fetched a pine armchair and helped Joan into it. 'I'll come and find you at the end of the class.'

For the next half hour, Joan moved her hands and waved her arms and turned her head from side to side, feeling like a puppet controlled with invisible strings by the athletic Sabrina. Opposite her, a lady with hair dyed the colour of a sinking sun was so stiff that a nurse was obliged to move her limbs for her. She submitted to this without protest, oblivious to Sabrina's encouraging calls, and then turned to her helper with a kind, uncomprehending smile – as if she wondered what possessed her to behave in this odd fashion.

They moved to the relentless rhythms of a strange cacophony that emanated from a small silver machine by Sabrina's side. A younger person might have identified it as house music, but to Joan it seemed only a brutal wall of sound, driving them on with relentless regularity like a metronome in a nightmare. Politely resisting the temptation to put her fingers in her ears, she thought sadly that a racket as dreadful as this was certain to drive the pedals away.

They took a break after ten minutes, and the lady with hair the colour of a sinking sun fell asleep abruptly, almost emphatically. Joan wished she might do the same. It was unexpectedly tiring, all this twisting and nodding. Lacking the courage to close her eyes, however, she had no choice but to submit to a further twenty minutes of exercise, after which she promised herself that she would escape to her room.

'Well I don't know about you, but I'm *pooped*.' Sylvia Fraser slipped an arm proprietorially through Joan's, just as she was standing to leave. Sabrina had switched off the CD player and was collecting the selection of plastic hoops in fluorescent colours that she had distributed earlier to her somewhat bemused audience. 'The breakfasts aren't very good,' Sylvia confided, 'but it's a lovely room we eat them in. You must join me.'

'I'm a little tired, thank you. I think I should rest.'

But Sylvia was not to be put off with such excuses. Dismissing Nurse Fleur, who had come to fetch her, she led Joan down the corridor and into a large, airy room that looked onto the garden. Like the others on the ground floor it was painted magnolia, which did little justice to its splendid panelling.

Various residents were sitting at scattered Formica-topped tables, and Sylvia pointed them out to Joan as they took their places by the window. It seemed that she did not only know everyone in the home, as Sister Karen had said, but had a firm grasp of their medical histories, too. 'That's George Chesterton,' she whispered, nodding at an angular octogenarian with dashingly parted grey hair. He was very thin, with a striking jawbone that suggested extreme beauty in youth. 'I can whisper, can't I? How's your hearing?'

'Perfectly functional.'

'Good. Well George is stage two Alzheimer's. Very debilitating. It makes him suspicious and argumentative. He doesn't recognise many people any more. Nurse Janet told me they had to remove the photograph of his family from his room. He recognised his wife and children, but not himself – can you imagine that? He got terribly jealous of the man who had his arm around his wife. Last week he hit Sister Karen in the face when she tried to wash him.'

The thought of someone hitting Sister Karen in the face brought a glimmer of a smile to Joan's lips, which she hastily repressed.

'I hope she wasn't hurt?'

'No, she's used to it. See that old woman there?' Sylvia indicated the lady with hair the colour of a sinking sun, now sitting by herself with a cup of coffee and some knitting on her lap. 'Her name's Katherine Ingelow. She's been knitting that scarf since she came here three years ago. Never lets that plastic bag out of her sight. And that one' – Sylvia nudged her hand in the direction of a large woman with pendulous breasts, whose starlet lipstick had been unfortunately misapplied – 'you don't want to get trapped with her. Doris Mitchell. She's only stage one, but by God she's a bore. She's got a scrapbook of her life, kept it for years, the old dear. Apparently it's got pictures in it of everyone she ever slept with. She'll tell you about them for hours, for *hours*.'

The conversation continued in this vein for some time. Sylvia, it transpired, was in her late sixties and had come to The Albany, after a serious car accident, only because she had no immediate relatives to care for her. She had been married twice but was childless. Her only surviving family, her sister Emmy's sons, lived in Charleston and had wives and children of their own. They were lawyers, with no time for foreign vacations.

Joan listened to her life story and murmured sympathetically when she paused long enough to indicate that some response was appropriate. How awful for this poor woman, she thought, to be trapped in a place where everyone is twenty years older than her and coherent conversation so hard to come by. Sylvia's loneliness was palpable, and the garrulousness it inspired at first tedious, then distressing. Joan began to yearn for solitude, and as the last of the other residents was fetched by a nurse and taken from the room, she got up.

'But I want to hear all about you!'

'I'm afraid I must telephone my daughter. The removals people who packed up my flat have forgotten to deliver something. She'll want to get on to them.'

'Let's meet for an hour before the Trivial Pursuit Club, then. There are only three of us who can play it now.'

'I have no general knowledge,' said Joan, emphatically. And then, because she felt sorry for the younger woman: 'But it has been so interesting to meet you. My life has been very dull by comparison. I'll tell you about it tomorrow.'

Sylvia looked at her, sensing perhaps that her headlong rush to intimacy had been too precipitous. 'Till tomorrow, then,' she said, quietly. 'We'll have a good long talk tomorrow.'

'That would be lovely.'

'Yes.'

Joan turned to go.

'You're very welcome to join the Trivial Pursuit Club. We have no competency threshold, you know.'

'Thank you, dear, but I don't think I would be much fun for the rest of you to play with.'

'What about bridge? We do that on Wednesday afternoons.'

Frank had played bridge, fanatically. 'I'm afraid I don't play that, either.'

'What about the library tour? We get taken once a fortnight.'

It seemed unkind to refuse further. 'You can count on me for one of those.'

'I'll put you on the list, then.'

'Please do.'

'You bet.'

Leaving Sylvia at their table, smiling bravely, Joan left the room.

Chapter 24

Despite Eloise's optimism, Claude did not call her the day Joan entered The Albany, and two weeks later she had still not heard from him. She thought back over their time in Paris, trying to gauge the length of his silences then. He had spent the month of June 1976 quite mute, she remembered, lost in an interior labyrinth from which he had emerged to complete his doctoral thesis in ten days. On that occasion he had been joyfully, even ethereally apologetic, had sold his moped in penance and spent the money on weekend tickets to Vienna. The memory of their three nights in a two-star hotel on the Laudongasse remained one of Eloise's favourite erotic scenarios, and she returned to it regularly in the company of her electric toothbrush – an altogether more stable companion than Claude himself.

Two decades in commodities trading had taught Eloise something about anxiety. She had wasted a lot of time, over the years, worrying about disasters that had resolved themselves in the end. She had also worried about many that had not; some, even, that had turned out worse than she had feared – and in each of these cases, her own emotional turmoil had not helped the situation. She was aware of her instinctive preference for action over inaction and wise enough to be wary of it; so quite systematically, because there was no concrete evidence to the contrary, she told herself that Claude's silence was indicative of intellectual exertion and that she should not distract him from it. Interrupting him from his mind-wanderings had led to dizzying rages before now.

The reward for her forbearance was a further collapse in osmium's price.

She observed its free fall impassively, aware of Carol's gimlet eyes on her and the consequent importance of nonchalant body language. Her outward calm reinforced Patrick, but as the days passed she began to see the serious flaw in the lie she had told her colleagues. As far as Patrick and Carol were concerned, the MaxiTech board was returning from its corporate retreat in Aspen on 25 May – a day safely distant when first selected, arbitrarily, by Eloise, but now approaching with relentless inevitability. As it drew closer she began to wonder whether, perhaps, Claude's silence had a different origin altogether. She recalled the message he had left before her departure for Bloemfontein: unusually late, his voice clipped and tense. Was he punishing her for not calling him back? Did he still do things like that? The thought began to preoccupy her and to remind her of his sulks, so impossible to bear in that claustrophobic flat with its dismal view of railway lines. Surely he had grown out of them now? He was fifty-five years old, for God's sake.

Observing none of this beneath Eloise's poise, Carol found that she could not restrain an involuntary leaping of her heart every time the telephone rang; and as day after day passed without incident she began to yearn for the fulfilment of the dark prophecy she had made at the start of the crisis. The intensity of her desire for Eloise's professional incineration alarmed her, but she was unable to resist it – though she knew that if Derby Capital went up in flames, her own job would go with it. She knew, too, that her husband would not pay their mortgage for long on the occasional thousand-word articles on 'The Male Meno-pause' and similar topics he wrote for the middle-brow dailies. And yet— Buried deep within Carol, in a secret compartment of her soul whose existence she barely acknowledged, was the thought that the pleasure of seeing Eloise fail would be worth this personal setback. She herself, after all, could always get another job; it would be Eloise whose reputation would be tarnished beyond repair.

Three weeks after Eloise's return from Bloemfontein, osmium's price touched $128.92 an ounce, leaving Derby Capital almost $62 million down on its previous high. 'We're going to need a realistic estimate from Pasquier, something we can use when clients start calling,' said Patrick at their morning meeting, cracking a biro in two.

'I don't know if he'll go on the record.' Eloise spoke evenly, feigning rapt absorption in her emails. 'Consolidated Platinum have just issued a profit warning. Don't we—'

'When we've got $130 million sunk in Consolidated Platinum, I'll give a shit about them. Until then it's osmium we're talking about.'

Carol looked up.

'Sure, Patrick. It's just that this is going to be very sensitive information. You know they won't leak anything until they're ready.'

'If you can't get a statement out of Pasquier, I'll get on a plane myself and bum-fuck it out of him in Boston.'

'What a charming image.'

'I'm not joking, sweetheart.'

It was clear from Patrick's red face and steaming brow that, indeed, he was not joking. Eloise saw that a confrontation she had been anticipating for several days was upon her and she stepped up to face it. 'You don't have any claim on Pasquier,' she said firmly, looking her boss directly in the eye.

'What the fuck are you talking about?'

'He leaked information to me, as a private favour. In case you're forgetting, you can only share inside information in the commodities market. Insider dealing in equities is illegal. That's why we bought however many fucking tonnes of osmium we did buy. If we'd bought shares in MaxiTech, you and I could go to jail.' She paused, allowing this fact its due enormity. Then she said, more briskly: 'Pasquier doesn't owe you anything, and if you get involved and start being your usual, obnoxious self, he's not going to have any desire to help you, either. If clients start calling, send them to me. But don't you fucking dare go throwing your weight around.'

'What are you suggesting I do, then?'

'Focus on something else. Follow the original plan. It's only May, for God's sake. If you're going to be this on edge until December, you'll need to be sectioned by the end of the summer.'

When Eloise left the office that evening, she did so quietly resolved to do whatever was necessary to reach Claude – even if that meant calling his mother or his wife. She walked quickly past the brightly lit buildings on Piccadilly, conscious of the need to act on this impulse before contemplating it further, and let herself into her flat with an expression of grim purpose. The pristine hush that greeted her suggested the recent attentions of Irina, but beneath the scent of a Pine Forest air-freshener was the faint but unmistakable stench of rotting wool.

Eloise knelt down and sniffed the recently replaced carpets, wondering whether bacterial cultures continued to flourish beneath them. It was difficult to trace the origins of the odour, so she opened the sitting-room windows as she hunted through her bag for her Blackberry. Finding it, she decided that there would be no need to bother either of the Mesdames Pasquier if she could reach Claude by other means, so she dialled his office one last time and was told again that her message would be passed to 'Dr Pas-kee-ay', who was 'very busy right now'.

Claude's cell phone rang twice then switched to voicemail with an abruptness that unsettled her. 'Hello, Claude,' she said, doing her best to keep the irritation from her voice beneath a suitably penitent tone, 'I'm so sorry we didn't speak before I went away. I was in South Africa with my mother. But I'm back now and would really like to talk to you—' She stopped speaking and pressed the star key. The 'really' was wrong; it sounded too anxious, so she re-recorded the message more briskly. Listening to this second attempt, she decided that it was not sufficiently apologetic – if Claude really was sulking, weary experience had taught her that the only way to coax him into communicating was to apologise with total, preferably tearful, sincerity.

It took a further two takes before she was satisfied and she ended the call with a heavy heart, wondering whom she should face first: Madame Angélique Pasquier, Claude's mother, or Ingrid, his wife. She decided to try his mother, then changed her mind, then changed it again. Where were all those numbers? There was a notebook, somewhere, with all the contact details she had ever had for the Pasquiers neatly written out in longhand. Only three (Claude's home, office and cell phone) had made the transition to her electronic database; it had not occurred to her that she would need the others again.

She got up, aware of the fact that even the tedium of an evening jog was becoming preferable to a conversation with the woman who might have been her mother-in-law. She had no idea where the notebook might be and could no longer remember the Pasquiers' address. Perhaps it would be better to take some exercise, clear her head; Claude was sure to call her back later that evening, or the next day. Why should she—? But she silenced this tempting train of thought. She was a grown woman. Angélique Pasquier had liked her, once. She would know where her son was and would, if anyone could, make sure he called her back. So she fetched a small stepladder and poked into the loft, where a number of dusty boxes – old bank statements, tax returns, very little of sentimental importance – were squeezed beneath the water pipes.

It took Eloise almost two hours of purposeful searching, by the end of which her bedroom and living room were strewn with papers and cardboard files, to locate the notebook. Joan had bought it for her at Liberty's as a parting present before her final departure for Paris, and its pattern of faded florals, so far from her own taste, brought her mother vividly to mind. In the last ten days, Joan had twice asked her to go to the storage unit in Hounslow to find a gift she had wrapped for her before their departure for South Africa, and twice she had lied and said that the facility was shut. She wrote the word HOUNSLOW in large letters on a pad she had taken from her room at the Volksraad Hotel and went to the kitchen, where she poured a Scotch and consulted the address book.

The neatness of her younger self's writing implicitly criticised the scruffiness of her notes to Irina, displayed on the fridge. She flicked to 'P' and found, as she remembered, the long list of Pasquier relatives: Monsieur et Madame Jacques Pasquier, Claude's grandparents; his sisters, Sybille and Marie-France; Marie-France's girlfriend, the artist from Varennes; Claude's great-aunt Mathilde (how he had doted on that cantankerous woman); town and country addresses for his parents, Albert and Angélique, for his aunt Céleste and her husband Guillaume; the birthdays of a host of cousins – Thierry, Hubert, Antoinette, Claudine, Christian, Sébastien, Jean-Jacques. She remembered some of these as children; they would be grown up now, with children of their own, probably hoards of children, for the Pasquiers were determined breeders. Others would be dead. She thought of Claude's grandparents, well into their eighties when she had last seen them. She had been rather afraid of his grandmother, the sharp-tongued Victoire, sister of the sharper-tongued Mathilde.

She sipped the Scotch and dialled the number of Albert and Angélique, half-hoping to find it out of date. When a recorded voice told her that it was, she dialled directory enquiries in Toulouse and gave the address listed, only to be told that it was *sur la liste rouge*, or ex-directory. She considered, briefly, braving his sisters, but decided against it. She had seen Sybille, who worked at the Banque Nationale de Paris, at a conference six or seven years before, and the encounter had not been a cosy one. Besides which, Claude would detect desperation in her efforts to contact two women who had always disliked her, with a resentment that had hardened into hatred after her rejection of their brother. No, she thought: the only way forward was Ingrid.

Claude had married Ingrid three years after Eloise left his apartment for good, following a courtship of four months' duration. She had gone to their wedding on St Croix in the US Virgin Islands, and at the rehearsal dinner, when a missed connection in Puerto Rico had delayed the arrival of her best friend, Ingrid had spontaneously asked Eloise to read at the service. Eloise paused over the recollection. Ingrid – tanned, blonde, Californian, with a smile of sharp white teeth – had embraced her, holding her tightly and looking at Claude. 'Our wedding's about our future *and* our past,' she had declared, squealing girlishly when Eloise, at a loss for alternatives, had said that she'd love to read, that of course she didn't mind her name not being in the Order of Service.

In the same box as the notebook, beneath a bound copy of Claude's master's thesis, was this Order of Service. Eloise took it out and turned to the page from which someone called Joanne Lampton was meant to have read. The passage Ingrid had selected was from *The Bridge Across Forever*, by Richard Bach. 'A soulmate is someone who has locks that fit our keys, and keys to fit our locks,' Eloise read, smiling at the incongruity of it. That Claude, whose shelves were stocked with the classic texts of Western literature, should have married someone who cherished the notion that 'When we're two balloons, and together our direction is up, chances are we've found the right person' was bizarre; that she should have read these words, with a straight face, at the wedding of a man with whom she had once intended to spend her life, was stranger still.

She took another sip of Scotch and dialled Claude's home in Boston. This, too, resulted in an answer service, but the message gave the cell-phone numbers of both Pasquiers. She tried Claude's once more, which went straight to voicemail; then, repeating the word 'Hello!' once or twice, in an effort to achieve lightness of tone, she dialled Ingrid's.

The younger Mrs Pasquier answered at the second ring. 'Yes?'

'Ingrid! Hello. Eloise McAllister. How *are* you?'

There was a pause; then Ingrid's voice, deeper than she remembered it. 'Hello, Eloise.' She spoke slowly. 'What can I do for you?'

'I was looking for Claude.'

'Were you?'

'Yes. I mean, if he's—'

'Well he's not here. I suggest you try him at the office.'

'I did, but his assistant—'

'I'm sure you'll get him then. Goodbye.'

'Goodbye.' But the line was already dead. *Little bitch*, thought

Eloise; and spontaneously, spurred to candour by Ingrid's hostility, she dialled Claude's cell phone again. Once again she was transferred to his voicemail. 'Claude,' she said, speaking quickly, 'I'm very sorry if you're in the middle of a project, and I'm disturbing you. I'm also very sorry I didn't call you back before I took my mother to South Africa.' She paused, clearing her throat; she could think of nothing else for which he might wish her to apologise. 'I'm trying to contact you because something's come up. Something important, which concerns us both.' Another pause. 'Me more than you,' she added honestly. 'So please call me back.'

Chapter 25

Ten minutes later, half alarmed by what she had done, Eloise rolled out her exercise mat. She did not believe in leaving emotional pleas on people's answer phones and was irritated with herself for ignoring this hard-won wisdom. The temptation of an evening jog, temporarily heightened by the prospect of a conversation with Angélique Pasquier, disintegrated as she contemplated the message she had left on Claude's phone.

She had not exercised in ten days. To punish herself, she extended her first set of stomach crunches to thirty, then to thirty-five; then she fetched the disc of grey metal from beneath her bed, placed it across her breasts and repeated the process. Breathing out to intensify each contraction, she did her best to clear her mind – but the image of Carol's smirk, sure to grow braver as the crisis continued, preoccupied her. What if Claude did not ring? She paused, counted a careful minute and began a third set, thinking how ridiculous it was to be waiting by the phone like an anxious teenager in her fifth decade of life.

As she completed her sixty-eighth stomach crunch, the telephone rang. She got up slowly, catching her breath. If it wasn't Claude, she would not mind. She went into the sitting room, repeating this sternly to herself, and paused with the phone in her hand as her breathing steadied. So successfully had she braced herself against disappointment that when Claude said hello she stumbled over her greeting like a gauche schoolgirl.

'Eloise? Is that you?'

'Yes! Hello, Claude.'

'You don't sound like yourself. Are you all right?'

'Yes, thank you. Thank you for calling back.'

'I am sorry I did not do so before now. I have – been busy.'

'Is everything all right?'

The answer to this was a strangled sob.

'Claude?'

But Claude was in the grip of such passionate tears that speech was impossible. Eloise had known him to cry this hysterically only twice before: once after visiting his great-aunt Mathilde in hospital during her final illness, and once several days after she had told him of her terminated pregnancy. His tears on this second occasion had succeeded a week of raging that had, effectively, ended their relationship. Now they drew from her an unexpected tenderness. 'What's wrong?' she asked gently.

'Ing – Ingrid has left me.' The confession prompted a further burst of violent sobs that took several minutes to abate. 'She threw me out a month ago. I tried to call you. I wanted some advice what to do.' Claude's English, usually flawless, lapsed occasionally in this way. Eloise had found such slips delicious in the days when she had loved him. 'She has kept the boys with her.' He spoke jaggedly, between caught breaths. 'She is taking them to her parents in St Croix for the summer. I have seen them only twice. Jean-Jacques has started wetting his bed, at twelve years old.'

'I'm so sorry, Claude.'

'It is killing me, Eloise.'

'Did she give a reason?'

'Apparently I am too obsessed in my work. She says I do not love her, that I stay with her only for the children's sake.'

'And is that true?'

There was silence. Eloise perceived that she had overstepped an invisible boundary; it was, after all, none of her business whom Claude loved, or how he loved them.

'I do not know what is true any longer,' he said at last. 'But I know that I cannot live without my boys.'

'Surely you won't have to.'

'She is being decent, and we do not wish to fight. Every second weekend, I can see them. But what is that?' Claude cleared his throat, as though against further tears, and spoke more levelly. 'You said something had happened? Concerning us?'

Eloise saw now that she had been grandiose to presume that Claude's protracted silence involved her. Understanding its cause, she did not wish to seem self-interested by launching immediately into her

161

professional anxieties, so she said, simply: 'I read the piece in *Science*. I was worried about you.'

'What piece in *Science*?'

'The one by Regan et al. of the LLNL.'

'Oh him. What does he say?'

'That osmium tetroxide's too toxic for industrial use. That all options for an industrial alloy have been exhausted.'

'I knew as a student that osmium tetroxide was toxic.' Claude clicked his tongue and the sound summoned his face: brows drawn decisively, as though by bold strokes of an artist's charcoal; lashes long and curled; neck tilted. She had found his intolerance for stupidity first terrifying, then exhilarating, finally infuriating. 'The only hope is the bonding of osmium and carbon.'

Eloise stood up and went to her desk, her pulse quickening. 'Is that right?' Above the word 'HOUNSLOW' she wrote: *Toxicity of Osmium Tetrox. no news. Direction of research: Os and C.* 'So the piece in *Science* has no real bearing on your research?'

'None at all. And unless he's done several million separate experiments, Regan's in no position to say all options have been exhausted.'

'Excellent.' She breathed deeply. 'So when will you be finished?'

'Hard to tell.'

'You said you were close to a breakthrough.'

'I did?'

'The last time you spoke to my mother.'

There was a pause; then Claude started to chuckle. 'Oh, *that*. Yes, I remember.'

'So?'

'So no luck yet.'

The cream carpet beneath Eloise's feet began to sway. 'But you've got all those people working on it.' She thought of the grey concrete dreamscape in which MaxiTech's research facility was housed. Claude had shown her his fiefdom with great pride during the World Metals Fair the year before. 'You introduced them to me.'

'Everyone who joins my lab has to spend six months working on osmium. It's one of the ways I evaluate their practical skills. We'll get there eventually.'

'This isn't funny, Claude.'

'I'm not being funny, Eloise.'

'But you told me you were close to a breakthrough.' Eloise was shaking now.

'We might be.'

'You said you *were*.'

'I didn't want to disappoint your mother.'

This is not happening, it cannot be happening. 'But you told me, too.'

'I didn't want Joan to think I'd been humouring her.'

'So you just lied?'

Claude caught something of her suppressed fury, still not understanding it. 'It was a kindness, not a lie,' he said gently. 'I wanted her to think she'd live to see it.'

'But I believed you.'

'A few more months, a few more years. What difference does it make?'

'I thought you were giving me a tip. I acted on it.'

'In what way?'

'I mean, I *invested* in it. In osmium.'

'But I never told you to.'

This, it occurred to Eloise, was true, and a hot flush began to spread outwards from the core of her being.

'How much did you put in?'

'A hundred and thirty million dollars.'

'*What?*' Now it was Claude's turn to be astonished.

'I've got $130 million worth of osmium sitting in a warehouse in Latvia, waiting for you to change the world.'

'You're joking.'

'How could you lie to me?'

'I did not *lie* to you, Eloise.'

'You told me a lie.'

'It was a kindness to your mother.'

'You always said you hated dishonesty.'

There was silence. Then Claude said, very deliberately, 'I was never as good at it as you.'

Eloise had been at this crossroads before and knew that further progress down the path towards mutual recrimination would have destructive consequences. Claude, so apparently controlled to those who did not know him, had no self-restraint when lost in a rage. She took a deep breath, drawing back from the point of no return. 'I just want to be clear,' she said, 'that you have no definite hopes of a breakthrough.'

'It's a question of trying every possibility. One of them will work.'

'But that could take years.'

'Maybe.'

'I see.'

There was silence. Eloise could hear Claude's breathing; it reminded her, suddenly, of his body in bed, heavy with sleep, of the way he slept curled up, with his mouth open.

'I'm sorry,' he said at last.

'So am I.'

'You should have told me what you were doing. I would have stopped you.'

'Yes.'

Another silence followed, in some subtle way gentler than the preceding one. 'Is it very bad, the situation you are in?' asked Claude.

'Yes.'

'I see.'

'We've got over a quarter of the fund in osmium. The value's tanking after that piece in *Science*.'

'Don't bother about Regan. He's a third-rate—'

'If some of our major investors weren't tied to lock-in clauses, we'd probably be out of business already.'

'I see.'

There did not seem to be anything more that could usefully be added. Eloise, who had long cultivated the ability to counterfeit calm, employed it now. 'I'm so sorry about Ingrid,' she said, more briskly.

'Thank you. It is something to know you care.'

'Yes, I do.'

Claude hesitated. 'When you said you wanted to talk about us, I thought— You said something important had come up, that concerned us both. I didn't think you were talking about osmium.'

'Well, I was.'

'Yes.'

Further silence ensued. It became clear to Eloise that she could not maintain her equilibrium much longer. 'I'd better go, Claude. Thank you for calling back.'

'I am coming to England at the end of August. MaxiTech is having a conference in London. Perhaps we could see each other?'

'Yes.'

'It would be good to see you.'

'And you.'

'If there's anything— I mean, if I can help in any way in the meantime.'

'Short of inventing a widely applicable industrial use for osmium, or finding $130 million, there's not a lot you can do.'

'I'm sure everything will work out. It always does for you.'

'Thank you. I'd really better go now.' The world was tipping dangerously. 'We'll talk soon.'

'Goodb—'

But the rest of Claude's farewell was drowned by the roaring of blood in Eloise's head.

Chapter 26

Joan rationed her grandmother's journal carefully through her first two weeks at The Albany. It was a talisman, she felt, against the despair that threatened to overwhelm her; a link with a past far harsher and more brutal than her present. When Nurse Fleur helped her out of bed each morning, she steeled herself against the indignity with the thought, somehow sanctioned by the appearance of Gertruida's black dress in her closet, that an important task remained for her. She ate her grapefruit, accordingly, with scrupulous neatness and carefully washed her hands before slipping on the white gloves she had stolen from the museum and removing the calfskin notebook from its cardboard folder. Sometimes she studied it, with careful absorption; on other days, she merely sat with it, absorbing its complex smell and paying silent tribute to the horrors it contained.

In this way, she read Gertruida's account of 1902 and learned what a comfort her own mother had been in the aftermath of Hannie's death. She read the passage recounting the devastating surrender of the Boer forces and followed her grandmother through the chaos of the war's end, the slow dismantling of the concentration camps and the return of their occupants to the blackened remains of their farms.

On the morning of Eloise's conversation with Claude, Joan sat down at her desk in sombre spirits, resolved to finish what she had begun. She closed her eyes, bending painfully over the cardboard folder, and asked her grandmother to forgive her for marrying an Englishman so readily. She thought of her mother's reticence, of her refusal to discuss the events of her childhood. Had she known them, Joan felt, she might have had a very different sort of life.

It is inconceivable, and not to be described Gertruida had written, her neat letters quivering with feeling, what it is to return to one's home to find it charred and in ruins, having nothing, literally *nothing* in the way of money or possessions to fall back upon.

I shall never forget the sight that awaited us when we reached the top of the first hill and looked at the valley below. Where the farm had been was field upon field on which no crops grew, for no one had planted fresh seed or seen to any land duties in all the time we had been away. As we came closer we found the bones of many animals that had been destroyed on that terrible day when we, too, were taken from all we knew.

As for the house – Cecilia did her best to calm me, but I would not be prevented from learning the worst. The walls were still standing, though burned and black. The roof was gone, and inside among the rubble, which comprised books, broken china, bricks, glass, quite anything that the British and the Kaffirs after them had thought unfit for salvage, was clear evidence that the place had had other uses during our absence. There were empty beer bottles on the ground, and the ashes of a recent fire. None of my children's clothes or dolls remained, and though we searched we could find nothing to remind ourselves of the dear ones whom God in His wisdom had taken from us.

'Strength comes as you need it,' said Cecilia to me, but on this occasion it did not. We had been careful, in the camp, to preserve our dignity and bearing in the presence of the English. Now, among my own kind, I gave way to my grief and begged God through my tears to bring back to me those I loved and had lost.

It was then, like a miracle, that Elsie was returned to me. She had seen us from the Kaffir kraal and was soon upon us, hugging us to her and asking after her brothers and sisters. She was almost a woman now, though terribly thin. We learned that she had been released from the Kaffir camp some time before, and had found shelter with her uncle Andries, our faithful servant. He alone, of all the men who once served us, remained loyal.

We spent that night, and many others, in the huts of the Kaffir kraal, more easily protected from the elements than we would have been in one of the windowless farm buildings. To think! That we, who had once owned some 2,000 sheep, should think it the height of luxury to sleep in a Kaffir kraal! But we did, and we were grateful to Elsie and Andries, who had preserved for us our family Bible and other goods in the trench behind the stables in which we had buried them. We subsisted on the cow's milk and some mielies that Andries had sowed on a small plot behind the ruined house.

It was then, truly, that I tasted despair. For I had no hope for the future, few possessions and no means to get more, no news of my husband and son. One day, walking in the stables, I came upon Hannie's organ, which Andries had wrapped in blankets and put in a dry place, to await our return. Oh, the tears a mother sheds! It seemed to me that Hannie sat at it still, with her hands on the keys, turning her gentle eyes upon me.

My only relic of my dearest firstborn girl, after the destruction of our home and possessions, was a letter she wrote to her former teacher, Miss Kleinhans, on the occasion of her eighteenth birthday. It was refused by the English censors and remains in my possession. I record it here, in part, so that it may be known what promise and hope was snatched from her by this terrible and needless war:

It is with something of a shock that I realise I am really and truly eighteen years already! It is so very hard to understand why I should have been so completely checked in the course of my studies just when it was all growing so immensely interesting. However, I have not at all given up hope yet. When the war is over I intend to become what you always thought I might be, dear Miss Kleinhans – a Writer of Fiction.

Were it not for my dear Cecilia, and the hope that I might one day see my husband and son again, I think I could have died of grief. I began to chide myself for failing in my duty to my children, lamenting bitterly that I had given up Naomi and Hannie to the English doctors. I remembered all that was whispered in the camp about the hospital, and what took place within its canvas walls. I felt that I should have given up my own life to preserve my dear ones from such barbarity in death.

I made applications to the authorities in Bloemfontein, for news of my husband, and learned that he had been captured and sent to Ceylon as a prisoner. The day he returned to the farm I hardly recognised him, nor the manly gentleman by his side, my own Jacobus, now fully grown. It was a hard duty to tell Martinus of the deaths of our four children, though he had expected the ruin of his forefathers' house, having heard of it from others.

Martinus said to me: 'I used to hear that if you burned a man's house you turned him into a soldier. Now I have seen it all round me, and I know that if you burn a man's house down you turn a coward into a hero.' Never have I heard such rage! Martinus wished to fight on and kill every English person he could find in the vicinity, but Jacobus and I dissuaded him with the help of our neighbours.

I make this testimonial, under oath, on the third day of October, nineteen hundred and three. As yet, we still have no home to call our own. Martinus and Jacobus have repaired the stable and begun to tend to the farm again. We live where our cattle once did, as we begin with God's help to build a new house at some distance from the first.

I must end by stating my gratitude to those English who condemned the actions of their compatriots. In our hours of darkness it gave us heart to know that there were those who cared for us and sought improvements in the conditions that faced us. The example of Miss Emily Hobhouse, who published to the world the true sufferings of the women and children of South Africa, is well known. It is thanks to her that some knew the truth, and acted on their knowledge.

I end this account by adding my voice to that of Miss Hobhouse, joining with her in my plea that the suffering of myself and other women, and of our dear little babies, should not be in vain. Let it be remembered what terrible things were done, that they may not be repeated – so that the very name 'Concentration Camp' may perish, because it has no meaning.

Gertruida van Vuuren,
Van Vuuren's Drift
Orange River Colony
This 3rd day of October, 1903

Chapter 27

Eloise's first thought, which made her want to be violently ill, was that she had to tell her colleagues the truth. Holding the idea in her head like a hot stone, heavy and scorching, she went to the window and drank in deep breaths of traffic-fumed air. She owed them honesty, at least – owed Patrick, especially, because it was his business, his life's work, that her own dare-devilry had risked. She picked up the telephone, but the impossibility even of phrasing an admission as dreadful as the one she had to make stopped her. A hot flush rippled over her skin, followed by another, then another – as though a volcano, deep within her, was spewing forth its lava at intervals of twenty seconds or so.

She had never felt so hot.

She leaned her face against the window pane, cooling it, then abruptly pulled away and went into her bathroom. She took off her clothes and turned the shower to COLD, watching the water surge and splash; then she stepped under the rose, gasping, forcing herself to stand beneath it as she counted slowly to thirty, then forty.

When she emerged, the scale of the catastrophe struck with renewed force and she stood motionless, naked and dripping, in the grip of a primal emotion: the need to blame someone. Claude had lied to her, brazenly. He had purposefully sabotaged her life – delayed vengeance, perhaps, for the circumstances of their parting, for the fact that she had driven him into the arms of a dumb little bitch who had now deserted him. She would get on a plane, go to Boston and have it out with him – for even now she had the capacity to wound him, to cast their past in a light that robbed him of all dignity. She rubbed her back savagely with a towel, determinedly ignoring a quieter truth: that Claude had not advised her to buy osmium; that he had not, in fact, known anything of her decision to do so.

She struggled against this unanswerable fact, but the part of her mind that provided an internal commentary on what she did, the insulated chamber in which Eloise often felt she truly existed, reminded her that Claude's previous tips had been given explicitly, without the possibility of misunderstanding or error. She dried her hair and went into her bedroom, where she began fanning herself with a copy of the *New Yorker*. How was she going to tell Patrick?

This question alone was enough to provoke another hot flush, which singed its way across her skin. A taste in her mouth reminded her, with sudden vividness, of childhood hours spent waiting outside her father's workshop while George was chastised for laziness or inattention. Once or twice she, too, had been summoned to these punitive rituals and they had left a lasting impression. No event since them had inspired the dread she felt now. Under its influence, her desire to blame someone abated and was replaced by a bitter self-questioning. She was chaotic about domestic arrangements, about business never; how could she justify having acted so confidently on a single phone call?

The likelihood of being subjected to an interrogation along these lines from Patrick provoked a wave of nausea that took several uncomfortable minutes to subside. He did not know that Claude Pasquier was anything more to her than one of several useful contacts scattered across the world's largest metallurgical firms. How could she possibly explain their history now, or the reasons she had for trusting him? She could not convey Claude's solidity, his unflagging constancy – or the circumstances of his falsely optimistic declaration to Joan.

Without warning, she began to cry. This was something Eloise had not done for many years, and once she had begun she found she could not stop. She sat on the edge of her bed, gulping for air as strange childlike yelps, almost animal in their intensity, emanated from within her. She saw herself, abruptly, the last time she had sobbed so helplessly: on a chilly afternoon in her late twenties, hunched at the end of the sofa in Claude's many-eaved apartment, two days before the final collapse of their life together. And with this vision came another; one she usually kept locked and unvisited, as far from her conscious mind as possible: the look in Claude's eyes as she told him a lie he did not believe.

She thought of her mother, of the tireless way she had always sought to make good her children's mistakes; but this only forced the realisation, too long postponed, that Joan was too old to help her now; that this crisis must be stringently kept from her. All she had to guide her was her mother's example, which pointed unfailingly but impossibly towards confession, apology and the making of amends.

She stood up slowly and moved towards the bathroom for tissues. She would have to tell Patrick that MaxiTech had decided, for reasons of its own, to abandon its osmium project within sight of its final goal. *Now why would it do that?* asked her inner voice, assuming its habitual attitude of inquisitorial hostility. She could find, for the moment, no answer more plausible than the generic catch-all that executives, like politicians, routinely act against their own long-term interests. She did not think this would wash with Patrick. *Think clearly, Eloise.* She went to the phone and picked it up, then put it down. She was in control of the information she possessed only until she shared it, and knowing this she hesitated.

Eloise had learned, through many crises, that there are always alternatives in life; that the trick is simply to see them. This, in fact, had been one of Claude's favourite maxims. She moved away from the telephone, resolving against rash action, and went into her kitchen, where she poured herself a second, larger Scotch. Outside, the light had slipped away and the street was quieter. Breathing deeply, she sat down on the kitchen floor, closed her eyes, and stretched her arms above her head. *The only enemy is panic.* She thought of other crises she had faced and survived: her over-extension on ruthenium; the collapse of iridium in the early 1990s. Neither of these had remotely approached the severity of her current position, and she brushed them aside. *Order your mind, Eloise; arrange the facts.* She attempted to do so, beginning with the most ominous admission of all: that a breakthrough in osmium was no more likely now than it ever had been, that the super-hard substance she had championed so fervently to her colleagues remained a pipe dream. She regulated her breathing as she followed the consequences of this unfortunate truth: that sooner or later, investors would learn of Derby Capital's overexposure and withdraw their funds.

Her stomach convulsed, momentarily. *Focus, Eloise. The only enemy is panic.* When that happened, what would follow? She preferred not to dwell on Patrick's immediate, dizzying rage and passed instead to the next inevitable consequence: the loss of her job, the incineration of her reputation. As calmly as she could, she imagined life without employment or prospects, and when she began to feel faint she stood up and went into the living room. Its discreetly expensive furniture confronted her sullenly, but she dismissed its reproach. She had been broke before; she didn't need an apartment this size, or a housekeeper, or, in fact, most of the irrelevant luxuries she currently possessed. *The only enemy is panic.* She concentrated on her breathing as she went into the hall, but a pale-blue envelope on the half-moon table by the door made her heart race. It was, she knew, a bill from The Albany. She opened it and scanned a pale-blue page, finding at the bottom a figure so decorously astronomical – Joan had been there barely a month! – that another hot flush was unleashed, another flurry of tears.

How could she possibly cope with Joan, with no money? It was this question that inspired the first, fine tremors of panic. She had signed a year's lease on the 'Prestige Apartment' she now occupied, which only Joan's death could break without a sizeable penalty; and even the price of a 'Standard Single' was far more than George would pay. The idea of Joan at the mercy of her negligent son as she grew older and frailer, more than ever in need of the best possible care, was unbearable. Eloise had no illusions that her brother would stump up the kind of cash needed to keep their mother at a first-tier geriatric facility like The Albany. He would put her somewhere cheaper, like that place with the concrete garden in Enfield; somewhere Joan would hate. She dropped the envelope onto the floor. She could not possibly let that happen. *Get a grip, Eloise. Think.* She went back into the sitting room, struggling against the claustrophobic certainty, from which a six-figure salary had so far shielded her, that she was completely responsible for another human being. It was a situation she had gone to great lengths to avoid; indeed she accepted her occasional loneliness willingly, as the price she must pay for escaping the trials and strains of Carol's life.

Now she saw that her precautions had been worthless; that though she had accumulated neither a husband nor a child, there was no escaping her obligations to a parent. And this realisation led to another: that the guiltless victim of what she had done would be Joan. Patrick, after all, had sanctioned the bet, the temptations of greed helping him to believe in Claude as she did. As she would probably have to make clear to him, in an encounter she preferred not to imagine, he shared some of the responsibility. That said, he had been siphoning money into offshore tax havens for years; whatever happened to Derby Capital, Patrick would be all right. So would Carol, the smirking cow; she'd find another job.

Her own position was rather more fragile. All her own money was invested in the fund, and this would be lost to her once it went under. She did not even own her flat outright, having preferred to borrow on a mortgage while interest rates were low and the commodity markets boomed. She looked about her, at the extravagant clutter of her apartment. So little of it was salvageable, or convertible into real money.

Her heart began to beat uncomfortably again. *Quantify the problem.* So she went to her desk, an eighteenth-century escritoire for which she had paid well over the catalogue price at a Christie's auction two years before, simply because she liked it. *Look at the numbers.* She took out a calculator, moving almost fearfully, like a competitive child beginning an exam for which she has not prepared. Derby Capital's peak value, on the morning of her trip to South Africa, had been $549 million or thereabouts. If osmium stabilised at its historic price of roughly $100/oz some time before Christmas, the fund would be down about $89 million.

She paused, absorbing the figure, her gambler's instincts reviving. Looked at in its simplest form, the problem was this: how to raise $89 million – call it $90 million to be safe – in the next seven months.

She inhaled deeply. This challenge, though far from insignificant, did not inspire terror in her. In a spirit she told herself was merely investigative, she began to consider various possibilities and the constraints of each, her mind turning with relief to the complex game of chance and discernment she spent her working hours playing and by which, using only her wits, she had so far lived very well for twenty years.

Her instinctive preference was for a single spectacular bet, on which everything was staked, but she interrogated this inclination and acknowledged its central flaw: that such a risk could only be taken, in the present *extremis*, if it wasn't a risk at all. A gamble of the size required to extricate Derby Capital from its current predicament could not be based on rumour. Only certain knowledge, which was unlikely to be legally available, would delineate a brave last stand from sheer insanity.

Eloise began to shake as the significance of what she was contemplating came to her. She stood up and moved away from the desk; and her first emotion was shame, weighted with the knowledge that Joan, too, would be ashamed of her. Her inner voice reminded her that she had not been raised a criminal, and as it did so her anxiety over The Albany's bill returned and grew. When it became suffocating, the only way of easing it was to turn again to the unthinkable, which grew more seductive, as though a glimmering, flickering light at the end of a sinuous tunnel.

There was no harm, she told herself, in simply thinking things through. She lay down on the floor, feigning unconcern, and let her mind drift idly over certain salient facts. The first of these, naturally, was the absolute necessity of concealing any further action she might take from Patrick and Carol. How could that be done? As she posed the question, for argument's sake merely, her inner voice refused to be taken in by her careful charade and expressed its horror of what she was contemplating in the freest terms.

She ignored it and pressed on.

Derby Capital's broker sent the tally of the day's trades at 6 p.m. each evening, to be reconciled against the records that she, Patrick and Carol kept of their transactions. This reconciliation, a tedious and painstaking chore, was usually left to Carol, and when she was out of the office Eloise did it. Patrick hated such administrative tasks and avoided them if he could, though he checked the full reconciliation of the company's total asset base carefully. This was performed on the last day of each month, and was one of his obsessions.

Eloise walked into the kitchen and poured herself a third Scotch. There was no way she could hide a significant transaction from Patrick for longer than a calendar month, but there was, perhaps, a way of making a single trade invisible for several weeks – so long as she, not Carol, reconciled the fund's transactions on the day it took place. She drank the Scotch quickly and the parameters of a plan began to form, like a dangerous genie squeezing from its lamp. All she needed was to find a piece of information not widely known; preferably something at odds with current opinion.

What bet might she place?

The question began to sound, siren-like, in her head. Suddenly fearful of it, and of the further horrors it had the power to unleash, she picked up the phone again; but again she put it down. If her gamble worked, Patrick would forgive her everything – because success always bought leniency. If only she could find an outcome sure enough to counter the weight of the risk ... What about some German government data? It always leaked in advance. She considered the possibility, but rejected it. News that others could obtain was useless to her; she needed something no one else could get hold of. Who could she ask?

Eloise did not often call in favours, though she kept a meticulous mental record of those to whom she gave them. She ran through several possibilities, each unsatisfactory in his or her own way. *There are always alternatives. The trick is to see them.* Her mind alighted on Akemi Hirukawa. They had been very friendly once, had almost, but not quite, slept together; and a decade before she had saved him from taking a career-ending short position on a firm whose takeover she was organising at Kleinberger Dresden.

What did he do now? She stood up and went to her computer, where she logged on to her home Bloomberg terminal. She typed 'Hirukawa' into the search box and frowned as his current employer came up: the Japanese Iron and Steel Association. Eloise did not, as a rule, deal in iron ore; that was more Carol's side of the business. She preferred commodities whose values fluctuated daily and did not follow the annual price negotiations between steelmakers and the mining giants that supplied their raw material. She wondered whether this year's iron ore price had been announced, and checked. It had not been. Further elementary research confirmed that a deal was anticipated in late June; that tight supply and booming demand had led the markets to expect a significant increase – as much as forty-five per cent.

She jumped up from her desk, like a child caught in the act of something more serious than mischief. It was true that there were always alternatives; that much she was well on her way to demonstrating. But she could not silence the knowledge of her mother's horrified disapproval; and the irony that she was contemplating such action for Joan's sake alone was not lost on her, and did not ease matters.

She went into her bedroom and stood in front of its floor-length mirror, addressing herself sternly. There was no need for an immediate decision. All she was doing was considering her options, exploring possibilities; nothing more. *Sleep on a thing before you do it.* This had been one of her father's dictums, and she fastened on it now. There was no need to rush into a decision. What she needed was time, and an upbeat presentation to Patrick the next day would buy that. She went into her bathroom and brushed her teeth, telling herself that she had done enough thinking for one night; that in any case a reassuring lie to her boss would not commit her irrevocably to any course of action.

She had, after all, seven months to find a way of telling him the truth.

Chapter 28

The next few weeks were among the most miserable of Joan's life. She spent them – or as much of them as she could – in bed, her fire-retardant duvet pulled up close under her chin, and did her best to sound cheerful during Eloise's daily telephone call. She did not show her daughter her great-grandmother's journal. Having done her best to instil in her offspring a respect for other people's property, she did not wish to confess to a theft at this late stage of life, and the fact that Eloise had made no real effort to reclaim the griffin chandelier from its resting place in Hounslow did not inspire further confidences. Joan had never known her daughter so self-absorbed; and unaware of the causes of her abstraction, she read it instead as evidence of a latent selfishness that spoke eloquently of maternal failure.

Among the many topics mother and daughter avoided was the subject of George, on whose answer machine Eloise had left several exasperated messages, and neither of them mentioned the fact that he had not contacted Joan since her return from Bloemfontein. 'I gather he's away on business,' was all Eloise said. 'He'll get in touch as soon as he's back.'

'Yes, darling, of course he will.'

In an effort to resist the temptations of resentment, Joan told herself that it was her own fault: she had not prepared adequately for the abrupt removal of self-determination that institutional life entailed. Indeed, she had given far too little thought to the reality of what she would encounter at The Albany – and the worst of it, in some ways, was how little she had to object to. She had to admit that the home was admirably run. It was, indeed, as its brochure had promised, staffed by 'dedicated professionals' who executed their duties fault-lessly. There was no cruelty, no squalor, nothing in fact that gave her any grounds to feel sorry for herself – and this meant that her self-pity was painfully tinged with the guilt it inspired.

The newspapers Nurse Fleur brought to her room each morning contained reports of suffering on a far more monumental scale than anything Joan had to endure. She read every day of horrors beyond her imaginings – of suicide bombers and women whose husbands and sons were taken from their homes in the dead of night, never to be returned. She looked at pictures of bombed buildings and screaming children and read of politicians who advocated the use of 'stress techniques' that amounted, frankly, to torture. What a terrible century the Anglo-Boer War had ushered in, she thought; how little attention had been paid to its lessons.

This sad fact did nothing to lift her spirits, which grew heavier with each passing day. At Wilsmore Street she had grown accustomed to ordering her life as she wished, a freedom she had taken for granted until it was too late. The Albany's nurses, used to confused and sometimes violent patients, wore their cheeriness like battle armour; they straightened her sheets and massaged her limbs and ignored her repeated requests to be allowed to stay in bed with impervious solicitude.

Offended by these limitations, the pedals abruptly ceased their visits, and on more than one occasion she woke to find herself in the small, dark bedroom she had occupied in the listless months after Eloise's birth, while Frank and his mother slept on the floor above. If only she had been stronger then! Perhaps Astrid would never have moved in.

'It's quite normal to feel a little out of sorts at the beginning,' said Sister Karen. 'If it goes on much longer, we'll ask the doctor what she can do about a spot of medication. There's a marvellous little pill that will make you feel right as rain.'

But Joan had had sufficient experience of marvellous little pills to be wary of them. She ignored the occasional appearance of the white porcelain box, painted with peonies, in which she had once stored her mother-in-law's orange painkillers, and observed with horror the reactions of her fellow inmates to the medication distributed with their morning tea. She had no wish to share their drugged docility – or even, she realised, to befriend those whose brains were in better shape than their decaying bodies. She came to dread Sylvia's cheerful visits. There was a desperate quality to her friendliness that seemed a stark indication of Joan's own social prospects, and she did not honour her promise to join a library outing.

'The problem with friendships in here,' remarked Sylvia one morning, as they waited for the aerobics class to begin, 'is that you're just getting started when the other person dies.'

Eloise spent Sunday afternoons with her mother; but these visits, marred for each of them by the strain of concealing their troubles from one another, were not a success. May ended; June began and continued. It seemed to Joan that time had never passed so slowly. Was it for this that she had lived so long?

Standing in the Recreation Lounge (Non-Smokers) one evening, waving Eloise goodbye, she remembered with something like wonder how badly she had yearned, years ago, for a child. It seemed hard to believe that that baby, longed for with such intensity, was now getting into a taxi and leaving her behind in this cheerless place. She thought sadly of the three miscarriages that had preceded Eloise's birth and overshadowed her twenties. It was these, she felt, that had so unbearably heightened her desire for children.

She closed her eyes, sifting her recollections for stable memories. It was so difficult to separate what one had really felt from the cosmetic touch-ups of subsequent experience. She had not, she was sure, thought much about children before meeting Frank. Certainly she had been sceptical of the lengthy sermonising of the vicar who married them, and of his stern insistence that the true purpose of Holy Matrimony was the continuance of the race. She remembered that: standing in the cold stone chapel of the little church in Clapham, wearing the fussy white dress (Astrid's choice) that she had never liked, listening to the priest's thunderous exhortations and doubting them. She had felt sure that God's purpose was wider – in the true sense of the word, *holier* – than simple reproduction, and had embarked on married life with a sense of thrilling adventure, inspired by the prospect of lifelong intimacy with another human being. It was for this, not for any future children, that she had sacrificed her musical career with a haste that seemed quite foolish to her now.

Watching Eloise's taxi turn the corner of Kingsley Gardens, Joan thought wistfully of that early excitement. With a candour provoked, in some mysterious way, by the ugly pine armchairs and beige paint of the Recreation Lounge (Non-Smokers), she admitted that it had not lasted long. On what slender grounds she and Frank had bound themselves to each other! She thought of his boyish face, and of all that it had masked. What folly, to marry on the strength of five months' acquaintance; and yet— Everyone had been in such a hurry after the war. No one had stopped to think.

She looked at the painted woman above her who impersonated the seasons so wistfully. There was no point in regretting the unalterable past. Besides which, Frank had taught her a truth for which others strive a lifetime: that a person's happiness is directly proportional to the discrepancy between their expectations of life and the reality of their situation. Things had been easier once she had accepted the unchangeable fact that her husband would never be otherwise than as he was. This was an insight that could help her now, she felt; and yet she could not quite reconcile herself to expecting from life only the bland, twilit surreality of a nursing home.

If only the pedals would return!

She left the window and went painfully to her room. All afternoon, as she listened to Eloise's bright babble, she had been distracted by a pair of doll's shoes with shiny buckles hovering an inch or two above the desk. Perhaps they would lead her to the pedals? But as she opened her door she saw that they had vanished; and in their place, unsettling to behold, was a sawn-off Golden Syrup tin full of what her grandmother had called 'night soil'. How very unpleasant. She turned away from it, filling a plastic vase for the tulips Eloise had brought her, and looked at her watch. It was 6 p.m. Sister Karen would soon be sending someone up to enquire why she was not at dinner.

Ignoring the improvised receptacle of effluent, she arranged the flowers and set the vase on the bookshelf, looking sadly at the pine armchair in the corner, so indistinguishable from all the others in the building. The homogeneity of the modern world, the mass-produced sameness of things, had infiltrated her daily life again – and without the pedals she was powerless to resist it.

She went to the window. It was still bright outside and a young couple was strolling contentedly in the road beneath her window. She could not get used to eating this early. The idea of the dining room, with its panels of fluorescent light and plastic tablecloths, depressed her. So did the thought of Sylvia, who would demand her attention as she rambled through an account of her latest operation, or gleefully retold the most recent excesses of a fellow resident in the advanced stages of dementia.

Having nothing better to do, Joan began to rearrange her photographs. She put Frank's picture on the desk and moved the snap of Eloise reciting Shakespeare to the top shelf of the bookcase, beside the flowers. She picked up the photograph of George, carefree and handsome on a beach; and as she wiped a speck of dust from its frame, something happened to her that had not happened for twenty or thirty years.

She lost her temper.

She lost it euphorically. From deep within her, from a place too long unvisited, a piece of her truest self exploded from the containing bonds of civility and self-restraint. It coursed through her, tearing her senses with exhilarating force and obliterating the tin of night soil. 'I will *not* go down to dinner,' she said aloud, her reflection in the window glass standing tall, eyes flashing. 'I will *not* attend another aerobics class. I will *not*' – she cast her eye around the splendidly functional room – 'stand this ghastly furniture a moment longer.'

She put the photograph down and added ten hours to six o'clock on her fingers. It was 4 a.m. in Sydney.

Picking up the telephone on her desk, she pressed '9' for an outside line and dialled George's number. The phone rang five times and switched to a machine on which his new wife's voice – a *hideous* voice, thought Joan – recited their telephone number and said that George and Lynda weren't available. She dialled again. And again. On the fourth attempt, a sleepy female answered and Joan, without greeting her, demanded to speak to her son.

'But he's sleeping, love,' said Lynda, her irritation tempered with relief that she didn't have to care for this senile old biddy on the other side of the world. 'It's 4 a.m. here.'

'Then wake him up.'

Joan heard sheets rustling and a throaty curse. Then George's voice, an octave lower than usual, came on the line.

'Mum? What's wrong?'

'After you were born,' she began, speaking fluently and without preamble, 'you didn't sleep through the night for four years. For the first eighteen months of your life, I never had more than an hour of uninterrupted rest. When you finally learned to go to sleep by yourself, you wet the bed continually. Then you would come into our bed and wake us up. On several occasions, you wet that too.'

'Mum? Is that you?'

'Yes it is me, George. When you went to school, your uniform stretched to more than sixty individual items of clothing. I stitched a name tape onto every one of them. I marked your pencils and their case, your ruler and your scissors. I filled your lunch box every morning and made sure you were never late for a single one of your sports clubs.'

'It's the middle of the night here.'

'What is eight times six?'

'What?'

'It is forty-eight, George. It is entirely due to me that you ever passed your Maths O level and when you were almost expelled for drinking behind the music schools it was only thanks to my intervention that the headmaster agreed to keep you on. I spent countless afternoons on cold sports fields, watching you play rugby. When you brought your noisy, ungrateful friends to stay in the holidays I cooked for them and washed for them and drove you all to the cinema and never once complained when I did not receive a single thank-you letter. I told you about sex and encouraged you to feel at ease around girls. When you got married I organised your wedding and made the cake. Sandra wanted icing flowers, do you remember? I made each of them by hand – two hundred roses, not counting the foliage – and when you left Sandra I helped her find a flat she could afford and moved her into it and consoled her when you wrote those despicable, self-justifying letters.'

'Hang on—'

'I have not finished. When you took up with your secretary I did not judge you. I continued to love you and care for you and to ignore the worthlessness, the sheer inanity, of the job to which you have devoted yourself.'

'What are you—'

'And then, having cared for you for over forty years, I accepted without complaint the fact that neither of my children wished to care for me in return. I went into the nursing home that Eloise has so thoughtfully arranged for me and where I will spend the remainder of my days. I did not blame you for your unconcern, nor did I once regret my tireless devotion to your well-being. I have accepted your selfishness, perhaps too readily, and I have continued to love you in full knowledge of your numerous and serious flaws. Despite all of which, and though I have been in this home for weeks now, you have never once telephoned to ask how I am, or to see if there is anything you can do to make this experience even a little easier for me to bear.'

'But Mum, I've been—'

'You have been selfish and self-centred and disloyal, George. That's what you have been. And that is what you have *always* been.' Joan paused. 'I am going to put the telephone down now. I have said all I wish to say.'

She replaced the handset in its cradle with a forceful gesture quite out of character in its theatricality. As she did so, there was a rap on the door.

'Dinner time!' called Sister Karen, opening it.

The appearance of this bustling autocrat inflamed Joan still further. 'I am not hungry and I am not coming down to dinner,' she said, with vehemence. 'And next time you knock, please wait for a reply before coming in.'

Chapter 29

'To tell you the truth,' said Sister Karen, with sympathetic candour, 'she's not doing as well as we had hoped. Stage one Alzheimer's can be difficult for family members to detect, particularly if they're' – she paused, as she always did before this part of the conversation – 'burdening themselves with unnecessary guilt. It is usually trained professionals who notice the early signs.' She looked down at the file of Joan's notes on her desk and took out a pen. 'Patients often suffer mild memory lapses – you've observed that, no doubt – and there are subtle personality changes. They forget social courtesies. They withdraw. They can become argumentative, even aggressive.'

At the other end of the telephone, Eloise scanned the small, open-plan offices of Derby Capital in search of somewhere private to have this conversation. 'Could I call you back in one minute?' she asked.

Sister Karen, unused to being interrupted in this way, waited disapprovingly at her desk until Eloise – now on the street, talking from her Blackberry – called back.

'As I was saying,' she went on, 'the changes can be subtle at first. Patients often lose interest in food. Joan, I'm afraid to say, has been unenthusiastic about meals for some weeks now, and the severity of hostility displays is variable. Last night, when I went up to fetch her for dinner, she was verbally aggressive. I understand from your brother that she has been making telephone calls to him at inappropriate hours of the day? That is all very much in keeping with the condition.'

'I see.'

'She seems unwilling to mix with other residents, too. You say she's always been outgoing? Socially extrovert behaviour is one of the first things to decline with Alzheimer's. You mustn't worry yourself if she seems subdued when you see her.'

'She says', said Eloise, 'that she wants her old things back.'

'That is not unusual, either. Patients often find it difficult to under-stand and engage with the rules of their new environment. It can be disorienting for them, at first.'

'Would it be possible for her to have at least a few of her possessions with her?'

There was a pause. Sister Karen was used to this question and knew that it must be met with firmness. 'I'm afraid not. We have strict fire policies that govern our fixtures and furnishings.'

'She wouldn't need to have many things. I can arrange for—'

'We have to put the health and safety of our residents first.'

'I quite understand that. But there are firms that specialise in fire-resistant coatings for wood and fabrics.' Since receiving her mother's hysterical telephone call the previous evening, Eloise had done some research. 'I would not think of asking you to have anything at The Albany that wasn't professionally treated.'

The conversation continued in this manner for some minutes. Sister Karen, accustomed to meek acceptance from the guilt-ridden families of her elderly patients, was not prepared for the politely implacable insistence of someone like Eloise. She parried her requests with increas-ing tetchiness, unable to express her most pertinent objection to the restoration of Joan's furniture: that she had a way of doing things at The Albany, and that there could not be one rule for one patient, another for everyone else. 'It would be very expensive,' she said at last.

'That's not a problem. I spoke to my brother last night. For once he's prepared to foot a bill.'

'Of course we do want our residents to feel as "at home" as possible.'

'I'm sure it will make her feel a great deal better.'

There was a pause. 'Very well.' Sister Karen conceded defeat in the tone of one who might say, '*Après ça, le déluge.*' She cleared her throat. 'But it is important to face facts, too. By the time your mother has reached stage two, she will most likely not be able to recognise her own furniture any longer. She will become confused about where she is, which will make her suspicious, argumentative, untidy and agitated. She will begin to forget acquired routines—'

'But surely that's a long way off,' interrupted Eloise. 'I was in South Africa with her six weeks ago. She seemed every inch her usual self.'

'Not forgetful at all?'

'No. Although— Now that you ask, she did intend to bring a

photograph with her on the trip. She forgot that, I suppose.'

'And did she do anything out of the ordinary?'

'No.' Eloise considered a moment. 'At least, she did buy someone a minibus.'

'A minibus?'

'Yes.'

'How long had she known this person?'

'About a week.'

'I see.' Sister Karen sniffed, significantly, and made a note in Joan's patient file. 'Could there have been any coercion involved? Alzheimer's patients are particularly at risk from unscrupulous individuals.'

Eloise thought of the grinning Simbongile. 'I doubt it.'

Sister Karen, in command of herself once more after her climb-down in the matter of Joan's furniture, resumed the sympathetic tone she reserved for the breaking of sad news. 'It can be difficult for family members to accept their loved one's ... diminished capacity. That's why it does her such good being here, with us. We have the staff and resources to respond to the situation as it develops.'

It took Eloise several minutes to compose herself before her return to the office, and she walked up and down St James's with the Nursing Manager's deft assurances ringing in her head. *We have the staff and resources to respond to the situation as it develops.* Where the fuck was George? Lying on a beach in fucking Sydney, fondling his new wife's plastic tits. The thought enraged her, as did the short and meaningless email she had received from him the day before. *Send mum my love. Tell her I think of her a lot. Hope she got my flowers.* What use were flowers when there were bills to be paid?

In the lobby of Derby Capital's building, she encountered Carol hurrying from the lift. 'Twins' sports day!' she called, in the cheery register in which most of their interactions were conducted. 'Ghastly. I was never any good at three-legged races.'

'Good luck!' Eloise smiled encouragingly. 'You'll be brilliant.'

'See you tomorrow!'

As Carol disappeared through the glass doors and into the crowds on the street, it occurred to Eloise that they had just had their longest personal conversation in several weeks, and her stomach seized again with dread. Carol had children to support, and a hopeless husband. When Derby Capital failed, her job would go and her kids would—

But she could not pursue this train of thought. Instead, she pushed the button for the lift and went back upstairs. On her desk, her Bloomberg monitor proclaimed the date as 14 June; behind it, a televised backdrop of trundling tanks heightened the apocalyptic mood, for osmium was now trading at $94.31/oz and falling daily, leaving the firm with losses in excess of $90 million.

Eloise had woken early in the morning after her conversation with Claude three weeks before, and spent several further hours tussling with her conscience in the darkness. Then, having decided to lie, she had done so convincingly; had told Patrick and Carol in their daily meeting that Pasquier remained confident of a breakthrough, that the focus of his research was carbon, not oxygen; that he had known since his student days that osmium tetroxide was toxic. She had seen to her satisfaction that Patrick, in need of reassurance, accepted her sparkling announcement of the good news from MaxiTech with almost touching credulity and that Carol, too, believed her: it was clear from the narrow-eyed fury of her glance.

Watching Patrick now, his head burrowed in a bond-issuer's report, her own persuasive powers alarmed her. *We have the staff and resources to respond to the situation as it develops.* Sister Karen's words, in which limitless expense was so subtly implied, began twisting through her head, and the visual prompt of Carol's empty desk combined with them to produce a violent shaking in her hands. Carol was rarely out of the office; her absence now might represent her only chance in months to handle the daily reconciliation. She glanced at the clock on the wall. It was 10 a.m., which made it 4 p.m. in Tokyo.

'I need a breath of fresh air,' she said lightly to Patrick. 'I won't be long.'

Eloise left the building for the second time that morning in something of a trance. For three weeks she had taken no further steps towards the acquisition of information to which she had no legal entitlement; all she had done, after a protracted routine of self-deception, was to locate Akemi Hirukawa's office number. This she now used, at the corner of St James's and Piccadilly, her heart beating a violent tattoo in her chest as she waited for him to answer.

At length he did so, and when he heard her voice he seemed genuinely pleased. 'Eloise!' Akemi spoke a precisely clipped Oxford English. 'Now this is a pleasure. How have you been?'

She told him that she had been well, that she hoped he had been too; they briefly reminisced and exchanged news of mutual acquaintances, now scattered across the world. Then Eloise asked him what his cell-phone number was, and Akemi, understanding that she did not wish to speak on a taped office line, gave it and went into the street. 'What's really up?' he asked, when she called a second time.

'I'm in serious shit.' It was something of a relief to be able to confide this in another human being.

'Yes? Worse than me that time with CHG-Andium?'

'By an order of magnitude.'

'Wow. That is serious.'

'Yes.'

'How can I help?'

Eloise hesitated, aware that asking for information made it more likely that she would receive it; that receiving it would, in turn, increase the likelihood of her using it. 'You're involved with the talks between Tintarco and Ichimura Steel Corp?'

'Yes. We're moderating them.'

'The market thinks there's going to be a hefty price hike.'

'Maybe.'

'People are talking forty-five to fifty per cent.'

Akemi was silent. 'I see,' he said at last. 'Let me call you back.'

He did so twelve minutes later, so drowned by background noise that she could hardly hear him. 'I'm on a public phone. We can talk more freely,' he shouted.

'The market expects forty-five to fifty per cent.'

'Yes.'

'Is there going to be a big enough differential to be worth betting on?'

'How much do you need to make?'

If the morning's figures were anything to go by, $90 million would no longer be sufficient. 'A hundred million dollars,' she said, keeping her voice level. There was an explosion of crackle on the line. 'Akemi?' She thought she had lost him.

But several seconds later Akemi said, 'You know I could lose my job over this, Eloise.'

'I know.'

'I could also go to jail. So could you.'

'Yes.'

There was silence again, broken only by the crackling connection. *There are always alternatives in life.* A part of Eloise – the moral being, perhaps, whose anxieties she had so duplicitously allayed – now began to hope fervently that Akemi would tell her nothing, and in so doing banish the temptation under which she laboured. But at length he said: 'Okay. I pay my debts and I owe you one. But you've only got one shot. You sure you want to make it this?'

'Yes,' she said.

'Then think higher than fifty-five percent.'

'How much?'

'Probably a lot.'

'How much is a lot?'

'Look. Buy a bunch of calls at fifty-five per cent. You'll be pleasantly surprised.'

'Are you sure about this?'

'What's certainty in life? There're only educated guesses, and better-educated guesses. This is a better-educated guess, but if you're worried try a combination spread. Sell some puts at thirty-five percent. That way, if the increase is anything between thirty-five and fifty-five you won't lose money. And if it's over fifty-five, as I expect, you'll rake it in.'

'You sure it won't be less than thirty-five?'

'As I said, there are only guesses. Obviously you're screwed if Ichimura gets Tintarco to accept only a twenty per cent increase – but you don't make this kind of money without taking a risk.'

'When will they make the announcement?'

'In a couple of weeks. Towards the end of June, I'd say. And now look' – the noise around him increased, as though he was holding the phone away from his ear and looking over his shoulder – 'I've got to go now. Buy a bunch of calls at fifty-five per cent and forget we spoke like this.'

'Thank you, Akemi.'

'No problem. Goodbye.'

She switched off her Blackberry and stifled an urge to fling it into the oncoming traffic. If she were to act at all, her inner voice remarked, she should do so immediately, without further contemplation. She had the information she needed, from as good a source as possible. *The problem could just go away.* Was that sufficient grounds on which to gamble not only her own future, but Patrick's, Carol's, her mother's?

Chapter 30

Joan left The Albany for the first time since her arrival under duress, in helpless thrall to the enthusiasms of Sylvia Fraser – who had insisted she honour her promise to join a library outing. She had gone to bed the night before feeling rather buoyed up, but the endorphins of anger had subsided during sleep and left her fretful and anxious on waking.

George had been such a gentle little boy. She should have protected that gentleness. But instead he had developed his own protections, and she had not intervened to alter them. Was it his fault, or hers, that he had become the man he was? There was no answer to this; nor any to the question of what Eloise would make of her strident demands for furniture and books, of her shrill insistence that she recover the box she had wrapped for her without delay. She leaned heavily on her stick as she descended the wheelchair ramp from the front door, thinking that this was not at all the mood she had envisaged for the passing on of the griffin chandelier.

'This way, ladies!' Sunil appeared from a grey minivan emblazoned with the *TranquilAge*™ logo in gold, and lowered an automated platform for wheelchair access.

The vehicle was not as smart as Simbongile's, thought Joan, noting the absence of a CD player with satisfaction as she took her seat in it. She thought wistfully of her friends in Bloemfontein. Perhaps Eloise would agree to her moving into the Volksraad Hotel permanently? She was sure that the fragrant Mr Engelbrecht would take excellent care of her.

This thought was momentarily cheering, but she acknowledged its impossibility. Moving to the other side of the world would be an unforgivable unkindness to her daughter, who deserved nothing of the sort; she could not contemplate it. Instead she smiled at the three other people who with her and Sylvia formed the totality of the party. One was Katherine Ingelow, the lady with the three-year-old knitting. She was silent, clutching to her chest a plastic bag containing needles and wool as though concerned for its safety. The other two, friends of Sylvia's, were commenting on how unusually warm the weather was for this time of year.

'Isn't it just?' cried Sylvia, patting Joan's leg.

Joan nodded politely, but the thought of entering a conversation of such staggering inanity was unbearable. Apologetically, she told her companions in a hoarse whisper that she had a sore throat this morning and really ought to conserve her voice.

'It's not unusual to get infections when the seasons change,' remarked Sylvia.

The library was two streets away – what a waste of petrol, thought Joan as they arrived – and the journey did not take long. It stood at the end of a neat row of Victorian terraces, an aggressive conglomeration of rain-stained concrete and glass; built in the 1960s on the site of an older building, damaged in the war and now demolished like so much else. She waited her turn patiently as Sunil helped each of them out of the van.

'You will find non-fiction and newspapers on the ground floor,' he said. 'Fiction is upstairs, but there is a lift. It is a little slow, so please be patient. Let me know if I can be of any help.'

The interior of the library was uncompromising in its ugliness. Threadbare carpets, in complex patterns of brown and orange, mutely demanded replacement. Scattered across them, like sepulchres in orange-tinted wood veneer, were free-standing bookshelves that seemed purposely designed to minimise the available space. Making use of her comparative mobility, Joan hurried across the room. Browsing the shelves around her, quite unaware of how fortunate they were to be able to move about so freely, members of the public stretched easily for out-of-reach books. It distressed Joan to think that, to these people, there was nothing to distinguish her from the lady with the everlasting knitting. She began to walk more quickly, using her stick as little as possible, as if to demonstrate her ability to move unaided.

In this way she distanced herself satisfactorily from the group with which she had arrived, but the effort tired her. Coming to a stop before a shelf on the far side of the room, she disguised her shortness of breath as best she could and took her bearings. A large notice informed her

191

that she had reached the section devoted to Geriatric Psychiatry.

Joan paused. The coincidence of this classification was striking, especially to a person alert to the possibilities of supernatural guidance. Looking behind her across the expanse of lurid carpet, she considered the numerous other shelves in front of which she might have stopped but had not. Each bookcase advertised its contents on a poster-sized card that was legible even from a distance. She had bypassed Biography, Parenting, Travel, Gay and Lesbian, and General Reference, she saw. Was there, perhaps, a reason that she had been drawn to a section so topically relevant to her current situation? The question seemed worthy of further investigation. God did not, after all, desert His children in their hours of darkness; she had forgotten that since her return from South Africa.

In a spirit of reverential enquiry, Joan closed her eyes, stood still a moment, and reached for a book. Her fingers connected with a plastic-coated dust jacket, which she took from the shelf with a tingle of anticipation. In her hands was a copy of *The Ageing Brain*, by Dr Lawrence Whalley. Feeling certain that Dr Whalley's work would contain some advice she was meant to find – she did, after all, have an indisputably ageing brain – she opened it at random and rested her finger on the page so discovered. To her satisfaction, the nail of her index finger had come to rest beneath the first word of a sentence. She held the volume at arm's length, squinted, and prepared for revelation.

'To be old and sad seems a not unreasonable condition for the last stage of human development', she read.

Perhaps because she had expected so confidently – it was ridiculous, she thought, deflated, how one demanded these little miracles of God – some sort of reassurance or kindly guidance, this gloomy pronouncement seemed spiteful in its patronising candour. Her eyes filled with tears at so brusque an articulation of a private fear. It is so unlike me, she thought, to cry like this all the time. She looked around the blurring room. Several people were standing near her, browsing the shelves; a middle-aged man sat at a nearby table, absorbed in the crossword. She could not bear any of them to witness her silliness; nor could she stand the thought of being comforted by Sylvia, to whom the opportunity would present itself as an irresistible treat.

One of the frustrating things about tears, thought Joan as she struggled for composure, is that the harder one tries to resist them, the more futile resistance becomes. She looked helplessly about her for the Ladies', but the route to that sanctuary was blocked by the attentive Sunil, gently pushing one of his charges in her wheelchair through lines of historical biographies. Where could she go? The panic of entrapment only made self-command more difficult. As sobs welled in her throat, she made her way hastily to the only available refuge and pushed the button for the lift.

It took an unbearably long time to come, and when it finally did its clunking doors opened and closed with agonising slowness. Once inside, Joan's feelings overwhelmed her. She stood in the steel cubicle, a copy of *The Ageing Brain* still in her hands, and cried as softly as she could. How long she cried for she could not afterwards remember, but in those few minutes the loneliness of her situation – abandoned as she was by her children; shunned by the pedals; denied the comforts of the piano by her beastly joints; separated from everyone and everything she held dear – consumed her.

The need for quiet only unleashed more tears. She had not cried like this for fifty years – not since that night in 1954 when her third pregnancy had ended, like the two before it, in a brightly lit hospital room full of sharp steel and grim doctors and blood. So lost was she in her grief that she did not press any of the lift's buttons, and when it began spontaneously to descend the shock of the movement almost unbalanced her. She thought with horror of how she must look and did her best to compose herself and wipe her eyes, but there was no time for the extensive attention her swollen face required. *Walk out of the lift*, she told herself, *as though nothing has happened. Affect nonchalance.* But as the doors opened she found, to her dismay, that her way was blocked by a young man with a large trolley of books. Moving past him, trying to do so with dignity, she barely noticed how ill-lit the hallway was, and it was only when she had proceeded some way down its length and the young man had run after her, calling out something in an American accent that the cavernous basement distorted beyond comprehension, that she finally stopped.

'I'm sorry, ma'am. This floor is closed to the public. You'll have to—' But seeing the state of her, the boy did not finish his sentence. From the depths of her embarrassment, Joan noticed that alarm and sympathy were mixed evenly in his wide blue eyes; and it was this sympathy, coming at a moment of such acute vulnerability, that dissolved the last vestiges of her self-control. She began to cry again, and from the centre of her fragile frame sobs rose up with overpowering force. She felt that she might fall, so unequal was her body to the task of sustaining this violent emotion – in which resentment, despair, and self-recrimination at both competed with each other for anguished prominence.

'I'm – so sorry,' she gasped, breathless as a child diving for pennies who returns to the surface after too long submerged. 'I don't—' But she could not finish this sentence, or do anything more than steady herself against the wall, waiting for the storm to abate.

Then the young man, who until this point had watched her performance with mounting discomfort, did something entirely unexpected.

He hugged her.

Joan felt thin arms around her shoulders, drawing her towards a scratchy pullover that hung loosely from a bony chest. The sweater smelled of trunks and mildew, as though itself discovered in the library's storerooms. The blades of the boy's shoulders poked from his back, but he had strength enough to support her, to hold her steady as her tears first welled, and then – slowly, too slowly – subsided, leaving her feeling curiously empty, but calmer, her nose and eyes streaming.

'Here you go, ma'am,' said the boy, reaching into his pocket and handing her an ink-stained tissue. 'If you'll just wait here a second, I'll get you some more.'

Chapter 31

The office in which Joan's unexpected saviour was being confined for the summer was dingy and ill-lit and smelled strongly of rotting fruit. The room owed its atmosphere of sweetly fetid decay partly to the large number of shrivelling banana skins in its overflowing bin and partly to the total absence of cross-ventilation. As Joan would learn in the weeks that followed, its occupier's diet consisted almost exclusively of bananas, supplemented by coffee and the vitamin pills that were his concession to his mother's worries. A number of mugs, long discarded, littered the table and shelves, the growths within them heightening the room's resemblance to an amateur germ-warfare laboratory.

The boy himself paid no attention to the microbial clutter. He found a grey plastic chair for Joan, who observed him shyly as she dried her eyes with the scratchy, Council-regulation loo paper he fetched for her. She was not quite sure how to begin a conversation after an introduction as unconventional as theirs.

He was tall, his height accentuated by his skinniness, as though a recent growth spurt had taken him by surprise. A thin layer of pale down covered his upper lip – he could not be more than sixteen, Joan decided – and a crescent of small red spots curved angrily across his pale chin. He had long, bony fingers and his hair was cut close to his head. As he leaned down to pick up a tissue that had fallen from her hand, she saw that the word 'Skull' had been painstakingly shaved across his crown, so that its letters glowed scalp-white from their background of black bristles.

'Yeah it's dumb, I know,' he said, catching her eye and indicating his head. 'I'm sort of waiting for it to grow out. My mom said I should shave my hair off and get rid of it that way, but I don't want to look like a cancer patient.' His brow furrowed, anxiously. 'You don't have cancer, do you, ma'am?'

Joan said that no, to the best of her knowledge, she did not have cancer.

'I only meant it as a joke. No offence intended.'

She assured him that she had taken no offence. 'My name's Joan,' she offered, to show that this was true. 'What's yours?'

'Paul Dhanzy, ma'am.'

'And what do you do down here, Paul?'

What Paul Dhanzy did each day, in the room that smelled strongly of bananas, depended on his mood – which the indignity of sequestration in a damp and loveless basement did little to lift. Occasionally, in rare but frenzied bouts of concentration, he worked diligently on his allotted tasks; more regularly, once the Head of Community Services had ticked his attendance sheet, he minimised the computer database on which he was compiling a painstaking catalogue and surfed the web looking at hardcore pornography. These excursions, though compulsively fascinating, were in other ways unsuited to his sensibilities, and over six weeks he had grown thoroughly weary of them. 'I'm cataloguing an artefact collection for the library,' he replied. 'And when that drags a bit, I read.'

'What sort of books?'

'Whatever's on the return trolleys. They don't let me wander round the rest of the library.'

Joan smiled at him. Her best efforts had never persuaded George to pick up a book for pleasure. 'I love reading,' she said, 'and imagining things.'

'Do you, ma'am?' Paul spoke warily, as though he had not for some time met a person who admitted to either of these activities. 'I read when I'm bored.' This was, perhaps, an understatement – for the circumstances of an eccentric early education had introduced Paul to the written word at an unusually young age, and his imagination was stocked with treasures not available to more conventionally raised children.

Paul had witnessed enough eccentric adult behaviour to find nothing unduly strange about encountering a weeping eighty-year-old woman in a basement corridor. He did not ask Joan what was wrong, and when it became clear that he did not intend to do so she began to relax. Really, he was a very considerate young man – though it was high time someone gave him a decent meal and scrubbed him vigorously.

'Would you like tea, ma'am?' Paul's Granny Rose had been an avid tea drinker.

'If it's not too much trouble.'

'Give me a second.'

He washed up two cups in a small corner sink, scrubbing them with careful vigour. There was a little kettle in the room and a jar of powdered whitener; he fetched the water from the basins of the basement bathroom along the corridor.

It was some time since anyone had gone to unpaid trouble for Joan, and she found the sight unexpectedly touching. 'Thank you, dear,' she said, taking the cup from him. 'Now where are you from?'

Paul considered the question. 'England originally, ma'am, but only up to age four. That's when my parents were together. After they separated, I went to live in New York with my grandma Hildy, but I spent vacations in Scotland with my other grandmother, Rose. Then both of them died and my mom remarried. I've been living with her and my stepfather in Texas for four years, but that hasn't worked out recently so now I'm back in England with my father.' Paul's vowel sounds illustrated the transatlantic nature of his upbringing and influences.

'Goodness,' said Joan, 'what a lot of travelling. Where do you go to school?'

'Nowhere, currently. I'm starting a new one in September.'

'I see.' It seemed to Joan that the circumstances of Paul's departure from the United States had been somewhat abrupt. Not imagining that he would wish to confide them to a stranger she asked instead what sort of artefacts he was cataloguing.

'Well, ma'am.' Paul rose from his low plastic chair and opened a door at the far end of the room, from which a smell of dust and damp emanated powerfully. 'One of my dad's friends from Al-Anon is the Head of Community Services. He got me the job here, unpaid, while I wait for school to start. Kind of a punishment, I guess. They've given me all the projects no one else wants.' He disappeared into the further room and switched on the light. 'Like this.'

It was fortunate, thought Joan, that her chair was so close to the desk. The availability of this sturdy support made it far easier than it would otherwise have been to get up, and she crossed unaided to the open door and peered inside. Water oozed through the stone of the far wall and had decorated it in undulating patterns of salt crystals; the three other sides of the tall, rectangular space were obscured by tottering steel bookshelves piled high with cardboard boxes and binders.

'But how do you get to the top shelves?'

Paul pointed to a small stepladder. 'Getting up's not so hard. The problem's the damp in here. Some of the boxes have rotted – and then everything falls out while I'm trying to get it down.' As if to illustrate his point, a large drop of condensation gathered in the centre of the ceiling and fell with an echoing *plop* to the concrete floor.

'How horrid for you. I don't suppose it's much good for the papers, either.'

'They're in kind of a shitty condition – sorry, ma'am. A *poor* condition.'

'What are they?'

'Family records, mainly.'

'Whose?'

'They were called Huntley. The dad started this library, apparently. I mean, gave the money for it to be built, etc., back in the nineteenth century. I guess he was a pretty rich guy.'

'What kind of things are in the archive?'

'Nothing valuable. Just books, letters, business files, family photos. They found it all in the basement of his old house when it was redeveloped. No one's touched it for years.'

'Do show me some.'

For two lonely months Paul had toiled doggedly, if sporadically, in his unvisited basement, and the chance to share his discoveries made him happy. 'Why don't we start with what I've already sorted?' he suggested, giving Joan his arm and leading her out of the storeroom. 'It's drier in the office, anyway.' There was something of the showman in the child, Joan thought; a certain precocity that implied youthful exposure to the elderly. He did not speak like any of the teenage boys whom she encountered on the television. 'Would you like to sit down, ma'am?' asked Paul, solicitously.

Joan hesitated; the admission of this strenuous desire struck her as undignified. 'Thank you, dear,' she said, at last. 'I'm quite all right standing.'

'Okay.' Paul went over to a shelf above the desk and took from it a green plastic folder. 'This is the census. I looked it up first, to help me make sense of things. My plan's to sort the papers by family member, with another category for Huntley's business.' He paused, anxiously. 'Do you think that's a good idea, ma'am?'

'Excellent.'

'The librarian wants me to put everything in chronological order, but I can't face that.' Paul peered at a photocopy of a government form annotated in clerkly copperplate. 'Do you know how a census works, ma'am?'

He was so obviously burning to tell her that Joan said that she did not.

'The census gets done every ten years in this country, but they only release the results a century later. That means the latest one we have access to is for 1901, but that's fine because according to the Land Registry the family built their house in 1893.'

Something in the young man's delivery reminded Joan of Claude. 'How clever you've been,' she said, and watched him colour with pleasure. It was distressing how much delight this simple piece of praise gave the child. 'Did they tell you how to do all that?'

Paul struggled briefly with his conscience, for he wished earnestly to deny all adult help in his venture, and to impress the strange but nice old lady who had wandered into his afternoon. Eventually, however, he said, 'The librarian told me about the census, but I thought of the Land Registry by myself.'

'Well that's very enterprising. Tell me what you've found out.'

He brought the form over and crouched eagerly beside her chair. 'On the night of April 5, 1901, the following people are listed as being resident. Gordon Earnest Huntley, Head of Household, a fifty-seven-year old merchant from Glasgow, Scotland. His wife, Clementine, aged thirty-eight. A sixteen-year-old daughter, Margaret, and a son, Thomas, aged eleven. Both born London. Also Surgeon Captain Leonard Vernon Huntley, Royal Army Medical Corps, aged fifty-four, born Glasgow. He was Gordon's brother.'

'Were they prosperous?'

'Prosperous is right. They had six servants, including a butler and a cook.' He turned the form to show her.

'Do we know anything else about them?'

'Not much about the servants, ma'am. There're only wage receipts for them, really. But there's plenty of the family's stuff.'

'How did Mr Huntley make his money?'

Paul had been hoping that Joan would ask this question. 'I ran his name through the database at Companies House,' he said proudly, for this had been his own idea. 'He had a chain of grocery shops called Huntley's Emporiums. Look at this . . .' He went out into the corridor where he had laid out seven large cardboard boxes and scrawled *Gordon, Clementine, Margaret, Thomas, Leonard, Business* and *Servants* in black marker on each. From the first of these he extracted a newspaper clipping, which he brought back to Joan. It was an advertisement, a cartoon sketch of a solitary pig weeping piteously in a large and empty pen. Nearby stood a sweet old lady, evidently moved by this picture of porcine despair. 'What ails you, little Piggy?' asked the lady. 'Sure, ma'am, I'm an orphan,' replied the pig. 'The rest of the family have gone to Huntley's.'

Joan chuckled at this macabre joke, and Paul too began to smile. He had not smiled in a very long time. 'Why don't you come sit out in the corridor, ma'am?' He spoke as though imparting a valuable freedom. 'I can show you things more easily that way.'

'Very well, dear.' Joan allowed herself to be led to a grey plastic chair, on which she now gratefully sat.

Paul switched on the corridor lights. 'Most of the stuff I've got through so far is just Gordon Huntley's business papers. I haven't found out much about Clementine yet, except that she seems to have been ill a lot. But there's a lot of the children's school books. Also a few journals of Margaret's, and some architects' drawings. I think Huntley developed most of this neighbourhood.' He paused. 'What would you like first?'

'Margaret's things, please.'

'Coming right up.' He removed from the appropriate box a pile of children's exercise books, and gave one to Joan.

'Goodness me.' She squinted downwards. 'What high-minded essays! '"*On tue les hommes, mais on ne tue pas les idées légitimes.*" "Both Vice and Virtue are born of Society. Discuss." I suppose they must have had a governess of some sort.'

'Miss Isabella Muir, ma'am. Born Rouen, France, to a Scottish father. She taught Mathematics, Latin, French, History and Moral Philosophy. I think Margaret was about as old as me when she wrote those.'

'And how old are you?'

'Fifteen, ma'am.' Paul wished that he could claim a more imposing age. 'Margaret did a lot of other writing, too, but I don't think she ever got published. She's my favourite Huntley so far.' He went back to the cardboard box and returned with another notebook, bulging with pages cut from a journal and laboriously pasted in. The first of these read:

MARGARET. – We thank you for your nice, creditable letter, and regret that the good sentiments you expressed in rhyme are not written in correct verse. They also lack original ideas.

'What a horrid thing to say about a child's work!' Joan turned another page, on which a second slip of paper had been glued:

M.J.K. – We never read anything so perfectly miserable as your poem. We hope it does not reflect your own state of mind.
There is little merit in it, though it will give you an outlet, if you persevere, for your melancholy thoughts.

'I'd like to give this editor a piece of my mind.' Joan closed the book. 'Oh I do hope Margaret was successful in the end.'

'She's not in the British Library Catalogue, ma'am, at least not under her maiden name. I guess she could have married.'

Joan sat forward. 'I must show you something, dear. It's a letter written by my great-aunt. She was close to Margaret's age. She also wanted to be a writer.'

'Where did she live, ma'am?'

'In South Africa. At the time of the Anglo-Boer War.'

'Captain Huntley was out there, with the Army Medical Corps.'

'Really?'

'Yeah. I've got a photo of him somewhere. Gordon was a big supporter of the war, but I think Margaret was against it. Now where is that map?' He went over to the box labelled *Business* and rummaged, a little careless in his excitement. 'Yes. Here it is.' He handed Joan an advertisement, a map of various British dominions arranged into the letters *Y, N, L, U, H, E* and *T. How the BRITISH EMPIRE spells HUNTLEY* ran the title.

Huntley's Emporiums play their part in the South African War, shipping over 85,000 lbs. of finest produce to our valiant troops. Doctors, nurses, officers, soldiers and newspaper correspondents unite in bearing testimony to the great popularity of Huntley's Emporiums' Invigorating and Nourishing Food, preparing the soldier for battle and aiding him to recovery when weakened by wounds and disease.

Beneath the map was a helpful explanatory note: '*The shapes are correct, but the sizes are not in proportion. Each number indicates a separate part of the Empire. HOW MANY PARTS CAN YOU NAME?*

The cheerful jingoism of the puzzle upset Joan. 'People who don't have to fight in them always think wars are such fun,' she said, a little sharply, setting it aside. 'You said Margaret was against the conflict?'

'Yes. So was Miss Muir. Margaret writes about her in this.' He picked a slim black leather book from the floor and flicked through it, finding a legible page. 'It's one of the worst damaged, unfortunately, but I've got bookmarks in the readable bits. Look.'

Reported in The Times *of this morning, Jan. 20, 1902,* Margaret had written in her scrupulous hand, *Mr Chamberlain declares that with 'a humanity absolutely unprecedented in the history of war, we, upon whom these Boer women and children have been forced, have executed the duty and responsibility in the name of humanity'. When all along civilian Boers are destitute only because British troops have burned down their homes!*

The three pages following had been torn from the journal. Joan returned it to Paul, touched by Margaret's human sympathy; and something in the oddness of their situation – sitting side by side in a dingy corridor, reading another person's private thoughts – inspired her to intimacy. 'My grandmother's house was burned down,' she said quietly, 'by the British. Four of her children died in a concentration camp. Her husband wanted to kill every last Englishman alive.'

Paul, who had gone to the boxes, stopped and turned.

'He said that if you burn a man's house down, you turn a coward into a hero. Do you think that's true?'

'It's happening in Iraq right now, ma'am.'

Joan thought suddenly – how could she have forgotten him? – of the young man with the blurred genitals whose picture she had seen in the newspapers, dangling before a fresh-faced girl. His image came swiftly, unsettlingly vivid, and brought with it the insincere, kindly-looking eyes of the man on the television set in the South African Airways lounge, the one who had talked about helping people. It struck her that his statement and Mr Chamberlain's had something in common. 'I will give you my grandmother's diaries to read,' she said to Paul. 'Then you can decide for yourself whether Margaret was right, or her father.'

'I was on Margaret's side already.' The young man opened the box labelled *General* and produced a disintegrating brown volume on which a mould had been dining extravagantly for decades. 'Would you like to see their pictures?'

'Yes, please.'

He put the volume gently on her lap. 'I think this is Gordon.' The photograph showed a man in a frock coat – portly, prosperous, with a thick black beard and an air of unassailable certainty – standing on a lawn while behind him, and a little to the right, a lady and two children reclined at a picnic. The lady was wearing a dress with innumerable buttons and a smart, though somehow cheap-looking hat on which a large imitation butterfly was perched at a jaunty angle.

'I expect that is the governess,' ventured Joan, pointing to the hat.

'I guess. Mrs Huntley was in bed a lot of the time, judging from her medical prescriptions.'

'And these are Thomas and Margaret?'

'I think so.'

The children were dressed, respectively, in a sailor suit and a confection of striped muslin; Tommy was fair but Margaret had thick dark curls that reminded Joan of Hannie's, in the photograph she had lost when those large young men carried her possessions away. The direction of the light and the angle of their heads made their expressions inscrutable.

'There are pictures of the house, too.' Paul handed her an ostentatious album of imitation snakeskin, on which *Starkey's Photographic Portrait Rooms* was stamped in wide gold letters. An ornate panel on the first page, beneath a frontispiece label of entwined 'G's and 'C's, made bold claims for this firm's status as the *'foremost makers of architectural and domestic light portraits'*.

'I love peeking around other people's homes,' confessed Joan, admiring a room with a vast canopied bed and a marble fireplace protected by a fender across which bronze children played, its walls decorated with painted flowers writhing through latticework.

'That's Clementine Huntley's bedroom but this is the best one.' Paul turned the page with the air of a concert impresario.

Even in black and white, the image was unmistakably gaudy. Joan knew enough to recognise the opulence of the *Louis Seize* style, though whether the clustered gilt sofas, chairs and ormolu tables were antiques or reproductions, she could not say. Their reflections in dazzlingly polished parquet amplified the salon's grandeur, while a curtain of lustrous brocade, suspended from the roof, was swagged extravagantly around a column like a detail in a painting by Alma-Tadema. From gilt panels in the elaborately corniced ceiling four women stared wistfully down at the splendours beneath them.

'Good heavens,' she said.

It was the Recreation Lounge (Non-Smokers).

Chapter 32

'Not good news, I'm afraid,' said Sister Karen briskly. 'We didn't want to call you until we'd found her, but I don't mind telling you I've got a few more white hairs today than I did yesterday.'

Eloise, getting out of a taxi in an industrial estate on the outskirts of the city, paid the driver and tried to keep the dread from her voice. 'What happened?' she asked.

But Sister Karen was not to be denied the pleasure of building towards her narrative's climax at her own pace. 'We put five staff members on emergency search duty,' she went on. 'We have excellent procedures in place for this sort of thing – it's not the first time it's happened, after all – but when they'd covered a six-street zone in every direction, I began to get anxious. Of course our journey facilitator, Sunil – you met him when your mother arrived – reported her disappearance immediately. But when lunch time came and went and we still hadn't found her, I must confess, I—'

'Where is she?' interrupted Eloise, who was beginning to share Joan's distaste for the Nursing Manager.

'She's safe and sound now, don't worry. I think she's in the Recreation Lounge. They do love a little telly, our old ladies and gentlemen.'

'So what happened?'

'Well they will get forgetful, as I said. Alzheimer's patients have a tendency to wander off on their own. The men, in particular, for some reason, just walk and walk – some of our residents would have got halfway to Timbuktu if we didn't have protective measures in place! It's only to be expected.'

'What is?'

'This walking they do.'

'Did my mother get out on her own?'

205

'Gracious, no. She decided to go on the library outing we organise once a fortnight. We always have a strict staff-to-patient ratio on these expeditions. She was with Sunil and three or four other residents.'

Eloise, familiar with the tactics of professional self-defence, was not moved by Sister Karen's insistence on the precautions she had taken for Joan's safety. 'What happened?' she asked again, more sharply this time.

'She disappeared from the library. She was last seen shortly after arriving, at 9.40 a.m. and we didn't find her until 4 p.m.'

'Where was she?'

'She'd wandered off into the basement, somehow. It's reserved for staff – you need a key to reach it via the lift, so we assumed she couldn't have got there. It turns out, though, that a young library worker found her and she followed him to his office. They got into a conversation, apparently, and neither of them thought it necessary to inform anyone else.'

'How is she now?'

'Absolutely fine. Chirpy almost, I'd say. I don't think her little escapade did her any harm – it's all of us who were worried to death.'

'The next time my mother goes missing, even for fifteen minutes, I expect to be informed immediately.'

'Well we don't—'

'Is that clear?'

There was silence at the other end of the telephone. Then Sister Karen, thinking how right she had been to put Eloise down as a tricky one, said that everything was clear.

'Please tell her I've gone to get her furniture. I'll come and see her this weekend, when hopefully it will have been sprayed.'

'I'll do that.'

'Thank you.'

Eloise put her Blackberry into her bag and looked about her. She was in an industrial no-man's-land of cheaply replaceable buildings, wire fences and billboard hoardings. Distracted by Sister Karen's call, she had allowed her taxi to drop her a considerable expanse of dreary car park away from Global Storage, Inc. She swore quietly and began to walk. She had dressed for heat but the day had turned unexpectedly cold around mid-morning.

A balding man in a prefabricated steel container observed her approach and gave a low whistle to attract the attention of his friend.

They were both in their mid-fifties, with voluptuously ponderous bellies. Moving swiftly, the friend took down the 1992 Pirelli calendar that was the office's sole item of decoration and dropped it into a drawer. 'Well,' he said, smoothing back the two or three greasy curls that remained on his head.

'Well, well, well,' said the other.

A few minutes later, having extended the client-verification process as long as they could, both men led Eloise to the container in which Joan's worldly goods were protected from rats and rain. It was usually the junior employee, Aubrey, who took clients out to the warehouse – especially if the weather was bad. On this occasion, however, his boss Reg shared the task, thinking wistfully what he'd have done with Ms McAllister's address details in his younger days.

Each of the men was keen to impress Eloise with his physical strength. This led to a great deal of picking up and putting down and shifting and grimacing as they looked for the items she had requested. Watching them work, oblivious to the excitement her presence had generated, Eloise found herself unexpectedly moved by the sight of these possessions, so redolent of her mother. When Reg dropped a box marked *Cookery Things*, the clang of utensils summoned the many afternoons she had spent at a low table in the kitchen, colouring-in with George, while Joan prepared their dinner or baked a cake. She remembered the Sunday-school lessons, the clothes Joan had made for her as a little girl. Her mother would be horrified to learn that the livelihoods of two innocent people had been risked for her sake; she would be scandalised by the smooth calculation with which her daughter had approved her own trade several days before. 'I'll take that little escritoire,' she said. 'And that bookcase, that chest of drawers and that armchair. There should also be a gift-wrapped box some-where. It was meant to be sent directly to her nursing home. Could you have a look for me?'

Reg and Aubrey, each secretly tiring, heaved and tugged and lugged some more.

'You'll be wanting a smaller container, once this lot's gone,' said Reg, stopping for breath a few minutes later and trying to disguise his panting from Eloise. 'Three-quarter size should do you.'

'Too much stuff here for a three-quarter size.' Aubrey squinted expertly at the items scattered across the asphalt. 'You'd have to get rid of something big to fit all this in a three-quarter size.'

'I can give you a very good price on a three-quarter size,' remarked Reg.

'It's okay, thanks.'

'You get fifty per cent off the cost for the first six months. Then £89.99 a month, £87.50 if you pay by direct debit. Best deal of your life.'

'Really, I'm fine. Thank you.'

'It'll cost you half what you're paying now.' Reg leaned towards her, as though confiding the secrets of the universe. 'It's a deal to attract new customers, see. They don't bother about the old ones like you.'

Aubrey's heart leapt at his rival's unfortunate choice of words.

'They reckon once they've got you, you're hooked in for life. Bastards. See, what we'll do is' – Reg leaned closer – 'we'll close your old account, get you out of the system, enter you in again as a new customer. Simple as that.' He smiled, allowing her to take in his munificence. He smelled of cheap aftershave, Strongbow and cigarettes. 'If you want, you could come back in five months and we'll do it for you again.' He was openly lascivious now. 'That way you'd get a whole *year* free.'

Reg's odour, the complex scent that told the story of his days – the fried food, the cider and fags, the hours of ball-crunching boredom with only Aubrey and a 1992 Pirelli calendar for distraction – rose strongly into Eloise's face, their horrors heightened by the wheedling hopelessness in his voice. If Derby Capital failed, she thought, she'd never get another job in finance and was too old to train for anything else. Perhaps she'd end up in a place like this, working for a man like Reg – though there were darker alternatives, too.

An image came into her mind, of Joan in the Recreation Lounge at The Albany, watching television with her new friends. The screen showed Eloise in a black trouser suit, walking down the steps of the Old Bailey, and Joan was clapping delightedly, pointing her out: 'That's my daughter! You've met her.' But her smile faltered as a BBC anchorman appeared, facing the viewer sternly: 'In what looks set to be a spectacular trial, disgraced former hedge-fund broker Eloise McAllister is facing ten years in prison and debts of a hundred million dollars ...'

The expression on her mother's face, reinforced by the sudden appearance of her possessions, was too much for Eloise. Fortunately Aubrey, who felt that Reg had monopolised her attention for too long, chose this moment to disturb her reverie and free her from it. 'Here's the box you're after,' he said. 'Some sort of present, is it?'

The striped paper was scuffed, but the bow was still intact. Eloise examined it sceptically. 'She said there was a card with it.'

'No sign of that now. Can't have been fixed very securely.'

Eloise hesitated. She was generally adept at ensuring compensation for poor customer service, but it was clear to her that neither Reg nor Aubrey had the authority to do anything more than apologise, and that securing even this meagre acknowledgement would be exhausting. 'I'll take it with me,' she said. 'You can deliver the other things to The Albany.'

'No problem.' Aubrey grinned toothily. 'We'll get that sorted, and I can fit everything into a three-quarter container for you, if you can find something to do with this.' He pointed to a large object, shrouded in blankets, that he had just expended a great deal of energy in trying to lift unaided.

'What is it?' Joan's image, only partially dispelled, lingered hauntingly as Aubrey set about showing her. Realistically, she admitted, her mother's shame would be the least of her worries: if Derby Capital folded and she went to prison, Joan would be completely dependent on George. Her own excesses now rose up before her. How wastefully she had spent her money! It was time to begin to economise; and here, perhaps, was her opportunity to make a start.

By the time Aubrey had pulled a sufficient quantity of blanket from the object to reveal its identity, Eloise had made up her mind – though she felt a moment's regret when she saw that it was her mother's organ that had to go. She examined it, sentimentally. The instrument had stood at the far end of the hall all her life; she and George had been allowed to touch it only on their birthdays, in a ceremony that had grown more intricate with the passing years. Until the age at which children abruptly lose interest in such things, they had loved to hear the story of its origins in the bridal trousseau of a fairy princess: a fiction devised at Frank's insistence, and never dispelled.

It occurred to Eloise that even now she did not know where the organ came from or how her mother had obtained it. It was hideous, really; heavy and ornate, in very dark wood. She opened its lid, with a thrilling sense of the forbidden, and touched a note. Silence. Of course, there was no air in it. But you'd need a chair, she saw, looking down, to work the pedals – and she did not relish the idea of spending much longer in the company of Reg and Aubrey. 'What can you do with it for me?' she asked, sweetly.

'I've got a friend,' said Reg, 'in the antiques trade. Reckon he'd have a use for it. Why don't I sell it to him on your behalf, use the money to pay the next few months' rent on the container?'

'How much do you think you'd get for it?'

'Couple of hundred quid, maybe. Maybe not. It's not my game.'

Eloise considered a moment longer. She had no way of knowing what the thing was worth. Maybe there were collectors who paid high prices for these pieces of rustic Victoriana. She touched the keys again. They did look like ivory. Perhaps she should . . . But the effort required to sell it to anyone else – transporting it, valuing it, advertising it – was unimaginable in the context of her current anxieties.

'Okay,' she said, 'that would be very kind of you.' And when she had signed two sets of papers, and been first taken out of and then put back into the system, she thanked both men for their help, called a taxi, and got into it feeling calmer. She had taken a small step away from her previous, thoughtless extravagance, and this struck her as appropriate.

Chapter 33

The morning after her adventure in the library vaults, Joan woke with the thought that the events of the day before were most probably a pleasant dream, sent by the pedals. Surely she could not have made friends with a fifteen-year-old who had the word 'Skull' shaved on his head?

But Nurse Fleur removed all doubt as she set out the grapefruit on her breakfast tray. 'You've got a visitor, Joan! A very smart young man named Paul. Is he your grandson?'

'Goodness me.' The news put Joan into a flurry. She wasn't properly dressed. Her hair was a mess; she had slept on it and now there was no time to wash.

'I could ask him to wait,' offered her carer, observing her confusion.

'No dear, don't do that. I expect he's come on one of his breaks. He won't have long.' Joan fumbled with the cuff of her blouse.

'Let me do that for you.'

Nurse Fleur began to fasten Joan's buttons. Joan had learned how useless it was to defy such attentions, and in the interests of haste and accuracy she submitted now without protest. Permitted to brush her own hair, she did so vigorously – for she had no wish to resemble the crumbling old people amongst whom she lived. Having applied a little careful rouge, she saw that the tin of night soil had disappeared under the tide of her rising spirits, and she went to the drawer of her desk and took from it a green folder and a pair of white gloves. 'Won't you show him up to the non-smokers' Recreation Lounge?' she said.

Paul was waiting on a pine sofa, beneath the Recreation Lounge's splendid ceiling. He stood up bashfully as Joan entered, unsure whether or not to help her.

'Good morning, dear,' she called briskly, to indicate that she could manage very well on her own. 'And how are you?'

'Good, thanks, ma'am. Yourself?'

'All the cheerier for seeing you.'

Paul was anxious to interest Joan in his researches, for she was the first likeable person to have broken the relentless tedium of his basement life. 'I brought some other things to show you,' he said, gruffly.

Joan reached an armchair, very slightly out of breath, and lowered herself into it. 'How kind of you. Would you like something to drink? Tea? Coffee?'

'Coffee, please.'

'There's a bell somewhere here.' Joan looked for it. 'There it is. Would you mind?'

Paul pushed the grey plastic button and a nurse appeared with sinister speed, as though she had been listening at the door.

'They have cakes too. Try one.'

Paul ordered a slice of the day's Black Forest gateau and a cup of coffee; Joan asked for tea. When the nurse had delivered them, Joan said, 'Did you get into trouble? With that pompous little man who interrupted us yesterday?'

'Mr Peabody?' Paul smiled. 'He was all right in the end.'

'I was the one, after all, who disturbed *you*.'

'Did you get in trouble then?'

Joan thought of Sister Karen's urgent greeting the evening before. 'It may be a black mark,' she admitted. 'How's your cake?'

'Delicious.' Paul wiped a spot of cream from his top lip with a grey cocktail napkin on which the word *TranquilAge*™ was stamped in gold. 'I hope you don't mind me visiting.'

'Goodness no! It's a treat.' Joan felt, suddenly, like one of the girls with whom she had once roomed at a boarding house in Johannesburg, entertaining a young man to tea and pleasantries. 'A real treat,' she said, in a different tone of voice.

'I brought some pictures to show you.' Paul took an envelope from his shirt pocket and handed it to her. 'I think the first one was taken in here.'

Joan put on her glasses and removed a photograph of a dark-haired, middle-aged woman in half-profile against one of the Recreation Lounge's extravagantly-swagged windows. She was staring into the street with an expression of mild surprise, tinged with horror: as though she understood that the fate of the Gothic church opposite was to become a row of concrete shops. She was swathed from head to foot in white: tightly, and yet in folds that contrived to billow. Her long neck rose through a stole of white ostrich feathers, which also bowed in theatrical supplication from the crown of her hat.

'It's the lady in the ceiling,' she said. 'And in the windows on the landing.'

'Clementine Huntley.' Paul nodded, grinning. 'This is her brother-in-law.' He produced a studio shot of a middle-aged man with wispy blond hair and a fastidiously tended moustache, wearing the braided dress uniform of the Royal Army Medical Corps and an expression of faintly alarming zeal. 'Surgeon Captain Leonard Huntley, at the time of the Anglo-Boer War.' He handed it to her. Beneath the image the words 'Schuster's Photographical Works, Bloemfontein' were stamped in blue.

'But I've just been there!' said Joan.

'What were you doing in Bloemfontein, ma'am?' Paul was a little disappointed to find that his new friend had visited the town, for he had spent half an hour that morning learning about it in case she asked for information. He felt that he had made a good impression the day before and was anxious to reinforce it, for he rarely made good impressions. 'It's the capital of the Orange Free State,' he told her, feeling a little foolish. 'It has a population of three hundred and seventy thousand and is one thousand, three hundred and ninety-five metres above sea level.'

'Really? I must say, I didn't know that.' She smiled at him. 'My daughter took me. We had a short holiday together and went looking for my grandmother's farm.' Joan leaned forward. 'It is a shopping centre now.'

'I'm sorry, ma'am.'

'So am I.'

They looked together at the doctor's photograph. 'I have one rather like this of my husband,' said Joan. 'A different uniform, of course, and a different war. I'd say Captain Huntley is a man of purpose. Look at the set of the mouth.'

'He looks a bit uptight to me.'

'That is another way of putting it. I can't quite decide if he's nice or not, can you? I'm not sure the doctors in those camps were always very nice to their patients.' She touched Paul's arm. 'I have something to show you too, dear. A statement written by my grandmother, describing her experiences during the war. I think it would interest you.'

The remaining minutes of Paul's morning tea break passed so quickly that when the young man had left, taking Gertruida van Vuuren's journal with him, the subsequent deceleration of time was obvious and burdensome to Joan. It took physical form in the painfully slow ticking of a large plastic clock that hung between the Adam-style bookcases; and as the second hand moved in relentless *adagio* across its face, she wondered how on earth she would fill another day.

She examined the photograph of Clementine Huntley that Paul had left her. She had a kind face; but there was something ineffectual about her. Her eyes registered a polite, passive, objection. Joan looked up at her portraits on the ceiling. The artist of these had caught the expression too, but conveyed it sentimentally as wistfulness. It was not wistfulness, thought Joan. It was— She paused, and looked closer, bringing the image up to her eyes. For all her finery, Mrs Huntley looked defeated, she decided, and resigned to defeat.

She turned to her brother-in-law. There was a sternness in Leonard's eyes, a gun-metal unconcern, that recalled the first, ominous indications of Frank's rages. She thought suddenly of the haphazard scars along the underside of her husband's arms and down his back; of his insistence on conducting physical intimacy in the dark. 'Dear me, no,' she said, and returned both photographs to the envelope, which she tucked into her bag.

Between the bookcases, the clock was still ticking. The room was empty. Her mother had always advised reading as a tonic for boredom, and neither the ghastly upright nor the large, silent television held any appeal. She inspected the collection of novels and magazines, without temptation; but as she turned away a spine of bright yellow caught her eye. She took it from the shelf. The book's back cover was missing, and the binding had gone; but this very shabbiness endeared it to her, because nothing else at The Albany was remotely shabby. She opened it at random. 'Such a dear baby!' she read. 'And yet I cannot be with him, it makes me so nervous.'

Joan looked over her shoulder, as though a shadow had stolen up behind her; but she was alone. She had never told anyone of the contradictory impulses of love and aversion provoked by the presence

214

of the screaming infant Eloise. 'Nobody would believe what an effort it is to do what little I am able – to dress and entertain, and order things.' Her heart began to beat uncomfortably. She thought of that charming little house in Turnham Green, chosen so optimistically with Frank in the days before optimism had deserted them both. It had taken ten years to fill it with the sound of a child's laughter. She had been so unprepared for anything but joy.

She put the book in her bag and walked briskly to her room, resisting this new direction of her thoughts – for there were worse states than boredom. But as she turned the handle of her door, she saw that the pillars with their dancing bas-reliefs had vanished. *It isn't real*, she told herself. *It's a story about someone else.* But this did not recall the cherubs; and though she went in, she did so warily, with her wits about her. The pine armchair remained by the window. She sat down heavily in it, staking her claim to tangible reality. *It is a book*, she thought, removing it from her bag, *a book called—* She put on her glasses and examined the frontispiece. *The Yellow Wallpaper.* Well, she had never owned any yellow wallpaper in her life.

This fact did not lessen the room's air of noncommittal possibility, and Joan was determined to behave as usual – especially since The Albany's walls were so stridently yellow themselves. The volume in her hands, she saw, was a modern reprint of a nineteenth-century novella by Charlotte Perkins Gilmore. It had belonged to a woman named Enid Delves, who had had bad habits as a reader, and its pages were dog-eared and occasionally flecked with marmalade. The spine was cracked and several sections were missing, but the effect suggested absorption, not neglect. 'I never saw a worse wallpaper in my life,' she read, picking up one of the loose sections. 'One of those sprawling flamboyant patterns committing every artistic sin.'

At once, the bed disappeared; so did the pine desk and the cherub-mounted doors. Joan stood up, fearful that the armchair would go too, and found herself at the entrance to her sitting room in Turnham Green. It was the room to which she had retreated in the years after Astrid's arrival; abandoning inch by inch the dining room, and the elegant dinners she might have given in it; her bedroom; the bathroom; the hall. Astrid had had clear ideas about the correct furnishing of a home, which did not at all coincide with Joan's; and Frank, raised on a diet of his mother's taste, had acquiesced in each of her decorative transgressions.

Now her mother-in-law's voice rang out, merrily autocratic. 'You need to recover, Joanie, and get well. I'll be here as long as necessary.' And yet, though Joan *had* recovered, though she had risen so admirably to the challenge of George's birth, and felt for him all that she should have felt for her firstborn, Astrid had remained; had left only twenty-six years later, when her corpulent body was carried down the narrow stairs in a coffin ornamented with heavy brass bows.

In the furthest corner was a Christmas tree, dense with orange tinsel and turquoise baubles. During Joan's two-week absence, presented to her family as a visit to a friend from Music College, Astrid had conquered the one outpost of the old order under the pretext of a 'Christmas surprise!' and rearranged the entire room around Frank's television set, brought in from his workshop next door. The floorboards had been carpeted in fuscous brown shag pile, the sofa recovered in a bold estimation of the psychedelic Deco style. The griffin chandelier had been banished to the attic, replaced by a raspberry shade that cast doleful mauve shadows at night. And the worst of it, Joan thought, standing aghast in the doorway once more, was the wallpaper: manic swirls of orange and fuchsia, impossible to ignore; a rampaging aggressor in whose presence she would now be obliged to play the piano, which alone remained unmolested in the space between the windows where it had stood before her departure.

'No!' she sputtered, but the scene had sharpened into unassailable solidity; and only the arrival of Nurse Fleur, forty-five minutes later, was sufficient to dispel it.

Chapter 34

The moment Eloise saw what it was, she felt despicable for having taken so long to collect it. She removed the dragon-scale shades carefully and placed each one on her bed; then she lifted the entire chandelier from the box and burst into tears. The sobs came so spontaneously, and so clearly indicated the intensity of her feelings, that she called The Albany at once, and when Joan was not in her room she asked a nurse to find her.

By the time her mother came to the phone, she was feeling calmer, but her mother's voice was sufficient to summon more tears. 'Mum,' she said, 'I can't believe it.'

'What, darling?'

'The chandelier. That you've given it to me.'

Standing in the reception area of The Albany with a plastic cordless phone pressed to her ear, Joan felt a moment's indignation that Eloise had not waited for the presentation to be made in person. This softened at once, and was replaced by a gentle regret. 'Oh darling,' she said.

'I love it. I'm going to hang it in my bedroom.'

'You know it was given to your great-grandmother for her wedding?'

'I did, I think. I'll treasure it.'

There was such sincerity in her daughter's voice, such an appropriate respect for the past, that Joan put aside her sorrow at a missed opportunity. It was useless to plan affecting scenes in life; nothing ever happened quite as one imagined it. 'Did you get the letter I wrote with it?' she asked.

Eloise hesitated; then lied with conviction. 'It was so lovely of you. I'll treasure that too.'

'I meant every word, darling.'

'Thank you, Mum.'

There was a moment's heartfelt silence. Then Joan said, 'There's something you could do for me, if you wouldn't mind.' Paul had now visited The Albany on three occasions, and Sylvia's enquiries had become unbearable. She wished to continue their meetings at the library, where she could help him with his catalogue, but Sister Karen's objections to the plan had been many and varied. She briefly explained her predicament to Eloise.

'Leave it to me.'

'You're an angel.'

'I'll call her right now.'

'My mother needs something to do,' said Eloise a few minutes later. 'She is volunteering for library work. What possible objection could you have?'

Sister Karen had many possible objections, but she knew that none of them would wash. 'None at all,' she said icily, folding another substantial bill for Joan's care and slipping it into an envelope. 'I just hope that the young man has the sense to call us should anything untoward happen. A fall, some sort of physical or mental episode.' She took a label with Eloise's address on it and stuck it to the envelope with satisfaction. 'I am concerned for her safety if she is left without experienced supervision.'

Official sanction thus procured, Paul began collecting Joan from The Albany each morning at nine-thirty, after she had breakfasted in her room. She took this meal now at the little escritoire that had stood in the hall at Wilsmore Street, for her furniture – bless Eloise! – had materialised within days of her strident demands for it: just a few old pieces, but the banishment of the varnished pine transformed her room and made it easier to bear.

Perhaps she should have ordered people about more, she thought, looking at her pretty things; it certainly seemed to get results. She had even received three large bunches of flowers and six concerned telephone messages from George. He had sent delphiniums, which rose with cheerful elegance from a tall willow-pattern vase, but she had not yet returned any of his calls. For the first time she began to understand Eloise's knack for getting what she wanted, which had hitherto been mysterious to her.

At Sister Karen's insistence, Joan moved between The Albany and the library in a wheelchair, pushed by Paul. It was undignified but, when all was said and done, handy. She did not object. In fact, she came to relish these daily adventures across rutted pavements, as the June weather grew warmer and the city drew in its breath in anticipation of the summer heat wave. She was sure she didn't remember London being this hot in her youth.

Paul's response to her grandmother's diary strongly confirmed her initial affection for him. There was something unguarded and generous about the boy's sympathies, a gentleness of disposition that his hunched shoulders and quick, aggressive movements could not disguise. Like Simbongile, and for broadly similar reasons, Paul had an instinctive fondness for elderly women. Mindful of his southern grandmother, he refused to call Joan anything other than 'ma'am' and treated her with painstaking respect, as though struggling to remember a way of being in the world that he had quite forgotten under the roof and influence of his stepfather.

Joan's tolerant interest drew from him the outlines of an unusual life story.

'My grandmothers raised me, mainly, ma'am,' he volunteered one morning, a few days into their friendship. 'I went to school in New York and lived with my grandma Hildy, who came from Charleston. In the holidays I stayed with my granny Rose in Glasgow, Scotland. She was my dad's mum.'

Paul's parents, it transpired, had parted ways explosively when he was four years old, having met in London nine and a half months before his birth: Michelle, an American graphic designer, and Douglas, a Scottish lecturer in cultural studies. They had both been young and theoretical, both stubborn, both ambitious, and the differences in their worldviews – so exciting in their frenzied first fortnight of cocaine-fuelled sex – had proved ultimately irreconcilable.

'How did your grandmothers come to take care of you?' asked Joan.

'I guess they got on better than my parents did, ma'am.'

This was true. In despair at their children's destructive bickering, Hildy Dhanzy and Rose Maclean had met for tea at the Thistle Hotel, Heathrow Airport, during one of Hildy's lay-overs on the return leg of a European trip. To their surprise, they got on extremely well; in fact, over four hours they conceived a more affectionate and practical relationship than their offspring would ever achieve.

Both women, Joan learned, were widowed; both, she imagined, had been lonely before Paul's arrival. The examples of their own children, educated at significant personal cost, had left them sceptical of the values of diplomas, certificates and degrees, and Paul's upbringing under their care had been somewhat unconventional.

Hildy – Valedictorian of the Class of 1943, Vassar College – impressed on her grandson an awareness of the slipperiness of words and a belief in the importance of getting to the bottom of things. She took him out of school to visit churches, art galleries and libraries as the mood took her, and with the solemnity of one bestowing the keys to a richer world she taught him to read biblical Greek and to follow the score of a Tchaikovsky ballet. She was an ardent believer in individual liberty and a dedicated writer of letters to her congressman.

Rose took her grandson on walking tours in the Highlands and alerted him to the matchless beauty of the sun setting over Loch Treigh. She let him sleep late and fed him meringues and home-made fudge and, thinking guiltily of Hildy's likely disapproval, encouraged him to read the romantic fiction from which she, herself, drew such solace.

Materialism was anathema to both women – 'Why', Hildy was fond of asking, 'do rich people only want to get richer?' – and they encouraged in their grandson a disdain for the uses of money beyond the satisfaction of a person's immediate needs. They did not provide him with Action Men or plastic guns; neither did either of them own a television set. Joan noticed that the young man did not mention any friends of his own age, and from this surmised correctly that he was not at ease around his peers.

'Your grandmothers must have been very proud of you,' she said one afternoon, watching him leaf through the pages of Gordon Huntley's business correspondence.

Paul coloured slightly, and looked away. 'I s'pose, ma'am.'

'Do you miss them?'

'Yeah.' He paused. 'They died a month apart, and then I had to go live with my mom and stepfather.'

'What are they like?'

Paul considered the question. Then, carefully folding the letter in his hand and returning it to its envelope, he went into his office and emerged with an orange-and-black lapel pin. This bore the legend '*Guantánamo Rocks!*' against a background of a map of the United States. He showed it to Joan. 'My stepfather owns a chain of supermarkets, ma'am. They sell pretty much everything, including stuff like this.'

'And what is it?'

'Haven't you heard of Guantánamo Bay?'

Joan felt certain that she had, but could not for the moment be sure in what context. 'Remind me,' she said.

'It's a US prison, ma'am, in Cuba. The government says everyone there's a "terrorist", but the detainees never get told the charges against them. People are kept chained up all day in the heat, or locked up in solitary for months on end. They get blasted with such loud music they can't sleep.'

In 1968, Frank had acquired a hi-fi and given his musical tastes free reign. 'How ghastly,' said Joan, feelingly.

'They're not allowed to appeal to an independent authority, or gather evidence to prove their innocence. They get the shit beaten out of them. I mean, they get brutalised by the guards, and when—' Paul stopped. 'Sorry, ma'am. I get kind of worked up about it. My stepdad thinks it's a good thing.' From Grandma Hildy, with whom he had read the Constitution and the *Federalist Papers*, Paul had derived a strong mistrust of executive power and its potential abuses. 'This isn't what the Founding Fathers intended, ma'am. My stepfather talks a lot about patriotism, but all he really cares about is making money. Look.' He went back into his office and emerged with a window sticker in orange, yellow and black. This was, apparently, a Terrorist Hunting Permit, valid until 2050.

'That's an awfully long way off,' said Joan, examining it closely. 'What does the small print say?'

'"No Bag Limit. Tagging Not Required." It basically says you can do whatever you like to someone, so long as you call him a "terrorist" – whether he actually is or not. It's a joke, but that's exactly what's happening.' Paul's voice rose. 'Robert sells these kinds of things, along with clothes and food and guns. He made me work at one of his MegaMarts in my Easter vacation. I said I wouldn't, but he made me. He kind of regrets it now, I think.'

'Really?' Joan leaned forward. 'Why?' On a shelf behind Paul, inspired by the young man's distressing revelations, the Golden Syrup tin of night soil had reappeared.

'Let's just say the Easter MegaSale didn't go to plan.'

'In what way?'

'I'll tell you later.'

'Tell me now.'

But Paul had disappeared into the dripping storeroom.

Chapter 35

A few days later, as Paul was pushing her wheelchair back to The Albany, Joan said, 'You must tell me what sort of mischief you caused your stepfather. I can't wait another moment.' They had spent the morning ordering a collection of crackled, jingoistic journals called *Black and White Magazine*, and the cover of one of these – a demonic image of the President of the Transvaal seated on a throne of children's skulls – intruded obstinately into Joan's thoughts. 'I need something to cheer me up after all that nonsense.'

It had been a cause of secret disappointment to Paul that his elderly friend had so scrupulously respected his reticence in the matter of his final expulsion from his stepfather's home. He was proud of his exploits and had hoped to be drawn on them sooner, though now he put up a further show of modesty in order not to seem boastful. 'You wouldn't approve, ma'am.'

'How will you know unless you tell me?'

'Promise not to be mad.'

'It is your stepfather, dear, who may or may not have the right to be angry. Not me.'

This was all the inducement Paul required, and he began his narrative with an eagerness that belied his earlier hesitation. Its length necessitated a diversion to a litter-strewn park where he stopped Joan's wheelchair beside a bench, applied the brake, and sat down. 'The first thing you should know, ma'am, is that my stepfather hates losing money.'

'Can we blame him for that?'

'You would if you knew what he sells to make it, ma'am.' Grandma Hildy had been a strict ethical consumer and had raised Paul to enquire closely into the provenance of his purchases. 'Robert goes to church every Sunday and prays for God's creation, but he sells beef raised on deforested land in Amazonia and garden furniture made of endangered woods. The cocoa he stocks is grown using child labour in the Ivory Coast. He doesn't care what he sells, so long as the margin's good.'

'I see.'

'He pays his check-out workers the minimum wage and doesn't give them benefits or health insurance.' Paul's voice was rising now, as he remembered fruitless conversations with his mother in which he had made these and similar points. 'Every once in a while he gets uptight about something. His latest craze is MegaMart's shopping carts – he's convinced the crack addicts are stealing them.'

'What is a crack addict, dear?'

'A drug user, ma'am.'

'I see. And by a shopping "cart" you mean a "trolley"?'

'That's right. Robert thinks they steal his carts to buy drugs.'

'And do they?'

'Couldn't say, ma'am. But a lot of the carts do get stolen.'

'I see.'

'Which is why he invested in the "Anti-Theft Ultraliner", at $2,000 a pop.'

'Goodness me.'

'They're meant to be theft-proof.'

'And are they?'

'I guess, ma'am. But they have other weaknesses.'

'Do tell.'

Paul smiled. 'You don't get a lot of technological sophistication for the two thousand bucks. There's just a sensor underneath the front wheels that detects light. When it passes over a bright colour, it activates a break.'

'And how is that helpful, dear?'

'There's a red line painted round the parking lot, so when you try to push a cart over the line it just stops moving. It's made of this dense steel alloy so you can't pick it up – especially if you're a crack addict.'

'Ingenious.'

'I wouldn't have done anything, ma'am, except he made me work in the "Patriotism Department". Selling shit like that terrorist-hunting sticker, and T-shirts saying "Guantánamo Bay is a holiday resort".'

'How horrid.'

'It's offensive. I said I wouldn't do it, but he made me.'

'So?'

o the night before the Easter MegaSale, I just painted a yellow
ae in front of the store doors.'

'I don't follow, dear.'

'Think about it, ma'am. A shopper tries to push an "Anti-Theft
Ultraliner" into the store . . .' Paul paused, expectantly.

'Yes?'

'But he can't.'

'Why not?'

'It won't go over the line, ma'am. The yellow paint activates the
break and the thing won't budge. Pretty dumb design, if you ask me.'

It took a moment for Joan to grasp quite what the young man
meant. Then she began to laugh.

'Eight hundred people were at the store for opening time that day,'
Paul went on, giggling now himself. 'It's the biggest sale of the year,
after Christmas. They spent six hours trying to scrub the paint off –
but you can't do that with rapid-dry gloss enamel. The manager only
figured out he could solve the problem by putting down a dark carpet
at about 4 p.m., by which stage everyone had gone home.'

'Goodness me.' Joan put her hand to her chest; the image was
wonderfully absurd and prompted more laughter. Each time she tried
to stop a fresh wave engulfed her. 'Oh!' she cried, for it was almost
painful, such hilarity. She clasped her sides, and as she did so, gasping
for breath, the pedals appeared – as clear as could be, glistening on the
grass in front of them.

Without thinking, for she had never confided their existence in
anyone else, she clutched Paul's hand and told him of their return.

It took two circuits of the park for Joan to explain, to Paul's satisfaction, just what the pedals meant, and as she did so, quite candidly,
she was a little surprised by her lack of embarrassment. It had something to do, she supposed, with the matter-of-factness with which the
young man absorbed the information. He did not once tell her that
they did not exist.

'So they let you play the piano?' asked Paul.

'That's one of the best things about them,' said Joan. 'But they do
more than that, too. I often find myself in rooms I've known or places
from my past, and generally I don't have any control over where I end
up. It can be very disconcerting. But if the pedals are with me, I can
choose my destination. And they let me transform things, and make

them as I'd wish.' She squeezed his hand, seized by an impulse to further confidence. 'Shall I show you?'

'Please.'

'I shall have to describe everything. You won't be able to see it yourself, of course.'

'That's okay, ma'am.'

'Does this all sound very silly, dear?'

'Not at all. It sounds fun.'

Joan looked at the young man carefully, and discerned no trace of mockery in his narrow face. How fortunate, she thought, that the last new friend she would ever make should be so delightful. 'In that case, let's go back to The Albany,' she said. 'It is greatly in need of improvement.'

'Sure thing.' Paul wheeled her out of the park and into Kingsley Gardens. As they turned the corner into the street, he leaned down towards her. 'Are the pedals still with us?' he whispered.

They were hovering on the ground a few yards ahead, as if eager to display their powers.

'Oh yes,' said Joan.

Chapter 36

Paul wheeled Joan up The Albany's ramp and into its reception area. It was late afternoon and the room was mercifully empty, and flooded with coloured light.

'Why don't we sit down?' Joan suggested. 'Perhaps in the corner over there?'

'Sure, ma'am.' Paul parked her wheelchair in the spot she had indicated.

Joan glanced at the reception desk, an inexcusable structure of marble-laminated chipboard assembled where an umbrella stand – a masterpiece of wrought iron, unfolding delicately from an entwined 'G' and 'C' – had once stood. 'How hideous this all is,' she said. 'Don't be alarmed if I tap my feet.' She knew from photographs in the Starkey album that a large fern had occupied the corner now taken up by the lift; that there had been an Elizabethan oak table by the door, beneath the space currently occupied by the noticeboard, and that various items of heavy silver had rested upon it.

'Tap away, ma'am.'

The pedals edged closer and Joan leaned forward to touch them, blinking and tapping her foot to indicate that she was ready to begin. She gave a cry of pleasure as the desk disappeared. With it went the grey computer screen, the printer, the visitors' signing-in book, the electric green EXIT sign that hung above the front door, and the receptionist's pink sweater, left dangling on her plastic chair – which went too. The sensation released a perfect cadenza in A major, played *velocissimo*. 'I've got rid of the desk,' she told Paul. 'Now I'm putting back the umbrella stand. You remember the one from the album?' She blinked and tapped her foot once more and it appeared, sparking a rampage of A major chords in the second inversion. 'There it is!' Another blink and tap produced a long oak table, bright with polish, and a run of finely balanced semiquavers. She removed, triumphantly, the noticeboard and the lift and the ugly carpet on the staircase. *That ridiculous stair seat should go too*, she thought, as it vanished.

It was many years since Joan had attempted the Mephisto Waltz, and many more since she had played it with focused panache; but these splashes of A major, at such speed, were an invitation she could not resist. Bless the pedals! And bless Paul for having made her laugh, and so tempted them to return! 'You really are a darling,' she said, seizing his hand. 'Now I can spend the whole afternoon playing Liszt.'

Paul was not used to demonstrative affection, and for a moment the old lady's cold smooth hands, clutching his, disturbed him. Grandma Hildy had not indulged in much physical contact; it was Granny Rose who had done the cuddling, and hers had been an altogether fleshier physical presence than Joan's was. He kept his fingers where they were, however, because he sensed the comfort they gave his friend; and after a moment he became more accustomed to the gentle touch of another human being. It induced a painful longing for the women who had brought him up. 'I'd better go, ma'am,' he said, embarrassed by the lump in his throat. 'Mr Peabody's due to check on me in fifteen minutes and I have to get back. Should I take you upstairs?'

'Thank you, no.' Joan shook her head, her left hand poised for a set of staccato chords. The pedals frowned on interruptions and she could not bear to lose them until she had played the waltz from the beginning. 'I can go up in the lift later.'

'Once you've put it back.'

'That's right.'

'Okay, ma'am. See you tomorrow?'

'I'll be waiting.'

She watched Paul leave, waving after him; and when he had gone she settled herself in her chair and bent over the keys. It had taken Joan several years to recover sufficiently from the trauma of Eiko Miyanishi's astounding performance of the first Mephisto Waltz to approach it herself. On her last visit to Nooitgedacht, in the weeks after her mother's death, she had let her hands stray idly over it for the first time, on the walnut upright on which her father had taught her to play Schubert; but sorrow alone had proved an insufficient stimulus and she had not picked it up again. Only Astrid's redecoration of her sitting room, many years later, had provoked the rage required to tame twenty-three pages of such unrelenting virtuosity.

On New Year's Day 1970, while Frank and his mother took the children to *Cinderella*, Joan had assaulted the piece, beginning with the syncopated C sharp minor chords on the second page – which she had played with terrifying violence beneath the orange-and-fuchsia wallpaper. So relieving was their cacophonic brutality that she had barely begun at the beginning by the time her family returned, necessitating an abrupt shift to Christmas carols; though when Astrid demanded an accompaniment to Ivor Novello's 'Shine Through My Dreams' she had pleaded tiredness and retreated to bed.

It had taken almost a year to match Eiko's technical certainty, and several months more to develop the physical dexterity required for performance. Frank's tolerance of her music had long since evaporated, and he had learned to silence her practice by turning up the bass in his workshop. Such interruptions had drastically heightened the challenge of the task. Now, blessedly free from them, she was just launching into the opening *acciaccaturas* when a hand on her shoulder interrupted her. It was the receptionist, recently returned from her tea break.

'Hello, love! Lost, are we? We'll soon find you your room.'

The music ceased. With traceless speed, as though they had never been, the umbrella stand and the oak table disappeared, replaced at once by the contents of The Albany's reception area. Joan glanced at the pedals, entreating them to stay. 'If I might, dear,' she replied, doing her best to keep the irritation from her tone, 'I'd prefer to go up to the Recreation Lounge instead. Do you think I could?'

'Not a problem at all.'

Joan tried to stand, but the younger woman pressed her gently into her seat and wheeled her to the staircase. 'No need to tire yourself out.'

'I'm not at all tired.'

'Of course not.' The receptionoist lifted her with a practised movement and strapped her onto the electric stair lift. 'Look at you!' The Recreation Lounge (Non-Smokers) was empty save for – what was her name? – the lady with the sunset hair and eternal knitting. The ugly pine armchairs had been pushed into a square, the remains of some class or other, and Joan was led to one in the middle of a row. She sat painfully – she *was* tired, now that she thought of it – and it was only when her self-appointed deliverer had left the room that she saw that she had been placed diametrically opposite the knitting lady.

Katherine Ingelow, she thought. That was her name.

Miss Ingelow was sitting perfectly still as always, her knitting in a plastic bag on her lap, hands neatly folded across it, staring straight ahead. Joan thought that she had never seen anything quite so empty as that stare; it was unsettling and now, thanks to the inattention of the receptionist, unavoidable.

Fortunately the pedals had accompanied her. She reached for them and tapped her foot, and at once the Adam bookcases filled with well-bound books; grilles of polished brass attached themselves effortlessly and the dusty magazines and romantic fiction vanished. It occurred to Joan that a splendid nineteenth-century drawing room was just the setting for Liszt, so she blinked and tapped her feet again, twice. Now the colours about her doubled, trebled their intensity. Above her head the plaster garlands threw off their modern drab and revealed them-selves as they truly were: a riotously colourful procession of wild flowers, marching above a pampas of gold leaf. She tapped again and found herself on a piano stool before a gleaming six-foot Bechstein. All about her were chairs and stools and settles with extravagantly detailed legs; in cases and on stands, on ormolu occasional tables, rare things shone expensively. Katherine Ingelow was sitting some distance away on a heavily ornate fauteuil, as unaware of the world as before.

Joan paused, gathering herself, and was about to begin when a loud cough eviscerated all traces of Liszt. Sister Karen stood beside her, accompanied by the receptionist, now bobbing anxiously. At once the pedals disappeared, taking with them the piano and a roomful of *Louis Seize* furniture.

'Everything's quite all right, Joan,' said Sister Karen firmly, causing Astrid's voice to ring out, shrieking the first verse of 'Deep In My Heart'. 'Don't you worry about a thing.' She took a mug from her colleague and leant down towards her. 'One of these will let you get some rest.'

She was holding, Joan saw, a small beige pill. Oh, the effrontery of it! 'Are you all right to take it by yourself? I've made you a nice cup of tea.'

The question was intensely provoking and filled Joan with loathing for the Nursing Manager's belligerent lack of imagination, and the false cheeriness with which she disguised it. She longed to assert herself against her looming bulk.

'Or should I do it?'

A delightfully mischievous solution occurred to Joan. 'Please help me,' she said, meekly.

Sister Karen sat down on an adjacent chair, dismissed the receptionist with a nod, and held Joan's tea for her to sip. Joan leaned back in her seat, settling herself as comfortably as possible, and focused her eyes on Katherine Ingelow's opposite; then she closed her mouth, resisting the temptation to giggle.

'Now just slip this down, and everything will be right as rain.' Sister Karen proffered the little beige pill in a large, damp hand.

Joan stared straight ahead, motionless.

'Come along, Joan.'

Vacantly, her heart warming to the task, Joan contemplated the fathomless depths of Miss Ingelow's demented stare.

'Now, Joan.'

But Joan remained impassive, lips tight shut. Sister Karen pressed a little buzzer to summon a nurse. Nurse Fleur came. 'Possible TIA,' said the Nursing Manager with controlled urgency, taking Joan's pulse. 'She may have had a stroke.'

Together, murmuring soothingly, the two nurses checked Joan's breathing and blood pressure, tilting her this way and that between them. They seemed puzzled to find that everything was in order.

'Come on, Joan! It's nearly four o'clock in the afternoon. You're tired and need to rest. Come on!' Sister Karen shook her shoulders with gentle but decisive vigour.

Joan sat on.

The nurses conferred for a moment, in inaudible undertones. Then Nurse Fleur began to tell Joan softly that everything would be all right while Sister Karen put her hands on her jaws and separated them. Joan was so taken aback by this assault on her dignity that she did not resist; and quick as a flash Sister Karen popped the little beige pill onto her tongue. 'Very good,' she said approvingly. 'Now have some tea to wash it down.'

At this point, something very odd happened.

Behind the backs of Sister Karen and Nurse Fleur, Katherine Ingelow winked. The shock made Joan jump, and it was only thanks to Sister Karen's experienced professionalism that the tea remained deftly in its cup. 'Just swallow it down,' she said, leaning close to Joan and putting one hand at the back of her head.

This time, however, her victim was ready for her. Joan waited until the Nursing Manager's nose was no more than two inches from her own, and for the mug of tea to be placed firmly against her lips. Then, with all the force in her, she jerked forward.

The effect of this was most satisfactory, and Katherine Ingelow winked again.

'On second thoughts,' muttered Sister Karen, her uniform now sticking to her, soaked in lukewarm tea, 'a petit mal seizure. Over to you, Fleur.' And wiping her hands on her skirt, she left the room.

Nurse Fleur leaned down to Joan, cooingly. As if lulled by her gentleness, Joan accepted a drink of tea and swallowed. 'Well done,' said the young woman. 'I'll come and see to you in a moment.'

Joan waited until she had gone, then removed from under her tongue a dissolving, but still intact, beige pill. She leaned painfully over to the next chair and slipped it under a cushion.

Katherine Ingelow winked again.

This time Joan winked back.

Katherine Ingelow winked once more.

Joan winked back.

But there was no further response to these tentative overtures. Abruptly, as though she had never left it, Miss Ingelow returned to her state of perpetual limbo.

Poor dear, thought Joan, congratulating herself on the success of her stratagem. She could not wait to tell Paul. If only the pedals would come back! She settled herself to wait for them and was startled when, after some minutes of absolute stillness, Katherine Ingelow moved again. Only her hands shifted; she continued to stare straight ahead, eyes quite empty, as she opened her knitting bag and felt within it for her needles. Then she paused, as if gathering her audience, and executed five perfect stitches in succession.

When Sister Karen returned some moments later, to check that everything was all right and to pat Joan's blouse with a damp cloth, the two old ladies were staring blankly into space. Katherine Ingelow had drooped forward on a high-backed armchair of pale-blue damask, and drool was gliding from her mouth to the knitting abandoned on her lap. Joan lay stretched out on an elegant *Louis Seize* daybed, having postponed the delights of Liszt to a time when she could be more certain of solitude.

Neither of them seemed at all aware of the Nursing Manager's existence.

Chapter 37

'I thought at first,' said Sister Karen, settling comfortably into her chair, 'that she was having a TIA, or what we call a transient ischaemic attack. But they don't usually last long, and your mother's has persisted for some hours now.' It was eight o'clock in the evening and Eloise was at the office. 'Her pulse, temperature, blood pressure and breathing are all normal, but she is extremely disoriented. I thought you would want to know.'

Eloise's attention, as she listened, was distracted by Patrick's opening and closing mouth. As Sister Karen paused, she saw that her boss was mouthing something to her. A moment later she understood what it was.

'Is ... she ... dead?'

Eloise shook her head. 'How is she? Have you called a doctor?'

'Our Resident Doctor will be paying her weekly call tomorrow morning, and we will keep your mother under close observation until then. She is currently sedated for her own safety and, as far as we can tell, quite contented. This is entirely as we'd expect in a case of developing dementia. Most probably, she's had what we call a petit mal seizure. They're relatively common in children and old people.'

'Should I come now?'

'Come tomorrow. She needs her rest now, and will be confused if she sees you. I understand' – Sister Karen sniffed, disparagingly – 'that you have an extremely busy schedule. But if I could suggest a visit at about eleven-thirty or twelve, when she's up and into her day. That would be best.'

'Of course.'

'And there is another matter, also.'

'Yes.'

'The boy. Paul Dhanzy, at the library. I am quite shocked by his negligence, and have communicated my concerns in the most emphatic terms to the Head of Community Services.' Sister Karen paused, gathering herself. 'As you will remember, I was far from happy about the arrangement in the first place, and it seems that prudence was indeed called for. The young man left your mother, in the middle of a seizure, sitting by herself in the reception area. He didn't alert a staff member, or do anything at all, in fact. He simply abandoned her. It was some minutes before our receptionist found her and was able to take the proper steps to ensure her' – Sister Karen paused again – 'survival and well-being. I am afraid I must insist that these unsupervised visits now cease.'

'Of course.' Eloise was not too proud to admit defeat in a matter as serious as this. 'But tell me, is she really all right? What are the long term consequences of this – episode?'

'As I said, this is par for the course for developing dementia, possible Alzheimer's. Now that she's in the proper hands, she is not in any immediate physical danger. We will have to wait and see if this was a single incident, or whether there will be multiple episodes over the coming days and weeks.'

'And multiple episodes would signify what, exactly?'

'Well, they will show how rapidly her dementia is developing. Some people have months, if not years, of lucidity left at this stage. Others have much less time with us. We will need to observe her.'

'Is she losing her marbles?' asked Patrick, with gruff sympathy, as Eloise put down the phone.

'She's had an episode of some sort. They don't know how significant it is.'

'I think it's easier for them, sometimes, to lose their minds. Saves them knowing what a burden they are on us.'

'Shut up, Patrick.'

Her boss looked up from his desk. 'Your parents aren't alive, are they, Carol?'

'No.' Carol did not intend to share the story of her parents' deaths with Patrick. 'I'm so sorry about your mum,' she said to Eloise. 'If there's anything any of us can do ...'

'Thanks. I'll know more when I see her tomorrow.'

'Sure.' Carol paused, allowing the mood to subside; then, reverting to business, she stood up. 'I've been talking to a friend of mine at Ichimura Steel Corp. He says, off the record, they're holding out for lower iron-ore prices this year. Last year's increase was crippling for the big steel manufacturers and they're not going to put up with another one.'

'So?' Patrick took a fresh biro from the pot on his desk and bit into it.

'So, the market's predicting a steep price hike. My contact tells me, though, that the producers are just briefing to bolster their position. It could be worth taking a punt on. The announcement's due in the next forty-eight hours. My guy says his side won't settle until the price comes down, and there's definitely not going to be anything like the forty-five per cent increase the market's expecting. They're thinking more fifteen to twenty per cent.'

'Eloise? Are you okay?'

Eloise coughed, as though the involuntary sound she had just made – somewhere between a horrified gasp and the bark of a frightened fox – had been the prelude merely to clearing her throat. 'Fine, Patrick. Thanks.'

'Anyway,' continued Carol, 'do you think we should go for it?'

'Could be risky. What do you say, McAllister?'

The only enemy is panic. Eloise tried to think what she could say that would not betray a suspicious knowledge of a commodity with which she had no regular dealings. Failing in this effort, she began putting papers into her briefcase. 'Not my field,' she said. 'You guys decide. But be careful – the market's not usually so wide of the mark.'

'Yeah. Cut it, Carol. We've got enough money riding on one man's word already. Our friend Pasquier's given me the—' Patrick's phone began to ring, and silenced him. 'Clive! How are you?'

There was only one Clive who had the number of Patrick Derby's direct line: Clive Stamp, the fund's second-largest private investor, whose $80 million was not bound by any lock-in clause. Watching Patrick's face, it took all Eloise's considerable self-control to compose her features and continue filling her briefcase with apparent unconcern.

'Look,' Patrick was saying, with the excessive geniality that those who knew him well understood as a front for rising alarm, 'Eloise has all the facts. This isn't the time to act stupid. What? No, of course not. I didn't mean to imply that. Best thing is . . . No, I know. Where are you staying? Great. Look, why doesn't Eloise take you to dinner tomorrow night? She can brief you fully. It's important . . . Yes, I realise that . . .'

The talk went on in this manner for some minutes, while total silence descended on the office as both Carol and Eloise, for different reasons, busied themselves with tidying their desks. Carol's heart was beating so fast she thought she would faint. At last! It had taken almost two months, but someone had seen through Eloise and was calling her bluff. The excitement somewhat eased her resentment at Patrick's dismissal of her iron-ore proposal, and she bent behind her monitor and closed her eyes. Though a lapsed Catholic, in situations of great tension her belief in divine intervention often returned, and now she prayed earnestly for her rival's professional demise.

At last Patrick put down the phone. 'That was Stamp,' he said, shortly. 'The cat, ladies, is out of the proverbial bag. You're having dinner with him tomorrow at eight, Eloise. Dress sexy. I don't have to tell you what happens if we lose him.'

Chapter 38

Joan spent the next morning overcome by painful regret for the worry she had caused her daughter. She saw it in Eloise's face as soon as she was shown into her bedroom by Nurse Fleur, in the expression of set brightness she wore to disguise fragility and inner turmoil. It was a face that always made Joan's heart ache.

'I'm absolutely *fine*,' she said, getting out of her chair unaided and hugging her daughter as tightly as she could. 'I was a little tired last night and the nurses wouldn't stop fussing, but I'm quite recovered this morning.'

'You may find her apparently normal,' Sister Karen had warned Eloise on arrival. 'Don't let that lure you into a false sense of security.'

'Oh, Mum.' As she had done as a child, on the rare occasions when she had chosen her mother's embrace over her grandmother's, Eloise buried her face in Joan's bosom. For some time the two women stood like this, while Nurse Fleur picked up Joan's breakfast tray and discreetly disappeared. 'They say you've had a petit mal seizure.' Eloise felt her throat gorge with tears as she spoke. 'But apparently it's nothing very serious, and all your vital statistics are fine.' She squeezed her mother gently and disengaged.

Joan, now in tears herself at the distress she had caused, contemplated confession. It would be excruciating, but preferable in the long run to the alternative. There was no reason that a delightful private game, followed by a little trick to avenge herself on the Nursing Manager, should cause her darling daughter such anxiety; and yet the prospect of sharing the existence of the pedals with Eloise was indescribably daunting.

Eloise reverted to the tone she had prepared during the course of a long and sleepless night. 'Sister Karen's not happy about your library visits,' she said, gently. 'This volunteer who's taking care of you, I'm sure he's very sweet, but he just doesn't have the experience to deal with problems if they arise. It's not fair to overload him with responsibility.'

Something about the firm set of her daughter's mouth as she spoke reminded Joan of a strict and terrifying convent nun of long ago. 'Let's sit down, darling,' she suggested.

Eloise helped her mother into her chair and took one herself, doing her best to drive from her mind the other demons that had robbed her of sleep. Joan was what mattered now; she would have to worry about the price of iron ore and her dinner with Clive Stamp later. *Fucking George*, she thought, noting the three vast bunches of delphiniums that stood on the Georgian table. *What use are flowers now?* Aloud, she repeated what she had decided in advance would be the core of her argument: 'It's just not fair to him.'

It was at this moment that Paul, who had been sent away by a duty nurse two hours earlier, knocked on Joan's door for the second time that day.

'Hello, dear! Come in and meet my daughter.'

As her mother made the introductions, the fact that she should seek out the friendship of someone so unprepossessing distressed Eloise, who detected social desperation in Joan's preference for a spotty child who had shaved the word 'Skull' onto his head. To disguise this anxiety, she greeted Paul with effusive friendliness. It was so lovely that he and her mother had met, she said. What was he doing in England? How long would he be here for?

'Indefinitely, I guess,' replied the young man, shyly.

'Well that's great. I'm just so sorry that Mum won't, you know, be able to come and visit you any longer.'

'Pardon, ma'am?'

'Don't mind Eloise,' interrupted Joan. 'She's a terrible worrier. I'm absolutely fine. The doctor's been this morning, just after you left. A sweet young woman, very capable. She assures me I'm fit as a fiddle.'

'That's great, ma'am.'

Eloise did not return to this topic during the fifteen further minutes Paul spent with them, but when he had disappeared to run an errand for Mr Peabody she gathered her courage and said, in her *friendly but firm* tone, 'You really can't go to the library any longer. Sister Karen absolutely insists and I'm afraid I agree with her. Paul is a lovely person, and he obviously feels very warmly towards you. But he's not a medical professional. He had no idea, when he dropped you off yesterday afternoon, that you were about to have a seizure. That's the kind of thing only trained doctors can be expected to anticipate. You must—'

But she was interrupted in mid-flow by an explosive snort from Joan, who had spent too much of her life abiding by the commands of an insidiously gentle woman. 'You will *not* tell me what I "must" do. You will not, Eloise. I quite refuse to be bullied by you into changing an arrangement I find most satisfactory.' What a revelation it was, thought Joan, this late discovery of her own assertiveness. 'I assure you, I *promise* you, that I am just as well this morning as I was the day before yesterday. I appreciate your care and concern but I have not lost the capacity to take decisions for myself.'

'Listen, Mum.'

'That is precisely what I refuse to do, on this occasion. My mind is quite made up. Please communicate that to Sister Karen.'

'I advise against it *very* strongly,' said Sister Karen half an hour later, secretly resolving to sedate Joan further. 'The young man may come here, if he wishes. I am sure the Head of Community Services at the library will excuse him, from time to time. But there can be no question of your mother leaving The Albany in her current condition.'

'She's very insistent.'

'That is not unusual, either. Believe me, Joan is not the first patient I have seen with developing dementia. But it would be an abrogation of my duties—'

'Okay.' Eloise had no wish to hear an extensive recital of Sister Karen's duties. 'What about letting him visit her for a week, and then reviewing the situation?'

'Impossible, I'm afraid.' Sister Karen looked at Eloise and considered making her 'I Am The Professional' speech – a talk she reserved for the home's most troublesome clients. Deciding, however, that she would have greater need of it later, with this particular client, she said, more soothingly: 'I understand how hard this is. Believe me. I'm quite happy to break the news to her myself. It's easier, sometimes, for the dear old things to accept a limit if it's imposed by a recognised authority figure.'

'That would be kind of you,' said Eloise, treacherously. 'I'd find it very difficult.'

'Of course you would. We can only do our best.'

'Thank you.'

'Do feel free to visit whenever you would like.'

'I'll do that.'

They parted, cordially; but by the time Eloise had considered going upstairs for a last hug with Joan, decided against it, left The Albany and given her office address to a taxi driver, she was on the verge of tears. Like an actress completing a costume change, her mind slipped out of one worry and into another, and she stared out of the window as she ran over the options that had kept her awake all night. Only two business days remained before the fund's full reconciliation. She could either keep her iron-ore bet open, and face the possibility of catastrophic ruin and a potential jail term if Carol's information was correct, or cancel it and ensure the collapse of Derby Capital. At any event, she would have to be at her persuasive best this evening, arguing a case she did not believe in to a shrewd, self-made billionaire whose hands tended to stray after a glass or two of Château Pétrus.

She found St James's flooding with the lunch-hour crowd, and as she paid the driver the certain realisation that she could not face either Carol or Patrick overcame her. She turned away from the office, up pavements thronged with suited figures gripping pint glasses and laughing. She pressed past these revellers like a shade, observing their carefree good humour as though from the far side of an abyss, separated from them by a Stygian river of fast-flowing anxiety that threatened to burst its banks and drag her into its dark depths. *The only enemy is panic.* She remembered a time – how long ago? two months, perhaps, not more – when she had done as they did, and now felt a paralysing envy for these blessed beings, so free from responsibility and care. The pavement began to tilt. She took a deep breath and tried to calm herself, but she had the agitated sensation that her brain could not alight anywhere with safety. The image of her mother, so small in her high-ceilinged room, pursued her, and with it came the smothered understanding with which she had ended her visit: that Joan wasn't happy at The Albany; that she preferred to spend her days in a damp basement rather than endure the extortionately expensive institution in which she was effectively trapped.

She thought of Claude. He would think it bizarre, sinful almost, that she had refused hospitality, the shelter of a home, to her own parent. Perhaps he was right. Joan had loved her selflessly, untiringly; did she not owe her the same in return? It seemed ridiculous, in any case, to be breaking the law only to keep her mother in a place she hated.

A desperate solution now occurred to Eloise, unanswerable in its combination of filial duty with fiscal responsibility. The idea made her shake, for it meant giving up everything she had chosen and worked for, and she put her hand on a railing to steady herself. Her inner voice, remarking her hesitation, judged it harshly and told her to make her mind up; but she could not. She stood still for some time, in indecisive agony; then, impulsively, she made a pact with Fate. If a taxi appeared in the time it took her to count to ten, she would hail it and go straight back to Wandsworth to liberate her mother. She would welcome Joan willingly into her home, would abandon her privacy and submit herself without protest to well-intentioned intrusion and advice.

She looked to right and left. The street was full of cars and people. She stood still and began to count. One ... Two ... Three ... There was no sign of an unoccupied taxi – of any taxi, in fact. Four ... Five ... How unusual it was, at this time of day, not to see a single cab. She began to count more rapidly. Six ... Seven ... Eight ... She forced herself to slow down. Nine ...

And then, just as she opened her mouth for the final element of the sequence, she saw one approaching from Bond Street like the oracle of an ancient God. She began to raise her hand, but she did not complete the movement. *It has to get to me with its light on*, she thought. *If no one's taken it by then, I'll hail it.* She stood quite still, her heart beating painfully in her throat. The lights changed to red. Surely someone would hail it now? But no one did. She began to shake as the lights turned green and the taxi started to move.

It passed so close to her that she could have touched it.

Watching it disappear, her inner voice remarked coldly that it was pretty clear how things stood now.

It took Eloise twenty-five minutes to complete a walk that usually took her six, and as she reached her apartment and fumbled for her key, she began to shake uncontrollably. She had not had a panic attack for a decade or more. A combination of regular exercise, early bedtimes and dedicated self-discipline had offered what she had begun to imagine was a permanent reprieve from such tortures. Now she understood that one was upon her, and that unless she acted at once she would lose the opportunity for any action at all.

This certainty imposed clarity of a sort, and with it came the sudden conviction that Carol had to be right. Iron ore was her field, after all.

In any case, Akemi's 'educated guess' had been exposed by Carol's informant as just that: a guess. She could not risk her own future, and those of two other people, on such a disputed premise. Nor, she thought, could she betray her mother three times in a single day – first by colluding with Sister Karen; then by failing to rescue her; finally by breaking every tenet of the moral code by which Joan had raised her.

She breathed deeply, aware of the necessity of sounding calm on the telephone, and went to her desk. She had her broker's direct line on speed dial, and in a close approximation of her normal voice she told him to close out her iron-ore options.

'You know something I don't, Eloise?' Dave Lieberman, Derby Capital's broker, was a dedicated pursuer of financial gossip.

'Just a hunch, Dave. Changed my mind.'

'Right you are. Consider it closed.'

She returned the receiver to its cradle with the curious sensation that the desk was rising to meet it. The distance between the sitting room and her bedroom had become unimaginably vast, and she sank to the floor and drew her legs up under her, curling into the foetal position as she tried to restrain her nausea. It struck her that, in the time it had taken her to get home, Derby Capital might well have lost another two or three million dollars. She could not face this thought, or the associations it unleashed, and she shut her eyes and held herself tightly. Watching her from above, the lucid part of her mind observed the pathos of the scene with sneering sympathy: a woman on the far side of forty, alone and unloved, reduced to hugging herself on the floor because there was no one else who would do it for her.

It was in mute contemplation of this depressing image that Eloise fell into a deep and relieving sleep.

Chapter 39

Carol usually supervised the breakfasts of her ten-year-old twins. They were calmer at the start of the day, almost adorable when tousled from sleep; she did not like to miss them in this state, particularly since she often returned from work long after they had been put to bed. On the morning following Eloise's dinner with Clive Stamp, however, she left them in the care of their harried au pair and went to the office early, anxious not to miss her rival's humiliation.

Reaching 144 St James's, it took an effort of will to disguise her anticipation and to regulate her expression to one appropriate to impending catastrophe. In the lift on the way to the fifth floor she pursed her lips and frowned, narrowing her eyes further when the result still failed to disguise a certain, suppressed, exhilaration. 'What's got you so wired?' Patrick was already at his desk. It seemed, from the glassy look in his eyes and the number of mangled biros in his bin, that he had not left it since she had last seen him.

'I'm just very worried,' she said, slipping onto her kneeler and logging into Bloomberg. 'That's all.'

'You're not alone.'

For some minutes they busied themselves, in silence. Then they heard Eloise's voice in the corridor, speaking to Emily, and Carol stood up. 'Coffee, Patrick?' She did not intend to be kneeling during the coming scene.

'No thanks. I've had four cups already.'

It was rare for Patrick to say please or thank you, and Carol read his unusual politeness, quite correctly, as a sign of profound inner turmoil. 'How's osmium doing?' she asked, though she had just checked it herself.

'Down to $86.76.'

'Shit.' Carol rarely swore, and did so now only to underline the extent of the crisis. She had done the sums already: Derby Capital was down $97 million, and this fact would shortly have to be made public in the fund's quarterly figures. 'What're we going to say in the investor report?'

'Let's see what McAllister has to tell us.'

At this moment the glass doors opened to reveal Eloise, who nodded curtly to her colleagues and went to her desk.

'How did it go?' Patrick asked the question in the tone of voice of one who knew how it had gone.

'Not well.'

'How not well?'

'First thing he said was that he'd be withdrawing $80 million by lunch time today. I told him we'd need notice to get that kind of liquidity. He said he didn't give a fuck about notice.'

'Christ.' Patrick switched off the television screen on his desk, silencing a reporter in a flak jacket shouting animatedly beside a burning car.

'Yes. He said he wanted to be the first man out of the fund, not the last. He was quite aggressive, actually.' Eloise turned to Carol. 'How are you this morning?'

'Fine, thanks.'

'You look chirpy.' Eloise went to the coffee machine and inserted a cup.

'How did you play it, Eloise?' Patrick rarely spoke quietly, and when he did it was invariably a prelude to unbounded rage. Now his question was almost inaudible. Quite unconsciously, Carol moved away from him towards the window.

'I took your advice and wore a sexy dress.'

'Yes?'

Eloise took her coffee and turned to face her boss. 'I'm not going to bullshit, Patrick. It didn't go well. I fed him two bottles of Pétrus, and that didn't work. I even' – she turned defiantly to Carol, who looked away – 'offered him a blow job. He wasn't having any of it.'

'You should have *given* him the fucking blow job, not offered it.'

'I tried, believe me. But he wants more than that.'

'What kind of "more"?'

There was silence. How like Eloise, thought Carol disdainfully, to use sex to try to save herself.

'What kind of "more"?' repeated Patrick.

Eloise took a sip of her coffee. 'There's no easy way to tell you this.'

'Does he want a share of equity, to stay in the game?'

'Worse, I'm afraid.'

'Worse?'

'For you, that is.'

'Christ, Eloise. What the fuck does the guy want?'

'I don't know how to put this, Patrick.'

'Yes?'

'It emerged, after two bottles, that our Mr Stamp doesn't like girls at all. He has a fetish for older white men on the . . . chunkier side of well built.'

A piece of black plastic, the remains of a masticated biro, fell from Patrick's open mouth. 'What the fuck are you talking about?'

'He said he'd keep his money in the fund until December, like the other big boys, in exchange for—' Eloise hesitated.

'For what?'

'For a pair of your used white briefs. He wants you to wear them for a week. You can't take them off, he was very specific about that. You have to go running in them for at least twenty minutes every morning, and sleep in them too. Then you have to send them—'

'For Christ's sake, Eloise.'

'You have to send them to the Plaza Athenée in Paris, where he'll be staying from Friday.'

'You're bullshitting me.' Patrick's voice rose tremulously. 'You mean a blow job from you wouldn't seal the deal?'

'That's the kind of remark that gets middle-aged men like you mixed up in sex discrimination suits, Patrick. Anyway, like I said, he's not into girls. The important thing to remember is that we're an equal-opportunities firm, and that means equal responsibilities, too.'

It took Patrick several stunned seconds, and Carol several more, to realise that Eloise was joking. When he did, the laughter that welled from inside him was so explosive that a picture on his desk – a group shot of his ex-wife and their two teenage children – fell over. Carol, in whom discomfort at Eloise's language was heightening the first notes of a bitter disappointment, did not know where to look or what to do.

'As it happens,' said Eloise sharply, 'I didn't wear a sexy dress and I didn't offer him a blow job. I simply put my arguments, the same ones I've gone over with you and Carol many times, and he came on board. The man didn't turn a packaging plant in Slough into a billion-dollar enterprise by passing out every time he took a risk.'

It was, as even Eloise's inner voice was compelled to admit, a stunning performance, though its professionalism alarmed her, too. So did the flawless confidence with which, the previous evening, she had counselled Clive Stamp to keep his money in a venture that could only end badly for him. She had woken the night before on her sitting-room floor, forty minutes before their dinner, looking very much like a woman who has cried herself to sleep; had changed and splashed water on her face and done her make-up in a taxi and proceeded to sparkle. In short, she had risen superbly to the occasion, and Carol's hate-filled eyes told her that she had done so again this morning.

She went to her desk, feeling sick, and logged into her Bloomberg terminal.

Patrick was still sputtering with mirth. 'You're going to fucking bankrupt me, McAllister.' He began to dry his glistening forehead with a handkerchief as his hilarity subsided. 'But I like you.'

'Knowing that, I can die happy.' Eloise picked up the remote control on her desk and switched on C-SPAN.

'So we're good for a few more weeks with Stamp?'

'He's in until he decides otherwise. He understands the strategy.'

'Good job. One less potential fucking disaster.'

'Yup.'

Observing this cosy intimacy, Carol moved to break it up. 'Well done, Eloise,' she said, crisply. 'But we've still got our investment report to worry about. We're down almost $100 million, and osmium's in free fall. It's going to take a lot of explaining.'

'At least we didn't do anything in iron ore yesterday.' Patrick clamped a new biro in his teeth. 'They announced the price three hours ago – it's up seventy-one per cent on last year.'

'*What?*'

'Biggest price hike in a decade. They're blaming the war.'

Relax your face. Don't show emotion. But Eloise's facial discipline, sorely taxed by the tension of recent days, was unequal to the task of hiding what she felt now. To her horror, her eyes began to fill with hot, pricking tears as she calculated the sum she might have made.

'Are you okay?' asked Carol.

It was in the region of $130 million. 'I'm – I'm fine,' she said.

'No you're not. What's wrong?' This was Patrick, who had risen from his desk.

The possibility of telling him the truth and throwing herself on his mercy flashed across Eloise's conscience, fatally seductive. Following it was the certainty of his fury, the uncertainty of what he might do with it, and after that came the shame of making such an admission in front of Carol, after the showy bravado of her morning's performance. She tried to pull herself together. *Focus, Eloise. There are always options in life.* It was only June, after all. They would survive for another five months, and that was an eternity in commodities. So she said, because it was the only explanation that was both convincing and sincere, 'I'm very worried about my mother.'

'You'd better go and see her then,' said Patrick with unusual gentleness, putting his arm around her. 'You deserve a day off after keeping Stamp in last night. We'll hold the fort here.'

Chapter 40

Joan's interview with Sister Karen, in which the Nursing Manager made a number of points quite painfully clear, took her forcefully back to her convent school, which was the last institution in which (on warm Tuesday afternoons, compelled to stay indoors as a punishment for losing her swimming cap) she had been confined against her will.

'You may go out whenever you like, of course,' said Sister Karen. 'But you must have a nurse with you, or Sunil. You can reserve a slot with him by signing in the book downstairs.'

It would be impolite, thought Joan, to mention that the thought of an excursion with Sunil held no appeal. 'What about my friend Paul?' she asked, tilting her chin slightly.

'He may come and visit you here whenever he likes.'

'But our work. We are cataloguing a collection of artefacts for the library.'

Sister Karen did not believe in extended discussions of this nature, or in making detailed individual compromises; neither, however, did she wish to receive another telephone call from Eloise McAllister, so she said, 'I will speak to the Head of Community Services. It may well be possible for Paul to bring some of the boxes here, to you. Then you can organise them together before he takes them back.'

'That's a great idea, ma'am,' said Paul, when Joan informed him of this compromise.

'But I shall miss your little room, dear.'

'Yours is much nicer.'

This, Joan supposed, was true; and the thought of standing up to the combined might of her daughter and the Nursing Manager unnerved her. She was not, after all, cut from Eloise's cloth. Perhaps it would be better to entertain Paul at The Albany, so long as she could keep him to herself, and not have to share him with Sylvia.

'Our work requires privacy,' she told Sister Karen, the morning after their conversation.

'Of course, Joan. I'll see that you're not disturbed.'

In this way, things were arranged, and Paul – to whom the idea of sanctioned escape from his basement was extremely appealing – brought the first batch of boxes from the library that afternoon. He stacked them in a corner and laid out cards on the desk on which he had written each of the Huntleys' names, for there was no room for the sorting crates that lined the library's basement corridor.

Together, with the aid of builder's drawings and architect's plans, they set about identifying the original layout of the house; and by the middle of July they had finished Gordon Huntley's correspondence and identified the rooms photographed so meticulously by Starkey's. The drawing room and the dining room had continued in use, but Gordon Huntley's study was a service hatch and the conservatory had been demolished. Sylvia Fraser occupied the larger part of Clementine's bedroom, its latticework wallpaper and clambering flowers long since smothered in magnolia, while the billiard room and smoking room were six smaller bedrooms. The nursery floor was given over to administrative offices and a first-aid station now operated from the butler's pantry.

These investigations involved a good deal of moving about, and at Paul's suggestion Joan accepted Nurse Fleur's offer of a wheelie. It was a funny little contraption, she thought, examining the collapsible triangular walking frame with its three wheels and plastic-gripped handles, its brakes so suggestive of the thrills and dangers of speed – as though, at any moment, she might freewheel off across the grey tiles of the Recreation Lounge (Non-Smokers). 'Do I look very silly on it?' she asked, anxiously.

'Not at all, ma'am. It's basically a bicycle.'

This was a helpful image, suggesting as it did the exhilaration of hair streaming in the wind, the delirious freedom of gliding down the steep drive of Nooitgedacht. 'In that case,' said Joan, 'I shall call her Cordelia. I once had a wonderful bike called Cordelia. My brother named her.'

'After the character from *King Lear*.'

Joan recalled the tuneless perfectionism of Eloise's schoolgirl recitals from Shakespeare. 'Indeed,' she said, suppressing a smile.

249

Paul's presence – unlike Sister Karen's, which banished them instantly – did not bother the pedals, which began to visit with delightful frequency. Really, thought Joan one afternoon, sitting in her armchair by the window as they hovered over her desk, it was not so bad being old. She closed her eyes in a prayer of gratitude, for now she understood that God had helped her that day in the library, after all: He had led her to Dr Whalley's awful book, which in turn had sent her into the lift, and so into Paul's life. It was further proof, she thought, of His mysterious workings; of the way one really could hear Him, if only one was open to the infinitely subtle murmurings of the universe.

Her back warmed by the sun, she prayed one by one for Paul; and Frank; and Eloise; and George, whom she hoped earnestly would honour his promise to visit. She had at last returned his calls and the ensuing conversation had been awkward; she felt sure things would be easier if only she could see him. She prayed for Nurse Fleur, who took such considerate care of her; and, reminding herself of Christ's injunction to love, for Astrid and for Sister Karen. Then, with far less reluctance, she prayed for Katherine Ingelow and Sylvia Fraser and the man with the blurred genitals, pictured in the newspapers; for the fresh-faced girl beside him, so chillingly brutal; for her parents and grandmother and each of her great aunts and uncles in turn; and for the kind English officer who had cried over the shooting of the van Vuurens' dog. She gave thanks for the pedals, last of all, and for the fact that they approved of Paul. Then she folded her hands in her lap, cast a fond look at the little escritoire on which they were shimmering, and went to sleep.

She was woken, how much later she did not know, by a coldness seeping down her chest. Outside, long blue shadows stretched across the wilting lawn, catching dust motes like glimmers of phosphorus in a sea at night. It took some time to make sense of the gurgling hum that filled the room – the sound of the shadows, she supposed – and to understand, first, that it came from a beige box mounted on the wall; then, that this strange device was an air-conditioning unit; and, finally, that she had drooled down her shirt and that it was the resulting dampness, chilled by artificially iced air, that had woken her.

She had the thrillingly mischievous sense that she had missed dinner and stretched her arms above her head. The room was hazy with early-evening light, as though the sun had left some behind as it slipped away, and the pedals had moved closer while she slept. She reached for them and tapped her foot, and beside her appeared a bicycle of gleaming chrome, with ranks of gears and a large bell. The original, gearless Cordelia, though much loved, had also, until shared adventure bred loyalty, been just a tiny bit disappointing. Now, incarnated in her fullest perfection, she had ten gears at least; no, twelve, Joan decided, throwing caution to the winds.

A further tap modified the ache in her legs into the stiffness that follows an afternoon nap enjoyed on hard, uneven ground after a long cycle across hilly country. It lent her room the semblance of a wooded glade of high, thin trees, and beside her on a tray appeared the remains of a picnic. She lifted a stainless-steel cover to reveal three slices of a dull brown meat whose dryness indicated, too strongly for easy transformation, its provenance in The Albany's kitchens; but as she replaced the lid it became a gleaming silver dome, keeping warm some richly flavoured mystery.

Joan paused, letting the magic settle over her. Then, looking further into the shadows, she saw the dim outlines of a door among the trees, dense with foliage beneath a high neoclassical pediment. The ballroom at Nooitgedacht had had such a door, and vines had crept over it, too. After the abrupt reversal of the van Hartesveldts' fortunes, her father had given up his attempts at refurbishment and the east wing had succumbed entirely to the estate's besieging flora. The roof had fallen in on one side, and the Cape's harsh rains had warped the parquet floor and prised the boards upwards, into giant splinters. She went to the door and tried it, and though it was locked she passed easily to the other side.

Rupert was peering into the black space between the rotting floor and the foundation, his dark blond hair tangled with gorse and leaves, shins bloodied from their scrambles through the marguerite bushes. He was laughing at her fear of darkness, and of snakes, and the memory of his disdain for cry-babies determined Joan to stand firm against tears, though it was sixty years since their last afternoon together.

It was Rupert who devised the complex games that prevented the isolation of the van Hartesveldt children from becoming loneliness, he who taught Joan to intone the poetry of Tennyson and so transform the algae'd reservoir into King Arthur's lake, his death barge waiting beneath the 'long glories of the winter moon'. The ballroom had been built, a hundred and twenty years before, three feet above the foundations of the original eighteenth-century house, and the space beneath the boards was large enough for human ingression. 'Who ever heard of a girl brave enough to explore a place like that?' He asked the question in the tone of affectionate challenge he reserved for his sister alone.

'I have.' Joan pulled at her white stockings and shoes. 'And it's me.'

'Go on, then.'

She approached the chasm, feigning fearlessness. A smell of damp earth rose from it and she wondered what creatures had made it their home. She had been bitten twice by a grass snake, and would risk being so again; but rats, and the thought of their tails running across her hands, alarmed her. She removed her shoes and stockings and began to lower her bare feet gingerly through the space in the boards – but her brother pulled her up by the arms, laughing.

'You're a chump, Jo-Jo, but a splendid one.' He set her down, approvingly. 'I'll get a torch and go in first. I only wanted to see if you would.'

'And I will,' said Joan.

'Which is enough.' He took her hand and rubbed it. 'I'll see if it's safe. Then we'll go in together.'

His rubbing continued; he rubbed and rubbed until he hurt her, quite unusually, his large fingers chafing the skin on her knuckles. She opened her eyes to find Astrid bending over her.

'Joan! Joan! We've brought you your dinner.'

It took Joan a moment to realise that it was Sister Karen who massaged her with such determined urgency. Anguish at the abrupt loss of her brother washed over her; she felt she was drowning in it. 'Rupert!' she called, in case he could hear her still, thinking of the afternoon they might yet, perhaps, spend together – for Rupert's investigation of the space beneath the ballroom floor had revealed no snakes or rodents, and suggested a far more private hideout than that provided by the abandoned piggery. For a moment the possibility lingered, as a dream does; then it cracked into shards so tiny she could never hope to reassemble them. 'I – I'm not hungry,' she said, faintly.

'You must keep your appetite up! You haven't even touched your lunch.'

'I really don't—'

'I'll be back in twenty minutes. Let's make sure it's eaten by then. We don't want it getting cold, now do we?'

Sister Karen waited, expecting an answer to this question. It became clear that she would not leave without one.

'No, Sister,' said Joan at last.

'Good for you.'

Chapter 41

'I wish we could find out more about Captain Huntley,' said Joan to Paul a few days later. 'There's nothing of his in all these papers.'

'There's still a lot to get through, ma'am.'

'Indeed. But there must be records somewhere. Official ones. We should at least find out if he was really attached to the camp at Bloemfontein. He may simply have had his photograph taken in the town, before being transferred elsewhere. I'm sure the librarian would help you, if you asked him.'

Paul did not wish Joan to think that he depended exclusively on the librarian for his information. 'I can find out on my own,' he assured her. 'I could do it this afternoon, if you like, or first thing tomorrow.'

'Would you, Paul? I feel I must know, after what happened to Hannie in the hospital tent there.'

'No problem.'

'Bless you.'

'I'll try to have something for you tomorrow.'

But the next day, at nine-thirty, Paul did not arrive. 'Your friend called an hour ago, before you were awake,' said Nurse Fleur as she set out Joan's grapefruit. 'He says to tell you he can't come this morning. He's gone to the National Archives at Kew. Is it to do with your cataloguing?'

'Yes, dear, it is.'

'How's it coming?' It was rare for patients at The Albany to be given as much freedom in the matter of furnishings and hobbies as Joan had, and Fleur was intrigued to know what grand undertaking she had involved herself with.

'Very well, thank you.' Joan had not so far shared her researches with anyone, and did not intend to begin doing so now. 'Would you send him up as soon as he gets here?'

'Of course.'

But the morning passed with no sign of Paul. Joan went down to lunch with Cordelia and endured half an hour with Sylvia Fraser, hoping to be interrupted at any moment; but she was not. Returning to her room, she saw that the pedals had not visited and settled fretfully in her armchair by the window, where she passed a tiresome afternoon unable even to nap. It was a swollen summer's day and the heat recalled the viscose dust of Bloemfontein, endured by her grandmother in the black dress that so often hung in her closet. Was it there again? She checked, but the grey plastic hangers held nothing unusual and she returned to her vigil by the window, turning occasionally to the photograph of Dr Huntley. He did not, she thought, look a kind man; but that did not mean he was a bad one.

Paul arrived just before tea time, anxious to convey the thoroughness of his researches. 'The army records are stored in the Royal Archive at Kew, ma'am,' he said, speaking quickly. 'I went this morning, but I didn't have any identification so I had to go back home, and then back out to Kew.' He smiled ruefully. 'I guess I must smell. The train broke down for forty-five minutes and I didn't have a seat, so I was pressed up against—'

'Don't worry at all, dear.' Joan could bear to wait no longer. 'Tell me what you found out.'

'Well, ma'am, what I found out is that all the records relating to the Anglo-Boer War were destroyed by a German bomb in 1940. The only ones that still exist are the courts-martial registers, but they're being restored. They'll only be available to the public again at the end of September'

'How *irritating*.'

'It's only eight weeks, ma'am.'

But eight weeks was a very long time in such weather, and Joan was crestfallen.

Paul observed her disappointment and sought to divert it. 'Do you want to see one of Clementine Huntley's medical prescriptions? Maybe you could give the list to your doctor and find out what they were for.' He removed from his rucksack a file marked *Clementine* and extracted a slip of ageing paper, which he handed to Joan.

When Mrs Huntley's bowels have acted well, it said, *and the evacuations have assumed a more healthy appearance, hydrate of chloral should be administered. Henbane is also a useful remedy, and chloroform is of great service. Hydrocyanic acid may also be administered in fair doses of 5 minims of the dilute acid every four hours.*

'It doesn't sound a very pleasant regime.' She gave it back to him.
'No.' Paul shifted in his seat. 'You will ask your doctor, ma'am?'
'Of course.'
'But I'm going to have to wait three weeks to find out.'
'Why's that?'
The young man hesitated. 'My dad's taking me hiking in the Dordogne,' he said at last, regretfully. 'He told me about it yesterday. It's a surprise. His therapist thinks we need to bond.'
Joan blinked. 'How – delightful.'
'It could be, I guess.' He sounded doubtful. 'Would you like me to leave the rest of this box for when I get back?'
'No, no. Work on.'
Paul's quiet industry was so comforting that Joan fell into a gentle doze, and when it was time for the boy to go she saw that his stillness had inspired the pedals' return. They said goodbye with great affection, and when she was alone she sat in silence for a moment, listening; but it was too hot to play the piano now. She thought of Clementine Huntley, an invalid in this monumental building; immortalised on its ceilings and in its windows. The paper on her bedroom walls had seemed friendly enough in the Starkey photograph, but she suspected that prolonged exposure to it might have been horribly claustrophobic – as though the latticework were the bars of a delicate cage, the writhing flowers trapped in an impossible bid for liberty.

When added to a cocktail of Brahms and Rachmaninov, Astrid's little pills had produced similarly alarming possibilities in the orange-and-fuchsia swirls behind Joan's piano, and she said a prayer for Mrs Huntley and the horrors she had perhaps endured. Then she got up slowly and tidied herself for dinner, making a plan as she did so. She would fulfil her obligations to the Nursing Manager and win for herself, by her appearance in the dining room, an evening's solitude in which to enjoy the pedals undisturbed – for though she had no energy for Liszt, a little Schumann would be relieving, and soothe the sadness of Paul's departure.

When she was ready, she pushed Cordelia towards the door and opened it. The pedals followed her discreetly and caused the hideously flecked carpet of The Albany to stretch into a Persian of pale rose and blue and green thread. Moving towards the stairs, she called gilt wall sconces into being and freed the cornice work from its suppressing beige. She banished the chair seat and the illuminated fire-escape signs, though a glimpse of Sylvia Fraser hurrying to the Recreation Lounge (Non-Smokers) briefly reconstituted the fluorescent strip lights. *I'll take the stairs*, she thought, *all by myself*; and she was just looking for a chain with which to secure Cordelia when a child appeared on the landing beside her. He was nine or ten years old and dressed in a sailor suit, but though he came right up to her she could not see his face.

Joan was, for a moment, nonplussed. Then, remembering her manners, she extended her hand. It was her habit to befriend curious phenomena; and perhaps it was not so very strange, after all, that her impromptu restoration of 17 Kingsley Gardens should have tempted the family's return. She felt sure that this was young Thomas Huntley. 'How do you do?' she asked, smiling. 'My name is Joan.'

The boy thrust his fingers towards her. His thumbs were black with bruises and the cuticles shredded and raw – so raw that when he put one to his mouth and began to worry it, driving his teeth deep into the tender flesh, blood leaked onto his lips.

This action threatened to transform the first-floor landing of 17 Kingsley Gardens into the narrow hall of the villa in Turnham Green. Beneath her feet, black grids shot out over olive-green-and-white shag pile, colliding haphazardly and solidifying as the wall-to-wall carpet Astrid had had laid over the wide oak floorboards. The walls picked up the green and the ceiling hurtled towards them, descending to the level of the false platform Frank had built to create three feet of storage space. Thomas Huntley's sailor suit disappeared and George now stood before her in his grey flannel school jacket, his teeth digging deeper and deeper into the swollen flesh of his fingers.

'*No!*' She grasped the pedals with savage strength and closed her eyes. She kept them closed and tapped her foot four times and when she opened them again she saw with relief that the little boy had gone, that she stood once more beneath a gilt cornice – though at the end of the corridor a stubborn EXIT sign in electric green remained. She hurried to the lift, the doors of which opened to reveal an elegant parlour hung in a William Morris print of autumn leaves, and this simple comfort inspired such gratitude in Joan that her eyes filled with tears, which complicated the pressing of the buttons; and when she emerged a few moments later onto a corridor of varnished wood, she understood that she had pressed the wrong one and gone up instead of down. She would never get to dinner at this rate, and yet her error permitted a moment's peace in which to regain control before submitting herself to the scrutiny of Sylvia Fraser. 'Calm down,' she said sternly, for there was no one to hear her; and when her breathing had subsided she summoned the lift again and was waiting patiently for its return when a low gurgle disturbed her.

The sound became a whine, and then a wail, and she drew the pedals tightly to her, for she was not equal to another encounter with the little boy. But the voice was a girl's, and she was weeping so uncontrollably that Joan could not ignore her. She listened more closely. The sound was coming from one of the many doors that stretched away on either side, and she moved from one to the next on Cordelia, trying each of them in turn. The first five were locked, but the sixth opened to reveal a narrow space cluttered with buckets and ladders and bottles of lurid fluids with menacing drawings on their labels.

On the window ledge at the far end, looking down at the street, was a young woman with the square shoulders and erect bearing of Hannie van Vuuren, wearing a white pinafore like the one Hannie had worn on the *stoep* of Van Vuuren's Drift in the photograph she had lost, her tumbling hair kept from her eyes by a white band. This resemblance transformed the walls of the room into blackened Free State rock, and roses began to clamber over them as they had in the ruined enclave in which Rupert's grave had once sheltered from the sun and the hot, dry wind. 'Hannie?' Joan called. But the girl was not Hannie, or at least not wholly Hannie; and this arrested the roses, and then dissolved them. She was hunched over a copy of the *Girls' Own Paper*, speaking to herself in an unmistakably English accent, and she gave no indication that Joan's presence disturbed her, or even that she was aware of it. Further observation revealed an envelope addressed to Miss Margaret Huntley, from which the young lady had taken the vicious rejection letter that had prompted her sobs.

'Margaret?' But Margaret merely rubbed her eyes vigorously and crossed the room to the door, which she opened and passed swiftly through. Even on Cordelia it was a challenge for Joan to keep up with her purposeful strides, but already a certain comprehension was dawning and with it came the possibility that by helping Margaret she might help Hannie, too, for both had wished to be writers. She spurred her bicycle on as the girl disappeared down the stairs, but lost sight of her at the bend of the staircase and stopped, panting, outside the lift doors. How enervating it was to be so slow!

She took the lift to the ground floor, railing against the tyranny of physical frailty, but Fortune smiled on her as she emerged from it – for Margaret Huntley was just crossing the hall and disappearing through a door at its far end. She knocked twice at it. Receiving no answer, she opened it boldly, preparing a little speech of introduction, but was wrenched by the loud clash of cutlery on china and a babble of modern voices into the hatch that serviced The Albany's dining room, where a group of gossiping dinner ladies stood laying trays and ladling soup.

The suddenness of this transition expressed itself in a vicious pain in her chest, but this died away as Nurse Fleur appeared and said, 'So you've ventured downstairs for dinner! Well done!' and led her gently into the dining room itself, the lifeless magnolia paint of which deterred the pedals from following.

Joan sat down at a Formica table, concentrating intently on her thoughts of Margaret and Hannie, which were fading dangerously and taking with them the opportunity of giving pleasure to two young women so sorely in need of it, just as Sister Karen's intervention had destroyed the possibility of an afternoon with her brother. The idea of spending the evening in The Albany's dining room, consuming The Albany's food, being spoken to by members of The Albany's staff, was insupportable. Her whole life, she thought crossly, she had done what other people wished her to do. She had fetched and carried and cooked and accompanied Astrid's vile singing. Hadn't she earned the right to do as she pleased? For an hour or two at least?

She looked about her at the blandly functional room, so choking to the imagination, and the intensity of her rejection persuaded the pedals to rise above their distaste for its blinding light and plastic tablecloths and rejoin her. She was reaching for them delightedly when a hand grasped her shoulder, vice-like, and then Sylvia Fraser's voice was in her ear, penetrating and eager.

'I've been so jealous of you with your handsome young toy boy.'

It was unfortunate, thought Joan, but not to be helped. She had no wish to be rude to the Chairwoman of the Entertainment Committee, in such desperate need of entertainment herself, but Sylvia was a mature woman, quite capable of amusing herself, and Margaret was a vulnerable adolescent in the grip of a confidence crisis. It was clear that, for once, inclination and duty combined; so she steeled herself for a monumental effort and tapped her foot twice, and when she opened her eyes she was, indeed, in Gordon Huntley's study, and Margaret was sitting at her father's desk, a handsome mahogany piece topped in red leather, tooled with gold. She was about to go to her when a braying sound caught her attention; and when she looked for its source she saw that Sylvia was with her still, standing by the sash window, staring in – and that would never do, for the pedals were *her* secret, hers and Paul's, not Sylvia's, and she would not share them.

Joan acted instinctively – she would marvel, later, at her quick thinking at this critical moment – and turned the full might of her attention on her pursuer, focusing defiantly on Sylvia's squat features and reducing them, shrinking her as Alice had shrunk after drinking the potion in Wonderland. A fanfare in C sharp minor rang out as she bore down on her absurd grin, reducing it to the size of a Christmas card; and when she was as tiny as she could make her, she called into being a pink dahlia in a pot of green faience, and with a yelp of triumph, like a child capturing an artfully darting fly in a jam jar, she put the dahlia in a window box, just where Sylvia's head was, and so obliterated every trace of the Chairwoman of the Entertainment Committee.

'Hurrah for me!' cried Joan. 'Hurrah for the pedals!' The pain had returned to her chest and she took a moment to settle herself and draw breath, letting it subside. Margaret was waiting for her father, whose tread was audible in the hall, and Joan caused a copy of the *Girls' Own Paper* to appear in her hands. The young woman held it uncertainly, as though it might spontaneously combust or otherwise injure her. 'It is better to have dared and lost', Joan told her, gently, 'than never to have dared at all.' She watched as the girl flicked nervously to the Correspondence section, thinking of the letter Hannie had written to her teacher; and as Margaret scanned it, and began to cry again, she summoned a breeze to ruffle the contents page and draw her attention to the lengthy poem which the editors, this time, had published with due prominence.

Margaret stood up. 'Oh Father!' she called. 'Oh Father! They have— It is— It is *published*!'

Chapter 42

The release of Derby Capital's Investment Report was followed by two days of eerie calm, which Carol punctuated with brisk remarks about the necessity of bracing themselves for the worst. This came at 9 a.m. on the third day, and by twelve o'clock Patrick's usually ruddy face was as white as the sheet of A4 paper on which he had logged each of the morning's harrowing calls. 'That's Morgan Christenson, Ribero Asset Management and the Parker Brothers out so far,' he said, taking advantage of a temporary telephonic lull and smiling wryly, 'and it's not even lunch time.'

'Between them,' volunteered Carol, 'that's fifty-eight million.'

'Your mate Pasquier better fucking deliver, Eloise.'

Eloise swallowed. 'He will, Patrick.'

'See if you can get him to make some sort of encouraging announcement. That's what we need to show these little fucks.'

This cannot be my life, thought Eloise. Aloud, she said, 'They won't want to say anything until their conference.'

'When's that?'

'In three and a half weeks.'

'We'd better have something then, or we're shafted.'

'I'll do my best.'

'Your best is pretty good, McAllister. You'll need to be on form for Birgir Lindqvist, too. I've arranged a lunch with him tomorrow. You'd better work some of the magic you weaved on Clive Stamp. How much has Lindqvist got with us, Carol?'

'About ninety-three million, Patrick.'

Eloise entered the lobby of the Connaught the next day, struggling against a rising nausea. The doorman, who knew her well, greeted her with friendly deference and led her to a seat in the lounge. She had chosen the establishment for its reassuring permanence: there was something soothing in its expensive ugliness that she hoped would add gravitas to her arguments. She was early and Birgir Lindqvist liked to be late, so she selected a deep sofa beside an air-conditioning vent and sat down on it. A hot flush was simmering just beneath the surface of her skin and she did not wish to be discovered drenched in sweat.

She ordered a glass of orange juice, no ice, and prepared her face for a smile of confident welcome. As she did so, a young man in tails emerged from a service door and sat down at the piano some distance from her. He had spent his break deciding what to play, and had almost begun with an Andrew Lloyd-Webber medley – which might have made things go very differently. As it was, he selected something a little tonier and began Chopin's Minute Waltz at a rattling tempo that suggested years of familiarity with the piece.

It was an unfortunate choice of soundtrack for a woman as close to the edge as Eloise, and the first hateful trill took her instantly back to the stuffy confines of Reading Town Hall, in which the final round of the Berkshire Piano Competition had taken place almost thirty-five years before. She had not thought of this adolescent episode for years, but now it came back to her clearly. She had been a nervous participant, coerced into taking part not so much by Joan herself as by her own intense desire to please her musical parent.

The day had been hot, like this one, the hall full of anxious parents, silently egging on their offspring. She had chosen the Minute Waltz carefully, and with good reason. It was an ideal concert piece: short; dazzling; well known. She had practised it painstakingly over several weeks, working on each delicate ornament with fanatical attention to detail, and the night before the competition she had performed it to her grandmother quite expertly. She had done so again the next morning, shortly before leaving the house, and George had spent the forty-minute drive to Berkshire singing it at her in a whining voice that quite spoiled her inner poise.

At Reading Town Hall, she had bidden farewell to her family and gone to the cubicle reserved for performers. She had hoped that she would be one of the first on the programme, but in fact she had been the last – and as the other performers disappeared, and bursts of applause drifted periodically through the panelled walls, she had succumbed to temptation and crept to the auditorium door to listen.

Eloise was the youngest finalist. The others, in their late teens, were dauntingly good. She listened to them through a crack in the door, her heart beating with the agonising certainty that she would shortly make a spectacular fool of herself. By the time her name was called, she was so petrified that it did not even occur to her to run from the building. She moved painfully onto the stage, her knees shaking so violently that she could barely walk; and on reaching the instrument she failed to adjust the stool correctly – so that she began the piece at the wrong angle, sitting too low over the keys.

Thanks to the exertions of sixteen nervous adolescents on an extremely hot afternoon, the keyboard was drenched in sweat. The ivories were in fact so wet that they caught the stage lights and reflected them distractingly. She should have wiped them before beginning – she understood this as she began to play – but by then she was already several bars into the piece, and going at a cracking pace.

Somehow, she made it through the first section. She stumbled over each of the ornaments but pressed on regardless. By the time she reached the middle section, however, she was shaking so violently that it was difficult to pedal – and she had not yet acquired the knack of feigning effortless unconcern at moments of crisis. As she reached the extended right-hand trill, she was almost in tears. How many bars had it lasted for? Five, she thought, though she could no longer remember. All she did know was that the required movement – a rapidly repetitive motion of the fingers from right to left – had clashed with the terrors of her body, which was shaking uncontrollably from left to right. The result was complete paralysis, her fingers locked above the keys.

The Connaught's pianist was just finishing, lifting his wrists with an affected flourish, when Birgir Lindqvist entered the room. Sweat was running down Eloise's face and her body was rigidly immobile. In these conditions, the assured smile of welcome with which she had intended to greet Derby Capital's most important investor became a haggard grimace, its lines harsh with fear.

'Are you ill?' asked Birgir, shaking her hand and ignoring the sweaty cheek she proffered for him to kiss. 'Would you like to postpone?'

Eloise did not go back to the office after lunch. She walked home, instead, while the pavements swam before her. She knew better than most the importance of initial impressions – and yet she had allowed herself to be discovered damp and wild-eyed, at the beginning of the most important meeting of her career. She wanted to cry, or break something, at the thought of this unforced error.

The handsome Swede, usually so charming and attentive, had replied very shortly to her questions about his wife and children, about whose doings and achievements she had an extensive knowledge, and refused even a glass of wine. He had chosen only one course and had not stayed for coffee, making it perfectly plain that he wished to end the meeting as quickly as was consistent with politeness. He had avoided any discussion of osmium and its glowing future; and though he had not said anything to suggest this, she knew in her heart that Patrick would shortly be adding Lindqvist's name to the list on his desk.

She walked quickly through Mayfair, the heat rising dizzily from the pavements, and as she crossed the traffic on Berkeley Square she wished – quite fleetingly; it was gone in a moment – for . . .

But she dared not put it into words.

Her breathing quickened. She had never had such a thought before. Wondering if it could be read in her face, she peered into an estate agent's window – but nothing in her reflection suggested the enormity of what had just happened. She had always embraced life's dramas; none of them had derailed her yet. Surely . . . *You need a shower*, she told herself, *and some time to think*. But thinking, as the last awful month had shown her, led only to alternating self-accusation and dread, and the minute inspection and re-inspection of her disastrous decision to cancel her iron ore trade. How useful $130 million would be now! The impulse to inflict physical injury on Carol, as punishment for diverting her at the crucial moment, was strong. She wanted to kick the little bitch, and the fact that she could not betray any sign of rage, or act on it, heightened it unbearably.

She turned right onto Berkeley Street, and the impulse returned – more strongly this time; louder. It was not that she wished to kill herself, she decided, examining the feeling out of the corner of her eye. It was more that she simply did not wish to be alive; that she could not face the humiliations and disasters of the coming weeks, the painful shadow they would cast over the long and penniless years that lay ahead. 'Pull yourself together,' she said crossly, aware that this instruction attracted the attention of another pedestrian, who looked at her with suspicion.

She hurried on, rifling anxiously through her head, looking for something happy to cling to; but she did so only half-heartedly, knowing that she had not had any happy thoughts for weeks. She was not accustomed to such extended failures of nerve and the tropical cheeriness of the weather further underlined the interior darkness from which no escape but one offered itself. By the time she unlocked her front door she was shaking uncontrollably. She went into the kitchen, filled a tumbler with ice and went purposefully to the cupboard in which she kept the whisky – but she did not open it. Instead, with a great effort of will, she retraced her steps and filled the glass with water from the filter jug. She should, she thought, have a shower or do some exercises, but she had no energy for either task. Instead she went into the living room and checked her messages.

There were four, in total: two from Patrick, asking where the fuck she was; one from George, enquiring after Joan; and one from Claude, who sounded better than he had done the last time they had spoken. 'I am arriving in London on 20 August,' he said. 'Are you free?'

She was just writing down the number of his hotel when the phone rang again. She was sure it was Patrick and steeled herself to answer it: she would have to speak to him sooner or later and it was better to face his wrath now. But the machine stopped ringing before she had collected her nerves. She sat down, tingling with relief, then jumped like a frightened child when her Blackberry sang to life a moment later. This time she answered. She would tell her boss the truth. She would say she was sorry; take responsibility for everything that had happened.

But it was not Patrick on the telephone.

'Your mother has had another worrying episode,' said Sister Karen, in the voice she reserved for the breaking of serious but not fatal news. 'Don't alarm yourself unduly, she's in very good hands. But it might be useful for you to come in and meet her doctor. Would it be possible to fit that in at some point in the next few days?'

Chapter 43

'Good morning, Joan. Time to get up. The doctor will be here at eleven.'

'The . . . doctor?' Joan's tongue felt heavy; it was hard to persuade it to form the desired sounds.

'You had a spot of bother last night,' said Nurse Fleur gently, opening her curtains. 'She's just coming to make sure everything's absolutely fine.'

Joan wriggled her toes. 'Where is Paul?' she asked.

'He's away with his dad.' Two hours earlier, Sister Karen had called the Head of Community Services to suggest that Paul refrain from disturbing her patient until she was stronger, and had passed the news of his timely camping trip to Nurse Fleur. 'It's probably just as well.' She plumped her pillows. 'You need some peace and quiet.'

'I feel perfectly all right, dear. Perhaps a little tired.'

'Let's get you breakfasted and washed, ready for the doctor.'

'Honestly, I'm fine.'

'Of course.' But this did not deter Nurse Fleur from cutting Joan's grapefruit for her, and watching her eat it; and this seemed to anger the pedals, who replaced the rack of steel spotlights above her head with the griffin chandelier as a gesture of solidarity against such undignified treatment. Their generosity palliated the dawning memories of the night before: the destruction of 17 Kingsley Gardens by Sister Karen, who had swept her from Gordon Huntley's study with a large damp hand; a confusion of voices and nurses and a paper cup in which two blue pills and one beige one had rattled like balls on a roulette wheel. Joan ate her breakfast beneath the grave stares of the chandelier's winged sentinels; and an hour later, once she had washed and dressed her patient, Nurse Fleur ushered in a plump, approachable young woman, who alone of all The Albany's staff addressed Joan with titular formality.

'Good to see you again, Mrs McAllister. How are you doing?'

Joan had not the faintest idea who she was. 'Very well dear, thank you,' she said.

'I'll leave you with the doctor,' volunteered Nurse Fleur. 'Just press the bell if you need anything.'

Dr Julia Walters, who had been up most of the previous night by the bedside of a terminally ill patient, gave Joan a smile of stoical cheeriness and put her attaché case on the bed. She had only two more patients to see before the end of her shift, and the lures of solitude and sleep were strong. 'I hear you had a bit of an adventure last night.'

'Hardly an adventure, dear.'

Dr Walters pulled up a chair and sat near her. 'You were a little confused at dinner time, I think. Are you having any trouble with your memory?' She asked the question respectfully, removing a clipboard from her case.

'None that I can remember.' Joan smiled at her own joke, but the doctor did not seem to notice it.

'May I ask you a few questions?' Dr Walters produced a pen from her bag and held it expectantly over the page in her lap.

'Of course. Anything you like.'

'Okay, good. What is the year?'

'Two thousand and four.'

'The season?'

'Summer.'

'The month?'

'It is July, my dear.'

'The date?'

Joan, whose succession of correct answers had induced a momentary overconfidence, considered the question again. Really, there was no need for dates at The Albany. She said as much, and Dr Walters made a note of this reply.

'And the day of the week?'

'Every day is the same in here, dear, except for Sunday afternoons when my daughter visits me.'

'I see. And does that make you feel that your life is empty?'

'No.'

'Excellent. Now, let's talk for a moment about where we are.'

'Very well.' Joan did her best to disguise from the young woman the tedium of her conversation. 'Ask away.'

Dr Walters blinked violently. She had performed the Mini Mental State Examination thirty-two times already this week, and it was not an exercise that improved with repetition. 'What city are we in?'

'London.'

'What part of London?'

'Wandsworth.'

'And the building we're in is called . . .?'

'It's called The Albany, dear.'

'Very good.' Dr Walters made a note. 'Now, if I could, I'm going to say three words. Please listen carefully. You can say them back after I stop. Ready?'

Joan nodded.

'Here they are.' Dr Walters paused impressively. 'Pony.' She waited a moment. 'Quarter.' And then, wishing earnestly for a cup of it, 'Coffee. Now, Mrs McAllister, what were those words?'

Joan, who had been distracted during this delayed sequence by the hope that Margaret's triumph of the night before had in some way been shared with Hannie, whom she so resembled, found that this interior diversion had removed all trace of what Dr Walters had said. 'Would you mind repeating yourself, dear? I'm afraid my hearing's not what it was.'

'Pony . . . Quarter . . . Coffee,' intoned Dr Walters. 'Now please say them back.'

What a silly exercise, thought Joan. Still, it was better to stay on the right side of the law. 'The first word was "Pony",' she said carelessly, as though it required no effort to remember it. 'The second was "Quarter", and the third . . .' But without so much as a by-your-leave, the third word had disappeared. How vexing.

It required a further repetition for Joan to master the sequence, and Dr Walters moved on to the numerical portion of the test. 'Subtract seven from one hundred and continue to subtract seven from each subsequent number until I tell you to stop,' she said gently, holding her pen at the ready. But for Joan, to whom mental arithmetic had always been a source of unprofitable anxiety, the path into the jungle of numbers was strewn with debris and decaying vines. She reached eighty-six before becoming hopelessly lost; and on her second attempt she made a wild stab in the dark, giving as the third element in the series the number seventy-seven, which she felt sure could not be right.

Dr Walters made more notes, and then rather meanly asked if she could recall the three words she had given her earlier.

From where Joan stood, in a dim thicket of numbers, at the mercy of a long line of sevens, it was impossible to make out the words that had been in her head just a moment before. They were there, still; she could see their outlines; but she could not quite discern their letters through the dense foliage of unresolved arithmetic. It was infuriating. 'I don't remember,' she said sullenly. There was so much she *could* remember, after all, and she yearned to tell Dr Walters just one of the many things she had learned in the last few months. 'I do know, however,' she continued, doing her best to keep the exasperation from her voice, 'that this house was built in ...' But when was it built? She could not, after all, be sure. 'That,' she began, trying again, 'Gordon Huntley's middle name was Ernest; that Miss Isabella Muir was born in Rouen to a Scottish father; that Margaret wished to be a writer and strikingly resembles my great-aunt ...' But what else did she know? 'That the doctors prescribed hydrate of chloral, hydrocyanic acid and henbane to Clementine Huntley.'

There, she thought proudly, was a triplet sequence she could recall with perfect accuracy.

'Very good.' Dr Walters made further notes. 'And what', she asked, holding up a pencil, 'is this?'

'It is a pencil,' answered Joan, testily; but her research mission now recurred to her. 'What would hydrate of chloral do to you, Doctor? Or hydrocyanic acid?' This was not a question frequently posed by Dr Walter's geriatric patients. She hesitated a moment. 'Chloral hydrate puts you to sleep,' she said briefly, 'but it can have unpleasant side effects.'

'Of what nature?'

'Well, it can induce nightmares and delirium. Are you having trouble sleeping, Mrs McAllister?'

Joan shook her head vigorously. 'What about hydrocyanic acid?'

'That's a really dangerous poison – I don't think any doctor can have prescribed it. It hasn't been used medicinally since the late nineteenth century.' Aware that time was running on, and that much of the Mini Mental remained to be completed, Dr Walters made an effort to return to the matter in hand.

'Please read the following and do what it says, but do not say it aloud.' She held up a card on which the words 'CLOSE YOUR EYES' had been printed in block capitals, and as she did so a thought occurred to Joan, who remembered (with satisfaction; it was further proof, after all, that she could still remember things) Katherine Ingelow's artful evasion of the second half of the aerobics class on her first morning at The Albany. Following the doctor's instructions to the letter, she closed her eyes, but she did so firmly resolved not to open them again until she had been left alone to think further about poor Clementine Huntley.

'Very good,' said Dr Walters. 'Now please write a sentence.'

Joan began to breathe rhythmically. Her mother had been a strict believer in early bedtimes, and she had learned to feign sleep convincingly as a child in order to avoid punishment for reading after lights out. She employed her best efforts now, allowing her head to fall forward on her chest for added effect.

This sequence of actions so precisely echoed Dr Walters' own inclinations that she could not quite stifle a yawn herself. At the bottom of her worksheet was an instruction to 'Assess level of consciousness along a continuum'. She placed an 'X' somewhere between 'Drowsy' and 'Stupor' and stretched luxuriantly in her chair. Then she roused herself and went downstairs, where she promised to call Sister Karen as soon as she had had a chance to finish her notes. 'If you could get her bloods taken and sent off for these tests in the meanwhile,' she said, handing the Nursing Manager a list, 'I'd be grateful. I didn't want to wake her now.'

A moment later she had driven her battered Renault Clio round the corner and pulled over into a loading zone. What a godsend it was, she thought, setting her phone's alarm and closing her eyes, when an appointment ended early.

Chapter 44

The instant the doctor had closed the door behind her, Joan sat up and opened her eyes. How she wished Paul were with her! But he was not; and neither, for the moment, were the pedals. Where was Clementine Huntley's photograph? She began to search for it, for the room was now cluttered with curiosities that Paul had salvaged from the Huntleys' boxes, and it took her half an hour to find it stuck between the pages of the yellow paperback by the bed. As she held it to the light, examining Clementine's eyes for evidence of drugged docility, Mrs Huntley's gaze seemed to extend beyond the window in the photograph, out of the image itself and down to the book beneath. Joan followed her glance. 'At first he meant to repaper the room,' she read, 'but afterwards he said that I was letting it get the better of me, and that nothing was worse for a nervous patient than to give way to such fancies.'

She closed the book sharply. Frank had refused point-blank to remove his mother's wallpaper and after two deliriously illicit weeks with Gian-Battista, she had lacked the inner moral authority to demand it of him. She sat down, her hands beginning to shake, but already it was too late – for in the corner a glass-and-steel table had appeared, and on it rested a porcelain box, painted with peonies.

Astrid had begun sharing her arthritis prescriptions as a friendly gesture, to give her daughter-in-law some 'oomph' in the numb months after Eloise's birth; but after Joan grew frightened of them she had pressed them on her with proselytising generosity. She looked at the box now, fighting the urge – as sometimes she had fought it for weeks, while Astrid's gifts so temptingly accumulated. *Take one*, said a delicious voice in her head, the voice of the white witch whose home had been the cypress tree on the oval lawn at Nooitgedacht. *Take three, for glee*. She had never taken more than four at once, deterred by the grave warnings on the black-and-yellow packet; but three had been heavenly, had soothed the impact of Frank's manic DIY and the stubborn banality of his music.

Astrid's painkillers killed many kinds of pain, and dampened all fear of the future. It was under their influence, on 19 May 1962, shortly after her mother's death and Frank's repainting of the ebony sideboard in the dining room, that Joan told her husband – so softly he had to turn the radio down to hear her – that committing herself to him, and having children by him, was the defining failure of her life. She had not yet been unfaithful to him, and might have said nothing at all had he not come home early from the office and violated her solitude. She had sent the children with Astrid to the park and taken three orange pills with a glass of sweet dessert wine, had just set her edition of Chopin on the music stand, when her husband entered the house and went straight to his workshop to hammer into being a chipboard bookcase for Eloise.

His banging unleashed in Joan – not fury, exactly, but an impulse to plain speaking that would not be resisted. She went to his workshop door and knocked, for she was forbidden to enter this sanctum without permission; and when he came to the door she smelt the liquor on him, rising above the fumes of varnish and turpentine, and said what she had come to say. She told him how passionately she regretted ever meeting him, how much she wished she could undo the past, and he did nothing but gulp at her like a trout taken from the water. She repeated her incantation over and over, under the spell of its truthfulness – until he turned abruptly from her, retrieved his hammer and went into her sitting room, where he brought it down on the highest note of her piano and cracked it beyond repair.

What possessed Joan in that moment she afterwards could not comprehend, for she had a horror of violence, but she threw herself at him. She did not expect Frank to flinch; and when he did, raising his hand to protect himself and revealing the scar that glimmered at his wrist, her anger left her. She was beginning to float, to rise inches above the carpet; and each movement was a swimming stroke through the warm evening air. She left her husband in possession of the sitting room and took her Chopin to the back garden, where she cleansed herself in B flat minor and listened to the First Nocturne, which had been her salvation in darker times than these. She listened to it over and over until the children came home; and when she had made their dinners the heaviness that marked the pills' retreat settled over her and she took it with her to bed.

She was disturbed, many hours later, by the smooth touch of nylon on her face; then woken by the intrusion into her mouth of the prune coverlet Astrid had bought after donating the Nooitgedacht linen to the Salvation Army. She protested, but the pills left her too weary for effective resistance; and the nylon in her throat made it as hard to scream as it was to breathe. Frank was pinning her arms behind her head, a look of blank indifference on his pale face, and though she kicked with her legs his weight was too much for her. The shock made her rigid, which in turn sharpened the pain. She had no name for the place of forced entry he had chosen; was grateful only that his stiff, angry little penis could not probe further into her, however hard he thrust it.

Joan's afternoons with the orange pills had henceforth been tinged with oppression and fear – and yet remained irresistible, with a fascination she could not explain. She looked at the box for a long time. *What harm could one do now?* asked the white witch, seductively; but Joan knew the harm it could do, and the thought of Clementine Huntley at the mercy of such intoxicants gripped her with a kind of frenzy and outweighed the agony in her leg as she stood. *I must help her*, she thought. But what could she do? In the absence of Paul her only ally was Cordelia, and she would have to suffice unless ... She closed her eyes and called for the pedals, reminding them that she did not do so lightly.

Then she opened the door.

The corridor outside was dark. She had been sitting in her chair far longer than she thought. But at her first tentative step the lights came on, as if they sensed her presence, and drenched her so forcefully in The Albany that for the moment she could do nothing against it. The passage was deserted. Where was Clementine? In bed, presumably. Joan knew from her explorations with Paul which door was hers and went to it, moving as quickly as she could. If a nurse appeared she would say— What would she say? That she was going to watch television, she decided, in the Recreation Lounge (Non-Smokers).

But no nurse appeared; and gathering herself together, she tapped smartly on Clementine's door.

At this moment, the pedals materialised at her side – as she had known, deep down, they would. She whispered her thanks as a voice cried 'Come in!' and opened the door to find Sylvia Fraser sitting on her bed, leafing through a copy of the *Radio Times*. 'Why Joan!' she said, beaming. 'What a pleasure to see you. How *are* you?'

'Fine, fine. And you?' Joan glanced at Cordelia, who maintained the form of a wheelie with admirable discretion.

'Oh I can't complain. Not like some of the old crusties in here!' Sylvia spoke cheerily. 'Why don't you sit down? Did you know that George Chesterton . . .' And with that she was off, recounting the latest developments in the medical histories of The Albany's residents with the enthusiasm of the relatively healthy. What a stroke of luck, thought Joan, that Sylvia's conversation should demand so little input from her. She felt sure she could summon Clementine's bedroom while providing the occasional interjections, the 'Ah's and 'Really?'s, that were the only encouragement her loquacity required, and she listened to a breezy account of Doris Mitchell's removal to a geriatric psych ward while the pedals inched closer.

When she touched one and blinked, the scrawled notes that littered every available surface disappeared. A further tap brought the cornices to life and eliminated the portable television. Now Sylvia herself had to be removed, and Joan stared intently at her face as she twitched her right toe inside her shoe. Once again, it was possible to shrink and distance her. 'Terrible,' she said. 'Do tell more' – and as Sylvia duly told more, she lifted her from where she sat and deposited her in a gilt frame, causing her skin to blur and crack as she became an oil painting.

There, thought Joan with quiet satisfaction, winking at Cordelia. Now that she was alone, she could operate with greater freedom. She grasped the pedals, closed her eyes and tapped her foot – not once, not twice, but *six* times – and when she looked about her again she was in the trellised bedroom that Starkey's had photographed. There, by the fire, was the bronze fender with its frieze of gambolling children; but the vast canopied bed between the pillars, luxuriously cushioned and blanketed, was empty. 'Damn,' said Joan aloud. 'Damn, damn, damn.' She mounted Cordelia and began to move. Clementine's medicine chest must be here, even if she herself was not, and she was determined to find it.

She went to the bed. Beside it stood a delicately scrolled chest of drawers through which she rifled hastily, discovering a series of brightly coloured modern magazines that seemed out of place in an invalid's

274

bedroom in the late nineteenth century. She crossed to the wardrobe. It took three taps to transform Sylvia's dowdy skirts and blouses into a collection of gowns suitable for a fashionable beauty like Clementine, and she began to pull them from their hangers – which remained an unfortunate grey plastic, with the *TranquilAge*™ motif stamped across them in gold. Soon she was surrounded by muslins and silks and scarves of the finest cashmere, but the medicine chest remained resolutely hidden. Did the doctor, perhaps, have it with him? She looked carefully around the room. But of course! There it was – on the window sill, right in front of her all along; a large bottle of poisonously green glass, the acid inside bubbling dangerously. She hurried over to it, heart beating. What could she possibly do with it? She had no experience of handling toxic chemicals.

Sylvia's open window suggested the solution, and bravely, scarcely considering the dangers involved, she grasped the bottle and began to grapple with its stopper. It was too tight for her aching hands, but she persevered and had almost succeeded when the door behind her opened.

'Now, Joan!' Sister Karen ran across the room and seized her shoulders, pulling her firmly away from the window, away from 17 Kingsley Gardens and Clementine's bedroom with its playful children, merrily motionless in bronze. 'Everything's quite all right!' But it was not, or at least not yet – and with all her might Joan threw the bottle of hydrocyanic acid into the street below. The sound of tinkling glass released the Chairwoman of the Entertainment Committee from her portrait. She appeared quite unharmed by her captivity; if anything, a little thrilled by it. Nevertheless, thought Joan, though an explanation was impossible, an apology was in order. She was about to make it when Sister Karen produced the porcelain box painted with peonies that she had spent all afternoon so bravely resisting.

'Now, Joan,' she said. 'One of these will make you feel a great deal better.'

Chapter 45

The first thing Eloise understood about Dr Julia Walters, and this came as an enormous relief, was that she was extremely nice. There was something jolly about her, and this jolliness combined with an aura of professional dependability to induce calm.

Thanks to the peaceful demise of her terminally ill patient, Julia Walters had had two nights of uninterrupted sleep, and she felt glad of them as she shook Eloise's hand in Sister Karen's office. Dealing with Family was one of her specialities, but it required immense energy. 'First of all,' she said, warmly, 'I've really enjoyed treating your mother. She's so sunny and optimistic, and she's using her wheelie wonderfully.' She looked at Eloise with unpatronising sympathy. 'I know this is hard for you. I sometimes think it's worse for the people who love them than for the patients themselves.'

'How bad is she?' The childish thinness of her voice alarmed Eloise.

'She's not in immediate danger, I'm glad to say. Physically, she's doing quite well. She's very mobile for someone in her condition, and the spontaneous Parkinsonism we've observed is quite mild. We would expect to see further rigidity and gait disturbance as things progress.'

'But she's all right at the moment?'

'Yes. Broadly speaking, yes.'

'So what's the problem then?'

'Well,' said Dr Walters, soothingly, 'this diagnosis would need to be confirmed by a CT scan of the brain – which I've organised for next week.'

'I'll go with her.'

'Of course. But we've already run a full biochemical profile on her bloods—'

'We get that done the same day,' said Sister Karen. 'It's best to know what's what as soon as one can.'

'Absolutely. Anyway, we've checked for erythrocyte sedimentation rate, urea, calcium, liver function, thyroid and so on. The results aren't conclusive, but her behaviour strongly indicates—'

'What?'

'That she's suffering from dementia with Lewy bodies – or what we call DLB.'

'Which is?'

'It's a kind of dementia that affects a significant minority in the elderly population. It has features of both Parkinson's and Alzheimer's, but isn't quite like either of them.' Dr Walters paused. Even now, eight years since finishing her training, she still found it painful to reveal to a patient's family the harsh truth of a loved one's situation. 'We can expect to see a progressive cognitive decline that broadly parallels that observed in patients with Alzheimer's,' she said gently. 'But there are a number of symptoms that set DLB apart. Sufferers often experience visual hallucinations and illusions, and in fifty to eighty per cent of cases something we call "fleeting misidentification phenomena" occurs, where patients confuse people around them with figures from their past. It is likely that we will see that in Joan as her condition progresses.'

'I see.'

'Patients with DLB have a tendency to noticeable fluctuations in cognitive abilities. Their attention span varies. Sometimes they're very alert, quite like you or me. At other times they're hardly there at all, and the condition can lead to delirious states that last for days – even, in some cases, for weeks. Am I going too fast?'

Eloise shook her head.

'Your mother's performance in the Mini Mental State Examination illustrates exactly what I mean. She began very well. She was chirpy and conversational, knew exactly where she was, what year it was, all that sort of thing. But as the test continued she became increasingly less coherent, and half way through she just fell asleep.'

'What form do the hallucinations take, Doctor?' Eloise's only experience of hallucinating had succeeded the consumption of a glass of suspect punch at a student party during her first year at university. She could not bear the thought of Joan being exposed to three-dimensional monsters of the sort that still returned occasionally to her nightmares.

'DLB sufferers generally hallucinate people or animals,' said Dr Walters. 'Sometimes objects of personal relevance. They tend to be realistic and well formed. There's also a tendency to spontaneous Parkinsonism. As I said before, we can expect to see increasing stiffness and problems with walking. There's a greater chance she could have a dangerous fall.'

'I see.'

'Yes.'

'And what can we do about it?'

'Well I'm glad to say that geriatric medicine has come a long way, even in the last ten years. Until quite recently most doctors would have put her on a strong tranquilliser – Haloperidol, say – which would have knocked her out. We wouldn't do that now, but DLB does present specific challenges. One of the problems is that it heightens patients' sensitivity to the medications we generally prescribe for rigidity. We could try her on a course, but the side effects are often worse than the original complaint and Mrs McAllister is relatively mobile at the moment. I wouldn't recommend that for the time being. The more immediate problem seems to be' – and here, with a slight inclination of her head, she indicated Sister Karen – 'that your mother's hallucinations are causing her distress. There's a new range of atypical neuroleptics that will help to keep them under control, without making her Parkinsonism worse as old-style tranquillisers would do. She has no history of epilepsy or cardiovascular disease?'

Eloise shook her head.

'Then I'd recommend we try clozapine to begin with. Of course we'll monitor her bloods on a regular basis, and we'll do our best to keep the side effects under control.'

'What kind of side effects might there be?'

Dr Walters raised a hand in mock protest and smiled kindly. 'If I told you everything that's listed in the *British National Formulary* you'd have a heart attack. Most people are fine on it, but there are risks associated with all these drugs: nausea, vomiting, agitation, paranoia, that sort of thing. There can be circulatory and cardiovascular problems, but she's in a place where she can be properly monitored, so any action that needs to be taken can be taken immediately. All that's really important is that she takes the medicine regularly. If she stops her treatment, or withdraws too abruptly, there's a risk of rebound psychosis – and that would be a serious problem.'

'Rebound psychosis being?'

'I'm sorry. Put simply, it means that her hallucinations will get worse – perhaps much worse – and paranoia will become a problem. She could begin to fear the people closest to her. We wouldn't want—'

'Rest easy, Doctor,' interjected Sister Karen, who felt that Julia Walters had dominated the discussion quite long enough. 'My nurses will make sure Joan takes her medicine like a good girl.'

Chapter 46

Thank goodness, thought Joan, as she examined the contents of the black metal box that Sunil had broken open for her, that Paul was away. She consulted the unmarked book on her lap; it was not the sort of thing that a child, however advanced, should see. 'Whilst they were in the heat of the action,' she read, 'guided by nature only, I stole my hand up my petticoats, and with fingers all on fire, seized, and yet more inflamed that centre of all my senses ...' She closed the slim volume, guiltily. It had looked so respectable, the neat black chest with the shiny lock, buried beneath a stack of ageing magazines at the bottom of one of the Huntleys' damp boxes. She had expected confidential business papers, at most love letters between Gordon and Clementine – but this!

Lacking Paul's experience of commercial erotica, Joan had no idea what to make of it. She had seen the colourful magazines confined to the top shelf of the newsagent's, of course; had scrupulously avoided eye contact with the women on their covers, all bulbous breasts and over-made-up faces. She had even overlooked the discovery of one such publication beneath George's mattress, many years ago. It was not, she told herself, that she was a complete innocent; she knew what pornography was. But the idea that such stuff had been written in proper sentences, and enjoyed between covers whose sombreness hinted so little at the technicolour excitements within, was shocking to her; shocking and, perhaps, just a little – exciting.

'For my part,' she read, scanning further on, 'I will not pretend to describe what I felt all over me during this scene; but from that instant, adieu all fears of what man could do unto me; they were now changed into such ardent desires, such ungovernable longings ...' Joan looked over her shoulder, to make sure that Sister Karen had not sneaked up on her. She closed the book, but this did nothing to silence the memories it summoned – of the man who had turned her own fears into ardent desires, who had taught her the delirious dangers of ungovernable longings.

She thought of Frank's pale, hairless body, so unlovely by comparison; of his anxieties about his own nakedness, which only drew attention to the scars he refused to explain. They had provoked tenderness in her, at first, these marks of past suffering; a tenderness that only his steadfast unwillingness to act on any sort of tactful instruction in bed had poisoned. She remembered his stubby penis and the thin, watery seed that sometimes dribbled from it during sleep, and the image prompted a violent churning of nausea that took several deep breaths to placate. Really, she was not feeling at all herself – had not, in fact, felt quite well since her visit to the hospital with Eloise, and her temporary incarceration in that funnel-like machine.

There were fourteen books in all, bound in plain brown leather and in markedly better condition than the Huntleys' other effects. She would have to ask Sunil to return them to the library before Paul got back, for she could not possibly share such things with an impressionable young person. Their spines and covers were blank, the typescript the same in each; only their varying widths made one distinct from another. Feeling less queasy, she opened the thickest and, finding it written in the masculine first person, a booming voice – manly and authoritative, with the faintest trace of a Scots burr – filled her head. It was Gordon Huntley's, she felt sure; and as she glanced at the words on the page he began to read them to her.

'We did not allude to our married condition,' he said. 'One evening lying face to face, kissing, I fingering her clitoris, she holding my prick, I put a question. She said no, her husband's prick was not quite as large as mine, very nearly she thought, and then, "Oh! don't let us talk about such things!"'

Joan dropped the book as though it had scalded her. How could Gordon possibly have known?

The scene returned with painful clarity: that cheaply tiled shower, with its leaking taps; the way Gian-Battista had looked at her, twisted lazily in the sheets, as she dried her hair in front of him for the last time. In a courtship of snatched afternoons, they had finally taken a holiday together; had gone to a bed-and-breakfast in Kent, in the shadow of Sissinghurst Castle, and spent two glorious weeks laughing and making love and reading in bed, while she sent postcards to Frank and the children describing a visit to a friend from her Royal College days. The hotel was cheap and the food greasy, but for the first time they had *had* time; and the explosiveness of prolonged intimacy had shown her that she could not much longer restrain her desire for more.

It was this that had made her afraid; this and the low malice of her final betrayal of her husband's physical shortcomings. She had only half-known, as she dressed, that she would not see her lover again; the possibility had hardened into certainty only as they reached London and parted at Victoria Station, beneath the festive lights.

In all the wild physicality of their affair, Joan had not once felt guilty until that day. She had returned to Frank and the children each afternoon, made their dinners, helped George with his homework, accompanied Astrid on the piano just as usual, the memory of what she had done – of what she would soon do again – a secret reserve of pleasure to see her through the week ahead. She had let Gian-Battista do things to her that Frank had never attempted; she had begged him to do them, and in all the time that he had known her body so intimately, she had never once felt bad – only joyful, almost giddy with the rapture of desiring and being desired. Her conscience, dormant so long, had been woken by words, not actions.

She thought of their last few hours together before the taxi came to take them to the station. Gian-Battista often teased her about what she put up with at home; and this morning he had asked, for the first time, slyly almost, what her husband was like between the sheets. She had told him, with spiteful candour. They had laughed and laughed while she measured the length of Frank's diminutive member against the thick, hairy shaft of her lover's erection, marvelling that something so large and solid could give such pleasure.

She picked up the book and smoothed the page on which it had fallen. 'Her first night with me', said Gordon, 'seemed the highest development of randiness and sensuous enjoyment I ever witnessed in a woman, who was what may be called chaste. Her long abstinence from a doodle, the effect on her physical organisation of the rocking of the boat, and my stimulating words acting upon her mind caused it.'

Joan remembered Gian-Battista's stimulating words, the wild sincerity of his declarations of love and lust. To think that she had turned away from all that! She thought of his astonishment as she told him it was over; the heavy, lonely trudge from the tube station through the winter mist as she tried to compose herself, her only solace the thought of her sitting room and her piano. By the Christmas of 1969 Astrid had been living with them for almost thirteen years; had already dealt with the linen and the china and the ground-floor carpets; caused Frank to rebuild the kitchen and lower the ceiling in the hall. Over Joan's objections, a pine laminate bedroom suite had been acquired and installed. Only her sitting room remained to her – an oasis of selfhood on the first floor, with its two pretty windows looking onto the street; its morning light; its piano and the few pictures she had salvaged from Nooitgedacht before its final sale.

The whole way home, pursued by the image of a grown man sobbing in a crowded railway station, she had wondered desperately how she might contrive to spend ten minutes alone before beginning the turkey. To her surprise, a miraculous silence had greeted her. Had her family gone for a walk, or to a matinée? She had paused in the hall, listening intently; but there was no trace of Astrid's singing, or Frank's banging, or Eloise's relentless declamation rehearsals. She sank to her knees on the olive-green carpet and gave thanks – for the anguish of terminating an alternative future demanded solitude, and she took the granting of it as God's reward for her resumption of uxorial duty.

She climbed the stairs slowly, and opened the sitting-room door.

The shock of what Astrid had done made her stumble. She gasped, and felt she might faint. 'Surprise!' Astrid cried. 'Isn't it comfy!' And again her voice rang out – but Joan refused to relive this moment twice in ten days, and Gordon Huntley's books suggested a potent alternative.

She licked her index finger and let her right hand fall to her lap, a quietly stimulating presence; and as she turned to the book once more the swirls of Astrid's wallpaper faded, and with them Gordon Huntley; and Gian-Battista's voice, rich and resonant, now spoke to her. 'She seemed almost mad with pleasure,' he breathed, standing behind her, his stubbled chin grazing her ear lobe. 'When fucking, her sighs were continuous, though she was quiet in tongue, until the crisis came on. The copious discharges she made were like a flood.'

Gently, but with authority, as he had done that first afternoon, in his kitchen at the end of her Italian lesson, he took her hand and drew it downwards, hitching her skirt up to her waist, guiding it beneath. 'She was a strong-scented woman. When she got hot, a sort of baudy, cunty, sweaty exhalation evolved from her. I shall always think it was that, among other things, which got me such an attack of stiff-standing, and that the aroma of her body excited me, though it somewhat offended me.'

That was it, thought Joan: his smell had excited her and offended her at the same time. He was not a conventionally good-looking man. It had taken time to see beauties in that strident nose, in the bristling eyebrows that loomed like awnings above his dark eyes. She thought of the dense foliage of his chest, his huge but gentle hands, and the intoxicating scent, almost obscene in its unashamed virility, that emanated so powerfully from his armpits. She shifted slightly in her chair, letting her legs part, and pressed her hand towards the place that Gian-Battista, with typically Latin hyperbole, had called *il centro dell'universo*. She moaned quietly. She would have to be careful and quick, lest she be overheard and discovered. Closing her eyes, she slipped her fingers beyond the absorbent crotch of her incontinence panties.

It was as though the aches and cares of sixty years were lifted from her. The pain in her joints became a gentle blur and her wrinkled breasts lost their lines and firmed, rising upwards as though cupped by two large, hairy hands with filed nails. A soprano began to sing – Gian-Battista had known nothing of music before they met; it had been a revelation to him – her voice rising high and clear in the *Laudamus Te* of Mozart's Mass in C Minor. *We praise you, we bless you, we worship you, we glorify you.* Why were human beings so afraid of physical pleasure? Would God have made such ecstasies possible if He did not intend us to enjoy them? Her breathing quickened as an alto joined the soprano in the glorious *Domine Deus*, their voices twining sinuously about each other as her smooth white legs had once writhed between Gian-Battista's thick brown ones. She became conscious of a stiffness in her wrist, but it served only to heighten the unfolding delirium of her return to a blessed state, unvisited for too long.

Walking through the years that parted them, crossing the days and nights, leaping the seasons with the leonine grace she had noticed the first time she saw him, handing out vocabulary sheets to an adult-education class, Gian-Battista came to her and pressed his body against hers, holding her close and drenching her in his heady scent.

Chapter 47

Joan ate only a few mouthfuls of dinner that night, and Sister Karen did not insist on her clearing her plate. In fact, she thought, the Nursing Manager had grown markedly more lenient since her experience inside that horrid machine at the hospital, with Eloise. She didn't seem to mind if she left the dried meats of her evening meal untouched (Pork on Mondays; Beef on Tuesdays; Turkey on Wednesdays; on and on in endless rotation) or if she had her food in her room; all she insisted on was that she ate the pineapple yoghurt she brought her each evening for dessert, and in this matter Joan acquiesced uncomplainingly.

She did so again now, to avoid a draining confrontation, but in truth she did not like the yoghurt. It made her tummy feel terribly tender. Was she developing some sort of allergy to dairy products? She suggested this possibility to Sister Karen, but the Nursing Manager pooh-poohed the idea and said simply that tomorrow she should have raspberry flavour instead. Nevertheless, though she fell asleep quickly enough, her aching stomach intruded on her dreams and woke her early.

She lay for a moment in the darkness, uttering a wordless prayer for clemency, then clambered laboriously from her bed and put on her dressing gown. The old gentleman who lived in the room next door was a great pacer. She could hear him now, and his movements irritated her as a constantly dripping tap might have done. With Cordelia's help she crossed to the window and drew back the curtains to find the cherry tree emerging from the night in a cloak of pale-blue shadow. How she loved the dawn! She opened the window and breathed deeply; the air was cool and damp, unusually sweet for London, but it acted violently on a stomach in no mood for innocent freshness.

From deep within her, unstoppable, the pieces of cold turkey and

285

tomato salad she had eaten for dinner rose up and made a desperate and successful bid for escape. Groaning softly, she gripped the window sill – oh the indignity! – as she vomited; but when the fit subsided, she was surprised at the meagreness of what her protesting intestines had expelled with such fanfare. Tonight, she promised herself, she would be firm about that awful yoghurt.

Wiping her mouth with her hand, she went back to the bed and pressed the button for Nurse Fleur, who appeared shortly and in a flutter of soothing coos helped her into the shower. Joan smiled to think of the many indignities to which life at The Albany had now accustomed her. She no longer thought anything of being dressed and undressed; or spoon-fed; or bossed about; told when to wake and when to sleep, when to bathe and when to rest. The force of the water beating down from above seemed too strong for her frail body; and leaning on the grey plastic rail as she soaped her breasts, she remembered with what fascination and excitement she had watched them grow, so long ago, and of how old people had seemed to her girlish fancy to belong a different, unmentionable race.

When she was dressed and alone, and Nurse Fleur had had the carpet cleaned, she looked for the pedals – but they had not visited for many days. The tin of night soil had reappeared on the desk, and Paul would not be back for a fortnight yet! A hot tear ran down her cheek and tempted others to follow, but this would never do. She must make her own luck. Summoning all her strength, she closed her eyes and tapped her feet four times, and when she opened them, though nothing else in the room had altered, her father's piano stood beneath the window.

'Thank you, God,' she said, quietly.

The piano was an upright in a case of French-polished walnut, made by the German firm of Carl Ecke and purchased in Cape Town in 1924, the year of her birth. No one had bought it at the van Hartesveldts' sale, and in order to prevent Cecilia from converting it to ready money by some other means, Peter had taught Joan to play it. She went to it now, but the thing was insubstantial and offered no resistance to her touch. She retreated from it, lest further interference should dissolve it altogether, and thought of the room in which it had stood – on the first floor of the tower, with its high arched windows overlooking the reservoir and the circling gulls.

They had begun with a Schubert Impromptu in B flat major, which her father had introduced as a window to heaven, very far from the grasp of mere mortals. He had played it to her with great skill, unconscious of the impact of this feat on his metaphor, and explained the moment at which one passed through the layer of cloud into the divine sunlight of the heavens. Every afternoon for two years Joan had abandoned her brother for an hour and a half and learned a bar; and practised all the other bars she had learned; and listened to her father as he showed her the possibilities of nuance and tone, as he exhorted her to be courageous with the black keys, and told her of an Étude he would one day teach her which would enslave them to her for ever. The time came when she had played each bar so many times that she could play them all together; and then she could share the journey with her father, who would take the bass line and keep a steady tempo while she learned how to make the smallest finger of her right hand sing above the others.

It was on this piano, in the time after Rupert's death, that Joan encountered the First Nocturne of Chopin and began her friendship with the key of B flat minor whose pure, unfettered melancholy became the only outward expression of her feelings in those dry-eyed, tight-lipped months.

In his grief, Peter lost interest in their lessons and left her alone while he assaulted the decadent undergrowth whose dark recesses had been his children's whole world. It was a brutal exchange, for Joan was compelled to observe from the window the destruction of the myrtle bushes and the derelict slave quarters, to hear the loud protests of the gulls; but without her brother to share them she felt that she had gained more than she had lost. It took her weeks to see beyond the deceptive simplicity of the piece's conception, to learn how to set twenty-two semiquavers in the right hand against twelve quavers in the left; and in the delicate unlocking of the music's secrets, she forgot – sometimes for hours – that Rupert would never dare her to leap into the reservoir again, or laugh delightedly when she proved herself equal to him. This forgetting transfused itself through her fingers and into the instrument itself, which became the confidante of her loneliness; and as autumn turned to winter, and then spring, she began to see that Chopin had pointed the way to her salvation all along, for the music he had written could only be played in a state of profound acceptance and peace.

Now she sought this grace again; tried once more to touch the instrument and was once more disappointed. But she was not wholly powerless. The nocturne began to sound in her head, as it had in the garden after Frank's assault on her piano; in the car on the way to her mother's funeral; in the darkness of a hospital ward in the hours after the loss of her first child, a little girl Frank had wished to call Astrid. She heard its delicate questioning, its reconciling of the irreconcilable, and her fingers twitched as the music rose and fell. She closed her eyes again, entreating the pedals once more; but when she opened them all that confronted her was the bland expanse of The Albany's yellow walls.

Chapter 48

'Tell me something positive.' Patrick spat a biro cap at a television screen across which a large tank was trundling, driven by a child barely older than Paul. 'Even if you have to make it up. I need some kind of fucking straw to cling to.'

It was late August, and the last three weeks had been the most harrowing of Eloise's professional life. 'Pasquier's arriving today,' she said, 'for the MaxiTech conference.'

'We're going to need that announcement.'

'I'll do my best.'

'Which was pretty good, once.' Patrick shifted in his seat, not meeting her eyes. 'You know' – he spoke meditatively, as though to himself – 'I considered throwing myself out of the window this morning. Why not make a dramatic exit, I thought.' He picked up another pen and chomped it in half. 'But then I reconsidered. We're only five floors up in this office. Worst thing you can do is survive something like that.'

This was not a train of thought Eloise wished to pursue, and understanding the volatility of her boss's mood she attempted levity. 'At least you didn't have to send Clive Stamp a pair of your used underpants.'

'There is that.' Patrick smiled faintly. 'D'you think Birgir Lindqvist might want them instead?' Two days after his lunch with Eloise, Lindqvist had withdrawn $60 million of the $93 million he had invested in Derby Capital.

'It's worth a shot.'

'Anything's worth a shot when you're totally fucked.'

They sat in silence for some minutes, watching the muted explosions on the television screen. 'Suicide bomber kills 70 outside a police station in Baquba, Iraq,' ran a ribbon of scrolling text, its words trickling distractingly beneath the carnage. 'President Bush insists victory is in sight.' The camera focused on a woman in late middle age, lost in a paroxysm of grief. It circled her, observing and concentrating her anguish, as though an unspoken agreement existed between the cameraman and his subject: that her rage and sorrow would be conveyed to the world only as long as its performance remained eye-catching. It was obscene, thought Eloise, that she in her well-appointed office should feel despair. What claim had she on the dignity of such an emotion? Aloud she said, 'How're we doing for liquidity?'

'Osmium's trading at \$72.01, which puts our losses in the region of \$108 million,' said Carol, smartly. 'We've had to dump most of our gold and all our titanium. That means—'

A crash, louder than the televisions' muted explosions, interrupted her. Patrick was standing over his desk, a vein on his neck throbbing so violently that she thought he was having a heart attack. Eloise had raised her hands instinctively, in a protective gesture, and in a moment she saw why: a piece of wilted lettuce had stuck to the wall several feet above her head, and on the floor were the shattered remains of a plate. 'It means', bellowed Patrick, 'that you'd better fucking sort this *out*, McAllister. Is that *crystal fucking clear?*'

Not since Frank had last beaten her, in punishment for pouring custard into Samantha Parry's gym shoes, had Eloise been in close proximity to physical violence. Claude had never hit her, though on one occasion she had sincerely believed that he would. He had never, in fact, come close to hitting her; but the same rage in a different sort of man would have played very differently, and this fact had made him terrifying. She witnessed violence all day, of course, on the television screens in her office; but its scale was too horrific to comprehend and had ceased to move her.

Patrick's treatment of his lunch, however, indicated powerfully his likely response to the truth she would soon have to share with him, and triggered in her a state she had not known since girlhood. She spent the afternoon vigorously focused on her work; conducted three successful trades; stayed late and chatted to Carol about the stresses and strains of mothering a teenager studying for exams; and all along she thought only of the fact that she now understood what true fear was. It was very different, she observed, from its weaker manifestations

– which tended too quickly towards the passivity of despair. True fear demanded action and brought with it a heightened awareness quite distinct from the numbing paralysis of panic. Under its influence, the outlines of things grew clearer; and as she did her best to restrain the impulse to run from the office and never return, she understood that she had reached the limits of her bluff.

Throughout the afternoon, in a repetitive monologue of exaggerated calm, her inner voice acknowledged that she had held disaster at bay, against considerable odds, for the better part of three and a half months; admitted, further, that this was an impressive performance that few others could have matched; commiserated with her on her astounding bad luck and unfortunate scruple in the matter of the iron-ore options; and proceeded to remind her that none of this mattered now, and that the game would shortly be up. If things went on as they were, it emphasised, there would be no holding out until December. With its gold reserves on the verge of exhaustion and all its titanium gone, the next major withdrawal would be the ruin of Derby Capital – which meant that it was probably days, not months, before she would have to face the confrontation she and Patrick had been having for weeks, so terrifyingly, in her dreams. After that, of course, her career would be over; her salary would cease; and her mother, now at the mercy not only of her body but of her mind, would have no source of financial support but George.

As she left the office and walked up St James's, conscious that Claude was now in the city, the white sharpness of her fear subsided, and with it went the quicksilver energy that had powered her through the afternoon. Deprived of this stimulant she felt she might fall apart, as though her mind was suddenly unequal to the task of containing the dreadful facts it had just sorted so deftly. *There are always alternatives in life; the trick is to see them*. But she knew the sophistry of this reassurance and no longer trusted it.

It was a beautiful midsummer's evening. In something of a daze, she wandered into Green Park and sat on a piece of parched earth, thinking how strange it was that of all the people who should witness her collapse it should be Claude. Since the end of their life together she had built herself into a stronger, less dependent person than the child she had been with him, and the thought of exposing herself to his sympathy now sent a hot tingle down her neck.

She stood up and dusted herself, and as she did so her Blackberry buzzed. 'Hello at last.' Claude sounded exuberant. 'I am sorry not to contact you earlier, I was giving a presentation. Even now I am having dinner with the board of directors – I am phoning you from the bathroom.'

'Welcome to England!'

'Are you free to see me tonight?'

'Of course.'

'I was hoping you were. You haven't been answering my messages.'

Since their conversation in June, Eloise had examined the issue from every conceivable angle and concluded that she could not legitimately blame Claude for anything that had happened. Having made this decision, she had not been able to bring herself to speak to him at all. 'I sent emails,' she said. 'I told you I was keeping the evening free.'

'Are you okay?'

'I'm fine.'

'So where do we meet?'

'Shall I come to your hotel?'

'No, no. Don't trouble yourself. Let me come to you. I'll just get a taxi.'

Eloise had agreed to this suggestion and ended the call before its full implications occurred to her. Once they had she felt uncontrollably nauseous. She hurried home and surveyed the state of her apartment with rising horror. Irina, in Pristina on her annual holiday, was not due back for five days. Eloise had not washed anything up or thrown anything away for three weeks. The bedroom, kitchen and study resembled municipal waste dumps, through which an observant investigator might trace the ethnicities of the takeaways she had consumed on those nights when she had eaten anything at all.

It was unthinkable that Claude should see the place in this state.

She went into the sitting room and opened a window, sucking in the traffic-fumed air of the street. The voice of her yoga instructor, whom she had not seen for months, came to her like a spirit message: 'Breathe in acceptance of yourself, breathe out acceptance of others.' It was a measure of Eloise's unusual desperation that for a moment she tried, quite sincerely, to follow this advice, while her inner self watched pityingly and washed its hands of her.

Trying to think methodically, she called Claude's cell phone to arrange a different venue – only to be told by his recorded voice that he was in London and would be checking his messages daily. Next she tried his hotel, but the receptionist did not know where the MaxiTech board members were dining. For half an hour she ran between the sitting room, the bedroom and the kitchen, carrying plastic cartons and glasses and making frantic resolutions to be tidier in the future. She was just disposing of a bonsai mould garden that had once been a carton of pilau rice when there was a knock on the door.

'*Salut, c'est moi.*'

'Claude?'

'I managed to skip dessert. I'm on your floor. The concierge let me in.'

'Right! Give me a moment.'

'Why this coyness?' The handle of the front door rattled. 'Can't I even see where you live?'

Eloise stood in the hall, calculating her options – which were limited, at best. She closed the bedroom door behind her and crossed soundlessly to the other end of the corridor, where she closed the sitting-room door too. Leaning down, she picked up the takeaway menus on the floor and stuffed them onto the hall table.

'What are you doing? Hiding a lover?'

She opened the door, her face wearing the expression of set brightness which Claude, like Joan, knew too well to be deceived by. 'Why don't we go out for a drink?'

But Claude had already moved past her and was standing in the hallway, looking at her with the expression of amused scepticism he had worn that second night, meeting her outside the locked door of Le Petit Trésor. His iron curls were still frizzy from travel, his face paler than she remembered it. He leaned to kiss her and she consciously resisted the impulse to retreat – for his smell was unchanging, and summoned the past painfully. 'Could I use the bathroom first?' he asked, mischievously.

'Of course.' There was a toilet off the hall, still in a presentable state because Eloise never went into it. She indicated it now.

'A glass of wine would also be great, thank you.'

She stood in the corridor, listening to the flush of the cistern, the running of the taps in the sink as he washed his hands. 'I'm out of everything,' she said apologetically as he reappeared. 'Let's go somewhere for a Kir, for old times' sake.'

But Claude only raised his eyebrow. 'So which is it? A lover or a corpse?'

'What?'

'That you have hidden in this mysterious flat with its closed doors.'

She laughed dismissively, but already he was striding away from her. From behind, barring the gun-metal curls, he looked almost like the lithe young man he had once been. 'Let's go out,' she tried again, but hopelessly this time, almost plaintively, because she knew that her shame would be revealed.

'I promise not to tell the police,' said Claude, opening the sitting-room door, 'whatever it is you're hiding.'

Chapter 49

Eloise woke the next morning to the sound of vacuuming. She reached for her alarm clock but found, to her surprise, that it did not occupy its usual space at the summit of the tottering books on her bedside table. The books weren't there either. She sat up in bed. The curtains were tightly drawn against bright daylight. Since Irina's departure, she had grown used to being greeted each morning by a harrowing scene of domestic devastation; but today, inexplicably, the cosmetics and mugs, the discarded clothes and half-read newspapers that usually cluttered every available surface had vanished.

She got out of bed, saw that she was naked, and reached automatically for a dressing gown that hung on a hook behind the door. She was conscious of a dull nostalgic thud, the half-pleasant echo of distant student nights. Her knees ached. It was decades since she had had a hangover of such monumental proportions, and she took careful steps towards the bathroom, which remained reassuringly chaotic.

'It is almost two o'clock in the afternoon,' said Claude as she entered the kitchen a few minutes later.

'What did you do to me last night?' The room was uncomfortably full of light and its dazzling surfaces made her squint.

Claude indicated two empty whisky bottles that stood by the bin, awaiting recycling. 'You did that to yourself. I stopped when we ran out of soda.' He smiled and stood up. 'I slept very comfortably on the sofa, thank you. I am worried that you do not seem to have a very attentive housekeeper, in these days.'

Eloise looked behind her into the sitting room, now a hallowed space of freshly plumped cushions and neatly stacked magazines. Long blocks of sunshine fell across the carpet, like a fleeting Mondrian in light. 'Thank you for doing this,' she said, weakly.

'Would you like coffee?'

'Yes, please.'

He poured a cup and brought it to her. 'Still milk and one sugar?' This was how they had both taken it, in the days when he had made it for her every morning.

'I don't take sugar now, thank you.'

'Neither do I.'

This made them laugh, though neither of them could have said why. It was so strange, thought Eloise, to be spending another morning drinking coffee in her dressing gown with Claude.

'Still stuck in your slovenly ways, I notice. Doesn't surprise me.' He said this tenderly, looking away from her.

'I did try to tidy up when I knew you were coming.'

'You can't have tried very hard.'

'I did. There just wasn't much time.'

'Dirty cow.'

She scrunched a sheet of newspaper into a ball and threw it at him, which he dodged, chuckling, as he placed a bunch of plump peonies at the centre of the table. He had made lunch, a crisp salad of spinach leaves, quails' eggs and goat's cheese, with a lime vinaigrette. 'I went shopping while you were sleeping,' he said, tossing it expertly. 'There is nothing in your fridge except some very old tomatoes.'

'I don't cook a lot at home.'

'Clearly.'

Details of the evening before began to return to Eloise. 'Did I embarrass myself last night?' she asked warily.

'Embarrass? No. But you were not as articulate as usual, perhaps.' Claude smiled. 'First you didn't say anything, hardly. You just got me to pour out my own troubles, which is easy enough these days. Then after three Scotches you began laughing with wild eyes and talking very fast. There was something about the price of iron ore in Japan, and Patrick Derby. Also the osmium situation. That's when you really started drinking.' He sat down opposite her, with a look of sensitive concern she recognised from long ago. 'What's going on?'

To Eloise's dismay, her eyes filled with tears as Claude moved his hand across the peonies and touched hers cautiously, like a child dared to put his finger through a candle flame. This quiet contact with another human being, which suggested so subtly that the intense private pain of the last months might be shared, and so eased, cut through the discretions of pride and ego and severed the last, tightly stretched sinews of her self-control. She began to sob as the impenetrability of her problems, the difficulty in choosing, even, where to begin an account of them, overwhelmed her. 'I – I'm in—' But she could not speak.

Claude watched her from his chair, unwilling to trespass on such grief, but as her tears welled he stood up and went to her and put his arms around her shoulders. He did not touch her hair, or wipe her eyes, or do anything more to recall their former intimacy than hold her shoulders, but he felt that he would remember the moment for the rest of his life.

'It's not your fault,' said Eloise, her breaths shallow and quick. 'I wish it was, but it isn't.'

'If you had only told me—'

'I know, but I didn't.'

'What is the situation now?'

'We're down a hundred and ten million dollars. It gets worse every day. I almost made everything all right, then I lost my nerve and couldn't bear my mother finding out and—' Between caught breaths, she told him of the loss of Joan's savings and her attempts to redress the situation; of her disastrous retreat from the iron-ore bet, the fund's haemorrhaging of clients and money, Carol's crowing hatefulness and the price of Joan's care and the fact, most fearful of all, that Patrick still believed that a breakthrough was on schedule. 'I thought, maybe, I could fix things before December. It didn't seem worth telling him straight away, I couldn't—' The sobs returned, but she fought against them. 'He's expecting you to make an announcement at the press conference, something upbeat about your osmium research. I – I've been telling him—' She stopped, because the truth demanded more explicit confession. 'I've been lying to him, Claude.' It was the first time that she had articulated this, and the verb sobered her. 'I've been going into the office every day for months and lying to Patrick, to our clients, telling them how well your work is going, what a fucking genius you are, how we can all rely on you. What a stupid—'

It was indeed, thought Claude, a very foolish thing to have done; but it was not lost on him that Eloise's first error, from which all her others followed, had been to trust his own word too implicitly – and this was supremely touching. In the weeks since June he had examined his polite lie to Joan, and his unnecessary repetition of it to her daughter, and now he saw the defensiveness in what he had done, and acknowledged his unwillingness to admit to Eloise that he had so little to show for decades of effort. He thought how closely they had once gone together in his mind: the eerily shining metal, so stubborn in its refusal to unite with other elements; the elusive girl to whom he had laid siege for eight years, on whom no intimacy could be forced. He had struggled to master them both, to subdue them to him and unlock their secrets, and when he had failed with the woman he had broken faith with the metal, and left it to the unimaginative attentions of juniors. 'There are always alternatives,' he said gently. 'The trick is simply to find them. What you need now, very badly, is some sleep. Come with me.'

She woke several hours later. It was early evening and Claude was sitting on a chair by her bed, reading. He was so absorbed that he did not see her stir, and for several minutes she lay watching him through half-closed lids. His posture had not altered. His straight back and tense shoulders were as she remembered; so were his dark, narrowed eyes; the half-frown so indicative of concentration, and his Adam's apple, still prominent in a thick, strong neck. His silhouette was different: not so stringy; heavier, with a belly that bulged over the belt of his trousers when he sat down. His skin had lost some of its suppleness; it looked greyer, and his smile lines were not, she thought, as pronounced as they should be – for the Claude she had known had loved to laugh.

She sat up and stretched towards him, touching his knee. He looked up from his book and took his glasses off, in a gesture so unchanged that she had the odd sensation, as sometimes happens in sleep, of re-entering the past. She did not move her hand; and quite naturally, perhaps because it was what he had always done with it, he turned it over and tickled her palm with his fingers. He had woken her like this in the mornings, and the action brought back their small bedroom with its sloping walls.

'Claude—' It was time, Eloise knew, to say what she had not said for twenty years.

'Yes?'

'I'm sorry.'

'For what?'

'For what I did in Paris.'

There was silence. Claude thought of Eloise's younger self taking off her raincoat in the cramped hall of their apartment, her body tense with portentous news. He had guessed at once that she was pregnant; had picked her up, overjoyed, and spun her round the kitchen, and been bewildered when she denied it. He had watched her undress and pour herself a bath and had known instinctively that she was lying, but he had found no way of saying this that did not sound ludicrous, absurdly paranoid. Now he said, 'I don't know why you did not trust me to be a good father. I have never known.'

But it was not Claude Eloise had thought of, sitting in a café on the rue d'Assas as she considered the news announced by the steadily creeping line of pink on the pregnancy indicator. It was Joan. Her mother's life, with its litany of sacrifices, its ceaseless self-restraint, had horrified her from girlhood; she had known it could not be hers and had acted on this knowledge alone, fearing Claude's persuasive powers and the exuberance of his joy. 'It wasn't you,' she said numbly, remembering his silence ten days later when she had at last confessed; her inability to explain as he set about breaking the china in the kitchen and smashing the frame of every photograph. 'I just knew that – that I couldn't sign up for my mother's life.'

Claude looked away. 'She, or he, would be twenty now,' he said thoughtfully. 'At university.'

'Or in rehab.'

'We would have had very different lives.'

'I know. I'm sorry.'

For a long time Claude did not speak; and when at last he did there were tears in his eyes. 'I appreciate you saying this,' he said thickly; and then, after a moment's hesitation, as though afraid of provoking her: 'It was left unsaid for too long.'

Chapter 50

Paul had spent three trying weeks making conversation by a campfire with his father, and his reunion with Joan was joyful on both sides. Nevertheless it struck him as unfortunate to discover with her, on his first day back, the most troubling Huntley artefact to date: Surgeon Capt. Leonard Huntley's copy of the *New Orleans Medical and Surgical Journal*, dated July 1894. This fell open, unhelpfully, at an article entitled 'Sexual Perversion in the Female', a case study of a two-and-a-half-year-old girl suffering from a 'nervous disorder'.

In order to be able to define, they read, *if masturbation were the true cause of the child's distress, I determined to put the girl to a practical test. Having her undressed and put on the bed, I first touched the external orifice of the vagina, then the labia minora, without any appreciable excitement on the part of the child.*

Paul observed his friend's white face with distress. The rapture of Joan's greeting had, in truth, alarmed him; for though she said nothing of them, he understood that events that greatly disturbed her had taken place in his absence. He began searching industriously for one of Margaret's essays, but Joan read on with shaking hands: *As soon as I reached the clitoris, the true phenomena developed. The legs were thrown widely open, the body twitched from excitement, slight groans would come from the patient. Being fully satisfied that the clitoris alone was responsible for this growing perversion, I decided* – 'No!' She seized Paul's shoulder – *to excise this organ.*

The nausea of the past few weeks, which had eased in recent days, returned powerfully. Joan took several deep breaths, for she could not bear the shame of vomiting in the boy's presence, but she continued boldly: *Assisted by my friend, Dr H. S. Lewis, I dissected up the clitoris and amputated it almost to its attachment to the pubes. Haemorrhage was controlled by simple pressure and the patient was allowed to get* up and play as soon as the chloroform had worn away; she never experiencing any pain. 'Do you remember ...' Joan began to tremble. 'They wouldn't let my grandmother into the tent, even when her daughters lay dying? Hannie's wrists were bruised. Do you think—' Her voice rose. 'Is it possible that something along these lines took place, that Hannie or Naomi were ... *experimented* on in some way?'

Paul had no immediate answer to this question, and as he hesitated it came to Joan that if Leonard Huntley were indeed guilty of abusing young women in this manner, then his niece might also be at risk. She turned to Paul, imploringly. 'When will those records be available? I *must* know more of Leonard. The pedals have stopped coming and I can't find anything out through them—' She stopped, for she did not wish to burden the young man with her troubles; yet it was true that the soul-destroying reality of The Albany appeared to have lost its mysterious fluidity, that its furniture and light fittings had assumed a morbid permanence.

Paul looked at his watch. 'Not for another month, ma'am.'

'But that's far too long. This is nothing but an excuse for fiddling with young children! And look how it's been pawed over.' Joan reached for Cordelia. 'Oh, I do hope he was never stationed in Bloemfontein!'

'We might not be able to find that out.' Paul spoke as soothingly as he could. 'And we can't draw any conclusions from this.'

Something in his tone troubled Joan, who scented a sweetly intentioned deception in the making. She took his hands and looked into his eyes, keen to impress upon him the significance of the pledge she was asking him to make. 'There may, indeed, be nothing in the archives, Paul, but if you *do* find anything, anything at all, I want you to promise to tell me about it. You must tell me everything. Don't spare me.'

'I will, ma'am.'

'Promise me.'

There was a moment's silence. Granny Rose had been extremely strict on the subject of promises, and the consequences of breaking them. Paul did not make them lightly.

'*Promise* me,' Joan repeated. 'I am not a lunatic. If you find something—'

'I'll tell you, ma'am,' Paul assured her; and then, because it was clear that nothing else would satisfy his elderly friend: 'I promise.'

Chapter 51

Claude and Eloise spent most of the weekend together, and on Sunday, after lunch at a Japanese restaurant in Soho, they began kissing in the taxi on the way home. By the time they were in the lift they were grappling with each other's clothes, and the wait as Eloise fumbled for her front-door key was unendurable. As Claude pushed after her into the apartment, both of them violent in the urgency of reawoken lust, Eloise found herself a girl again, a nineteen-year-old in a strange man's flat. For a moment she held this image, almost wistfully, against the truth declared by her veined hands as she gripped his trembling shoulders. But as he lifted her onto the hall table and began to kiss her neck, his fingers sliding down her back, rediscovering their old haunts, she knew that there were certain pleasures available only to Experience – and the force of them incinerated all desire to exchange the maturity of middle age for the innocence, however firm-fleshed, of youth.

On the perilously narrow hall table, her head jammed uncomfortably beneath the sharp-edged light fitting behind her, Eloise understood for the first time what her mother had long known and struggled to teach her: that there is a beauty in the present. This truth, channelled in some mysterious way through Claude's fingers, was nevertheless independent of them – and it washed over her, bathed her in itself, made her want to scream for joy.

She did scream, as Claude attempted to hoist her over his shoulder: an effort frustrated by the fact that he was no longer as strong as he had once been, nor she as light. These failed heroics made them laugh, and they went more sedately into her bedroom, where he undressed her with the flawless expertise with which he had once removed Madame Récamier's purloined bra. It took several minutes to locate a condom – *Fuck Eloise's messiness*, thought Claude, concentrating to preserve his erection – and when she had found one, and fitted it, they began to move more quickly, each abruptly aware of the enormity of what was happening and the consequent necessity of avoiding conscious thought.

Eloise noted the changes in Claude's body as he laid her on the bed, the small scar above his collarbone, the softened contours of his torso, and wondered what similar etchings of passing time he had discerned in her. She regretted her many missed jogs and arched back to flatten her stomach; but as Claude – reciting the periodic table backwards from Zinc, in an effort to avoid an unfortunate mishap – began to kiss her neck, his lips as soft as they had always been, their lost spontaneity returned to them both and obliterated all else.

Free of the present and its implications, they recovered their intuitive feel for each other's rhythms; and when they returned to themselves it was dark outside and the day had died, leaving them pooled in sweat as the shockwaves subsided: breathless, wordless, lost in the shimmering glory of the moment.

Claude was the first to wake, and as he did so he was conscious of feeling more himself than he had felt for – he tried to decide accurately, because accuracy was important to him, but found that in the languid half-clarity of the early morning he could not pinpoint precisely the last time he had felt so – what was the word? *Vigoureux*, he decided.

Yes: he felt vigorous, full of unrealised possibilities.

Beside him, Eloise had fled in her sleep to the furthest corner of the bed, just as she used to do. The sight was profoundly touching. It permitted the illusion that they had never parted, that he had not wasted two decades of his life (they were not a waste; he had his boys) with a woman chosen simply because she could not be less like his first, life-changing, love. He looked at Eloise tenderly, at her body that resembled its youthful self so closely when dressed, that displayed in its nakedness now, in its bumps and marks, the occasional saggings of skin, the fact that she was middle-aged, that she would one day be old.

That she had staked $130 million on him was immeasurably romantic. He leaned back into the pillows, thinking wryly of the twists and turns of life, and saw with a start that they had made love under the chandelier of gilded griffins that had once hung in Joan's sitting room at Wilsmore Street. He pulled the duvet over his chest at once; there was something scandalous about being naked and aroused beneath an object so redolent of Joan.

Eloise had waited two years to introduce Claude to her family, and had prepared him as best she could for her father's extreme Francophobia. 'He speaks French perfectly,' she told him, 'but he'll pretend he doesn't. It's got something to do with the war.' In the event, Frank had been civil, his natural taciturnity a helpful disguise for the complex emotions aroused in him by his daughter's passion for a Frenchman. He had spoken English resolutely with Claude, but restrained his tirades on the French national character out of respect for Eloise; and though relations between the men were carefully cordial, nothing in the first four years of their acquaintance suggested that Claude would one day be the recipient of Frank's darkest secrets.

They were in Paris when it happened, on a quest for cheeses. It was 1981, and Frank and Joan were visiting for Eloise's birthday. Claude had already bought and plucked the duck he intended to cook, but the meal would be incomplete without a sharp little Spanish goat's cheese, available only at the *fromagerie* on the rue de Lubeck. Frank had so far shown no interest whatsoever in leaving the apartment. As a *politesse*, Claude suggested that he might like to accompany him and sample a delicious *vacherin* – an invitation which led to harsh whispers in the bathroom between Frank and Eloise, and a grudging acceptance.

Frank had been on the rue de Lubeck once before, in the summer of 1944. Parachuted into occupied France by the Special Operations Executive the previous June, he had found the Gestapo waiting for him on his pre-arranged landing ground beside the Maille woods. He was twenty-four years old, a shy, red-faced young man whose father, a schoolmaster, had spoken French to him with a heavy Glaswegian accent throughout his childhood. In his pocket were French cigarettes, two thousand francs, and a *carte d'identité* proclaiming him to be *Monsieur Marcel Juneau*, a haberdasher from Poitiers.

Frank had never been to France and knew very little about haberdashery. Even had he not been carrying a wireless transmitter in an imitation pigskin suitcase, his accent would have betrayed him at once – and the fact that the Gestapo knew his code name, 'Albert', the name of the circuit he had been sent to join, and the address of the Baker Street offices in which he had received his final briefing, rendered useless his carefully rehearsed speech about the accessories trade.

Nevertheless, he continued to repeat it, to the amusement of his captors.

They drove him to Paris in an open Mercedes with his hands cuffed behind his back, having relieved him of his cyanide capsule. Nothing in Frank's life had prepared him for the beauty he encountered, or its scale; and though he had no words for what he saw, no means of identifying the baroque or the neoclassical, the boulevards of Haussmann or the façades of Perrault, he was profoundly affected by them nevertheless. As they crossed the Pont Alexandre III, tears filled his eyes – and in them was no fear, only dazzled wonder.

This memorable journey gave no indication of the squalid violence that awaited him at 3a Place des États-Unis, a large private mansion requisitioned by the SS for purposes of interrogation and torture. Frank had spent the early part of the war as a training instructor in the Royal Engineers, had never seen armed combat or faced any situation more alarming than his mother's irritation when he brought a girl home to meet her. On arrival, he was taken into a small interview room and asked if he was 'Albert'. He replied, in heavily accented French, that he was Monsieur Marcel Juneau, a haberdasher from Poitiers.

'Ah, you poor fellow,' said his interrogator, in perfect English – for he had been a silk salesman before the war and had visited London many times. 'Come with me.'

Frank was taken to another room and strapped to a chair. A large, red-headed man appeared and proceeded to punch him with astonishing force all over his body – battering his stomach, his testicles, his jaw, which dislocated on the second impact and introduced him to an indescribable agony.

'Are you sure your code name isn't "Albert"?' asked the officer, solicitously.

'I am Monsieur Marcel Juneau, from Poitiers,' replied Frank.

The next twelve months were a blur. He had memories of being strung up by his arms with piano wire, and beaten further; he had bled so much from the wounds on his wrists that he almost died. Cigarettes had been extinguished on his body and small incisions made with a knife, on which salt was poured and rubbed in and left for days. Until the end of his life he would scream in his sleep, trapped once more in a bathroom full of pretty young women: Gestapo secretaries summoned to observe his repeated near-drowning in a porcelain bath that had once belonged to a well-known actress.

Eventually he told them what they knew already, but this only reduced the frequency of the torture, because he refused outright to work for them. He was kept for months in solitary confinement in a small windowless cell, which he had no choice but to soil repeatedly. He tried to hang himself twice, but was cut down each time and revived. Finally, on 10 April 1944, he was summoned for transfer to Germany, driven in a van with other agents via Maastricht, Düsseldorf, Leipzig and Dresden to Breslau. At Breslau, the men were separated from the women and taken to the concentration camp at Ravitsch – where, on 19 May, a day that never again passed without him drinking himself into a stupor, he was woken at 1 a.m. and told to get dressed. *At last*, he thought, *the end*. But it was not the end. He was driven, with two others, to Berlin, and flown back to Paris for reinterrogation. At 3a Place des États-Unis once more, he was soaked with water and left alone, freezing in the rat-filled dark, for several days; then kept awake for seven nights in succession.

Now he began to tell his captors all manner of things, anything he thought they wished to hear. None of it was true, but all was believed, and as a reward he was given a job tending the flowers in the garden. The sentry on duty at the back gate was a Georgian, with no natural sympathy for the Nazis. He and Frank spoke, formed a tentative friendship; and on a blistering August day, Frank overpowered him as he leaned down to pick a flower, took his *mitraillette* and shot him in the leg with it; then stole the keys from his belt and let himself out onto the street.

It was down this street, the rue L'Amiral d'Estaing, that Claude led Frank on a bright November day thirty-seven years later. The door through which he had escaped was still there, the wall now concreted over and painted grey. Beside himself with terror he had stopped a civilian at the corner and attempted to requisition his car. When the man refused to relinquish it, he had shot him in the face, at point-blank range, and taken it. *At the end of this street*, he thought, as he and Claude turned right onto it, *you see the Eiffel Tower on your left*. And there indeed it was, a masterpiece of engineering so breathtaking that even on that day, in a car drenched with blood, he had marvelled at it.

He said nothing as Claude made his purchases, only hoped that they would not go back the way they had come. But they did, and when they reached the Place des États-Unis, Claude suggested that they take a seat on the bench beneath the statue of Washington and Lafayette and enjoy a glass of wine together, perhaps some bread and cheese.

For Eloise's sake, Frank did not refuse, understanding that to do so would cause unbridgeable offence. He sat down on the bench, unable to reconcile the present with the past. A blind rage overcame him, of the sort that only the methodical planing of wood, or the construction of a kitchen unit, could soothe and divert. Claude's efforts at conversation riled him further; he found himself wanting to break the bottle in his hand, to assault with it the man who had bought it – for a second-class Croix de Guerre, accepted only at his mother's insistence, remained the French people's sole acknowledgement of the suffering he had endured.

The inscription on the base of the statue, a piece of flowery gratitude for French aid to the Americans at the time of their revolutionary struggle for *independence et la liberté*, was the spark that lit the fuse; and with barely coherent venom he launched into a diatribe so furious and apparently baseless that Claude grew first alarmed, and then indignant.

'It's the bloody French who should be thanking the United States,' shouted Frank, who had emerged from hiding only after the American liberation of Paris.

'Perhaps gratitude is appropriate in both directions,' Claude suggested, as pacifically as he could – for though his intellectual principles deplored unthinking nationalism, he had a personal allegiance to the land of his birth that would not brook the groundless defamation of it. He listened with mounting irritation as Frank lamented Gallic ingratitude in the most strenuous terms; then, when he lost his own temper, he began to shout back.

They almost came to blows, but the very idea so offended Claude's sensibilities that he gave ground and apologised for raising his voice. Such unexpected humility deflated Frank; and in quiet, heavily accented French, he told the younger man what had happened to him.

Claude frowned at the memory and kissed Eloise awake. 'Why don't we go and visit Joan?' he said, quietly.

Chapter 52

Two hours later, there was a knock on the door and Sister Karen popped her head round it, beaming. 'A gentleman's come rather a long way to visit you, Joan! Would you like a minute to get ready?'

Joan struggled to her feet. She knew in her heart that George had come at last. 'Oh Paul!' she said, as the Nursing Manager disappeared. 'It's my son!'

'Should I go, ma'am?'

'No, no! You must meet him!' Joan hurried to the mirror and brushed her hair. Fancy George giving her no notice! She looked fondly at the latest flowers he had sent, a magnificent arrangement of hydrangeas, and toyed, momentarily, with the possibility of being just a little stern with him. He had, after all, behaved quite shoddily when she first arrived at The Albany. And yet . . . Her expression softened. He had come an exceedingly long way, after all. Perhaps his visit would tempt the pedals back. At any event, he would be able to offer her some advice on what to do about their absence; he was so much less intimidating than his impatient sister. She decided to tell him everything.

But when the knock on her door came and she cried 'Come in!' and patted a hand to her hair, it was not George who opened the door, but Eloise; and when she said, 'Oh, where is he? Where is the darling boy?' it was not George who appeared, but Claude.

'How did you know he was coming?' Not for the first time, Eloise suspected a telepathic connection between her mother and Claude.

But Joan did not answer. Her energies were too completely absorbed by the challenge of first grasping and then coping with the fact that Claude was not George. To Paul's extreme discomfort, his friend begin to cry. 'I'd better go,' he said, hurriedly, not wishing to intrude on this family scene.

'Well if you'd rather.' Eloise made way for him at the door.

'Goodness me, how silly I'm being!' Joan waved the young man goodbye, mortified that Claude might think she was not pleased to see him. 'I'm quite overcome.'

'I have thought of you so much these past years, Joan. I am overjoyed to see you again.' Claude put his arms on Joan's shoulders and kissed her delightedly on both cheeks; it was clear to Eloise that he was thrilled by this tearful reception.

'And I', said Joan, revived by this gallantry and recovering herself somewhat, 'am delighted to have my old cooking partner back.' She wiped her eyes with the back of her hand; thank goodness she didn't wear mascara nowadays. 'I only wish you had come a few months earlier and I could have given you dinner at Wilsmore Street. I'm afraid the food in this establishment is *ghastly*!' She said this jokingly, for she and Claude had loved to criticise other people's cooking together, and was horrified to be alerted by a sharp little cough that Sister Karen was in the room. How had *she* slipped in?

'Do let me know if there's anything you'd like sent up,' said the Nursing Manager, smiling to show that she was used to all manner of insults from demented geriatrics. 'I know the chef has made an excellent carrot cake this morning.'

Claude stayed for an hour or more and under the flurry of his conversation Eloise observed Joan carefully. Her hair needed cutting, and her lipstick was a little too vaguely applied, but otherwise she seemed entirely her usual self – or, rather, the self she usually was with Claude. It was amazing, she thought, how quickly Joan and Claude could resume their former intimacy. Soon they were making faces at the over-strong tea and wincing at the inexpert icing of the carrot cake – 'Too much sugar, too little carrot!' cried Joan, chuckling – and the general hideousness of The Albany's cuisine. It pained Eloise slightly, but did not entirely surprise her, when her mother sent Claude delving into the depths of the wardrobe to find – what else should it be? – a framed picture of them both, pissed as lords, standing in that tiny Paris kitchen, high on mutual appreciation. *She's going to start talking about the fucking duck*, she thought.

'Do you remember? It was for one of Eloise's birthdays!' Joan clapped her hands, rapturously. 'I've never tasted anything like it. *Perfectly* succulent, just rich enough but not too rich. Crisp, not fatty.

It was' – she angled her chin archly, always a sign that she was about to attempt a foreign language – '*complètement merveilleux!*'

'But that little piglet', returned Claude, entering into the spirit of things, 'that you cooked – when was it? It must have been the New Year's Eve of 1981. It haunts my dreams, I tell you.'

And they were off, screaming with laughter, quite oblivious to her presence. It was almost a relief to Eloise when her Blackberry pinged in her bag, a welcome reminder that there were those in the world who did seek out her company. 'Excuse me a minute,' she said, standing up. 'I'll be downstairs if you need me.'

When Claude returned to The Albany's reception area half an hour later, Eloise went up to her mother's room to say goodbye. She found Joan in the old chair that had been her favourite at Wilsmore Street, staring out of the window at the sky. How restful it must be, she thought, to be old; she had not had such a peaceful afternoon in years. 'Claude was so happy to see you,' she began, cheerily.

'And I him, darling. What a treat he's come to visit you.'

'He's not visiting me, Mum. He's in London for a conference. His company sent him over here.'

'I see.' Joan smiled discreetly, for she had promised herself that she would not pry. 'But it seems you two are getting on well?' This, she felt, was not a question so much as a statement, and therefore permissible.

'Yes, thanks.' Eloise did not wish to be drawn, and leaned down to give her mother a gentle hug. 'I'm sorry I didn't come yesterday afternoon. I should have called.'

'Don't worry at all, darling. I lose track of the days of the week in here. One's so much like another. Seeing you is what's important.'

'I'll be back next Sunday.'

'That would be lovely.' Joan hesitated. A strong impulse to share her sorrows remained with her, and emboldened by Claude's effusive visit she had decided, in a leap of faith, to tell Eloise. Now that her daughter stood before her, however, the prospect of confiding the existence, and subsequent disappearance, of a mysterious pair of pedals that allowed her to travel to all manner of places, even to venture into The Albany's past and to meet its former residents, was daunting. Eloise was so tall and well dressed and forbidding; she had so little patience for what she could not see. It was why she was such a dreadful pianist. She could never be expected to understand the curious bond that linked the fortunes of Margaret Huntley and Hannie van Vuuren, for Joan barely understood it herself; but the thought of her grand-mother's endurance, and the need to live up to it, made her brave. 'If you could spare a moment, darling,' she said, hardly faltering, 'there's something rather important I need your advice about.'

'Of course, Mum.' Eloise sat down on the desk chair. 'Fire away.'

Joan swallowed. 'I know', she began, trying to put herself in Eloise's position, 'that this is going to sound very strange.'

Sister Karen had advised Eloise not to discuss Joan's condition with her – 'It's upsetting for the dear old people to know too much about what's happening to them. Your mother's lucidity is variable. It's kinder to gloss things over' – and it was only when Joan was halfway through her narrative, which seemed to involve a pair of magical piano pedals and an array of invalids, Victorian children and dubious doctors, that Eloise, unable to bear it any longer, took her hand and gently began to explain.

It took Joan some time to understand the extent of her daughter's treachery.

That Eloise had permitted the hateful Nursing Manager to medicate her without her knowledge or permission was – oh, it was insup-portable. She began to splutter with rage. Sister Karen's audacity in suggesting that *she* was out of touch with reality was staggering – this from a woman who described the morning's regrettable carrot cake as 'excellent'! As Eloise spoke, measuring her words, careful not to alarm or excite her, it seemed to Joan, who for decades had scrupulously avoided making this admission to herself, that they had never really got on and that now they never would. It had been like that from the beginning, she supposed. In her entire life she had never felt such violence towards anyone. She wanted to scream and punch, to kick, scratch and bite Eloise – but of course she could not do any of these things.

What on earth had she done to merit such vengeful treatment? She thought of Sister Karen, and the habit she had of metamorphosing into Astrid. Could there be a link between *them*, too, as there was between Hannie and Margaret? What could it be? Why should it matter to anyone if she freed herself from this ghastly place for an hour or two, or controlled where she went and what she did? She was an adult, after all, at the height of certain powers of which the young and middle-aged could only dream!

Joan put her hands in her lap and did her best to control her breathing. That Eloise – whom she had yearned for, and cared for, and loved as well as she could; for whom, when she might have left with George, she had remained – had betrayed her, was unbearable. Only forty years' practice of concealing her wounded feelings from her husband and his mother enabled her to say now, in a tone of voice that betrayed none of the ferocity she felt, 'Thank you, darling. You've put my mind quite at rest. I see how silly I've been being.' She watched her daughter's face closely, to gauge her reception of this untruth.

'Not silly at all, Mum.' Eloise took her hand and stroked it.

Yes, thought Joan, *she believes me*. 'What is the name of the medication?' she asked, innocently.

'I believe it's called clozapine.' It was always best, thought Eloise, to be open with the people one loved; of course it was. What did Sister Karen know about human relationships?

'And how', asked Joan, looking nonchalantly out of the window, 'are they administering it to me?'

'In your yoghurt, I think. Some patients won't take their medicine, and get worse. I'm sorry I let them, you know, give it to you without—'

'Darling, please don't apologise.' Joan turned and looked straight into Eloise's aquamarine eyes. 'I know you acted from the best intentions.'

'Thank you, Mum.'

Oh the chilling calculation of it! As her daughter leaned forward to hug her, and she returned her embrace, it occurred to Joan how vital it was that the Nursing Manager, whose motives remained murky, should never know that she knew what she knew. 'Please don't tell Sister Karen about any of this,' she said. 'I'd hate to worry her.'

'Of course not.' Eloise squeezed her tightly. 'I'll see you next weekend.'

'I'll look forward to it, darling.'

Chapter 53

'Listen, George' – Eloise did her best to keep the exasperation from her voice, wary of her sibling's stubbornness – 'she's not well. She needs to see you.' It was unfortunate that Patrick should be in the car to overhear this conversation, but it could not be helped: George rarely took her calls and never returned her messages; having reached him, she could not waste the opportunity. She looked at her watch. The MaxiTech press conference was starting in twenty minutes and they were still stuck in traffic. In some ways it was a blessing to be distracted from looming disaster by George's selfishness; at least it spared her from having to talk to her boss. She listened as her brother's excuses – so apparently reasonable, as always – flowed and expanded.

'It's just not possible,' George was saying, his voice full of regret. 'I've worked my arse off for three years to get this contract – we're shooting the ad in six weeks' time and they want Sylvester Stallone or Vin Diesel. I've got to go to LA on Tuesday to meet with their people. Otherwise it's going to have to be Jean-Claude van Damme. Then there're the print adverts, which we can't even begin until we've got the star. It's a big deal for me, E.'

'Believe me, Porgy, I don't underestimate the importance of a new range of muscled soldier dolls to the continuation of life as we know it.' She had not called him 'Porgy' for years; it was a nickname derived from the nursery rhyme about Georgy-Porgy pudding and pie who kissed the girls and made them cry, and it resurrected the image of her brother as a fat and spotty twelve-year-old, victimised by the other boys in his class. 'But Mum's all over the place. There's only so much I can do.'

'She sounds fine when I talk to her.'

'How often do you do that?'

There was a pause. 'When I can,' said George at last. 'The time difference makes things hard.'

'Right. Well her lucidity's variable. Sometimes she *is* fine, but the last time I saw her she was completely out of it. She thinks her nursing home's full of children. The doctors say they don't know how quickly the condition will progress. By the time you've shot your fucking advert—'

The conversation continued in this circular fashion for some time, and had reached no satisfactory conclusion when the car slowed outside the vast modern hotel in which seven hundred and fifty Maxi-Tech employees were gathered for the firm's annual conference. 'Look, I've got to go,' said Eloise.

'You're a star for doing this, Sis. I'm going to save my leave and come for a month as soon as the campaign's in the can. We'll be together as a family.'

'Fuck you, George.' She threw the Blackberry into her bag and smiled at Patrick, who was grinding his molars ominously.

'Tell me your guy's going to come through for us, McAllister.'

'I've been telling you that for months.' Eloise got out of the car, her pulse rate rising. All Claude had said as they parted the day before was 'I'll see what I can do,' and their physical intimacy had prevented her from asking for more – because it was not for professional reasons that she had spent the weekend in bed with him. If this was the end, she thought, smiling bravely, then it was the end; there was nothing more she could do.

The hotel's Jubilee Suite was crowded and hot, and the plastic grilles in the ceiling released only tricklings of blood-warm air. In an effort to restrain her soaring body temperature Eloise fanned herself with the glossy MaxiTech prospectus and took a bottle of complimentary mineral water from a trellised table in the corner.

'This doesn't say anything about osmium,' said Patrick, examining his own copy. 'It's all about synthetic paint fibres and petrochemical processing. They're—'

'For God's sake, shut up.'

'What?'

'I've just had my brother whining at me for an hour on the phone. I can't handle another whingeing male voice.' It was some time since Eloise, in whom anxiety and guilt had combined to induce an uncharacteristic passivity, had talked to Patrick like this. He seemed calmed by the treatment and fell silent as they took their seats.

'Get the doctors to give her some barbiturates,' he suggested as the lights dimmed. 'Painless way to go.'

'I'll bear that in mind.'

The CEO of Maxi-Tech, sporting an incautious tan and a suspiciously full head of hair, now appeared and launched into his welcoming address. The ardour in his eyes as he discussed the enviable position of MaxiTech 'stakeholders' was faintly alarming; he looked like an Old Testament prophet, Eloise thought, specially groomed for a twenty-first-century appearance; or a psychopath. She knew that Claude did not like him. As the flashbulbs that greeted his appearance subsided, the technology correspondent of the *Wall Street Journal*, arriving late, scuttled to her row and sat down next to her.

The CEO ended his speech, and her blood pressure began to climb. The Chief Operating Officer succeeded him at the podium; then came the VPs of Marketing, Sales and Brand Identity, each resolutely gleeful about the state of the company. She sat very upright in her seat, as the tension she had woken with mounted unendurably. A promotional video was played, and only as the assembled journalists began to stir and think of lunch did the CEO rise once more and introduce in euphoric tones the Head of Research and Development. To a smattering of polite applause, Claude appeared and took his seat on the stage, scanning the room, perhaps for her.

A cold chill began to spread upwards, from Eloise's feet.

The press had been waiting for Claude, and a thicket of raised hands now blocked him from her view. He began fielding questions, his replies unhesitating and fluent. She had forgotten how impressive he could be in public; how his certainty in his own capacities communicated itself to an audience. Even Patrick was affected by it; his shoulders relaxed and he leaned forward, visibly less febrile. As Claude spoke, Eloise could not resist calculating her own distance from the door; the number of people past whom she would have to squeeze to escape her boss, in the event that Claude said nothing about osmium, or too little. Her inner voice, observing her childish desire to run away, informed her sternly that this was not something grown-ups did, and reminded her of other responsibilities from which she could not flee.

Joan came to her mind, raving about piano pedals and doctors who had been in her great-grandmother's concentration camp. She tried to focus on what Claude was saying, but his dryly technical language was impenetrable: *electron densities ... Fermi-liquid ... metathesis reactions ...* She caught the phrase 'diamond-like tetrahedral structures' and restrained an involuntary shudder; he had not yet mentioned the critical word, and Patrick was beginning to shift dangerously in his seat. Her mother returned to her, waving her hands. Claude had not said anything after their visit, but she knew that he disapproved of Joan being put into a home, and this quiet knowledge had led her to hold forth on the advantages of The Albany with an enthusiasm she did not feel. She thought of her childhood illnesses, of the way Joan had plumped her cushions and fed her cough syrup and read to her or played the piano, and her inner voice resumed its long-running monologue detailing her many and varied filial failings. She was as bad as George, it said – worse, because her brother's unconcern lacked the hypocrisy of pretended devotion.

On and on Claude spoke, Patrick's knuckles whitening as he gripped the arm of his chair. She became conscious of the blood in her head. There was only one decent thing to do with her mother, and their last conversation had proved it conclusively. If Joan was losing her mind, she needed to be with people who knew and loved her; she should not be trapped in a building that frightened her, surrounded by 'professionals' like Sister Karen, however expensively expert they were. She belonged at home, with her.

The idea distracted Eloise with good resolutions, deceptively achievable – but her inner voice, abruptly changing its tune, set about undermining them with relentless accuracy. If Derby Capital failed, it pointed out, she would have to get *some* kind of employment. What was Joan to do all day while she worked? She would be left alone with nothing but satellite television for company – and Joan hated television. What if she fell? Or began to hallucinate? Eloise had been through similarly tortuous thought cycles many times before, and gave way to another with helpless resignation. There was no way of combining a full-time job with the care her parent needed; that was the fact of the matter, and unless Derby Capital survived and prospered, allowing her to leave with some sort of cash bonus, she would never—

She looked at Claude, and made a silent pact with herself. If he somehow saved the firm she would resign and care for Joan at home; she would abandon all she had worked so hard for and do the right thing. She closed her eyes, mindful of her broken word in the matter of the taxi on Piccadilly. She would not renege this time. If a home nurse became necessary she would get one; but *she*, Eloise, would be the primary care-giver – and she would love Joan, and tend to her, and spend time with her, without once resenting her or considering her an imposition.

When she opened her eyes, Claude was looking at her. 'There is one more thing, ladies and gentlemen, which I wish to share with you.' He spoke briskly, but it seemed there was the faintest flicker of a smile at the corner of his mouth. 'For some time, we have been working on a new range of ultra-incompressible compounds which will have extensive industrial uses. I am pleased to announce that we are now approaching the end of the laboratory phase and that we anticipate beginning full product testing within the next eighteen months.'

The correspondent of the *Wall Street Journal* raised his hand. 'Anything further you can tell us, Dr Pasquier, about these compounds?'

'We are currently making significant experimental steps using osmium.'

Patrick gripped Eloise's arm.

'With all its toxicity issues?'

'Osmium has an exceptionally high valence electron density, which is why we used it as our starting point. Our goal, of course, is to produce an effective, non-toxic alloy, and I am pleased to announce that we are making great progress. I hope to be able to make a more formal announcement later in the year.' Claude stood up. 'Thank you very much for your time.'

Chapter 54

The impact of Claude's public announcement on the price of osmium was immediate and marked. Three hours after the close of the MaxiTech conference the commodity's free fall stopped, and two hours after that, as Eloise took him to the airport, it passed $90/oz and began climbing steadily. Patrick called from the office with this news and yelled it so joyfully that Claude started to laugh. 'I take it he's happy,' he said.

'He's wetting himself.' Eloise smiled. 'Of course all Carol can say is that we're still $94 million down, but at least the figures are moving the other way.' She turned to him, forcing herself to make eye contact. 'Thank you, Claude. I can't thank you enough.'

He raised his hand to interrupt her. 'It is I who should thank you. I feel returned to myself.'

'But how're you going to get out of it?'

'Out of what?'

'The commitment you made this morning.'

'Oh that—' He looked at her mischievously; it was the expression he had worn that first evening, observing her across the Formica table of a Left Bank café. 'I do not need to. It is possible to combine osmium and carbon, Eloise. I am sure of that.' He took her hand tenderly and held it to his lips. 'The question is to find the best method, and that needs motivation – which I have not had for too long.'

They sat in companionable silence as the car weaved its way through the traffic and the memories of the last dark months, like scenes from a slowly fading nightmare, heightened the world's new hopefulness for Eloise. As they passed Hammersmith she thought of her panicked walks through crowded streets; of those long and lonely nights of wide-eyed wakefulness amid the domestic devastation that was the outward sign of slow internal collapse. How suddenly unlikely they seemed, these chastening reminders that she had exceeded the limits of her emotional endurance. And yet she had exceeded them. She knew that she had, and there was no pretending that uncomfortable truth away.

With uncharacteristic humility she acknowledged that she owed her renewed equilibrium, temporary though it might prove, not to any rediscovered reserves of her own but to the love and care of another person; to the loyalty – God, how strange this was! – of Claude, whose impulse to protect her had once been so unbearably stifling.

They parted at Heathrow with a lingering kiss in the middle of Terminal Four; and in that wordless embrace both felt that much was said – though they would not, perhaps, have agreed on precisely what it was. 'I'll be in touch,' whispered Claude, running his fingers down the back of her neck. 'And in the meantime, try to wash something up, just once maybe, before we meet again.'

She watched him go, his curls visible through the crowd of shorter travellers, and as she turned away she felt a surging of the fondness she had once had for him, a rush of the joy they had known together. She felt like singing, or skipping down the pavement; and had she not been in such a public, dreary place, she might have done both.

As it was, she walked smilingly to her car, thankfully unaware of the conversation her mother was having in The Albany's Recreation Lounge.

'Can you credit it?' Joan folded her arms, having told Paul what she knew of her daughter's co-operation with the Nursing Manager's maleficent scheme. It did not seem to her that the young man was as outraged by Eloise's perfidy as he should have been.

'I'm sure she was doing what she thought was best, ma'am,' he said gravely. 'She's probably worried about you.'

'If she were truly worried about me, dear, surely the first person to consult on the subject would be *me*?' Joan looked at the boy, his mouth a little overfull of chocolate fudge cake, and decided to restrain herself. He was not even sixteen and could hardly be expected to appreciate the complexities of the current situation. Indeed, she could barely comprehend them herself, and Sister Karen's motives remained obscure to her. 'Perhaps you're right,' she said, resolving to act alone. 'I'm sure the pedals will return at some point, in any case.'

'I hope so, ma'am.'

This was not something Joan intended to leave to chance, and when Paul left she returned to her bedroom, resolved to put into action the plan she had been formulating ever since the visit of Eloise and Claude. When Nurse Fleur appeared with her dinner tray an hour later, she clapped her hands delightedly over the three slices of boneless turkey that rested beside the inevitable side salad and dessert bowl. It was important to feign compliance convincingly – for it had become Nurse Fleur's habit to sit chatting with her while she ate, and Joan suspected that this had less to do with friendliness than covert surveillance. 'I'm terribly peckish,' she told her, with marvellous enthusiasm. 'But would you mind terribly, dear, if I ate alone? It's too hot for company.'

Nurse Fleur hesitated, fussing over the cutlery as she weighed Sister Karen's explicit instructions against her patient's simple request. In the end it was the thought of herself in Joan's position, making a similar bid for personal autonomy, that decided her. What harm could it do to let the old lady keep a little dignity? 'Of course,' she said kindly, at length. 'I'll come back for the tray in twenty minutes.'

'Thank you, dear.' Joan tucked into the turkey with gusto as the nurse departed, but as soon as she was alone she put her cutlery down and leaned for Cordelia, her hands shaking with excitement. 'Now now,' she warned them sternly. 'Less haste, more speed.'

She picked up the white dish of yoghurt and began to move with it to the bathroom, infuriated by her stiffly uncooperative joints. How difficult the simplest things were nowadays! The operation required the concentration and precision of her most demanding concerts in times gone by: the steady breathing; the focus on posture and heart rate; that curious trick of not thinking about what one was doing as one did it, of relying instead on past practice to guide a complex motion that conscious thought would only impede. It was a little like playing the beginning of the Mephisto Waltz, she thought. *Allegro vivace (quasi presto)* was required, in case Sister Karen came to check on her; but it could only be achieved by calm confidence, undimmed by the distracting fear of failure.

Like a true professional, Joan made it to the bathroom, put the yoghurt down on the basin shelf, lifted the loo seat, retrieved the white china dish and spooned its contents carefully into the toilet bowl. As she leaned on the flush button, the cascade of water chimed with the rapturous applause of a concert hall and she took a modest bow, a faint half-flush across her cheeks the only indication of inner triumph. 'You'll be a bicycle again in no time,' she told Cordelia as she returned to her chair to tackle the haggard turkey.

She would have to eat her dinners from now on, lest the nurses suspect that she did not touch the yoghurt – and poultry of this weight and dryness was not something that could be entrusted with safety to a toilet bowl.

Chapter 55

Claude glanced at the notebook on his desk, made a neat annotation, and returned to the glovebox. Before putting his hands into the gloves he checked that his materials were in order: a cylinder of argon, to provide an inert atmosphere; pressurised containers of helium, krypton and xenon. Within the glovebox were an oven, a laser, an ion gun and three industrial diamonds. These last would be the substrate; above them in a chamber, ready for sputtering, was a large chunk of osmium.

It was too long since he had rolled up his sleeves in a laboratory. He felt like a student again and thought affectionately of his old Professor Heimlich, the tight-lipped Austrian whose unsentimental encouragement had spurred his early ambitions in the field. How happy he would be, he thought, never to attend another board meeting or brief another research team.

He went to a CD player in the corner of the room and pressed a button as the strange, unhurriable quiet of approaching concentration settled over him. From concealed speakers in the vaulted roof came Mozart's Twelfth Violin Sonata in E flat major. He had played it with Joan and chose it partly for this reason, partly for the subtlety of its transition from the first movement's confidence to the introspection of the second. This was precisely the emotional progression demanded by the task in hand, and he pressed the *Repeat* button on the CD player lest any break in the music disturb the regulated focus of his mood. It was late afternoon and the day had been cold, full of crisp autumnal light. He had sent his staff home early and the solitude of the laboratory, with its polished concrete floor, its pristine workbenches and rows of neatly labelled chemicals, pleased him.

It had taken several evenings of dedicated searching to locate his student notebooks in the cluttered self-service storage unit in which most of his possessions currently languished. He had gone back to them instinctively, unwilling to rely on the work of juniors when so much was at stake – for he had a high estimation of his own talents, and did not intend to tie his chances to the careless inaccuracies of his underlings. He put on his protective perspex glasses and slipped his hands into the openings of the glovebox. In this way he could handle toxic substances safely, observing his actions through strong glass and the soothingly inert atmosphere provided by the through flow of argon. It was not dissimilar, he thought, from the manner in which he had handled his memories of Eloise during his sons' infancy and childhood: he had observed them, but from a distance, having taken suitable precautions.

He worked methodically for several hours, as the light from the windows disappeared and was replaced automatically by sunlight-sensitive electric lamps. He moved carefully through the experiments recorded by his youthful self in the notebooks, and as he did so he found that passing time had brought perspective. Osmium atoms, packed tightly together, had somehow to be insinuated between the more widely spaced but strongly bonded atoms of diamond. A metal and an insulator had to be coerced into forming a stable bond; and only by doing so could they create a new substance, greater than the sum of its parts.

The metaphor was too tempting for a person of Claude's essentially romantic disposition to resist. He proceeded systematically, taking the oven in gradual increments to 1000°C in an effort to weaken the diamond's atomic structure; then he tried more rapid heat cycling, all the while sputtering atoms of osmium down onto it, occasionally sputtering the diamond too. As he worked, like a child transforming a plastic soldier into a vast army, he co-opted the materials before him into his own life's drama: the osmium, tightly closed, capable of sudden and unexpected toxicity, was himself of course; and the diamond – glittering, beautiful, infuriatingly self-sufficient – became Eloise. The jewel must be persuaded to accept the metal into her very being. A bond must be forged between them that would be more stable than their first effort had been, twenty years before. Success would lead to a union of rare potential; and failure— Well, it was not a possibility.

His attention trained calmly on his goal, Claude spent many long nights in this way. At length, he grew tired of the Twelfth Violin Sonata and switched his allegiance to the Eleventh, then the Tenth. With patient scrupulousness, he attempted a dizzying range of temperature combinations and catalysts: boron carbide, silicon carbide, helium, krypton and xenon, taking each new material systematically through the full range of heat and pressure options. He had high hopes of krypton and xenon. Though they had failed him and others before, he was sure that their bulky atoms could be made to smash diamond's defiantly imperturbable structure, and he fired them at ever greater speeds into a succession of gems.

In this way, the summer ended and a glorious New England fall arrived, hardly noticed. He saw his boys at the weekends, but only then, and the functional solitude of his new bachelor apartment held few attractions for him. His reputation for professional devotion grew and his social life, never extensive, dwindled; with no one to cook for but himself, he lost interest in food and spent little time in his new, cheaply fashionable kitchen. His needs for social interaction were answered by his children and by osmium, diamond and the other visitors to his glovebox – each of which had a discernible personality, with tastes and habits, idiosyncratic inclinations.

Halfway through September, in a bid to change the intellectual atmosphere decisively, he abandoned Mozart and switched first to the Pet Shop Boys, and then (but only late at night, when there was no one but the building's security guards to hear him) to a range of increasingly glossy mood sustainers: Duran Duran, Madonna, the Trammps, Rose Royce; twice even, in desperation, to Jean-Michel Jarre. Each of these artists briefly sustained his energies, but for increasingly limited stretches of time. He was alert to the dangers of thinning self-belief, had learned to discipline the fear of failure – which only paralysed a person's thinking and did nothing to aid it. So he pressed on, doggedly, and emailed Eloise weekly (confidently at first, then more diffidently) and twice issued cautiously optimistic press statements that buoyed the osmium market and raised excitement levels in MaxiTech's own boardroom.

It was fortunate that his bosses considered Claude a genius, for they left him to his own devices and did not demand from him any participation in the corporate deep-sea-fishing events around which their own lives appeared to revolve. In an attempt to maintain his physical fitness he hired an expensive personal trainer; but after six sessions he came to feel – it was a dangerous sign, he knew, but he could not help it – that he had no time for such distractions. He passed his days and evenings with osmium and carbon, who joined him again as he slept. His nights were spent roving fitfully about his large and lonely bed, a sputtered atom of osmium in search of a resting place in diamond's unforgiving lattice; and on some mornings he found a foothold and woke exultantly, only to discover that his triumph held no real world value.

Eventually, Claude stopped listening to music altogether and worked with feverish intensity – like Mozart, he sometimes thought, finishing his Requiem. Ever the self-dramatist, he began to think that perhaps he would die in the attempt to unite osmium and carbon, or himself with Eloise, as Mozart had died, struggling to complete his final Mass. There was something pleasing in the idea, for he had always been drawn to tales of sacrifice, and it returned to him at odd moments like a soothsayer's prophecy: he was a knight on a quest, attempted and abandoned by many. Only death could alter his course.

Claude's pile of notebooks grew, dizzying memorials to heroic efforts. He bombarded diamond with ever larger and heavier atoms, at ever greater speeds, and took his oven as high as 1500°C. He switched sources of carbon and replaced diamond with graphite, hoping that it might prove more amenable.

Still nothing worked.

Chapter 56

Joan hoped that Paul's ordering of the Huntleys' papers might yield more of Dr Leonard Huntley's possessions, and when it did not she placed her hopes in his further investigation of the National Archives at Kew. She did not suspect that the young man, checking each box before bringing it to The Albany, chose only those that contained the driest of Gordon Huntley's business accounts – which he began to catalogue with such painstaking scrupulousness that their progress, never rapid, slowed further.

Paul started at his new school at the end of the first week in September, and at Joan's request he came to show her his uniform on the afternoon before the fateful day. 'How smart you look!' she cried, noting with approval that the world 'Skull' was no longer discernible among the boy's lengthening bristles. His black suit and dark tie resembled an undertaker's livery rather too closely for comfort, she thought, but she did not share this with Paul. She was concerned, however, that he should not feel burdened by any sense of duty towards her. 'You'll have far too much to do, dear,' she said, 'what with homework and all your new friends, to visit me so often.'

But Paul's feelings about returning to the undiluted company of boys his own age were decidedly mixed, and he had no intention of giving up his happy hours with Joan. 'I could bring my homework over, if you like,' he said. 'I have to carry on with the Huntley stuff anyway – the library's started paying me now.'

'You should do just as you wish. Of course you're very welcome to visit whenever you like, but you mustn't feel that you *should*.'

'I don't.' And indeed Paul did not seem to, for he came most afternoons and his company made the imaginative barrenness of Joan's days much easier to bear.

Eloise came frequently, too, and Joan detected in her manner a

326

lightness she had quite forgotten was in her. It reminded her of the person she had been before she started dabbling with rich people's money, and she suspected that Claude's visit was responsible for this new exuberance. But she forbore from asking questions. The revelation of her daughter's complicity with the Nursing Manager had introduced a distance between them that she was not inclined to bridge; and though she did not at all begrudge her her happiness, she was conscious that everything she said to her might be reported to Sister Karen, and so kept her own counsel.

For a month, Joan evaded her yoghurt undetected; and when, at last, the Nursing Manager arrived in person to watch her eat it, she consumed it meekly and kept it down until she had been left alone and could vomit it undetected into the trusty toilet bowl. This was a painful sacrifice, but she felt sure it would be rewarded; and indeed, she woke the next morning to a room full of possibility. She got out of bed slowly, hoping for the pedals. There was nothing on her desk, or on the shelf beside her ugly bed; but as she turned towards the window, something sparkled in the sunlight on the sill.

She looked again. The light was cheerful, almost mischievous. It was shining into the face of a cherub at the base of a pillar, who was shielding his eyes against the glare as Rupert had done, dripping dry on a towel beside the dark-green waters of the reservoir. She held this thought carefully within her, letting it breathe; and when she was ready, she raised her left foot and tapped it against the wainscoting.

The room quivered.

Joan tapped again.

Now the pillars began to shimmer, and two oak book cases appeared on the facing wall, where no book cases had been before. From these she understood, with relief, that the morning's destination was not to be Turnham Green – where all the shelving had been of chipboard, constructed by Frank. She tapped once more, and the chair beside her sprouted into a small, straw-stuffed sofa. A clock struck in a tower, and a pair of mating gulls hooted.

Now she knew where she was, and her gratitude was sufficient to dispel all traces of The Albany. The two arched windows of her father's study had become one, but in all other respects the room was as she remembered: a space devoted to cheerful disorder, scattered with books and letters and cushions covered in dog hair. It was from her grand-father, she understood, that Eloise had inherited her inability to put anything away. She smiled, and a wonderful possibility came to her – so wonderful that she stopped herself, in case consideration withered it. The room should be quite solid before she acted; so she waited, as details she had long forgotten recurred and took their accustomed places: a wrought-iron carriage clock on the mantelpiece; her father's patched mackintosh, thrown carelessly over a chair.

Is Rupert alive? The question slipped from her, like water from cupped fingers. *Is he in the garden now, waiting for me?* She rose, her heart fluttering. Soon Fleur would come with her grapefruit, bringing with her the tedious unanswerability of a day at The Albany. *I must act*, she thought. So she stood and went to the window, ready to open it and call for her brother; but the luxuriant jungle in which she and Rupert had roamed was no more. A bonfire of marguerite bushes smoked in the shadow of the disused slave quarters, and the syringa trees that had once hidden the courtyard of the servants' wing were in ashes. Her father had destroyed the garden after his son's death, as if in violent retribution for the tragedy; and the desecration beneath her declared, without equivocation, that she had come too late.

She leaned heavily against the window frame. Heaven only knew when she might be here again. She turned to the piano for consolation, for its music stool was as full as ever; and as she did so her nanny emerged from her bedroom far beneath her, and placed a small tin bath in the shade of the jacaranda tree in the servants' yard.

'Beauty!' called Joan, for she had loved her dearly.

But Beauty did not hear her, and she turned away and began to unfasten the clasps of her dress, which fell from her sturdy shoulders as she stooped for the soap.

The action troubled Joan, though she did not know why. She tried to turn, but her feet were weighted and would not obey her. As she watched the young woman wash herself in the sunlight, a tremulous fear crept over her and the gulls began to caw. They had been disturbed, and were protesting. Against what?

And then she saw him.

Her father was creeping along the wall of the servants' yard, to the place where the cement had crumbled between the bricks. The spot was shielded from the main house by the piggery, and when Rupert was alive he and Joan had often played in the secret passage beneath the undergrowth. Now denuded of foliage, it was secret no longer; and there was nothing to shelter her father from her gaze as he bent down and put his eye to the aperture in the masonry.

'No!' cried Joan; but no sound escaped her. Peter van Hartesveldt had put his right hand in the pocket of his trousers and was rubbing himself urgently, as if possessed by a violent itch. It was the explanation she had chosen at thirteen, but it did not survive the scrutiny of adult interrogation. She went to the piano, as she had that day; but as she opened it her father's study became oppressive to her, for it could not contain the enormity of what she had seen. It was not for this that she had so bravely vomited, and now a choking indignation arose within her. '*No!*' she cried again; and again, as in a nightmare, she made no sound.

But the pedals heard her.

They appeared above the window sill and she gripped them tightly. At once the room darkened. The servants' yard beneath her disappeared; and with it went the smoking myrtle bushes and the piggery, the faint tinge of sea salt in the air. If she could not see Rupert, she refused to spend another instant in her own life; and the pedals, sensing this, obeyed.

Behind her a door opened, above which cherubs were strumming a harp, and through it walked Gordon Huntley: magisterial in his black frock coat; but damp, too, as if from strenuous exertion. He crossed to the window, oblivious to Joan's presence, and she saw that in the garden below, in the shade of the cherry tree, a young woman in a hat sewn with jaunty butterflies sat on the lawn. Miss Muir! she thought, giving thanks for this diversion. But as Gordon passed her, she saw that the previous scene had leaked, somehow, into this one; that Mr Huntley's face was furrowed and red, as her father's had been; and that he, too, was rubbing himself with obscene vigour.

The shock of this, a second time, was too much to bear. A jolt of fury shot from her and condensed as a tight, white light. Gordon Huntley stopped, startled by the strength of her feeling, and turned towards her. His eyes widened, and the redness in his cheeks turned puce, and then purple. He opened his mouth, perhaps to protest, but a horrible rattle sounded – as though in the brightness he could not breathe. He began tugging at his cravat, but the light was choking him. He sank to his knees. 'Oh Cordelia!' called Joan. 'Go to him!'

But it was no use.

Before her very eyes – soundlessly, helplessly, unable to grasp what afflicted him – Gordon Huntley died; and as he breathed his last, 17

Kingsley Gardens vanished and Joan was left, cowering and aghast, conscious only of Sunil standing before her with a shaker of sugar in his hand.

'Nurse Fleur's not well today,' he said gently. 'Is it okay if I do your breakfast?'

Chapter 57

Joan woke a few hours later with the sickening realisation that she had done a truly monstrous thing. She had fallen asleep in her chair, and it took some time for the events of the early morning to arrange themselves in traceable sequence: the abrupt appearance of Sunil; her efforts to behave as though nothing unwarranted had occurred; the invincible exhaustion that had succeeded his departure.

She stood up, her limbs trembling, and told herself that it could not have happened. It stood against all reason. She had not even been born when Gordon Huntley lived in this house. Time travel was impossible. Or was it? She went to the window, as half-remembered facts began to creep from distant mental crevices. A gentleman named Einstein – Isaac? Esau? *Albert*, she decided; Albert Einstein – had devised a theory, the theory of … Whatever had he called it? *Relativity*. And that theory had proved something about time and space. There had been a famous formula. She rather thought it was $E = mc^2$, but whatever were E, m and c?

She could not remember. Who but God could say, with certainty, what was possible and what was not? Over the course of her own lifetime, previously unthinkable marvels had come to pass: space travel; long-distance telephony; even the ghastly wonders of the atomic bomb. Science was limited only by the scope of human ingenuity. What if, unbeknownst to herself, she had succeeded in moving about between centuries, in accomplishing a feat that was not impossible but merely undemonstrated? 'I do wish', she said to Cordelia, resolving to put everything before him as soon as possible, 'that Paul wasn't at school today.'

In fact Paul was not at school. He was sitting on an airless train, wearing his jacket despite the heat in case anyone should see, through his white shirt, the phrase 'GRANNY FUCKER' inscribed in thick black capitals on his back. His eyes smarted with tears and his lips were clamped shut, his chin thrust stridently forward in aggressive self-defence. A bruise was forming on his jaw where it had met the ground as Liam Cormack sat on his head, while Lee Anderton and Sean Ward pulled his shirt up and set to work with a marker pen stolen from the art-room store.

The task of the morning's double English period had been to write a composition entitled 'My Best Friend', and in a spirit of fatal candour Paul had written a heartfelt eulogy of Joan. Asked to read it to the class by Miss Brett, he had endured a painfully humiliating break period, during which twenty boys surrounded him, cheering on the three who pushed him to the ground, sat on him, and recorded their opinion of his essay in terms calculated to inspire maximum embarrassment during the afternoon's swimming session. Hard experience had taught Paul the dangers of putting a foot wrong in the first month at a new school, and when his current fury abated he knew he would be left with nothing but self-recrimination and regret. For the present, however, he burned with a righteous rage that kept his tears at bay.

He reached Kew Station dry-eyed, and as he got off the train he took his school tie out of his pocket and put it in a rubbish bin. This piece of defiance soothed him and he walked the short distance to the Archives imagining himself, in his black suit and white shirt, a young office worker in his lunch hour. The cool of the archive building calmed him further, and he produced his reader's ticket and went to the appropriate room feeling almost cheerful, his mind straying pleasantly to thoughts of vengeance.

As he asked whether the Anglo-Boer records were on public view once more, he imagined kicking Liam Cormack's fat face until his nose bled. Informed that they were, he filled out a request slip, thinking how satisfying it would be to dangle Lee Anderton from the art-room window. He took the lift to the first floor, wondering what he should do to Sean Ward, but as the doors opened the memory of his grandmothers intervened and Hildy remonstrated sternly against such tit-for-tat violence, while Granny Rose spoke gently of the necessity of turning the other cheek.

He sat at an empty desk, waiting; and in the quiet, ordered room his anger sputtered and died, leaving behind it only an aching loneliness he knew too well, and a dread of the following day. He could not share the morning's events with Joan, and the thought of confiding them to his father was deeply unappealing; he couldn't wait, he thought, his skin prickling, to be old enough to live by himself.

At length a librarian appeared with a handsome folio bound in red leather, its bindings newly stitched. 'This is just the registers of courts martial,' she said. 'Everything else for the period was destroyed by bomb damage in the Second World War.'

'I know.' Paul sounded self-conscious; he did not want her to think he had no experience in the field.

'Right then.' She fetched two further volumes in dark-blue, water-marked satin and left him.

He opened the first and scanned the hand-filled columns. The names were not in alphabetical order and there were hundreds of them, each brief entry divided into *Rank and Name*; *Regiment*; *Where held*; *Date of Trial*; *Proceedings submitted to the Queen*; *Nature of Charges*; *Sentence as approved by Her Majesty*. He scanned the *Where held* column, ignoring all offences not committed in Bloemfontein – because Joan had asked him to check Leonard Huntley's connection to that city only, and he did not intend to range more widely in his searches than he had promised. Returning empty handed would help his friend relax a bit, he thought, and he moved quickly through the lists, his lips pursed in concentration.

Some entries were in pencil, others in pen. On 29 January 1901, near Bloemfontein, a Lieut. J. P. Milne-Hume had 'Knowingly done an act calc'd. to imperil success H. M. Forces (Showing white flag)' and been dismissed for it, though there was a recommendation to mercy. On 15 May 1901, a Lieut. G. Fitzgerald had 'endeavoured to enter a railway carriage specially set apart for ladies at Bloemfontein station and ...' The rest of the charge was thickly crossed out and aroused his curiosity, but he scanned on. He had reached the halfway point of the third volume when he stopped, for on the page was a name he recognised: 'Captain John Bryars, Reserve of Officers, Bloemfontein, 14 May 1901, Stripped and exposed naked against his will and subjected to indecent treatment a civilian.' This, he thought excitedly, was the man who had ordered the burning of Van Vuuren's Drift, and he wrote the details on the back of a request slip to show to Joan. What had happened to him? '*Not guilty*' read the entry, but Paul was not persuaded. He turned the page, and then the next, relieved that Leonard Huntley appeared to have kept himself out of trouble; and then, among the last ten entries, he saw his name: 'Surgeon Capt.

L. V. Huntley, Rl. Army Med: Corps, Bloemfontein, 19th January 1902, For disgraceful conduct of an indecent kind, Guilty, Discharged with ignominy.'

'Fuck,' he said softly, under his breath.

Joan was sitting in her chair by the window when Paul knocked on her door, the day's feverish worry having summoned the Golden Syrup tin of night soil and a pair of gasping, white-tinged lips that flitted on the edges of her vision. 'Come in!' she called, and when she saw it was the dear boy she could have cried with relief, so eager was she for an outside opinion.

She was about to confess what she had done, or perhaps not done, to Gordon Huntley when Paul said, 'I went to the National Archives for you, ma'am. I've found a couple of things,' and this made her hesitate, for she wanted the unexpurgated truth.

'Do tell.' She patted the seat beside her.

Paul had struggled with his discovery all the way back from Kew, and twice had almost thrown away the photocopies he had made of the ledger entries for Leonard Huntley and Captain Bryars. In the end, however, the indignity of lying to the person who was, perhaps, his only real friend had stuck in his throat and left him resolved to keep the promise he had made. He showed the papers to Joan, who put on her glasses and looked them over, hands trembling.

'I have done something terrible,' she said, when she had examined them. 'I have left the children in their uncle's clutches, with no one to protect them.'

'What, ma'am?'

It took some time for Joan to explain to Paul what had happened, and as she did so the reality of what had taken place grew more resonant. 'I can't explain it,' she finished, 'and I did not intend it, but I think I have caused the death of an innocent man. Whatever can I do?'

Paul hesitated. It did not seem that dismissing Joan's fears out of hand would be the most productive way to tackle them. 'Perhaps he's only injured,' he suggested.

'Oh no, dear. He died. At my feet, with the most dreadful look in his eyes.' Joan's voice started to shake. 'It was a terrible thing to witness. And now that you've found – Well, we always knew what sort of a man Captain Bryars was. But Leonard Huntley! He must have returned to this house after his – what was it called? – "ignominious discharge".'

'We don't know that, ma'am.'

'Why would his papers be here, if he hadn't come himself?'

'He might have sent them for safe keeping.'

'No, no. *Look* at them.' Joan leaned in the direction of her desk, where Leonard's pamphlets were still piled. 'See how heavily used they are. And of course! He's in the census. Goodness knows what he did to the children in the camp. What if—' Joan stopped, as an awful coherence dawned. 'Leonard came back here, after Bloemfontein, Paul,' she said, 'to this very house. Maybe he drugged Clementine with all those medicines, to keep her out of the way so that he could *experiment on the children*.' The phrase, once uttered, assumed a ghastly solidity. 'The only person who could have protected them was Gordon and I – I – killed him. What if Leonard attempted to—'

At this moment, there was a smart rap on the door and Sister Karen entered the room. She took in Joan's tears with a brisk frown and switched on the air-conditioning unit, which began to gurgle. Then she looked at Paul and said, in what she thought of as her jocular manner, 'Someone's supposed to be at school, young man. The head teacher has phoned your father, who has just phoned us. I thought you might be here. You may wait in my office until he collects you.'

'Were you meant to be at school, dear?'

Paul nodded, collecting his things. 'Yeah, ma'am.'

'You're not to bunk out on my account.' It was the first time since Rupert's death that anyone had played truant for Joan, and she could not quite inject the appropriate sternness into her tone. Neither, however, could she bear to be parted at this critical juncture. 'Might he wait with me until his father comes?' she asked the Nursing Manager. 'We were just talking.'

But Sister Karen shook her head. 'I'm afraid not. It is against the law for children to run away from school. He will need to wait in my office, where he can be supervised.'

'Just a few moments, Sister. Please.'

'I'm sorry, Joan.'

Joan's hands began to shake, and Paul, understanding the futility of further resistance, stood up. He leaned down to hug his friend, and as he did so a thought occurred to him. 'If something did happen last night, ma'am,' he whispered into her ear, 'surely you can *un*make it too. Reverse it, I mean.' He squeezed her shoulder. 'Then the children will be safe again.'

Chapter 58

Claude's patience with himself and his own limitations finally and abruptly snapped at 3.17 one chilly morning. Calmly, he removed his hands from the glovebox. He cooled the oven and disabled the through flow of argon, tidied the surfaces around him and switched off the lights. He left the building, saying a polite goodnight to the security guards as he did so. Then he got into his car and drove to his rented apartment.

Quite methodically, he began to sort through the untouched boxes he had brought from the house he had shared for seventeen years with his soon-to-be ex-wife and took out the set of cut crystal glasses that his grandmother had given them as a wedding present. He put them on a tray and took the tray into his living room. The floor was tiled in terracotta – the development was conceived in a Spanish style, wholly inappropriate to New England – and he took the first glass and dropped it with calm indifference.

There was something relieving in the finality of its shattering: a precious object needlessly destroyed, impossible to reconstitute.

He picked up a second glass and dropped it in the same manner; then took a third and threw it at the television set. Missing its target, it broke dazzlingly on the wall behind, so he threw a fourth glass and missed again; and then a fifth and sixth until the seventh, at last, connected with the screen. He broke the rest of the set on the edges of tables and doors, or by throwing them against windows of thick modern glass, and when they were all in splinters he went back to the kitchen and found the decanters that matched them and broke them, too. He worked purposefully, in a soothing trance of destruction. Later, reaching down to crush the intact neck of a port decanter that had survived its collision with the floor, he pricked his finger on a shard of glass; and this pain, puncturing the last remnants of his self-control,

336

provoked in him an ungovernable fury of the sort that Eloise had witnessed only once but never forgotten.

Claude permitted himself one liberating howl of rage. Then, afraid of being interrupted by the police, he cried no more but set to work with grim determination on the other boxes. A bang on the wall from the residents of the apartment next door registered hardly at all as he opened the crate that contained his wedding china and began breaking it systematically, plate after delicate plate. Ingrid had chosen the pattern, gold-rimmed and wafer thin. He hated it. He hated it like he hated osmium and himself and all those stupid, time-wasting catalysts that had promised so much and delivered so little.

When all his china was broken and the living room and kitchen were glittering with crystal and glass, finding that his passion demanded further outlet he went into his bedroom and set about searching for his climbing axe. Now where had he put it? His quest took him through suitcases of mountaineering gear, disturbing evidence of a previously well-ordered life, now catastrophically overthrown, and ended beneath his bed. Seizing this implement, he turned to the eighteenth-century mirror he had inherited from his great-aunt Mathilde and flung it, squarely, into the centre of the glass – which splintered into a spider's web, distorting the reflected room and giving him, at last, a fitting visual metaphor for the self-disdain that rose up so chokingly within him.

He loved that mirror. He had admired it as a precocious child, playing bridge with the old woman, and her children had been politely horrified when she had left it to him and not them. Its destruction sobered him, and he sat down on a pile of ski clothes and licked the bloodied tip of his index finger.

Oh well, he thought, *j'ai fait de mon mieux*.

As Mathilde had so often told him, one's best was all anyone could do.

Chapter 59

Joan contemplated Paul's suggestion all day. What a resourceful young man he was! By the time Nurse Fleur appeared with her dinner tray she had resolved on a course of action, and she tucked into the breaded lumps of processed flesh on her plate with every indication of enthusiasm. When the nurse had gone she disposed of her yoghurt and settled to wait impatiently; and though it took some time for the pedals to appear, she knew with absolute certainty that they would come. 'Aha!' she cried, as they materialised, glinting over the Golden Syrup tin on her desk. 'Follow me, Cordelia.'

The corridor outside was deserted, and it was neither Joan nor the pedals who transformed it into 17 Kingsley Gardens but Miss Muir, who appeared from nowhere and hurried along it. She was wearing black skirts and a bonnet, and as she went all trace of The Albany disappeared behind her, with the curious effect that 17 Huntley Gardens appeared to trail in the governess's slender wake.

From the hall rose subdued murmurs, as though of a great gathering of people, and it seemed to Joan that she had returned to the house at a moment of crisis. She went to the head of the stairs and peered over the banisters. From where she stood only a partial view was possible, but it was enough to confirm her worst fears: swathes of black crêpe were draped extravagantly over every available surface and a multitude had assembled.

She had arrived, she knew, at Gordon Huntley's funeral.

She went to the lift and took it impatiently to the ground floor. As the doors opened she made a decisive effort to see The Albany's receptionist, for it was vital to know the enemy's whereabouts, and was pleased to discover her in the act of packing up her bag and putting on her coat. 'Have a good evening, dear,' she called, congratulating herself on the faultless sincerity of her delivery.

'See you tomorrow!'

When the receptionist had left, Joan made her way through the throng of people, looking curiously about her at the clothes and faces of the ladies and gentlemen. It was odd, but she seemed to see them only in the aggregate; no matter how hard she focused, she could not look at them directly. She had a strong sense, however, of black dresses and black-edged handkerchiefs; of fans of black ostrich feathers on tortoiseshell sticks, and black hair ribbons, and though she could not hear the words, the conversation was sombre and subdued.

Responding to this atmosphere, Cordelia twisted a piece of black crêpe about her handlebars as she led Joan to an ornate, mock-Elizabethan hall chair to await developments, the pedals hovering attentively beside her. The Albany had quite vanished; indeed, it seemed suddenly unlikely that it had ever existed or ever would. Tenses, Joan thought fleetingly, were so difficult to manage when one had no idea which century one would find oneself in from one moment to the next. Only by the greatest effort of will did she keep hold of the fact that, though she might not see Sister Karen if she should appear, the Nursing Manager would certainly see her. She kept her hands resolutely in her lap and did her best to calm their anxious trembling. *Oh when would something decisive happen?*

Now a hush fell over the waiting crowd. She had a sense of a hundred necks twisting and turned her own in their direction, towards the radiantly lit staircase; and what she saw almost made her faint.

She herself stood at the turn of the stairs, in the dark wool suit she had bought for Frank's funeral. She was younger by twenty-two years and moved with the thoughtless nonchalance of people whose bodies remain at their sole command. At her side were Eloise and George, in their late twenties, supporting her as they had done on the steps of the church. But this was quite wrong! Frank's death had marked the end of his tyranny and she would not undo it for anything.

She closed her eyes and began to tap, fearful of the possibility of reversing something so essential to her own well-being, and when she opened them Clementine Huntley stood on the landing in deepest mourning, her arms about her children's shoulders. Behind her towered her own tripled image, reflecting the glowing hall lights, and Margaret was sobbing uncontrollably.

It was not a moment, Joan knew, to lose concentration. She closed her eyes, then opened them – but narrowly, focusing her energies on the few square inches of Clementine's face. She had once transformed Sylvia Fraser into a pot of dahlias; might she not at least bring some colour into Mrs Huntley's haggard cheeks? She doubled and redoubled her efforts as Clementine began to move down the staircase, and as she did so the terrifying conviction grew that she had only a few moments in which to work; that as Clementine reached the hall, full as it was of her husband's mourners, all would be lost.

God, help me! Joan had never prayed so fervently – not even for the safe delivery of Eloise. *Help me, Lord.* She could not, she knew, accomplish a task of this magnitude alone – only Jesus, after all, had been able to raise Lazarus from the dead. *Help me, help me!* And just as He had helped her on that miserable day in the library when He had led her to Paul, God intervened at this moment too and sent into her head some lines from a poem that she had memorised as a child – what was its name? She could not remember, but such details no longer mattered. 'Sir,' she said, like a priestess reciting an ancient rite,

'twas not
Her husband's presence only, called that spot
Of joy into the Duchess' cheek.

That was it! She must call a 'spot of joy' into Clementine's cheek. This should not be a funeral but – a *ball*, she decided, clapping her hands. A ball for Clementine's birthday!

At once, Mrs Huntley's cheeks began to glow.

Joan leaned forward and clapped again. The sound of her hands coming together, heightened by the ache of her arthritic joints, had a stimulating effect on the people around her. She clapped once more and a fan, somewhere to her right, burst into a riot of peacock features. *That was better!* She continued to focus her efforts on Clementine, whose eyes lost the expression of resigned horror they wore in her portraits on the drawing-room ceiling. Joan clapped again and her dress of deepest black taffeta began to lighten, became the colour of the sea at night, and then, catching the tone of the peacock fan, a beautiful aquamarine, with a low neck that revealed pert and powdered bosoms rather like the ones that she herself, in better and lovelier days, had possessed.

The conversation around her grew louder. Someone laughed. *Don't ever touch that medicine again!* cried Joan, giving Clementine the strength to act on this advice; and the knowledge that she had saved a woman from a life of drugged numbness gave her glorious strength. She clapped again and tapped the pedals and Margaret's hair, until now brushed straight down her back and tied with a black bow, spun into tresses – this was her first grown-up party – while a necklace of small, perfectly matched pearls appeared at her neck. An orchestra began to play a polka by Strauss, and she saw that the guests around her were eager to dance, to carouse the night away in revelry. It was for this, after all, that the house had been built! Not for sad old people and belligerent staff nurses. Not for pompous death but for joy and laughter and social display!

As if to emphasise their complete accord with her, the interior furnishings now began to gleam with a magnificence she had not yet seen. The hubbub of conversation grew louder still, forcing the orchestra's volume up with it, and the black crêpe disappeared. Fur stoles slid across the ladies' shoulders and their necklines plunged. Jewels appeared – yellow diamonds and emeralds, an amber brooch in a delicate setting of platinum roses. The gentlemen, of course, wore white tie and tails, with gleaming dress shoes and slicked-back hair. To Thomas Huntley, allowed to stay up until supper, she gave a sailor suit and a neat side parting, and at Clementine's bosom she placed a large gardenia, her mother's favourite flower. Admiring the effect, she put one in her hair too, now piled in complex coils and curls.

It seemed to Joan as if so many of the bad things she had done – the little lies and occasional meannesses; the small deceptions; even her mocking description of Frank's sexual equipment and expertise – were expiated by this monumental effort she made to bring and give joy. It became clear that Gordon Huntley was not dead at all, merely late for his wife's party, called away on urgent business but hurrying home for the first dance. She tapped her feet and clapped her hands – she was almost dancing herself – and as she did so more jewels appeared, and more furs, and the coiffures of the women complicated and shone. Clementine was no longer alone on the stairs with her family; she was at the centre of a group of laughing guests, moving from the drawing room to the ballroom. Even the servants were enjoying themselves. There was the butler, tapping his foot discreetly in time to the music's infectious rhythms; and Miss Muir, in purple and diamonds lent by Clementine herself; and there, in the distance— God, it could not be—

Astrid now entered the hall, bringing with her a wave of Ivor

Novello that clashed horribly with the Strauss. 'No!' shouted Joan, but even the pedals could not remove her. *She wants me to resurrect Frank*, she thought suddenly, stunned at the audacity of it. *But I won't, I won't.*

'Joan!' called Astrid. 'Joan!'

'Take your hands off me! I'll never do it. *Never.* Cordelia!' At once the wheelie sprang to attention, moving swiftly back and forth between Joan's hands and Astrid's short fat legs.

'Joan! Everything's quite all right!' Astrid began to shake her.

Joan knew that unless Gordon Huntley entered the room immediately, Astrid would use the scene's dramatic potential for her own ends. It was understandable that a mother should wish to raise her son from the dead. She would do the same for George – but she would *not* raise Frank. 'How dare you?' She attempted to stand, playing for time. Around her, people had begun to dance across the entrance-hall tiles. Outside, she heard the unmistakable sound of a carriage drawing up and knew – *Oh, she could never have done it alone!* – that Gordon was raised from the dead, if he had ever been dead at all; that he would shortly enter a room full of his friends, and gather his lovely wife in his arms.

Gordon, dear, do come in! I must see you! She clapped and silenced the Novello; but another clap, not her own this time, and then the gradual spreading of heat across her cheek, set it off again. Now Astrid was launching into the first verse of 'Every Bit of Loving in the World'.

'Shut *up*!' cried Joan, who had never once criticised her mother-in-law's singing. 'You're horrifically flat! Can't you hear?'

But this resulted only in another slap, which stung more sharply than the first. She pushed her away with all her might; but as the butler went to admit Gordon Huntley, Astrid's damp palm connected once again with her cheek and the force of it a third time was destabilising, disastrous for concentration. The door began to open – *Come in! Come in!* – but as it did so the dancers around Joan grew formless. Their jewels stopped blazing and through their rosy cheeks and shimmering gowns noticeboards appeared, and a computer monitor; and then, with the suddenness of a tragedy, 17 Kingsley Gardens disappeared as swiftly as a dying fountain jet.

'You bitch,' she said, looking straight into her mother-in-law's eyes. 'You vicious *bitch*!'

Chapter 60

'She needs complete rest,' said Sister Karen to Eloise. 'She got violent last night, which is a worrying sign, and the young man's visits excite her unduly. She was crying the last time I saw them together. He is also playing truant from school, in order to visit her. I have told him he is not to come for the time being.'

'Right.'

'Yes.' Sister Karen sniffed. She had been expecting Eloise to kick up a fuss, and had been quite prepared to employ her 'I Am the Professional' speech. 'Well, good.'

'How is she?'

'It has been necessary to sedate her a good deal, as you saw. I'm afraid', said the Nursing Manager, adjusting her tone appropriately, 'that the rapidity of your mother's deterioration is alarming. She stabilised briefly on the clozapine, but ultimately there are no guarantees with any of these drugs. Each patient goes at their own pace. Some have years before their cognitive faculties truly fail, but Joan's condition seems to be progressing more quickly than is usual. Of course, it may have begun gradually, almost unnoticeably. She may have been ill for years before she came here. Dementia patients are often highly skilled at hiding the severity of their condition from others. Even' – she paused – 'from family members who are close to them.'

'Have there been any problems with her medication? Has she been receiving the right doses? The doctor said if she ever stopped—'

'I am quite aware, Ms McAllister, of what Dr Walters said,' replied Sister Karen, superbly, 'and I can assure you that your mother has been receiving the best possible care. We do not make *mistakes* at The Albany.'

'I understand that, Sister.'

'Excellent.' In Sister Karen's experience, it was best to nip complaints in the bud as soon as they appeared; failure to do so allowed them to develop dangerously in the minds of family members, where they often became fixed. 'We will, however, be arranging regular supervision for Joan. We do that as a matter of course when patients reach a certain stage.'

'Thank you.'

'I appreciate your co-operation.'

When she had put the phone down, Eloise tried for the tenth time that week to get hold of her brother. She called his office and was rebuffed by his assistant; then his mobile phone, on which she left a message; then his home phone, which transferred her to a shrilly defiant fax machine. These options exhausted, she summarised her conversation with Sister Karen in a short but pointed email, which she read through with glaring eyes before deleting the 'Mum' of the subject line and replacing it with *SELFISH SHIT*. There, she thought, hitting the *Send* button: she had done all she could.

It took Joan some time to comprehend the movement of the days, and more to understand that so many of them had been and gone without a visit from Paul. Once she was strong enough to ask for him, Sister Karen's assurances that he was 'too busy to come' inflamed her. Of all the lies to tell!

Without Paul's advice she could not hope to understand the curious properties of this strange, malleable house in which God had ordained that she spend her final days; for though the pedals had taken her on extraordinary journeys when she lived at Wilsmore Street, it was only since her installation at The Albany that people had begun to appear to her. She did her best to think things through. Astrid had been dead for more than twenty years, but was free to roam the corridors of 17 Kingsley Gardens at will. The Huntley children, too, were very much alive, though they had been young a century before. It appeared that time operated differently here, in a less lineal fashion than elsewhere. But surely that was impossible?

It was, however, the only explanation that fitted the facts, and its plausibility increased as Astrid assumed more and more of the Nursing Manager's duties. She took to delivering Joan's meals in person, as she had done in the months following Eloise's birth; and as a punishment, presumably, for Joan's refusal to resurrect Frank, she went to great lengths to ensure her daughter-in-law's consumption of the yoghurt that made her queasy and banished the pedals.

Eloise had always adored her grandmother, and an appeal to her was useless. As a consequence, Joan was obliged to play a subtler game; and though she ate her poison each evening and held it down until she was alone, and had been checked on twice, she vomited it up in the bathroom as often as she could. This was not always possible, for sometimes Astrid sent an underling to guard her for hours at a time, and on the days that followed these evenings of forced pleasantries with Nurse Fleur the pedals did not visit. Nevertheless, Joan used the endless hours of her imprisonment wisely, and at length discovered that such temporary defeats could be turned to her advantage: that if she consumed her yoghurt obediently for two or three days in succession and *then* stopped, her powers would return with greater force than ever.

Chapter 61

Claude fell asleep in despair on the hard terracotta tiles of his sitting room, surrounded by shattered objects he had once loved. He dreamed first of his great-aunt Mathilde, who deplored this senseless tantrum; then Eloise came to him, wearing the green cotton dress she had worn that lush midsummer's night in 1991 when they had seen each other for the first time since his wedding.

He had arranged a business meeting in London as a pretext for visiting the city, though of course he had not told her so; had not even admitted it to himself, for such clandestine chicanery offended his sense of honour. She had come straight from work without showering, and as he kissed her cheeks a sharp, unanswerable longing stirred so powerfully within him that he was afraid.

I'll never do this again, he told himself as they sat down. *This will be the last time.*

But Claude had not kept this promise. He had seen Eloise as often as he dared, sometimes once, sometimes twice a year; and when the urge to hear her voice became unbearable, he had called and given her professional advice, replacing the receiver with shaking hands. Now his dream conjured her sparkling eyes, the fullness of her lips as she smiled. He found himself stretching for her, but then she was running away from him, her hair tangled in the wind. He chased her across the fields behind his great-aunt's house, through which he had wandered as a boy. Still she eluded him, laughing. He ran and ran, and when at last she stopped, panting, he threw himself at her – but again she slipped from his grasp, defiant now, and vanished down the rue de la Chapelle.

He woke, shivering, on the cold tiled floor; and as his dream left him he saw with devastating clarity the error he had made.

It was not coercion that was required. It was *seduction*.

He sat up, shaking himself awake. How had this simple truth evaded him for so long? He went to the bathroom and splashed cold water on his face. He had been thinking too big, seeking to conquer diamond, to subdue her to his will and break her open with ever greater violence. What a fool he had been! He splashed the water into his hair and let it run down his neck. It was brutally cold and heightened his focus. It was not to the massive atoms of krypton to which he should have turned – he went back into the sitting room, his feet crunching over china – but to tiny ones; to atoms that had insinuated themselves into carbon before.

He went straight to the door, patting to check that his car keys were in his pocket. Outside, he was half surprised to see that it was light, and that his most fitness-conscious neighbours – a gay couple, who had always been extremely friendly but who looked at him now with undisguised suspicion – were already setting out on their morning jog. He smiled at them wildly, like a madman, and got into his car. He drove quickly but carefully to the offices of MaxiTech and let himself into his lab. Catching sight of his reflection in the glass doors, he saw that shards of china littered his shoulders like dandruff. He brushed them off and went over to the glovebox. He was shaking with certainty. It was all he could do to discipline himself as he went through the procedures, checking that the argon was flowing, that the materials he needed were in place.

Then he put a block of osmium in a chamber and sent a stream of charged ions into it. Beneath it, where its dislodged atoms would fall like dust motes, he heated a large diamond – just enough to warm it gently, to set its molecules chattering. He had learned his lesson: brute force was not the way. Then he withdrew his hands from the hood and went to a distant counter, where the hydrogen was kept.

Hydrogen, hydrogen. Why had he not considered it before?

He wheeled the cylinder to the glovebox and attached it to a long rubber tube, which he fitted to an exterior valve. Putting his hands once more into the container he turned the nozzle and began to cool the diamond with a gentle breeze of the gas – delicately, gracefully, as he and Joan had once supervised the building of flavours in a *jus*. He withdrew his hands and turned away. He could not bear to look. He walked once around the laboratory, then twice more. The first lab assistant arrived for work and he sent him away. Another arrived, and he dismissed her too. Then he took a felt tip pen and wrote 'Do Not

Disturb' on a sheet of paper, which he stuck to the laboratory door with a piece of chewing gum he had flicked into the bin the night before.

He walked another eighteen times more around the lab, pausing with elaborate nonchalance to examine the labels on the ranked bottles of chemicals. He forced himself to wait: for an hour, then two, then ten minutes more. Only then did he return to the tank, and even now he kept his eyes closed, giving the elements time.

Claude did not believe in God – it was one of the few points on which he and Joan had vehemently disagreed – but before he looked he found, to his surprise, that he was prepared to accept the existence of a deity if only his greatest wish would now be granted.

Chapter 62

George was standing in the corridor outside his father's workshop, worrying the cuticles of his left hand. His mouth moved furiously between thumb and index finger as Joan watched him, the small white teeth they cleaned together each evening gouging viciously into the torn flesh. He stood quite still, his only movement the extension and contraction of his arm and jaw. Joan looked at her watch. Gian-Battista would be outside already, waiting in his car around the block.

Frank performed his punishments on Sunday, as if to make clear to the children that there was no God. Joan had become accustomed to returning from her observances to find her son in tears in his bedroom; but in recent months a fierce taciturnity had replaced the tears, which troubled her greatly. She looked at George as she put on her gloves at the top of the stairs. His eyes were glazed and unseeing, as though his spirit had sought refuge elsewhere.

I could just leave, she thought. *I could take him and never come back*. The possibility began to throb at her throat; it made her shake so violently that she could not button her gloves. She pulled them off and stuffed them into her bag. In a moment Astrid would appear, and then Frank. *Act now*, said a voice in her head, *and never look back*. But what of Eloise? She thought of her daughter, twelve years old already; soon to become a young woman. She would never come with her quietly; would make such a fuss about packing her clothes and taking her homework books that Frank would hear, and then . . . There was no saying what might happen. *Act now*, the voice repeated, urgently. *Save one*.

Joan's heart began to thump wildly in her chest. Was it for this that she had so cunningly evaded the Nursing Manager's potions? 'I will *not* leave Eloise,' she said aloud. 'I am her mother.' And as if moved by this maternal dedication, the pedals appeared within reach and she seized them and began tapping furiously with her feet.

When she opened her eyes she was in her room at The Albany once more, surrounded by dancing yellow children. She had never been so happy to see them. Her lunch tray waited for her on the escritoire. Outside the leafless cherry tree swayed in a sharp wind. Even the grey towel hanging behind the door, across which *TranquilAge*™ was stitched in gold, was a comfort to her. 'I'll lean on you, if I could,' she said to Cordelia, getting up from the chair; and she was just feeling more herself when the sound of Astrid's singing began to seep after her from the scene she had left behind. Soon she was shrieking 'We'll Gather Lilacs' so penetratingly that the house in Turnham Green began to loom once more; and though Joan resisted, her mother-in-law's throbbing flatness sent the yellow children racing away, their hands over their ears, and deposited her once more on the green, white and black carpet Astrid had chosen.

Frank now emerged from the kitchen and the shock of their first encounter in twenty-two years was overwhelming, and temporarily paralysing. George began to bite more savagely into his fingers. *Take him. Run right now*, said the voice in Joan's head. 'I can't,' she shouted, for Eloise would be in her bedroom at the top of the house, learning her Shakespeare declamation; she could not possibly get ready in time.

'Aren't you going to church?' asked Frank.

Joan walked down the stairs, into the hall. 'Yes,' she replied – for she had indeed 'gone to church' that day, had left George in his father's hands and slid into Gian-Battista's car, driven with him to his flat, made frantic, violent love to him and returned three hours later with a story about an unexpected parish lunch.

'Well go then,' said Frank.

But age had given Joan resources that would have been unimaginable to her in her forties. As Frank turned to their son she grasped the pedals and sent them all – George, Frank, herself – hurtling into the nineteenth century, where they emerged, shaken but quite unharmed, in the Music Room at 17 Kingsley Gardens. George was Thomas Huntley now, and easier to bear as someone else's child. Clementine Huntley occupied her own place, and was also drawing on her gloves. 'I'm going to church, Leonard,' she said, addressing the man who had been Frank.

'Well go then,' he said.

He was wearing the dress uniform of the Royal Medical Corps, in which he had once sat for his portrait in Bloemfontein. Joan examined him closely, expecting the wispy blond moustache he had sported in his photograph; but to her alarm she saw that her husband's features remained unaltered.

'Frank?' she cried. But as she did so, Clementine Huntley said 'Leonard?' in just the same tone of anxious surprise. She repeated herself. Again Clementine Huntley spoke over her. *No, no*, thought Joan. *This will never do*. But Frank remained in Leonard Huntley's uniform, and Clementine planted a kiss on his cheek and departed.

A terrible fear now gripped Joan, and she watched as Thomas began to move heavily towards Captain Huntley's study. Had she somehow infused Frank into Leonard Huntley, whose sadism even the British government had censured? Had she given them both a fresh lease of life? The boy's fingers were bleeding so profusely that sharp red drops hit the floor. *Help us!* she prayed, and at that moment a door opened. Was it Paul, come to her aid? No. It was a man, burlier than Paul. For a moment she thought it was Gordon Huntley, raised from the dead to protect his child.

But it was not Gordon. It was George.

Standing behind her brother, Eloise gave a cry of alarm and brushed past him. 'Mum! Are you all right?'

Leonard and Thomas began to shimmer, and with them the door into Captain Huntley's study, which had so recently been the entrance to Frank McAllister's workshop.

'Thomas!' cried Joan. 'Stay here!'

But already Leonard was shoving the child through the door. She should never have summoned the Huntleys and confused their drama with hers, for there was no telling where such meddling might lead. In exculpation of her error she began to shout, and as she did so Astrid appeared, speaking urgently into a walkie-talkie. But the prospect of another tuneless rendition of 'We'll Gather Lilacs' gave Joan strength. She threw herself at Captain Huntley, scratching the face that was still Frank's with all her might.

For a person in the ninth decade of life she was amazingly vigorous. The assistance of both Nurse Fleur and Eloise was required to get Joan onto her bed without injury; and once she was secure Eloise sat down beside her and stroked her hair soothingly. The effect of this gentleness was alarming, and Eloise was sufficiently human to feel just a tiny bit annoyed that their mother should give no sign of gratitude, now that

George was at last available to witness it. Quite the opposite, in fact – and the more frenzied Joan's screams grew, the more determinedly her daughter stroked her hair.

Sister Karen's production of a large medical bag wrenched Joan forcibly back to The Albany. She looked about her, dazed, and to her astonishment saw her son. 'George?' she called, not trusting her eyes; for he had been a little boy moments before and was a grown man now; capable of defending himself – and her. Eloise was gripping her head, trying to break her neck, and Astrid stood beside her with an evil-looking syringe. 'George!' she cried again. 'Help me!'

But he did not move; and the possibility that he now preferred his grandmother to her, as his sister had always done, induced in Joan a profound, ungovernable exhaustion. She felt her limbs slacken and her frame deflate. 'Help me,' she cried hoarsely, fixing her eyes on his.

But she had not helped him, and now he did not help her.

'Quieten down,' said Astrid. 'Everything's going to be right as rain.'

'Stop her!' cried Joan. 'Don't let them—'

But George did not move, and though there were tears in his eyes she understood that he would not, whatever she said.

The pain of this realisation dwarfed all the sorrows she had ever known. Both her children, in league against her! 'I did try,' she whispered, but she knew as she spoke that further protestation was useless. She barely felt the sting as Astrid plunged the needle into her arm, unopposed, and half-wished the dose would kill her; that, if it did, she would discover that there was no eternal life after all.

As a cold lightness crept up her arm she was seized by a desire to make plain to George the immensity of her regret. Since his birth, maternal tact had prevented her from referring, even obliquely, to the truth she wished to convey; but now she raised her voice and spoke it without shame: 'I have never loved anything – or anyone – as much', she said, her eyelids growing heavier with each syllable, 'as I have – loved you, George.'

Chapter 63

Even Sister Karen, so accomplished in the presentation of dementia to the families of The Albany's residents, did not allude to what Joan had said. It was clear from Eloise's clenched nonchalance that tactful sympathy might have unpredictable consequences, so she put away her speech on the importance of not taking things too much to heart and offered instead to call the McAllisters a taxi. She left them to wait for it in the entrance hall, without making her usual offer of a nice piece of cake. All she said was: 'You're so unlucky to have caught her on an off day. She has better ones quite frequently. Do let me know when you'd like to visit again and I'll make sure she's ready to see you.'

It was a cold November afternoon and the light was failing. George bit his cuticles and immersed himself in The Albany's professional literature as they waited for the taxi to arrive, and when it came Eloise gave the driver her address and retreated into a silence so palpable that her brother feared to break it.

George knew better than to offer sympathy, and because nothing else was appropriate he said nothing as the car turned into Wandsworth Bridge Road and slowed to an inching, rush-hour crawl. As they edged towards the river, he stifled a yawn. It was warm in the cab and the chug of the diesel engine was heavily soporific. He had left Sydney an hour into the launch party for the Liberators and Tyrants range and barely slept for five days before that; he had also missed a private dinner with the CEO of Boys' Toys' parent company, an invitation he had spent three years angling for. In consideration of this painful sacrifice he permitted himself a full yawn, conducted discreetly behind a clenched fist.

As they reached Wandsworth Bridge, Eloise said, ' "Never was a truer word spoken," I suppose.'

It took George a moment to understand what she was talking about, so fuddling was the car's drowsy heat. 'Come on,' he said sleepily, when he had. 'Who knows what was really going on in Mum's head? Don't take it personally.' In the last six months he had dispensed good humour in such industrial quantities that his supply was exhausted; he noticed this with regret and tried to rouse himself, conscious that his sister deserved a shoulder to cry on. 'Honestly,' he added, pinching her arm.

Why was it, wondered Eloise, that she so badly wanted to gouge George's eyes out? It was not his fault, after all; he had not asked Joan to love him more. 'I'm not taking it personally,' she said, moving her hand away from his.

'Well that's good.'

Nothing further was said until the cab had ground up Piccadilly and dropped them in Stratton Street. George leapt out to pay, an act of apparent generosity rather spoiled by his asking for a receipt.

'So you're expensing this trip?' remarked Eloise dangerously, as they waited for the lift.

'I've got one or two meetings. Couldn't handle economy class on the way down here.' George grinned, but stopped when he saw the expression on his sister's face. 'I could've done the meetings any time, though. I'm here for Mum.'

'Of course.'

They stood silently in the lift and when they reached Eloise's floor, as she rummaged in her handbag for the keys, George put his arms awkwardly around his sister's shoulders. They had been physically demonstrative as children and their fights had often ended in this way, but the movement now felt ungainly. 'Thank you for taking care of her, E,' he said. 'I really appreciate it, and I know Mum does too.'

Eloise found the keys, unlocked the door and walked into the sitting room. 'How would you know what Mum appreciates?'

'She never stops saying how well you've – arranged things.'

'I spent every second Saturday for nearly a year and a half taking her around old people's homes, George. I didn't just "arrange" it.'

'And you've got her into the best. I read that The Albany has a three-year waiting list. How did you—'

'You can always get private medical attention if you're prepared to pay for it. Sadly, Mum's care isn't something I can write off as a business expense – unlike your only trip to see her. Would you like a drink?'

'Have you got Scotch?'

'Give me a sec.' Eloise went into the kitchen and took two tumblers from a cupboard, which she filled with ice and whisky. She longed to tell George that Joan had never pushed her away before, but could think of no way of doing so that would not sound defensive.

'If it's a question of money,' he said on her return to the sitting room, 'I can always chip in.'

'How kind of you to offer. Mum's only been at The Albany since May.' She put the Scotches down on the coffee table and went to the bureau, where she fished among the letters and bills for a pale-blue envelope. 'When do you think you'd've got round to "chipping in" if you hadn't turned up in time for a major psychotic episode?'

'I paid for her to get her furniture sprayed, remember?'

'And I paid for her house to be packed up, for everything to be boxed and stored, for her holiday in South Africa, for—' But Eloise stopped; she would not play tit-for-tat.

'She's got money of her own, anyway.'

'You know the dot-com fiasco wiped everything out.'

'Not everything, surely.'

Eloise found a pale-blue envelope and tossed it onto his lap. 'In the context of expenses like these, there's basically nothing left.'

George examined the envelope and the bill it contained. 'Isn't this going overboard?'

'I didn't think money should be the first consideration when deciding how to look after our mother.'

'I'm just trying to be practical.'

'If you wanted to be practical, the time to start was two years ago. Perhaps if you'd seen some of the other places available, you'd think The Albany was worth it.'

'It's just that she could live another ten years. We have to plan for the long term.'

Eloise hesitated, standing at the juncture of two very different evenings. Then she said, 'Don't you fucking tell me what we have to plan for, you selfish little prick. You haven't lifted a finger to do a single fucking thing for Mum since you went off to the other side of the fucking world and left me to handle her by myself. If you start fucking lecturing—'

'What do you want from me, then?' It was a question George regularly asked women who raised their voices at him, and he put it now more shrilly than usual.

'An apology would be a good place to start.'

'I – I'm ...' But apologies had never come easily to George. 'I do live thirteen thousand miles away,' he said, exasperatedly.

'I know. Add to which the fact you've never really given a shit about anyone but yourself, and you have a perfect explanation for your behaviour.'

'Oh please, Eloise. Spare me the martyr sequence.'

'You haven't even taken my calls for a month. She's been getting worse by the day.'

'I told you I couldn't leave before the campaign was launched. Boys' Toys are our biggest client – it's a major deal for me, getting this account. There wasn't any point fighting with you on the phone.'

'There's never any point fighting with you. You always talk yourself so smoothly out of trouble.' Eloise stood up and went to the window, alarmed by her strong desire to pull George's hair. *You're forty-eight years old*, she reminded herself. 'I don't know why I'm even surprised. You shirked your duties when you were a child, you shirk them now. The only difference is it's not the cat-litter tray that needs emptying any—'

'Don't get on to our childhoods, Eloise.'

'Believe me, George, I stopped counting all the things I did for you years ago. What I've—'

'You're just wound up by what Mum said.'

This barb, so nonchalantly flung, grazed the truth too sharply and Eloise's desire to inflict physical injury on her brother dramatically increased. She paused, restraining herself. 'It's ironic', she said at last, 'that the child she always loved most should abandon her in her old age.'

'I told you, she was out of it this morning. You shouldn't take everything she says so personally.'

'I've had forty-six years to get over it, George. I can live with the fact Mum loves you more.'

'Life's not a competition, Eloise.'

'Don't patronise me, you little shit. It's not a competition for you because you won it.'

'What? The war of our mother's affections?'

'If you like.' The unfairness of it choked Eloise, without warning. Paul had become Joan's boon companion in the course of a single afternoon; so had Simbongile, half a world away; and there was apparently nothing George could do to make Joan love him less. Yet her own efforts to become her mother's friend had failed devastatingly. Why? For a moment she felt that the weight of this unanswerable question might crush her – until George, his own ire rising, said, 'What about Dad? Are we going to take *his* preferences into account?'

'Dad was always fair.'

'No he fucking wasn't.'

'Yes he was.'

'Dad worshipped the bloody ground you walked on, Eloise. At least give me that while you sit in judgement.'

'Dad lost his cool with you sometimes, George, because you behaved like a spoilt brat. He didn't love you any less.'

'Lost his cool with me "sometimes"? Have you forgotten Sunday mornings in his workshop?'

'Oh for God's sake, get over it.'

'Easy to say if it never happened to you.'

'I got punished too.'

'Not like me.'

'That's because I didn't behave like you, Porgy.'

Both siblings had the sense that they were sliding towards the speaking of things that could not be unspoken. To both of them, the idea was no longer wholly unappealing. There was silence; then George said, in a very different tone of voice: 'You know what he used to do.'

'He taught you how to work with your hands. It's how fathers bond with their sons.'

'He set me impossible tasks and when I made mistakes he hurt me, Eloise. He used to hammer my fingernails.'

'Bullshit.'

'You think I injured myself *every single fucking week*?'

'It wasn't every week.'

'I spent my whole bloody childhood with bruises on my thumbs. Didn't that strike you as odd? If we're going to do some straight family talking, let's admit Dad was who he was.'

'And who was that, George?'

'A mildly unintelligent man with a very conservative view of the world and a penchant for corporal punishment.'

'Dad loved us, George. He did everything he could for us.'

'He loved *you*, Eloise.'

'He was trying to toughen you up.'

'He was a sadist.'

She went to her desk and picked up the framed drawing of a roast chicken that stood beside a photograph of Astrid. 'You know why this is rusty brown?' She showed it to her brother.

'Why?'

'He drew it in his own blood. While he was in solitary confinement in Paris.'

'How do you know?'

'Granny told me. She gave it to me two days before she died.'

'Maybe Dad should have done some more drawings then, seen a shrink. *Dealt* with it.'

'He thought it could all happen again. Don't you see? He wanted you to be able to cope if there was another war.'

'He was a fucked-up drunk, Eloise. But you'll never see anything you don't want to see.'

'You needed a disciplinarian.'

'And Mum? Did she need one?'

'What?'

'Do you think our mother needed a "disciplinarian"?'

'Dad never hit her.'

'Just roughed her up every now and then. Pushed her around. And when he wasn't doing that he was belittling her and finding fault with her every chance he got. He set his mother on her.'

'Don't bring Granny into this.'

'Why not? Mum fucking hated her.'

'She was the only one who knew Dad before—'

'What? The Gestapo got hold of him?'

'Exactly. He needed her. She was a wonderful woman.'

'Well maybe he should have married her, then, and left Mum free for someone else.'

Eloise hesitated, tempted by this diversion. In the end, however, she decided against it. 'Okay, George. Let's go with your little version of reality. Mum and Dad had an awful marriage. Dad was nasty to you. Does that make your abandonment of our mother okay?'

'It was *work*, Eloise. I had *work*! You know? A major professional opportunity? I don't get them as often as you. A real chance to prove myself. Mum wanted me to go for it.'

'Which is why she called you last June, screaming at you in the middle of the night?'

'She apologised for that. She said she wasn't herself.'

'Which is exactly my fucking *point*, George!'

Now the telephone interrupted them with shrill urgency, and the thought came to both Joan's children that it might be Sister Karen, calling with bad news. Eloise ran to the desk and picked it up. 'Hello?'

'Is something wrong?' asked Claude.

'Thank God it's you. I'm just here with my brother.'

'George?'

'There's only one.'

'Tell him hello from me.'

'I'll do that.' She leaned away from the phone. 'Claude says hello, George.'

'Are you two fighting?' asked Claude, softly.

'Yes.'

'On a severity rating of one to ten?'

'Twelve and rising.'

'I see. You should get back to it. I just wanted you to know I will be in London next week.'

'Can I see you?'

'I was hoping you'd say that.'

They began speaking quickly in French, and when Eloise put down the telephone, George, who had cooled during this interruption, saw an opportunity to change the subject. 'Was that Claude Pasquier?'

Eloise nodded.

'*The* Claude Pasquier?'

'The same.'

'So you two are getting cosy again?'

'We're becoming friends, slowly.'

'Friends my arse. I heard you whispering sweet nothings.'

'I was telling him what a dickhead you were, in French.'

'No you weren't. You were murmuring sweet nothings. You—' As a teenager, George had displayed an indefatigable interest in Eloise's burgeoning romantic life and had spent many hours bombarding her for information concerning it. Now he seemed to catch himself. 'Why did you two break up, anyway?' he asked, changing course. 'I never really understood it.'

'I got pregnant, Porgy, and had an abortion. Claude took that as the end of the road.'

'I never knew that.'

'No, you didn't.'

'Was it the end of the road?'

'Maybe.'

'You didn't want him to be the father of your kid?'

Eloise went to the window and looked out onto the darkening street. 'It wasn't Claude.'

'What was it then?'

'That's none of your business.'

'We're talking about everything else tonight, Sis. Go on. After you're done I'll tell you all about Mum's affair, if you like.'

'*What?*'

'With that Italian lecturer.'

'Bullshit, George.'

'You remember how nutty she got about Dante – then never touched him again? The football field at school backed on to the council car park. I used to see them nip out the back of the adult-education centre for a quick snog between classes.' He smiled. 'But I want to talk about you and Claude.'

'You can't start dropping bombshells like that.' Eloise turned from the window. 'You—'

'Let Mum have her secrets. Tell me why you wouldn't make her happy with a grandchild. She never wanted anything more than that.'

This was too much for his sister's stretched self-control. The truth flashed into her mind, where she looked at it more directly than she had ever done before. Then, very slowly but quite intentionally, she spoke it. 'I had an abortion, George,' she said, 'because I couldn't bear the thought of having a child like you.'

Chapter 64

It was the only terrible thing that Eloise had ever said to her brother, and it sobered them both. A determined politeness overcame them and George hovered attentively as his sister made up the sofa bed and gave him a fresh towel.

'I'll call the office tomorrow and organise some extra leave,' he said. 'But I can easily move to a hotel. Give you a bit more space.'

'You're very welcome here, you always are. I'm sorry for what I said.'

'Don't be. We've had a difficult day.'

The phrase showed Eloise what their fight would become, if they did not address it now: a few regretted words at the close of 'a difficult day' that smouldered on, nevertheless. It seemed an appalling end to four and a half decades of sibling intimacy, but she could think of nothing to say that might alter what had happened, or make it better. She covered her sorrow by showing George how to use the shower in the second bathroom and fussing with his sheets, in the manner of their mother. Then they embraced, stiffly, and she went into her bedroom and undressed and lay in the dark, listening to him moving about.

From the ages of four to nine she had shared a room with George. Joan had always read to them, after their baths; and when she was old enough she had taken on the duty herself and continued the habit long after her brother had learned to read and she had graduated to the guest bedroom on the floor above. She wondered whether this would be the last night they ever spent under the same roof.

Their mother had hated them to argue; she had been at her sternest when compelling them to co-operate. It was ungraspable, somehow, that she should have no jurisdiction over them any longer; that she should not be there to goad them into mutual apologies and the making of amends. Eloise thought of Joan's parting words and saw how easily the day's pain might coalesce into lifelong resentment, into a bitter grudge that she could hold against her until her own death. She gripped her shoulders. The heating had switched off and the room was cold and dark, its atmosphere conducive to seeing things as they truly are. It came to Eloise that Joan's preference for one child did not mean that she had not loved her firstborn, too, and this prompted the recollection of certain friends who continued to blame their inadequacies on their parents, though they were well into middle age. Her mother did not deserve that. She had never intentionally wounded her, had sought always to advise her well and do her best for her. It was only as her brain disintegrated, quite literally, that the truth had come out – and how was she responsible for that?

George woke the next morning as his sister was finishing breakfast. He saw her through the door to the kitchen and hastily closed his eyes. He could not face further confrontation and an exchange of tense pleasantries would be worse, so he slowed his breathing as he heard her leave the table and tiptoe into the hall.

Only once the front door had opened and closed did he stir, and then he got up and dressed quickly and did his best to remove from the room all trace of his presence in it. He stuffed his sheets into the washing machine and dragged his bags into the hall, with the furtiveness of a naughty child covering up the evidence of his misdeeds; and when everything was ready he wrote a note thanking Eloise for her sofa bed and promising to let her know the details of his hotel. He left this, after some consideration, by the kettle; and at the bottom, as an afterthought, added 'Lots of love, G.'

Harrison Beacher, whose Youth Media department George ran, had an arrangement with a boutique hotel in South Kensington, and once he was safely out of his sister's building he booked himself a room there at a sizeable corporate discount. At once he felt calmer; and on his way to deposit his bags, he rang Sister Karen and asked if she thought his mother would be able to see him.

'Well—' The Nursing Manager hesitated, judiciously. 'She's a little groggy from last night. We had to sedate her, as you know.'

'Right.'

It struck Sister Karen, quite correctly, that George was more biddable than his sister. 'But I'm sure she'd love to see you,' she said, with greater warmth. 'One can only hope for the best.'

'Yes.'

'We look forward to welcoming you.'

Having left his bags at the hotel, George took a bus towards Wandsworth, and for the first time since he had gone to sleep his sister's words came back to him. He put them away as best he could, for he did not share Eloise's tireless zeal for self-examination, but they returned each time he attempted to suppress them, and with them came the look with which she had uttered them. With nothing but such brutal sincerity to distract him, he began to find the bus oppressive; and as it crawled along the Cromwell Road he lost patience with it and got off. Siren-like, a bittersweet memory led him across the lanes of traffic towards Exhibition Road and the haunt of many boyhood adventures with Joan.

He paused outside the Science Museum. His mother had often brought him to see the electricity exhibits as a child, while they waited for Eloise to finish her twice-weekly ballet lessons in Thurloe Square; and on an impulse he joined the queue and entered the building, moving slowly towards the model of the solar system.

George was not a person who put his own feelings into words, though he was expert at articulating the unsuspected desires of potential consumers, and his progress through the museum's exhibits was soundless. He spent almost two hours staring at the rings of Saturn and then queued with all the other parents and children for the space ride, holding on to the side of the shaking box while an American voice explained the mysteries of supersonic flight. When he emerged, he went to the cafeteria and bought a cup of tea and a slice of chocolate cake, and it was the taste of this indulgence – he remembered, suddenly, that Joan had made him and Eloise a chocolate cake every second Saturday afternoon – that punctured the morning's false calm.

To the astonishment of the young mother sharing his table, he burst into sudden, gut-wrenching sobs, and when these had abated he abandoned his tray, stumbled out into the street and caught a taxi. '17 Kingsley Gardens,' he told the driver. 'It's a nursing home called The Albany.'

Deposited forty-five minutes later at the foot of The Albany's wheel-chair-access ramp, he strode up it, past a workman gouging tiles with a jackhammer on the entrance steps. He entered the building and hurried across the hall and up the stairs, beneath the eerie Gothic fantasy of stained glass in the window. *Really*, he thought, *they should get rid of this old stuff*; it made the place creepy.

On the first-floor landing he met Sister Karen, emerging from the Recreation Lounge (Non-Smokers) and she greeted him effusively and led him to Joan's room, pressing him repeatedly with offers of fruit cake which he politely declined.

'Very well.' The Nursing Manager knocked on Joan's door and ushered him in. 'But if you need me at all, for *any* reason' – she nodded significantly towards her patient, sitting in her armchair by the window – 'you'll call, won't you?'

George assured her that he would and waited until she had left. Joan was staring acutely at the locked door in the wall, and he said nothing until a surreptitious glance in his direction confirmed that she was, at least, aware of his presence. Then he went to her and took her hand – it felt so fragile in his, its skin so waxy smooth – and said, 'Mum, it's me. It's George. Your son.'

Joan's fingers hung limply in his.

'Mum, it's me.' He paused. 'George. Remember?'

But nothing in his mother's face suggested that she heard him, and Eloise's words sounded forcefully in his head: *I couldn't bear the thought of having a child like you.* 'Mum,' he repeated. 'It's George. Me, George.' The sound caught in his throat and his earlier tears welled again – quietly at first, then more loudly; the guttural sobs of a cheerful man unused to public emotion. When he looked up he saw that tears were running down his mother's cheeks, too. 'Mum? Can you hear me?'

It was all Joan could do to resist the temptation to take her son's head in her hands and cradle it against her breast.

'I'm sorry, Mum,' he said. 'I'm so sorry.'

What if George were sincere? What if he had forgiven her, and come to make amends for his behaviour the night before? The thought made Joan's heart race. Oh, she could not bear it! She, who had always believed in giving people second chances.

She had spent the morning waiting anxiously outside Leonard Huntley's study, gripped by the traumatic possibility that had come to her the previous afternoon: that she had somehow twinned him with Frank, and brought about the vivification of a monster. The door was locked. No matter how hard she tugged, she could not open it – just as Frank's workshop had always been locked against her. Even the pedals could not help her; and when, around mid-morning, the sound of brutal and prolonged hammering had begun to shake the building, she had almost fainted.

How she needed a man of George's vigour now! But she had watched Astrid, with her own eyes, lead her son into the room and address him in low tones at the door. Was he now wholly on his grandmother's side? She couldn't believe it; and yet she had seen what she had seen.

'Mum,' said George again, stroking her hair, 'say something to me.'

But Joan sat on, immovable.

Chapter 65

A week later, after a particularly miserable day at school, Paul set out for the library as usual, and as usual took a route that led him past The Albany. Sister Karen had promised to let him know as soon as Joan was well enough to see him, but he had been waiting for her call for a month and had begun to doubt – quite correctly – that it would ever come. The Huntleys' boxes had been returned to the library by Sunil, but even the discovery of a chest full of nineteenth-century erotica had not stimulated him or eased his loneliness. He missed Joan sorely, and the prospect of facing Lee Anderton and Sean Ward the following morning made him miss her more.

As he turned the corner into Kingsley Gardens, the nursing home's receptionist appeared at the door of number 17. She was holding a packet of cigarettes and looked guiltily from left to right, but failed to register the presence of a shabby schoolboy. Satisfied that no likely visitors were in sight, she slunk down the entry ramp and disappeared behind the trunk of a large oak tree on the pavement.

Paul stopped.

A moment later, a wisp of smoke twisted towards him and suggested a thrilling possibility. He advanced cautiously, as silently as possible, and in a confident movement copied from the heroes of innumerable action movies, he leapt up The Albany's stairs and entered the hall. The reception area was deserted. Heart thumping, he crossed it and bounded up the staircase. The first-floor corridor was empty too, and he reached Joan's room without incident. He knocked at her door and received no answer. He knocked again and waited, but now the creak of an arriving lift overrode the obligations of good manners and he opened the door and slipped through it, closing it softly behind him.

Joan was in bed, fast asleep, in a pink cotton nightdress with bows on the shoulders. Paul had been in the room with his granny Rose the night before she died, and the similarity of that scene with this brought a lump to his throat that quite silenced his pride in his own daring. Joan was lying on her back, as though crushed beneath a heavy weight. He stole up to her bed and touched her hand. 'Ma'am?'

Joan stirred.

'It's me, Paul. Try to wake up, ma'am.'

Joan opened her eyes. 'R – Rupert?'

'It's me, ma'am.'

'Dear ... Rupert.'

'Can I get you something?'

The sudden fear that this might be a dream roused Joan from her pillow. She shook her head as vigorously as she could and prodded him. 'Is it really – you, Rupert?'

Paul hesitated, moved by the tremulous joy in his friend's voice. 'Yes,' he said at last.

'Are you in heaven?'

'I've just come from there.'

Joan began to cry softly. 'Has God let you visit me?'

'Yes,' he said; and then, with sudden inspiration: 'The pedals sent me.'

'Bless them.'

They sat in silence as the tears trickled down Joan's lined cheeks. 'I'm not really crying,' she whispered, lest he think ill of her. 'They're happy tears. I'm not scared.'

'So long as they're happy tears.'

She reached for his hand. 'I'm afraid I've done an awful lot of stupid things since you died. I just didn't expect it. I thought we would always—'

Am I one of her old boyfriends? wondered Paul. But Joan's next remark was revealing.

'I broke my word to Granny,' she told him, her voice shaking. 'They buried you at Die Ou Plek. Elsie planted roses for you. I went to say goodbye before I came to England, and she made me promise I'd never marry an Englishman and – I did.'

'That's okay.'

'No, no it's not! She made me promise. And I didn't even think of it when I—'

'You mustn't let it trouble you.'

'But— You didn't know Frank. What he was capable of. I thought he'd be like you. He was so – sweet-looking. A companion. I thought he'd be a companion.' She reached for his hand, and squeezed it with unexpected strength. 'But there was something – broken in him. He understood violence, not love. He used to hurt George. I couldn't – protect him. I should have. And then his mother moved in. She said she was staying a month, but she lived with us – for almost thirty years. Astrid. And—' Joan now sat up, with a superhuman effort. 'She's here now, watching me. She gives me drugs. I can't – move. And I've done the most terrible thing.'

'What have you done?' asked Paul, gently.

'I've killed Gordon Huntley. I tried to undo it but Astrid— She stopped me. And then, I – I brought Leonard and Frank to life again. As the same person. I didn't mean to. I don't know how – but they're alive. I must – find them. And stop them, for the children's – the children's—'

But the energy to complete the sentence deserted Joan, and she closed her eyes and fell back onto the pillows, which were damp from where she had dribbled.

Chapter 66

Two weeks later, the price of osmium crossed the \$110/oz mark to reach its highest value since the start of the crisis, though this did not prevent Carol from pointing out that Derby Capital still had losses in excess of \$70 million. 'I think we should start liquidating assets,' she said at their morning meeting. 'We don't want a last-minute scramble when the lock-in clauses expire.'

'What's your view, McAllister?' Patrick was hunched forward in his seat, the biro in his right hand as yet untouched.

'Run me through the list.'

'Zeus Capital, fifty million. Roderick Parker, forty million. Steven Reid, twenty million. The Walker Group, fifteen million. The Emir of Qatar, sixty-five million.' Carol reeled the names off, her eyes darting from Eloise's to her computer screen and back again.

Eloise adopted an expression of brisk purposefulness. 'I think it's worth meeting with each of them before we do anything drastic. No one's taken any money out since MaxiTech's conference, so there's no reason they should start now. I'm seeing Pasquier later today. I may be able to talk him into making another statement. If everyone stays calm, I'm confident we can keep them in.'

'I'm with you.' Patrick bit decisively into the pen.

Watching him, Eloise wondered whether she believed what she said. Since Claude's visit to England she had found that her fragile internal calm could not withstand prolonged consideration of the future, and had studiously avoided it. Her brother's presence in the city and the harrowing visits that they made, together and separately, to The Albany had consumed her available energies. She looked at Carol, so eager to see her fail, and smiled. 'I'm sure Pasquier will come through for us. There's no point losing faith now.'

*

Claude was waiting for her as she left the office, sitting in a café across the street, and she did not see him until his arms were on her shoulders. 'I thought we were meeting later,' she said, laughing as he spun her round and kissed her.

'I wanted to surprise you. I had something to show you that couldn't wait.' He pressed her into a doorway and kissed her again, oblivious to the stares of suited passers-by who seemed astonished that middle-aged professionals should behave in this way. 'I have a gift for you.'

He reached into his pocket and felt within it for a perspex box, identical to one he had given her many years before. He had planned this moment meticulously and his head was full of fine phrases, but Eloise's physical presence somehow inhibited them; there was something in the set of her mouth that deflated the possibilities of romantic language. Instead, he took out his package and handed it to her, almost bashfully. In the box was a lump of something dazzling blue, about two inches thick. 'As far as I am aware,' he said quietly, 'this is the first nugget of osmium carbide that has ever existed.'

Eloise looked at the box, then at Claude, then at the box again. Her hands began to shake.

'I made the first crust weeks ago,' he went on, 'but I wanted to have something larger to show you. Of course there will have to be more trials, but every indication is that it is completely safe, and that industrial replication will be straightforward. I—' He paused, hoping for something from her, and when she said nothing he added, very softly, 'It was all about hydrogen and seduction, in the end.'

Eloise could not speak. She had the disorienting sensation of watching herself from above, pushed into a grimy doorway on a crowded London pavement. Claude's face, lit from behind by an orange street lamp, seemed curiously suspended, as though independent not only of his body but of their joint past.

She felt no elation; for a moment, in fact, she felt nothing at all – as though she, too, were suspended in a place beyond herself and the natural world. Then relief came, like the first jet of water through a cracking dam. It spurted through her, caused her to lose her balance, and she stumbled against Claude, grasping for words. 'Thank you,' she said, 'thank you, Claude,' conscious of the quotidian inadequacy of the phrase; and then, as the full enormity of what he had done for her dawned: 'This means I can have my mother with me. At home where she belongs.'

This was not at all what Claude had expected. He had imagined delight, perhaps shrieks of triumph as Eloise proved herself to those who had doubted her; but filial affection, so spontaneously admitted, was too much for him. His eyes filled with tears. There was a time, long ago it seemed, in another life before marriage and children and ranks of white-coated assistants in palatial labs, when he had known how to access Eloise's gentleness. Long before their parting – years, if he were truthful – he had lost his way to that secret place within her, and his stumbling upon it now felt almost sacred. '*Viens*,' he said, pulling her into the street. '*Il faut fêter ça!*'

But Eloise shook her head and drew him in the opposite direction, away from the lights of Piccadilly. She moved urgently, for at last she saw the truth and it liberated her from her pain. It did not matter that Joan loved George more. What mattered was her *own* love, which she could now demonstrate as never before.

She began to run, pulling Claude with her, and when they reached Derby Capital's building she pushed through the workers streaming from the lift and touched the button for the fifth floor. The elevator was empty but for them, and she dried Claude's eyes with the sleeve of her blouse and kissed his hand, holding it tightly in hers. 'Time to take a bow,' she said, stepping away from him as the doors opened.

Carol and Patrick were in the boardroom, examining a list of figures. As Eloise entered they looked up, surprised to see her, and the flicker of disguised dislike in Carol's eyes heightened the moment's sweetness. 'Patrick,' she said, 'you know Dr Claude Pasquier? But I don't think you've had the pleasure, Carol.'

Carol shook her head, smiling politely. She had spent so long analysing Claude's research history and prospects that the sight of him, familiar from a thousand pixellated web images, was oddly unsettling – as though a reflection in a mirror had stepped down into the room, suddenly tangible. She saw that his features were more agile than his photographs suggested; that his eyes were fiery, full of intelligence and humour. 'I've heard a lot about you,' she said, offering her hand.

Claude shook it, gallantly, and in a tone as level as she could make it, Eloise said, 'Dr Pasquier has succeeded in creating a new compound. A super-hard, non-toxic alloy called osmium carbide. He has been kind enough to show us one of the first examples. Here it is.' She took from her pocket the perspex cube and placed it on the table between them.

For a moment no one spoke; then from Patrick came a roar that silenced the screaming civilians on the television screens. His face, usually red, turned scarlet, then purple, then a flaming cerise, and in his rush to go to Claude and seize his hand he knocked the pen pot from the desk and spilled biros over the floor.

'We will begin full testing soon,' said Claude, smiling as Patrick swung his arm up and down, 'but initial results in terms of strength and hardness are very promising, and it is stable at temperatures up to 1500°C. There is no evidence of any long-term health risk.'

'What a brilliant achievement, Dr Pasquier,' offered Carol, as her boss attempted a movement somewhere between a fiddler's jig and a dervish dance.

Patrick ushered them into the main office. 'Any idea when you might be able to make an announcement?' He was panting, unused to such exertion.

'In the next few days, we will go public about the compound's existence.'

'Fantastic.'

'And we will issue regular updates as the practical trials continue.'

'Let me get some champagne.' Patrick reached for his phone. 'Emily!'

But Claude had no intention of celebrating an occasion this momentous with Eloise's boss, and excused himself politely. 'I must be getting back to the hotel. I had a very uncomfortable flight.'

Eloise saw him to the door and asked him in whispered French to wait for her downstairs. Then she turned to her colleagues and said, very briskly, 'I'm delighted this has all worked out, Patrick. I'm sure you two will do an excellent job from now on.'

'What do you mean?'

'I'm resigning.'

'What?'

Carol put her hand to her mouth, then abruptly removed it. Patrick turned stupidly towards Eloise. 'What're you talking about, McAllister?'

'I'm resigning. I need to look after my mother.'

'Don't be a stupid bitch—'

'Goodbye.' Eloise leaned down and kissed her boss's cheek.

'Look, I know you've taken a lot of heat from me these last few months. I'm the first to admit your bonus should reflect that.'

'I know you'll be generous, but it's not about the money.' Eloise turned to Carol. 'I wish you all the very best.'

'What do you mean it's not about the money?' It had never before occurred to Patrick Derby that there existed other, higher motives for human action. 'Of *course* it's about the fucking money!'

'It's not, Patrick. It's about me and my mother and doing what's right.'

In the building's lobby, twenty minutes later, Eloise told Claude what she had done. 'I'm going to get her first thing tomorrow morning,' she said, linking her fingers through his as they stepped into the darkness.

'And between now and then?' He looked at her almost shyly, as though they were meeting for the first time.

'It's my last night of freedom. Help me enjoy it!'

Chapter 67

'I'm sorry,' said Sister Karen firmly, 'but her family is visiting her this morning. Perhaps we can start your visits again in a couple of weeks.' She crossed her arms, to emphasise the finality of this judgement.

'It's been six weeks already.' Paul swallowed. 'I can't wait any more.'

'I *beg* your pardon?' Sister Karen resolved, in future, to take a stricter line against unsuitable outside liaisons formed by The Albany's residents.

'I can't wait any more,' Paul repeated, raising his chin defiantly. 'I have to see her. She needs me.'

'She is quite well looked after here, thank you.'

But Paul had not expected an easy victory. 'If you don't let me,' he said calmly, with assiduously rehearsed assurance, 'I'll wait in the street every weekend until I meet her daughter. Her name's Eloise. She'll help me.'

'She will *not*.' But the possibility of such an encounter alarmed Sister Karen, who arranged her face into an expression of indulgent leniency. 'Ms McAllister entirely supports The Albany's decisions for Joan's welfare 'but it is good of you to care.' She coughed and made a show of consulting the clipboard in her hand. 'Perhaps you could visit tomorrow morning at nine.'

'Thank you, Sister.'

'No more than fifteen minutes.'

'I promise.'

'Well good, then. Run along.'

But Paul hesitated, for he had more to say. 'You have to stop giving her that medicine. It's making her worse.' The words came out in a rush. 'She's searching for someone she—'

'Searching for whom?' asked Sister Karen, sharply.

'For a man called Leonard Huntley.'

'And who is he?'

'He was a doctor in the concentration camp at Bloemfontein where her grandmother was interned during the Anglo-Boer War. His brother built this house. She's worried that he's twinned somehow with her husband, Frank, who—'

'Who is dead, as I understand it.' The Nursing Manager, alarmed for a moment by the thought of unchaperoned members of the public evading the Visitors' Register and wandering the building at will, relaxed visibly. 'We must help the dear old people not to lose themselves in nonsense,' she said, firmly. 'The things she sees aren't real.'

'They are to her. She think's her mother-in-law's—'

Sister Karen raised her hand to silence him. 'Which is precisely why she needs her medicine.' It was not her job, she felt, to explain The Albany's palliative-care systems to children who had no connection with those who paid the home's fees. 'It's good of you to trouble yourself,' she repeated, her tone signalling the imminent termination of their discussion, 'but you must leave these things to people with experience. If you continue to alarm Joan by entertaining her delusions, I'm afraid we'll have to end your visits for good.'

It took two large slices of Victoria sponge cake to restore Sister Karen's composure, but by the time she greeted Eloise, George and Claude in the entrance hall an hour later she had wholly recovered. She received them warmly and led them to Joan's room herself. 'People to see you, Joan!' She knocked and opened it. 'What a lovely crowd you have today!' She made way for them as they filed in and remained discreetly in the corner, in case medical intervention should be required.

The sight of her visitors made Joan's heart flutter, but she reminded herself that God did not ask more of His children than they were able to endure. She remained motionless as they greeted her, wondering why none of them seemed at all surprised to encounter a woman who had been dead for twenty years. Did they know the secret of Astrid's rejuvenation? Had they sided with her? She glanced at Claude, who had turned to talk to her mother-in-law and was nodding gravely, as he had once done when eliciting her own opinions on the correct phrasing of a Mozart violin sonata. She had always assumed that he shared her distaste for Astrid's music and furniture, though she had never put him in the awkward position of having to declare himself. To do so would have been grossly unfair to her daughter, now also conversing with her grandmother in whispers. Even George had joined the gaggle around Astrid – as though she, his own mother, were not even there! She watched them bitterly, thinking of the many evenings on which Eloise, at Astrid's request, had performed for the family one of her prize-winning declamation speeches. In Joan's opinion, these victories relied more on the poverty of the other contestants' talents than on any innate feeling of Eloise's for the subtleties of language and nuance. Her daughter's penetrating voice, inherited from Astrid, had amply filled the assembly hall at St Monica's and was uncomfortably loud in the confined space of her sitting room. Nevertheless, she had praised her, and encouraged her, and driven her to and from regional competitions without complaint. It seemed callous of Eloise to have forgotten all this, and to have deserted her now.

She looked closely at her mother-in-law, who glanced at her occasionally with patronising sympathy. Had Astrid brought her children and Claude to flaunt their new allegiance to her? To underline the fact that, having conquered her house, having driven from it every object of beauty, she had now assumed total authority over her family and banished her last remaining friend? The possibility, once conceived, became compelling – and infuriating. *If the time has come for a confrontation*, thought Joan, *so be it*.

But now Eloise dislodged herself from the cabal and came towards her. 'You remember Simbongile, don't you, Mum?' She thrust onto Joan's lap a photograph of a young man standing by a silver minibus, emblazoned with the words 'Miss J's Maxi Taxi At Your Service!' Joan peered at it, wondering what on earth it might mean. 'He writes to say he's doing well and business is booming – thanks to you. He's been able to put a down payment on an RDP house for his mother. That stands for "Reconstruction and Development Programme". He says to tell you it has an inside toilet.'

An inside toilet? This struck Joan as a bizarre subject for conversation. But the phrase unlocked an image, and then a succession of images, and all at once she knew exactly who Simbongile was. 'I'm so glad,' she said, despite herself.

Her words excited everyone in the room but Astrid, who slipped behind a pillar as George and Claude rushed over to her. Her visitors began talking at once, but in the end – as so often before – it was

Eloise's voice that prevailed. 'And I've got another piece of good news!' She took her hand. 'I called the carpenters this morning and they're removing the bookshelves in the second bedroom. You remember that Sanderson fabric you used to have in the guest room at Wilsmore Street? Maybe we should get that for the wallpaper.'

There was such tenderness in her daughter's tone, so little of the impatience that usually filled it, that Joan was temporarily disarmed. 'You've lost me, darling,' she said.

'I'm sorry. I should have explained first. You're going to come home and live with me. Where you belong.'

'What?'

'I'd like you to come and live with me,' repeated Eloise. 'I've given up my job so I can care for you. I can't bear the thought of you in a nursing home.'

It took Joan a moment to comprehend the audacity of Astrid's plan. So she had persuaded Eloise to tempt her from 17 Kingsley Gardens and the wonders she was capable of accomplishing in it! With her gone, Frank could exist without fear in the person of Captain Huntley. She would never be able to undo what she had done.

'Claude will be with us some of the time too,' continued Eloise. 'Just as you always wanted.'

'And I'm going to come over once a month,' George blurted out. 'We can go to museums and art galleries, like we did when I was a kid. You shouldn't be cooped up here.'

At last, thought Eloise, *some spontaneous humanity from George.* 'That's right,' she said. 'We're going to look after you for a change, just like you looked after us for so many years. I can't promise we'll do as good a job as you did, but we'll do our best.'

'But I'm very happy here,' said Joan, parrying this thrust.

'There's no need to be brave any longer. We've arranged for you to leave tomorrow.'

I will not, thought Joan; and something in the passion of Eloise's gaze reminded her of a particularly unfortunate rendition from *King Lear* which Astrid had insisted on hearing every night for a week. 'Th'untented woundings of a mother's curse pierce every sense about thee,' she said quietly, adapting the language to the requirements of the moment.

'What, Mum?'

Joan repeated herself more loudly, and the confusion wrought by this dramatic denunciation was supremely satisfying. The lines now materialised with crystal clarity in the camera obscura of her memory, and she pointed her finger at Eloise and raised her voice. 'Away, away!' she cried.

'Mum, please,' began George.

'Vengeance, plague, death, confusion!' How wonderful this language was, thought Joan, how potent and true. 'Away, away!' she shouted. 'Here I disclaim all my maternal care, propinquity and property of blood. And as a stranger to my heart and me hold thee from this for *ever!*'

She watched them retreat, beaten back by her energy and force; and when they had gone at last she began to cry – because she had never yet been purposely cruel to her children, and the justice of it did not ease her pain. 'Upon such sacrifices, my Cordelia,' she murmured, pulling the wheelie towards her, 'the gods themselves throw incense.'

Chapter 68

'With all due respect,' said Sister Karen, who had been saving this speech for just such an occasion, 'I am a professional. Believe me, once the old dears have settled down it is unkind to move them.' She was used to dealing with grieving family members and her tone of voice was superbly appropriate.

'But she always – wanted to be at home.'

'I know, Ms McAllister. But that was during her settling-in period, when things are often difficult for our ladies and gentlemen. What can be hard for families to appreciate' – here Sister Karen stood up and moved to the window – 'is that the elderly *enjoy* the company of their own age group. Joan has settled in very well at The Albany.'

'But Mum needs her children more than ever now.'

'No one is suggesting she doesn't. We're extremely flexible about visiting hours, as you know.'

'That's not what I mean.' Eloise attempted to control her tone. 'I don't want to visit her. I want to live with her, take care of her.'

It could be a challenge to fill The Albany's Prestige Apartments, and Sister Karen did not intend to relinquish one of her most profitable patients without a struggle, particularly after the morning's trying encounter with an insolent fifteen-year-old. 'Might I suggest that what you want is rather less important than what Joan needs?' she said reasonably. 'And that is routine, stability, familiarity.'

'Let's talk about it at home, E,' said George.

'Yes,' agreed Claude, squeezing her shoulders. 'Nothing needs to be decided now.'

'Maybe we could ask her friend Paul to mention it to her?' Eloise abandoned her dignity now. 'Perhaps if it came from someone else, it would be better.'

'I would not advise outside intervention, at this stage.' Sister Karen made this point very firmly.

'Do you know how I can get hold of him, at least?'

The Nursing Manager hesitated, then decided that full disclosure was the only course available to her. 'He came to see me this morning, as it happens. He was very anxious to see your mother, and I've said he may come tomorrow at nine for fifteen minutes before she has her breakfast. Of course if you wished to speak to him then—' Sister Karen left the sentence eloquently unfinished, as though this was all such a foolish suggestion deserved. 'But I must insist that Joan is left in peace for the rest of the day. I'll give her a little something to quieten her down.'

'Of course.'

The Nursing Manager smiled and rang a bell. 'Now what about a nice slice of Victoria sponge? We've all had quite a morning of it.'

Sister Karen's 'little something' did not only quieten Joan down; it sent her into a turbulent, dream-filled sleep that persisted until the early hours of the following morning, when she was shaken awake by an unseen force in the grip of a terrifying rage. The sharp square handles of the built-in bedroom unit Astrid had chosen dug into her back and made her cry out in pain as she was thrown against them. 'He's only a child,' she gasped; and it seemed that she could hear George crying. He was wailing as he had done when a little boy, before the onset of thin-lipped taciturnity. 'It's not—'

'Never undermine me!' Frank threw her back onto the bed so violently that her chest wall nearly gave way, and though she could not see him his voice was unmistakable. He reached into her and grabbed her heart, rattling it viciously; and when at last he relinquished it and flung it back to its rightful place she lay on her back, sobbing, as the tremors subsided.

It took some time to establish that she was at The Albany, surrounded by dancing children, and not on the prune nylon coverlet of her marital bed; that the only remnants of her husband were the yellow walls that recalled so painfully the sideboard he had once painted over and ruined. When her breathing had steadied, she pressed a button in the control panel and a third of the mattress swung abruptly upright, taking her with it. Her mouth was dry and her ears were ringing, but she was alone. *One of these days*, she thought, switching on the light, *I am going to die.*

It was not, of course, the first time that Joan had acknowledged this truth, but she had never yet done so with any immediate urgency. She did not fear death, but the possibility that it would come when so much remained to be done troubled her greatly. God had blessed her with special gifts. He had sent the pedals and led her to Paul and allowed her to perform wondrous feats; but by tampering with what she did not understand she had revived two men who were better off dead.

She moved stiffly to the window, thinking things over. What would happen if she died? Only Paul knew that she had killed Gordon Huntley, and that his children were at the mercy of their uncle; and no one but she suspected the ominous fusion of Frank and Leonard. Paul would not rest until the children were safe, but it would be decades before he was old enough to travel through time and space as she had done and set things right. Such a burden might overshadow his whole life. 'We can't have that,' she said to Cordelia. 'How I wish I could speak to him!' But she could not reach him in the middle of the night, and Astrid had kept him from her for weeks. She might never see him again. *I'll write to him*, she thought, *and ask the pedals to deliver it.*

It was some time since Joan had written anything longer than a line or two by hand, and explaining everything to Paul required a great deal of exertion. Her handwriting had been beautiful once, but as her fountain pen leaked over her fingers she knew that the young man would need help in deciphering the haggard letters on the page. 'When I'm gone,' she told the pedals solemnly, 'I bequeath you to my friend, Mr P. Dhanzy. You're to appear to him on the morning after my death and give him this.' Their throbbed assurance calmed her, but to be quite sure she made the crucial assurance in unmistakable capitals: 'I WILL TAKE CARE OF EVERYTHING MYSELF.'

Then she put the letter on her desk and went again to the window. It was deep night outside and the horizon glowed orange with the lights of the vast city. She looked at her watch: several hours remained before the arrival of her breakfast tray, and the prospect of solitude sent a shiver of freedom rippling over her skin, which quite dispelled the fear with which she had woken. She would confront the dark forces ranged against her, but there was time for that yet. Perhaps ...

She glanced at the wheelie, who sparkled suggestively. Perhaps she might allow herself one final pleasure.

Joan had performed the Mephisto Waltz only once in concert – to the fourteen-year-old George, on the sturdy upright piano in her sitting room. She had coaxed from this unexceptional instrument a performance of which she was quietly proud: a small triumph that eased the tragedy of the fact that no one but her own son would ever hear it. Now a grander plan occurred to her, and she reached for the pedals and tapped her foot.

As she did so, the poisonous yellow around her faded. A second tap removed the partition walls. Now the room assumed a certain lofty grandeur and the cherubs above the doors strummed their harps. A powerful optimism seized her. She flexed her fingers and found them marvellously free from pain. She had, indeed, been better than Eiko Miyanishi once; surely she could be so again. She stood up. With a wonderful *rapido* movement, her nightdress crinkled into the concert gown of pale-green satin her mother had sent her as a graduation gift, and her skin tightened across her cheekbones. Her hair darkened and twisted into a chignon at the nape of her neck and a fireplace appeared, above which hung a large mirror framed in ivory. She went to it and examined her reflection, acknowledging her restored beauty with a boldness that would have shocked her youthful self.

The greeting of the crowd surpassed in volume and rapture anything she had ever heard at Wigmore. Through the dazzling lights she saw Eiko in the front row, a look of disguised envy on her small, beautifully made face, and beside her sat Gian-Battista, his eyes shimmering with pride. Neither Frank nor Astrid was anywhere to be seen, but Paul and Simbongile and Eloise and George were there – and Claude, she decided, forgiving him his equivocal behaviour of the day before. She bowed deeply and went to the piano, a Bechstein in a case of polished ebony.

The room held its breath.

She flicked her wrists and began.

Joan took the opening *acciaccaturas* at a dizzying pace, on the fast side of *quasi presto*, and threw into them all the countless little confrontations she had had with Astrid, and lost; all the useless politeness that had failed her for so many years. Her frustrations erupted in a clanging confrontation of C sharp minor chords, which gave way to the theme she had always thought of as her own; and when she reached the D flat major section, played *espressivo amoroso*, she far surpassed in tender nuance anything that Eiko had ever achieved. The music swelled unstoppably from her, expressing all the tenderness of her love for Gian-Battista, and the return of the manic triplets of housework and wifely duty provoked a terrible fury.

As Joan played, the splendour of her own performance lifted her from her body; allowed her to range with godly freedom as she observed her dizzying movements from above. The lights of the concert hall dimmed and dirty canvas began to flap; and then she was in the hospital tent in the concentration camp at Bloemfontein and Hannie was strapped to a bed, her legs forced open. On the cot beside her lay Margaret and Thomas Huntley, their wrists bound. Leonard was bending over Hannie, peering *into* her; but the return of A major *con fuoco*, or with fire, sent a blistering force through Joan's fingertips that freed the captives from their bonds and gave them life, while Captain Huntley's uniform burst into flame.

Their liberation filled her with joy; and when Gian-Battista's theme returned, demanding repeated strikes of the same note at lightning speed while the whole was played *sweetly, expressive of love*, she thought of the tap of his fingers between her legs and pleasure built within her once again. It gave her the energy to laugh in the face of the *pesante* octaves in the bass line, so redolent of Frank's heavy, philistine assaults, and as she finished in a flourish of A major chords she felt gloriously, supremely herself.

Joan had done nothing with the power unleashed by her first performance of Liszt's masterpiece. She had made baked Alaska for Frank's dessert and eaten dinner with the family; had later accompanied Astrid as she sang 'Dark Music' and not once mentioned to anyone what her triumph meant, or even that it had taken place.

Now she rose from the piano and seized the pedals, for she would not make the same mistake again.

A jolt of pain shuddered through her, as severe as any she had ever known. Her body began to tingle and to shed its human form, but through the agony rose the conviction that she was equal to whatever she must face. She closed her eyes and gave instruction, and then she was in the corridor of the house in Turnham Green, outside the locked door to Frank's workshop. It was barred against her once more, but Joan was no longer the woman who had submitted to the tyrannies of her husband and his mother. She was a tower of light, and she flung the door open, mighty and unopposed.

George was kneeling on the floor, grappling with the lid of a paint tin. The nails of his thumb and index finger were black and blood had dried on his lips, where he had torn at the cuticles. Frank stood over him, a hammer in his hand, and on the floor between them, on a bed of newspapers, lay the griffin chandelier – half of it now a ghastly, sullen beige.

'Who are you?' cried Frank, staring upwards in horror.

'I am your Nemesis,' she thundered.

Chapter 69

Seven hours later, Eloise climbed the steps of The Albany resolved to put away her own bruised pride. George was right: life was not a competition. It was a blessing that her mother had a friend like Paul, and she could not – would not, did not – begrudge her that solace. She checked the Visitors' Register and saw that he had not yet come. Settling herself to wait for him on a chair of turquoise plastic, she looked at the extravagant entrance hall and hoped that she would not see it very many times again. She knew in her heart that Paul was going to make things all right. He would help Joan understand the intensity of her children's love, the sincerity of their gratitude for hers; and this thought soothed her.

Despite the harrowing events of the previous day she felt more peaceful than she had in months – as if the anxiety and solitude of a tense and lonely year had somehow refined her, aligned her priorities more correctly than before. The sensation was deliciously calming. Joan had always loved Christmas and its festivities. Soon she would celebrate one with both her children again, secure in the knowledge that she need never return to the care of strangers.

Paul arrived ten minutes later and Eloise approached him almost shyly, for her limited experience of young people left her uncertain how best to proceed. 'I want to thank you', she began, 'for all the care you've shown my mother. I know how grateful she is to have you as a friend.'

Unused to adult gratitude, Paul found his eyes drawn irresistibly to the floor. He forced them upwards. 'She's my best friend,' he said, simply.

'Is she?' Eloise swallowed. 'Well I know you're hers.'

There was a brief silence, which Eloise broke by beginning the speech she had prepared in the taxi. 'I wanted to ask you something, Paul. A favour of sorts. My mother has always wanted to live with me. She never wanted to go into a home, but it wasn't – possible for me to look after her.' She looked frankly at the boy. 'I've resigned my job now. I can have her with me, but she seems frightened of moving. I'm sure she can't have changed her mind. Not really. Do you think you could—'

'Persuade her?'

'Something like that.'

Paul shifted from his right foot to his left, mindful of his obligations to his friend. He did not intend to share Joan's marital regrets with her daughter and looked again at Eloise, trying to gauge her likely response to the Huntleys' drama. Then he said: 'The thing is, she has unfinished business in this house.'

'Of what kind?'

Paul began to explain, but warily, as though resigned to not being believed; and indeed, at the mention of a Victorian family, Eloise's face assumed the expression of set interest adopted by adults who did not think much of what he was saying. 'She won't go', he finished, 'until she's fixed things.'

'Couldn't she do that at my apartment?'

'I don't think so. The Huntleys live here.'

'I see.'

But it was clear to Paul that Eloise did not see, and he doubted that she ever would. 'I'll do my best to convince her,' he said, politely.

'I'd appreciate that.'

They moved together up the stairs and past their heavenly guardians, beneath the stained glass and the burglar bars that protected it. As they reached the landing, Paul touched Eloise's arm. 'If she does go and live with you, will you still let me visit her?'

'Of course.'

'Every day?'

'With pleasure.'

This seemed to relax the young man. It was wonderful, thought Eloise, that her mother could inspire such genuine affection despite her infirmities.

When they reached Joan's door, Paul knocked. There was silence. He knocked again. 'She might be asleep,' he whispered, 'but she doesn't mind me waking her.' He turned the handle very gently and pushed the door back softly on its hinges. 'Ma'am?'

Joan was lying across the bed, face down, her hands grasping the pillow with savage strength.

'Ma'am?' Paul moved towards her, tiptoeing silently.

'Mum?' Eloise brushed past him. 'Where's the panic button?'

'Over there.'

She slammed her palm against it and leaned over her mother. 'Mum? Are you all right?'

But Joan did not stir.

The corridor outside now filled with the sounds of running feet in rubber soles, and in a moment Nurse Fleur entered the room, followed swiftly by Sister Karen. It was clear at once to the Nursing Manager what had happened, but she understood the delicacy of the situation and for Eloise's benefit she performed the appropriate steps, taking Joan's pulse and putting her hand on her chest, feeling for movement. Together she and Nurse Fleur lifted their patient and laid her on her back. 'I am so sorry,' she said, at last. 'Do try to think of it as a release.'

Eloise took a step backwards. She felt she might fall. At her feet, she saw, was a cracked photograph of her brother, grinning and shirtless on a beach somewhere. There were scattered sheets of paper, too, covered in densely impenetrable shapes. Nurse Fleur leaned down and began to tidy them.

Only Paul recognised the signs of a desperate struggle, and as the nurse slipped her patient's doodles into an empty drawer he stepped forward boldly and asked for them. He had been so silent as the women fussed over Joan's body that the adults in the room had almost forgotten he was there. Nurse Fleur looked at Sister Karen, who nodded, and she gave the sheets of paper to the boy.

'Does any of it make sense?' asked Eloise.

Paul glanced at the pages in his hand. Long lines of ink, heavily blotted, ran into and out of one another, climaxing occasionally in a half-formed word. He saw the name 'Leonard'; then his own name beside the word 'pedals'; and then, several pages on, more completely formed than any other, the last sentence that Joan had ever written.

'Your mother died a hero's death,' he said.

It was a curious choice of words, but Eloise did not question it; and Joan's face did, indeed, wear an expression she had not seen on it before – a sort of triumphant serenity that dignified her frail body in its stained, pink nightdress.

'I'll be waiting in my office, when you're ready,' said Sister Karen tactfully. 'Do take as much time as you need.'

*

Afterword

Most of what Joan and Paul find in the archives of the Huntley family is historical. Margaret's rejection slips, Clementine's medical prescriptions, the advertisements for Huntley's Emporiums and Gordon's erotic literature (with the exception of the excerpt from *Fanny Hill*, which was published in 1748) were all written by Victorians, and I have altered only the occasional detail in the interests of the Huntleys' peculiar story. Leonard Huntley's medical papers, too, are taken from periodicals published in the late nineteenth century, and the cliterodectomy described in the *New Orleans Medical and Surgical Journal* was indeed performed on a little American girl in 1894.

Although Gertruida van Vuuren's journal is a work of fiction, everything that happened to her happened to someone – and much that she describes, including her conversations with her husband and the letter written by Hannie to her former teacher, is recorded in contemporary memoirs of the Anglo-Boer War.

I dedicate this book to my great-grandmother, Naomi Cecilia de Klerk, who was incarcerated in a British concentration camp as a young child. Several members of her family died in captivity, including her mother and her favourite sister, Sarie.

Richard Mason

Acknowledgements

To thank every person who contributed to the research and writing of *The Lighted Rooms* would be almost impossible. I would, however, like to express my particular gratitude to the staff of the Mitchell Library, Glasgow, especially Joe Crawford, Tom McDonald, Joseph Fagan and Lorna Kerr; to Maralyne McGinty and Paul McCaffer, the exuberant hosts of the Mitchell's cafeteria; to the staff of the National Library of Scotland, the British Library, the Imperial War Museum, the National Archives at Kew; and, of course, to everyone at the Museum of the Anglo-Boer War in Bloemfontein, especially Elria Wessels (who bears no resemblance whatsoever to the assistant curator in the novel).

Any errors in the text are, of course, my own. I am, however, deeply grateful to Dr John Klepeis of the Lawrence Livermore National Laboratory, who patiently explained the complexities of metallurgy to a non-scientist and checked the plausibility of Claude's research (though the views he expressed are his own, and not the LLNL's); to Professors Robyn Jacoby and Guy Goodwin of Oxford University, for their insights into geriatric psychiatry and pharmacology; to Dr Marcus Harbord for being at the end of a phone when I needed a medical question answered; to Professors Elizabeth van Heyningen of the University of Cape Town and Ian Smith of the University of Warwick, who shared their work on the Anglo-Boer War so generously; to Jani Loder, for the benefit of his experience in hedge funds and for his diligence in checking my figures; to Madame Lise Graf, for recounting her experiences as a member of the French Resistance; to Sarah Helm, for her excellent work on the Special Operations Executive; to Christina Parker, for verifying the accuracy of my French; to my mother, for checking my Afrikaans; to Ella and Robin Shaw, in whose house I decided to write this book; to Matthew Sweet, for his gripping investigations of Victorian culture; to Sister Janet Allyson of the Trianon Nursing Home in Cape Town and Sister Margaret McMullen of St. Wilfrid's Nursing Home in London, for being *much* nicer than Sister Karen; to John Thwaites, for playing the Mephisto Waltz to me and discussing it at length; and to the writers of the nineteenth-century books, journals, letters and articles that helped me imagine the world of the Huntleys and the van Vuurens, particularly Trooper Victor Smith, Private W. Puttland, Private Tucker, Private Stanton, E.W. Smith, P.J. du Toit, Hendrina Rabie van der Merwe, Lady Pamela Glenconnor, Charlotte Perkins Gilmore, Emily Hobhouse, Gertruida van Vuuren, Ellie Conje and E.M. Roos.

What is best in the book owes much to my remarkable editors: Victoria Wilson at Knopf; Helen Garnons-Williams and Kirsty Dunseath at Weidenfeld & Nicolson; to my agents, Kathy Anderson and Patrick Walsh; to Frédéric Chopin and Franz Liszt; to my partner, Benjamin Morse; and to many elderly friends, whose candour and companionship have been invaluable. Among them are Eileen Hershaw, Polly McAllister (who allowed me to borrow her surname), Isobel Harper, Margaret Page and Marjorie McMillan. My friend Bob Stanton died, aged 88, shortly after reading the first draft, but his memory remains with me.

A letter from the author, founder of the Kay Mason Foundation

Dear Reader,

When I was growing up in South Africa, it was illegal for children of colour to attend the excellent schools that the Apartheid government had built for white children like me. Instead, they were compelled to study a simplified syllabus, and to receive their education in poorly-built schools where as many as fifty students had to share a single textbook.

South African schools are now open to all, but the fees charged by the best ones make it virtually impossible for many from disadvantaged communities to receive the education they deserve. With the royalties of my first novel, *The Drowning People*, I tried to address part of the destructive legacy of Apartheid; and in memory of my sister Kay, who died when I was ten, I set up the Kay Mason Foundation.

We began by educating two boys and two girls at two of South Africa's elite, formerly 'whites-only' schools. By 2003, we were helping thirty exceptional kids to attend nine of the nation's best schools. Today, under the patronage of Nobel Laureate Archbishop Desmond Tutu, we are helping more than fifty children to receive the first-rate education they need to fulfil their true potential.

The KMF works in partnership with parents and the kids themselves. Parents pay as much as they can afford, and we make up the difference while also providing counselling, extra lessons, uniforms, textbooks, stationery, pocket money and help with transport. We even have our first school bus. With just one exception, all KMF scholars have graduated from high school and gone on to university, where they are pursuing studies in fields as diverse as medicine, law, politics, charity work and gourmet cuisine.

The donations made by readers like you have transformed the lives of our scholars and their families. Please visit www.kaymasonfoundation.org to learn more; and if you're moved by what you see and read, click the DONATE button and join in!

With very best wishes,

Richard Mason

A letter from Nobel Peace Laureate The Most Revd. Desmond M Tutu, Archbishop Emeritus of Cape Town

Dear Richard,

Thank you for coming to see me. I am very pleased to be the patron of the Kay Mason Foundation and I commend you most warmly for your initiative in wanting to make a difference in the lives of young South Africans.

Sadly a very small minority of children in South Africa have access to quality education. Education is the key to the future and the Kay Mason Foundation seeks to change the lives of just a few young people, to enable them to realise their potential and to unlock the leadership capacity within them. It is focused assistance around the needs of a selected few, a relationship in which I believe both parties will find that they are greatly enriched.

The world has been changed by individuals. We have a role model in former President Mandela. I am convinced there are others if they only had the opportunity. I urge our international friends to join you in transforming the life of a young person. What could be more worthwhile?

Desmond M Tutu

Archbishop Emeritus